Yorkshire all his life. For twenty-five years he ran his own building and civil engineering company. During this time he also worked as a freelance artist, greeting card designer and after-dinner entertainer. He has appeared on television, radio and as a comedian on the Leeds City Varieties' *Good Old Days*.

Writing is now Ken's first love – not counting of course his wife Valerie, to whom he has been married since 1973. He has five children and twelve grandchildren.

Visit Ken McCoy online:
www.kenmccoy.co.uk

By Ken McCoy

Nearly Always

Ken McCoy

piatkus

PIATKUS

First published in Great Britain as a paperback original in 2016 by Piatkus

1 3 5 7 9 10 8 6 4 2

A CIP catalogue record for this book
is available from the British Library.

ISBN 978-0-349-41023-4

Typeset in Bembo by M Rules
Printed and bound in Great Britain by
Clays Ltd, St Ives plc

Papers used by Piatkus are from well-managed forests
and other responsible sources.

MIX
Paper from
responsible sources
FSC
www.fsc.org FSC® C104740

Piatkus
An imprint of
Little, Brown Book Group
Carmelite House
50 Victoria Embankment
London EC4Y 0DZ

An Hachette UK Company
www.hachette.co.uk

www.piatkus.co.uk

Chapter 1

'You okay, love?'

The weather was seasonal for Yorkshire – cold, miserable, wet. Just like the shivering girl. She wept as she walked by the light of a guttering gas lamp over treacherous stone flags, awaiting just one careless step. She tripped over a crack and gave a cry of anguish, almost going headlong but recovering her balance at the last second. The man who'd been passing by at the time showed his concern but she didn't answer. He muttered, 'Suit yersen, love,' and hurried on.

Of course she wasn't all right. How could anyone be okay in this cruel world? One that had just forced her to do the most awful thing a person could ever do. She wasn't being rude, just dumb with despair. What she'd just done – what she'd been forced to do – was making it difficult for her to breathe, much less answer a stranger's question, no matter how well-meaning.

She passed darkened windows that reflected her own mood of desolation; her wet hair plastered to her scalp; her eyes were focussed somewhere beyond the pavement

1

passing beneath her boots. She almost tripped again. She blinked away a few tears and remembered to concentrate on where she was going.

Tread on a crack marry a rat, tread on a line marry a swine. That's what kids used to say about walking on stone flags. It'd never apply to her. She had her own motto: Never trust a man with testicles. She'd got that from Marie Garside who lived next door but one. She hadn't really known what testicles were but, when Marie explained, it had seemed a good motto. Marie pronounced her name 'Marry' as in Marie Lloyd the Music Hall star, but it took all the class out of it somehow.

William pronounced Billy, that's what they'd call him. Billy was okay, she didn't mind Billy. Bill would be even better ... stronger.

She really and truly wished she were dead.

A loud, grating engine noise had her glancing over her shoulder at a double-decker bus, the number 33, coming into Leeds city centre from Menston. The driver, in his enclosed cab, was having trouble changing up from second gear to third, and was cursing the mechanics at the depot who were supposed to have fixed the problem. He was crouching over his steering wheel and peering forward to make out whatever lay beyond his labouring windscreen-wiper. All the passenger windows were lit up cheerfully against the dark night, two tiers of misty figures staring out at the foul weather into which they'd soon have to venture. None of them could possibly have known of her misery.

All she had to do was throw herself in front of the bus. The heavy vehicle would squash this wretchedness out of her in the blink of an eye. All gone ... so tempting. She stepped up to the kerb and felt all emotion drain from her as she waited for it to arrive. Decision made. Here it came. All she had to do was step out smartly in front of the lumbering vehicle. Three quick steps, no more. Then an upsurge of guilt because she could see the driver and it wouldn't be right to make him carry her death on his conscience. Plus there was the sudden and terrifying thought that death might not be the end of it all. There could be further repercussions – God might not be too pleased with her, for instance, although at that moment she wasn't too pleased with God.

Maybe death was too easy ... Her momentary hesitation gave the bus chance to pass her by. Its wheels splashed through a puddle, soaking her, but couldn't add to her cup of misery, which was already overflowing. She walked on, soaked to the skin, eyes to the ground, sad to be alive.

Her two-week-old baby would have been found by now. Even as she'd hurried away from the empty Wellington Street bus station people had been arriving. He was such a beautiful baby that he'd have no trouble finding parents who would look after him a lot better than she ever could. She'd left a note with him, telling them his name was William. Maybe she should have told them his birthday. Too late now.

The baby's father – her stepfather – was away at sea and due home soon. The very thought of that monster made her retch. But she had to go home. She had nowhere else to go but to the house where it had all happened, and would continue to happen when he returned. Unless she did something about it – unless she stabbed him in his sleep.

Oh, the delight and the joy and the sheer relief that would bring! A knife through his putrid heart would take away his life and restore hers. Surely they wouldn't hang her for killing an animal like him. She might get out of prison before she was thirty if she told them why she'd had to do it. The way she felt now, it wouldn't matter if they did hang her . . .

She was walking up Briggate when the distress became too much for her and she fainted, collapsing on to the pavement. An ambulance was summoned to take her to the Leeds Public Dispensary on North Street, where she was kept overnight before she was brought home by her mother the following morning.

Her name was Helen Durkin and she was fourteen years and six months old.

Scotland
1944

Leading Wren Helen Durkin was a military messenger, more commonly known as a dispatch rider, based at HMS Ambrose, a shore establishment near Dundee. She had left school without her School Certificate at Christmas 1936 – three convenient months before William was born. Two months after she'd left her baby at the bus station she had got a job at the Leeds Grand Theatre as a general dogsbody: clerical assistant, stage hand, runner, walk-on actress, and anything else the theatre needed her for. She was a pretty girl, which always helps in such a job. The work was modestly paid but she enjoyed the atmosphere, especially once she started getting the odd minor part in productions as she grew older. The theatre wasn't the real world but the real world wasn't for her. Not after what the real world had done to her. She spent part of her meagre wages on acting lessons and her future was pretty much mapped out. Or at least it had been until war was declared which was when she'd volunteered for the Wrens, subsequently to become a dispatch rider. It was a skill that might prove handy once the war was over. Acting wasn't the most secure of jobs.

She was riding her Triumph Tiger along the coast road, heading east towards Carnoustie, when she heard the aircraft above. Its engine was spluttering and the pilot was obviously trying and failing to maintain height. She slowed down and watched as the plane's engine cut out completely and the propeller slowed right down until it was just idling in the moving air. The pilot swung his now gliding aircraft out over the Tay Estuary and then back to shore and into the west wind to pick up air speed for the safest landing possible. It was a big, cumbersome biplane, a Fairey Swordfish, nicknamed the Stringbag due to the jungle of bracing wires holding it together. It was a relic from the First War, but still in use as a torpedo bomber. This one didn't look as if it would be in use for much longer.

Helen gazed across its prospective landing area. The narrow strip of shingle beach didn't look too promising. She could see the airmen quite clearly, three in line, no doubt bracing themselves for a very nasty landing ... or worse. She opened the bike's throttle and rode parallel to them, keeping up with them, looking down at her speedo – fifty-five miles per hour. The pilot brought the nose up, the wheels touched the beach; the Swordfish bounced twenty feet into the air and came down again. This time the wheels dug into the shingle, the nose dipped, the tailplane cartwheeled over the nose several times, with bits of the superstructure flying off all over the beach, before the stricken plane came to a halt, right side up but with flames licking outwards from the engine.

Helen gasped with shock and rode straight over a grassy mound leading to the beach. The pilot was still in the cockpit, motionless. The other two men – the observer and the rear gunner – had been thrown out of their seats on to the beach but were still in grave danger should the aircraft explode; they were making no move to save themselves. Helen abandoned her motorbike and ran straight for the aircraft. She yanked at the pilot's arm but he was still strapped in.

'Oh, hell!'

She took a step back from the searing heat to recover then ran in again. Her crash helmet, goggles, gloves and riding leathers staved off the worst of the flames. This time she unclipped his safety harness and pulled him halfway out before the heat got to her again. She stepped back once more then went in again. She got a good grip on him but he was unconscious, a dead weight. All the time she was cursing at the top of her voice.

'Move yourself, man! Come on, move your bloody self!'

With no help from him, she dragged the pilot clear. By now one of the other airmen had got to his knees. She grabbed him under the arms and hauled him away from the flames. She then went back for the third man, whose flying suit was already on fire. Helen flung herself on top of him to put out the flames before dragging him clear. Exhausted by then, she sat down beside all three of them, coughing and gasping for air.

Other people had arrived on the beach by now, most of them having witnessed Helen's bravery. All four of them were helped well clear of the blazing wreckage. She had recovered some of her strength and went to retrieve her bike but she was in no fit state to ride it. An ambulance arrived, as did police and RAF personnel. Helen sat still, reliving what she'd just done. There was praise for her bravery, all of the spectators amazed that it was a mere woman who had put her life at risk to save three men, but no one was more amazed than Helen. She didn't regard herself as brave, merely uncaring for this damaged life of hers thanks to her stepfather's callous treatment of her. She hadn't been scared of dying just now, though she'd wanted to avoid the pain of being burned to death.

All three airmen survived. The pilot needed extensive plastic surgery but it was better than being dead, and she received a wonderful thank you letter from his wife, plus similar letters from the mother and the fiancée of the other two airmen; letters she treasured even more than the British Empire Medal awarded to her by the King at Buckingham Palace three months later. Helen didn't feel that she deserved it.

Chapter 2

Leeds
23 May 1954

Billy's grey flannel bags flapped around his ankles, almost obscuring the size eleven boots bought from the Army and Navy Stores. His haircut was a short back and sides with not much on top, and his green jumper had been knitted by one of the many women whose hobby it was to help kit out the mentally handicapped children of the Archbishop Cranmer Children's Home. Billy's jumper had been made by one of the less talented knitters.

It was a fine, blustery day. Lucy and Billy were walking up Harehills Lane. A lone tram rattled past, as did a horse-drawn cart driven by a dishevelled man, shouting, 'Aaraggabone! Any owd raaags?' A woman loudly chastised him for breaking the ragman's rule of not working on the Sabbath. He shouted back and stabbed a grimy finger at a row of medal ribbons on his shabby overcoat, which apparently gave him divine dispensation to work on the Lord's day. She hurled a string of unchristian profanities his way. He accepted defeat and clicked his unkempt horse into a trot, quietly pleased when the animal took his side by treating her to a farewell fart.

Cars, almost exclusively black, passed by at infrequent intervals, some struggling up the incline and belching out blue exhaust smoke. Cyclists laboured wearily up or free-wheeled happily down. Branching out to either side of the road were crowded rows of brick-built terrace houses, constructed in the late-nineteenth century and liberally coated with early-twentieth-century soot from the many engineering works and industrial chimneys scattered around the city. Clothes lines were strung out across the cobbled streets, festooned with drying washing flapping in the spring breeze – another rule of the Sabbath broken, but this was the first decent drying day in over a week.

They passed a school and the Hillcrest Cinema. *On The Waterfront* was showing, but not on the Sabbath. A poster depicted a defiant Marlon Brando sitting in the back seat of a car next to Rod Steiger, who was pointing a gun at him. Lucy stood in front of it with her hands on her hips, head angled slightly to one side, absorbing the story it told her.

'Look at Marlon Brando. He doesn't look a bit scared, does he? You can't scare Marlon Brando, you know. It's a well-known fact that you can't scare Marlon Brando. Even when he's acting, he can't act scared. He doesn't know how.'

Billy stood beside her and looked at it with less appreciation. It was a picture of two unsmiling men. He didn't know them, nor did he want to know them.

'I wanna go an' see that,' Lucy said. 'Our Arnold's seen it. He says it's a great picture but it's an "A" an' I'm only fourteen so I'll need someone who's sixteen or over to take me in.'

'Am I sixteen or over?' Billy asked.

Lucy looked up at her seventeen-year-old companion. 'Not really,' she said.

'Oh, I thought I was.'

'You might be one day, with a bit of luck.'

They moved on, with Lucy planning the freeing of a dog which she'd found in the woods and had kept there as a pet until it had been picked up by a dog van two weeks previously. Billy was wondering why he wasn't sixteen or over.

'Did you sing in church this morning?' Lucy asked him.

'I did. They give me two bob to sing me songs.'

'Two bob . . . where is it?'

'Missis keeps it for me.'

'What did you sing?'

'Don't know what it's called. I only know the words. I know four songs now.'

'They're called hymns.'

'I know but I think that's daft. It's same as calling 'em hers.'

Billy had a beautiful counter tenor voice and had been singing solo in St John's Church since he was fourteen years old. Lucy thought it was a miracle that he'd learned the words to four hymns when he couldn't remember what he'd had for breakfast.

*

As Lucy and Billy were talking about hymns, Ethel Tomlinson, another resident of Archbishop Cranmer's Home, was talking to a man who had smiled at her in the street and stopped for a chat. This never happened to Ethel. People never stopped to chat with her. They usually walked straight past, maybe giving her a wary glance as if people such as she weren't safe to be near. Sometimes they sniggered, especially the younger ones; sometimes they called her cruel names, such as Daft Ethel. What they never did was stop for a chat with her. Most girls would have been on their guard with such a man but Ethel didn't have a guard.

She was a year older than Billy and like him was classified as mentally sub-normal. She was also a very friendly girl who wasn't aware of the advances being made to her. The man was telling her how pretty she was and asking if she would like to take a walk with him in the wood behind the home. She went with him but still didn't understand what was happening when he tried to kiss her. Ethel had never been kissed before, nor had she ever had anyone try to put his hand up her dress. She knew that was wrong. She'd been told that was wrong and to report any of the boys at the home who tried to do such a thing. Which was why she began to cry.

*

Lucy and Billy walked on in silence. 'If somebody doesn't rescue Wilf they'll just kill him,' she said, at length.

'Why do they want to kill him?' Billy asked.

''Cos I bet they think he's ugly and he's not been taught proper. Wilf never does as he's told, and he slobbers a lot, and he nearly bites your hand off when you give him sausages.'

Billy laughed. 'Wilf likes sausages! Missis never knows I nick 'em, y'know.'

Lucy glanced at him sidelong and despaired at the way he'd been dressed by the home. It was the era of the teenage Teddy Boy – drape jackets with velvet collars were worn with drainpipe trousers; beetle-crusher shoes with inch-thick crepe soles were the only kind to wear, and hair had to be styled into a proper DA – the polite way of saying Duck's Arse. Even Lucy's brother Arnold, who was hardly a follower of fashion, wore Levi jeans with fifteen-inch peg bottoms and had his hair styled in a Tony Curtis quiff, which she thought was ridiculous. Like Lucy he'd inherited their mother's Irish complexion and fair hair. Arnold's would be better described as ginger, although he referred to it as auburn.

'It's better than nickin' sausages from the Co-op,' Lucy said. 'The coppers'd have us for that an' lock us up.'

'They won't lock me up,' said Billy.

'Why not?'

''Cos I'm a potty.'

'Don't they lock potties up?'

'No.'

'Who says?'

'Missis says. I once nicked some currant teacakes from Mr Sizer's shop an' when the police came to the home, Missis said they'd have ter let me off 'cos I'm potty, and they couldn't do me for it. Din't even tell me not to do it again 'cos Missis says I know no better.' He grinned and added, 'So they know I know no better. I bet you can't say that.'

Lucy didn't try. She knew he'd have been practising it. Billy did that. He practised phrases he heard people use and stuck them into conversation, usually out of context. Not this one. He'd got this one right and he knew it, which pleased him.

'It must be great being a potty,' she said, 'and getting away with all sorts o' stuff. I never get away with nowt, me.'

12

''Snot bad.'

Then he laughed because he'd said snot.

'D'yer gerrit? I said "snot bad".'

They'd been walking for an hour and Lucy still hadn't established if Billy was going to help her or not. It had started out as just a walk as she didn't want to complicate things too much by giving him a destination and a mission for them to accomplish. Best to break it to him in stages. That would have been Arnold's advice. She made a start now by bringing the subject up.

'I bet you wouldn't even get into trouble if we got caught rescuin' Wilf.'

'I bet I wouldn't as well.'

'So, you're gonna help me?'

'How d'yer mean?'

'Are you gonna help me rescue Wilf?'

'I don't know what that means.'

'It means we're going to get him out of the dogs' home and take him back with us. And I need you to help me.'

Billy gave this some thought, then asked, 'Have yer got any sweets?'

'I've got two sherbet lemons. You can have 'em both as a reward if you help me.'

He shrugged again. 'Okey-dokey.'

Lucy handed over the sherbet lemons. Billy stuck them both in his mouth at once and carried on talking. 'How d'yer know his name's Wilf?' His voice was more garbled than ever, talking through a mouthful of sherbet lemons.

'What?'

He repeated his question. Lucy caught the gist of it. 'I've told you sixty-three times,' she sighed.

13

'I never heard you tell me sixty-three times.'

'*I* called him Wilf. It's what me dad was called.'

'I didn't know you had a dad.'

'Blimey, Billy, I've told you that as well.'

He opened his mouth to comment but Lucy cut him off before she could get involved in another numbers argument with Billy, who struggled to count up to ten. A sudden gust of wind almost knocked her off balance.

'Blimey!' she said. 'It's a bit windy today.'

Billy wet his forefinger in his mouth and made a show of holding it in the air to test the wind. He'd seen it done and it was a clever trick in his opinion. 'It's not as windy as what it was before it was as windy as what it is now,' he said.

Lucy tried to unravel this but gave up. It made sense to Billy so it was okay by her. Billy didn't understand her most of the time so why did she need to understand him?

'I haven't got a dad any more,' she said. 'He was blown to pieces by the bloody Germans and him only five foot six in his socks, is what me mam always says.'

'Does she always say that?'

'Nearly always.'

Billy fell into deep thought then said, 'I don't know what that is.'

'What what is?'

'Nearly always.'

'It's when stuff happens a lot but not all the time.'

'That's me, that is. Stuff happens to me but not all the time. I nearly always do daft stuff but not all the time.'

'All lads do.'

'Who's that man what lives in your house? Is he yer dad?'

14

'Billy, me dad's dead.'

'Aw, I'm sorry yer dad's dead. I didn't know he were dead.'

'No, yer won't know the next time I mention him, neither.'

'I haven't got no dad,' he said. 'I haven't got no mam neither.'

'You might have. They sometimes just bugger off when you're born and give you to someone else to look after. They shouldn't be allowed to do that, y'know.'

Billy nodded vigorously as he tried to absorb this baffling piece of information. 'Who's that man then?' he said.

'That's Weary Walter. He just thinks he's me dad.'

'What's he like?'

'He's a vegetarian.'

'Is that like being a Meffodist or a Cafflic?'

'No, it's like being full of wind.'

'Right,' said Billy, who hadn't a clue what she was talking about. After that he didn't say a word, just followed Lucy, who was three years his junior and the only kid on the estate with any time for him. Most of the others made fun of him, but not when she was around.

'She's a right mouth on her has young Lucy,' was what his house-mother, Mrs Sixsmith, said. 'If she's on your side, you'll come to no harm.'

Billy just called his house-mother Missis. He couldn't quite get his tongue around Mrs Sixsmith. It was Sunday afternoon and the stray-dog centre in Crossgates would be open until half-past four. It was where Wilf had been taken when he was picked up as a stray. One of Lucy's friends had seen the dog van pick him up and they'd read the address on the side. Lucy's brother Arnold had 'cased the joint', to quote him. He told her it would be easy to nick a dog from the centre. What you had to do was unbolt a kennel door when no one was looking and throw the dog over the wall which wasn't all that high. Lucy wasn't all that high herself which was why she'd asked Billy along. He was six foot tall and very strong due to his labouring job on a building site for which he was paid two shillings and threepence an hour – half the going rate for a general labourer.

All they had to do was get past the woman at the reception desk. Arnold had told his sister to talk sense and be polite. If a kid did that it always impressed adults no end.

'I'll do all the talking,' said Lucy. 'Don't you even open your gob.'

'Is that 'cos she'll think I'm potty?'

'She'll know you're potty – all lads are.'

'Good job you're not potty as well,' said Billy.

'That's 'cos I'm not a lad.'

They came to the York Road and ran over to the central reservation where the tram tracks were. A number 18 was rattling towards them, advertising both Tizer and its destination – Crossgates.

'Tizer tram,' said Billy as it stopped at a shelter. 'Good trams, Tizer trams.'

Lucy nodded, impressed that he'd recognised a word. 'They're your favourites, are they?'

'Yeah. I like Tizer trams, but I don't like Tetley's Bitter trams. Oh, no! Missis says Tetley's Bitter makes you pass wind, but I don't know what that means.'

'It's . . . er . . . when you fa— oh, never mind.'

16

They crossed to the far side of the road and made their way to the dogs' home, which was down a quiet street just off the main road. Arnold had given detailed instructions on how to get there. They'd walked four miles from the Moortown council estate where they both lived – Lucy with her mam, Arnold and her stepfather, Walter. Billy's children's home was on the same estate. The sound of barking dogs guided them to a compound halfway down the street. Lucy gave Billy his final instructions.

'If I tell the woman names that aren't ours, you're not to say anything.'

'Is that tellin' lies?'

'It is, yeah. Sometimes it's okay to tell lies.'

'Okey-dokey.'

The only entrance to the compound was through a wooden reception building painted dark green, with a sign over the door reading *East Leeds Animal Centre*. Underneath was a list of the opening hours, which Lucy examined. The centre closed at 4.30 p.m. She didn't have a watch but she reckoned it couldn't be any later than a quarter to far so they were here in plenty of time.

Lucy opened the door and the two of them went into the office. It had a faint whiff of disinfectant, wet sawdust and cigarette smoke, which Lucy didn't find at all unpleasant – it was just how a dog place should smell. There were posters on the wooden walls – mainly instructions to would-be dog owners, and a large and incongruous picture of Blackpool Illuminations. The floor was covered in worn, brown lino, which still held a trace of yesterday's muddy footprints.

A woman of around sixty was sitting on a high stool

behind a counter, smoking a Woodbine and reading the *News of the World*. She was wearing glasses which were apparently only good for reading as she looked over the top of them to peer at the visitors – or rather kids – a lad and a young girl. Up to no good, probably. Having made this assessment she told them to bugger off and returned her attention to an item in the paper: apparently a bill that proposed to give eighteen-year-olds the vote had just been defeated in Parliament.

'I should damn well think so!' she muttered. 'They know nowt at eighteen.' She shook her head, wondering why they printed such boring rubbish in a sex and scandal newspaper. She looked up at Lucy again.

The girl smiled, politely, as per Arnold's instructions. *Be polite and well-mannered to grown-ups and it always throws 'em. They don't expect kids to be polite and well-mannered.*

'Hello,' she said, 'I'm Maggie Butterworth.'

Maggie Butterworth was Lucy's sworn enemy at school.

'Are yer really?' said the woman.

'Yes, my dad sent me to look at the dogs. He says if I can find one that's not too much trouble, we can keep him.'

The woman glanced up at Billy, then back at Lucy. 'So this dog's for you?'

'Yes, this is my friend George. He's just come to show me where the dogs' home is. I didn't know where it was but George's been before.'

'Is he all there? He doesn't look the full shilling ter me.'

Lucy didn't like the observation though it was true Billy had a vacant smile and a slight cast in his left eye, which didn't help his appearance.

'No, he's not all there, he's all here,' said Lucy.

Billy nodded his agreement. He was good at nodding his agreement. Lucy's cheeky reply was made with a disarming smile and she got away with it. The woman concentrated on her.

'How old are you?'

'Fourteen.'

Arnold had told her that they don't let kids have dogs, only adults got to take them away.

'If I see a dog I like, my dad'll come back with me. He's got a van and I'll sit in in the back with the dog – that's if you have one I like.'

The woman put her newspaper down and placed her cigarette on the edge of an ashtray. 'Well, with it being Sunday I'm on me own so I can't show yer round. But I suppose yer can take a look on your own, if yer like.'

Arnold had told her about the woman being on her own on a Sunday. He was in the sixth form, studying A-level physics and chemistry, and destined for university – that's if his stepfather didn't try to make him go out and work for a living. Lucy knew that wouldn't happen, though. If the subject came up, Arnold had an answer ready for it. Arnold had answers for pretty much everything. He was annoying in that way, but very handy to have on your side.

'The kennels all have numbers,' the woman told her, 'so, if yer see an animal yer like, just come back and tell me the kennel number and I'll tell you all about the dog. Whatever yer do, though, don't let it out.'

'I won't,' lied Lucy. 'How much does it cost to buy a dog?'

She had no intention of buying one as she had no money and wouldn't be allowed to keep Wilf at home. On top of which she didn't have a proper dad. She'd kept her mam out of the subterfuge just in case things went wrong and the police thought she might be involved. Lucy always tried to think things through beforehand.

'Yer don't actually buy it,' said the woman. 'There's an administration fee of seven and sixpence, which includes a year's licence.'

'Yeah, that's what my dad said. Well, he said three half crowns, but that's the same, isn't it?'

Arnold had told her to embellish her story to make it sound more authentic. Lucy trusted her brother. He was a big daft lad but he always looked out for her.

'It's through that door,' said the woman. 'The dogs might start barking when yer go through, with 'em thinking it's me comin' ter feed 'em, but as soon as they see it's not me they'll quieten down.'

Lucy had one more question. 'If they don't get bought, what happens to 'em?'

'We keep 'em here for two weeks, then, if they're not claimed nor bought, we have to put 'em down.'

Lucy stared at her, not immediately knowing what *put down* meant, then she realised.

'That's hard luck for the dogs,' she said.

'They don't feel nowt,' said the woman, picking up her cigarette and returning her attention to her newspaper. 'There's two due for the chop tomorrow, unless yer want one of 'em.'

There were twenty-six kennels in all, twenty-four of them occupied. Lucy wondered which ones were due for the chop. If they started with the ugly ones, Wilf didn't have much of a future.

As the woman had forecast, the dogs started barking the second the visitors entered, then calmed down very quickly as if a secret message had been passed between them. Wilf, the stray mongrel Lucy had found, was in kennel 12 near the end of the first row. The compound was in the open air although each kennel had its own undercover sleeping quarters at the back. There was a brick wall surrounding the area, maybe six feet high. Her heart sank when she realised Arnold hadn't told her about the strand of barbed wire running along the top of this. It would be hard to get Wilf over without injuring him. Lucy carried a small shopping bag. Inside this were a dog collar and lead plus a juicy bone. She intended to throw the bone over the wall with Wilf. The idea was to keep him there, chewing the bone, until they went out to collect him. It had not occurred to her that he might just run off with the bone, never to be seen again. She just assumed that Wilf would wait for her, which he probably would.

Then she noticed a wooden gate in the wall, locked by a sturdy bolt to keep intruders out. All the kennels had similar bolts and it was the work of two seconds to release Wilf. He immediately recognised her as the girl who had looked after him for two weeks before he'd been picked up by the dog van. His tail wagged excitedly. He flung himself at her, jumping up and trying to lick her. Lucy squealed with delight and hugged him, despite him slobbering all over her.

'I think we should lerrem all out,' said Billy. ''Snot fair jus' lerrin' Wilf out.'

He was already sliding back bolts and opening doors as Lucy ran to the gate in the wall and unbolted that. The dogs that Billy had released charged past and out on to the street. She was panicking now, trying to slip the collar and lead on to Wilf.

'C'mon, Billy, we've got to go.'

But Billy wouldn't go until he'd unbolted all the kennels. The receptionist, alerted by the cacophony of barking, appeared and screamed at them. Lucy, having managed to secure Wilf on the lead, turned and ran. Billy ran after her. The street was full of racing, barking dogs, all delighted to be free. Many of them ran as far as the York Road, creating traffic mayhem; others just scattered amongst the myriad of side streets. Lucy and Billy ran down one of these and then up another, hoping to lose the woman. But she had given up the chase before it properly started and was now ringing the police station.

*

He had his trousers down now and had pushed Ethel to the ground. He put his hands around her throat to choke off her screams. No one could see them. If he could keep her quiet, he could have his way with her and no one would believe what she said. She was just another nutter from the home.

Ten minutes later he left Ethel lying unconscious on the ground, with her knickers missing and her dress up over her waist. He knew that when she woke up she wouldn't have a clue what to do. She would probably go back to the home, not telling anyone what had happened; even if she did, no one would believe her. His only worry was that he might have made her pregnant. He'd hate to think he was the father of a nutter's kid.

*

Lucy and Billy eventually emerged half a mile down the York Road. A tram was approaching. They joined the queue. Dogs weren't allowed on trams, Lucy knew that, but she could also see that the conductor was upstairs collecting fares. The tram driver didn't care who or what got on, that was the conductor's job. It was largely empty downstairs. Lucy led the way right to the front and tried to hide Wilf under the seat. From behind she heard the conductor's voice.

'Fares, please.'

'Billy, have you got any money?'

'No, spent me money yesterday.'

'On sweets?'

'Yeah. I like sweets, me. That woman were mad, weren't she?'

'Serves her right for telling us to bugger off.'

The tram stopped again, more people got on.

'C'mon,' Lucy said. 'We'll get off here.'

'Okey-dokey.'

Like all trams it had a front and a back door. This was an older model with both doors permanently open to the elements. As the new passengers got on at the back, Lucy, Billy and Wilf got off at the front. The driver smiled and winked at them. They weren't the first kids to play this trick and they wouldn't be the last.

The three of them were now a safe distance from the scene of the crime. Half a mile up the road the dogs were still creating havoc; they'd caused a crash that had badly damaged two cars. The police had arrived at the compound and were taking details. What they weren't doing was chasing the dogs. They hadn't spent all that time at training college to end up chasing strays. Neither of the two officers was sure just what crime had been committed. Nothing had been stolen so far as they could tell, and no violence had taken place. Two kids had been allowed into the kennels and had let all the dogs out, causing a road accident.

'Delinquency,' suggested one of them, 'juvenile delinquency.'

His colleague nodded his agreement and got his notebook out.

'Delinquency, that'll do. How d'you spell it?'

*

Lucy watched the tram rattle off into town, then looked at her two companions, one canine, one potty. 'Well, we walked here, we can walk home,' she said. 'We'd better avoid the main roads just in case coppers are looking for us.'

'It's all right for Wilf,' said Billy.

'What's all right for Wilf?'

'Walkin'. He's got four legs, we've only got two.'

A clock above a shop doorway told her it was just after four. 'You're not due in for your tea until half five, are you?'

'Five o'clock's teatime on a Sunday. Better not be late. Miss me tea if I'm late.'

'How do you know when it's five o'clock?' she asked, curiously.

He shrugged. 'Dunno. I allus get back before, then Missis tells us when it's teatime.'

'Well, we'd better get a move on or Missis'll be playin' pop with you for being late.'

*

24

In a small house in the south of the city a woman looked at herself in her bathroom mirror and frowned because she could see behind the image in the glass to the wound that her stepfather had inflicted upon her – an invisible wound that wouldn't heal. Her reflection was beautiful but she saw the deeper ugliness beneath; an ugliness masked by a veneer of loveliness which had never been apparent to her. She was thirty-one years old and had never had any form of relationship with a man, other than the abusive one inflicted upon her by her stepfather more than half her lifetime ago. Helen was now an actress who spent more time at her back-up job as a motorbike courier, which paid better than her stage work.

She hadn't seen her son since he was two weeks old and prayed every night for him to be leading a happy life. Once again she pictured him as he might be now. Adopted by a good family – anything less would be unthinkable. Maybe he didn't know he was adopted – that would be okay by her. He'd be seventeen years old now, tall and strong, possibly sporty, studying for his A-levels and opening the batting for his school cricket team. Her boy Bill would no doubt have a girlfriend or two.

Tears flowed, as they always did when she pictured her boy Bill. His hair would no doubt be fair like hers, his eyes blue. His features would be strong and handsome and he would be clever and he would laugh a lot because he was a happy boy – her boy Bill. She'd named him William after her real father who had died of tuberculosis when she was three. How she wished her son could be with her now. Did she regret abandoning him? Sometimes – no, often. Then she told herself that his quality of life couldn't possibly have been better had he lived with her. But would her life have been better had she kept him and loved him and brought him up alongside her? That was a question she often asked herself.

And then she thought about the horror of his real parentage, and shuddered at the thought. How on earth would she have coped with divulging that ... perhaps if her stepfather was dead it would have been possible. Oh, how she wished he were! Her mother had suggested that he might well be, but Helen knew different. The vile bastard was still about somewhere. His continuing existence tainted her life. Not for the first time she envisaged killing him. One day perhaps. God knew, it would be justified.

Chapter 3

Ethel lay in the woods for almost two hours before she was found by two twelve-year-old boys out playing Cowboys and Indians. They stood, transfixed, and stared at her from a distance, neither of them wanting to go near. She was showing more of her body than either of them had ever seen of a woman before.

'It's daft Ethel,' said one. 'D'yer think she's fell asleep?'

'Ethel!' shouted his friend.

'Ethel!' they both shouted.

They stood about ten yards away. Ethel didn't seem to hear them, nor did she move a muscle. A light wind blew through the trees, ruffling her hair and her dress, which was pulled up above her waist. Below that she wore nothing. Neither boy felt inclined to approach her, any prurient interest overcome by fear.

'She's not dead, is she?'

'Dunno.'

'Should we dial 999 or summat?'

'Think so. It's free from a phone box.'

'There's that one outside the pub.'

'Maybe one of us should stay and help her. See if she's alive.'

'I'll go, you stay.'

'I'm not stayin'! Whoever did this to her might still be around.'

'What? You think someone did that to her?'

'Did what?'

'How should I know?'

With no further discussion the two boys galloped to the phone box outside the pub and dialled 999.

'Emergency. Which service, please?'

'There's a lass in the wood behind the kids' home on Cranmer Bank, Moortown Estate. She's half undressed and she might be dead.'

The operator asked a few questions to satisfy herself that this wasn't a crank call, then said, 'The police and an ambulance are on their way. Will you be able to wait outside the children's home and direct the police when they get there?'

'Er, yeah.'

A black Wolseley 6/90 police car arrived first. No blaring siren, no skidding to a halt – maybe an indication that the police didn't think this was much of an emergency. The boys looked at each other, apprehensively. Two uniformed officers got out of the car and approached them.

'You the lads that rang 999?'

'Er, yeah,' said one of the boys.

'There's a lass in them woods what looks like she's dead or summat,' said the other.

'Right, lads, you'd best show us where she is, then.' The officer gave the impression that only seeing would be believing.

The boys took the two constables into the wood. One

of the officers took off his helmet, kneeled down beside Ethel and pulled her dress down to restore her modesty.

'She's breathing . . . just,' he reported to his colleague. Then he asked the boys, 'Does either of you know who this is?'

'It's Ethel,' said one.

'It is, it's definitely Ethel,' confirmed the other. 'She lives in the 'ome.'

'She's not all there,' said his pal. 'None of them are at the 'ome.'

'Do you know her surname?'

'No,' said one.

'I think it's Ethel Tomlinson,' said the other boy.

'That's right,' confirmed his pal.

There was the sound of an approaching ambulance. The policeman kneeling over Ethel looked up at the boys.

'Could one of you lads go back to the road and tell the ambulance people where we are?'

'Okay, mister.'

As one of the boys galloped off, excited to be an active part of the drama, the policeman leaned right over the girl and spoke to her. 'Ethel, I'm a policeman. No one's going to hurt you any more. Can you tell me who did this?'

Ethel's eyes flickered open momentarily. Her mouth opened and closed as she tried to speak.

'It's okay, Ethel. Take your time. We need to find this person and make sure he never does it again. Tell us who did this to you.'

Ethel's lips opened and closed. They were blue, her face bloodless. Red abrasions were visible on her neck. With a supreme effort she forced out just one word – a name.

29

'B ... Bill ...'

The other policeman was leaning close to hear her reply. He knew corroboration might be called for.

'Bill? Was it Bill who did this?'

Her glazed eyes stopped flickering; her whole body shuddered and was still. The officers looked at each other; one checked Ethel's pulse and shook his head. Together they confirmed the time and date of death as 18.24 hours on Sunday 23 May 1954.

'Did you get that name, Ronnie?'

'Bill,' said his colleague. 'We're looking for someone called Bill.'

'There's a big kid called Billy Boots at the home,' called out the remaining boy, who had heard this conversation. 'He's not all there either.'

'Best call it in,' said Ronnie, sitting back on his haunches. 'Looks to me like she was strangled.' Then he called out to the boy. 'This Billy Boots, you say he's a big lad?'

'Yeah, he's really strong is Bootsie.'

'Okay, we need you and your pal to give statements, but we'll want your parents with you at the time, so where do you live?'

*

Ronnie called the crime in to the station at Chapeltown. A detective inspector and a detective sergeant were sent to investigate. The boys were being interviewed in their homes by one of the uniformed men; a forensic team arrived to examine the body as Detective Inspector Bradford knocked on the door of the children's home. Mrs Sixsmith answered. He identified himself and asked for her name. She already knew there was something going on, with the police cars and the ambulance, but hadn't yet been told that Ethel was dead.

'Do you have a resident called Ethel Tomlinson?' asked the DI.

'Er, yes. She didn't come in for her tea – not for the first time either. Do you know, I've got all on trying to keep track of these kids ... why, what's she done?'

'She hasn't done anything. A young woman's body has been found in the wood to the rear of your premises and I wonder if you might be able to help with the identification. The body is still in situ.'

'What does that mean?'

'It means it ... erm ... hasn't been moved. It's still there.'

'So you want me to look at a dead body to see if it's Ethel? Oh my God!'

'And do you have a resident called Billy Boots?'

'What? Oh, you'll mean Billy Wellington. Boots is what the local kids call him. It doesn't bother Billy.'

'Is he inside?'

'Er, yes. Why do you want him? He's a really good boy is Billy. Oh my God, I hope it's not Ethel. She wouldn't harm a fly, wouldn't Ethel.'

'Has he been out today?' asked the sergeant.

'Who?'

'Billy B ... er, Wellington.'

'Erm, yes. He went out after lunch and came in for his tea about quarter-past five. He were quarter of an hour late which isn't like him at all.'

'Did he say why he was late?'

'He just said he didn't know the time, which I can't argue with. No point giving him a watch. He can't tell the time.'

'So he's in now, is he?'

'Yes, he's in the day-room, listening to the wireless.'

'We need to take him to the station to ask him a few questions and it would be helpful if you came with him as a responsible adult.'

'Me?'

'Yes, but first I'd like you to take a look at the body.'

Oh, my Good Lord!' said Mrs Sixsmith, reaching for her coat.

She tearfully identified the body as that of Ethel Tomlinson, and asked repeatedly why she and Billy were needed at the police station.

'It's just routine,' said the sergeant, 'to rule him out as a suspect. Then we can get on with the job of finding out who did this to poor Ethel.'

'Oh, my Good Lord!' said Mrs Sixsmith. 'And you reckon she were strangled to death?'

'Well, she didn't die during the attack but strangulation was definitely involved.'

'She had a weak heart did Ethel, we had to be very careful with her. If someone really scared her I think her heart'd give out before long.'

'I'll put that in the report we give to the pathologist. Weak heart or not, it's still murder.'

'I should flaming well think so, poor girl.'

Billy responded to Mrs Sixsmith's request that he should come to the police station with the words, 'They can't do me for it, 'cos I'm potty, me.'

'Do you for what, Billy?' asked the sergeant.

'Nothin',' said Billy. He knew that if he admitted releasing the dogs he'd be getting Lucy into trouble, so the best thing to say was nothing.

*

The interview room at Chapeltown police station was sparsely furnished with a table and four chairs. Billy and Mrs Sixsmith were sitting opposite Detective Chief Inspector Bradford and Detective Sergeant Boddy. Bradford was never happy interviewing suspects with mental problems. First he needed to establish Billy's background. He addressed a question to Mrs Sixsmith.

'Does he have any family we need to contact?'

'No, he was abandoned at birth. Found in a bus station. No one knows who his parents are.'

'Wellington Street bus station,' added Billy. 'That's why they call me Billy Wellington. Some people call me Boots but that's all right by me. Wellingtons are boots what yer wear when it's rainin'.'

'I see,' said Bradford, looking at him. 'You've been a naughty boy this afternoon, haven't you, Billy?'

Billy folded his arms and pressed his lips together, indicating that he wasn't going to answer.

'If you don't talk to us, we'll have to lock you in a cell.'

'Billy,' said Mrs Sixsmith, 'be a good lad and tell them what you did this afternoon.'

'Not much,' he said, defensively. 'Didn't do nowt much.'

'I think you did a very bad thing,' pressed the sergeant.

'Wasn't bad and I did it on me own. Nobody was with me. I did it all on me own.'

Mrs Sixsmith exploded. 'Billy Wellington, you stupid boy! Of course you weren't on your own. What about the poor girl?'

Billy's face folded into a deep frown. He didn't know they knew about Lucy being involved. She was probably in more trouble than him, with her not being potty. Mrs Sixsmith was screaming at him. 'You know not to hurt girls!'

'I didn't hurt her,' he mumbled. 'Anyway it was her idea. She took me there an' she wanted to do it. I didn't 'cos I know it's naughty.'

'Didn't hurt her? Billy, she's dead. You killed her.'

Billy stared at Mrs Sixsmith. 'I never did nowt to her, Missis. She were all right. She was laughin' and stuff. I never hurt her, honest, Missis.'

'When a policeman asked her who did it she gave him your name,' said the sergeant. 'Last thing she ever said was your name – Billy. Two policemen heard her say it.'

'Well, I never hurt no one.'

'You're a strong and powerful young man, Billy,' said Bradford. 'You probably don't know your own strength.'

'I do,' said Billy. 'I can lift a bag of cement on to me shoulder and carry it up a ladder – fourteen steps. If I din't know me own strength I wouldn't know that, would I?'

The DCI shook his head, sat back in his chair and rubbed the back of his neck. He looked at Mrs Sixsmith, then at his colleague. The sergeant opened his mouth, about to speak, but was stopped by the inspector's staying hand.

'Look, I'm not sure this interview is going to be of any

use, with Billy being, erm, mentally troubled. It could be that this was a grotesque accident, but the public have a right to be protected from such accidents. Mrs Sixsmith, we'll be holding Billy here pending a hearing at the magistrates' court, which will possibly declare him unfit to plead and remand him to a hospital for reports. But that's their decision to make, not ours.'

Billy smiled. Hospital wasn't so bad. He'd been in loads of hospitals.

'What does that mean?' asked Mrs Sixsmith.

'It means this is out of our hands. We'll continue our investigation tomorrow, to check for any witnesses, but I suspect we already know the full story.'

Mrs Sixsmith heaved out a sigh. 'None of it'll bring Ethel back, though.'

Billy was wondering what Ethel had to do with this. People nearly always said stuff he didn't understand. In fact he didn't understand most of the conversations that went on around him so he saw no reason to wonder why Ethel had anything to do with him letting the dogs out.

'No, it won't bring her back,' said DCI Bradford.

'No,' said Billy, nodding his agreement. He was good at nodding his agreement.

*

It was a different police officer who came to see Mrs Sixsmith the following morning. The fact that he was an aging constable arriving alone on a police bike was a measure of the diminishing status of the investigation. It was a crime that had been solved. All that was needed were a few last details.

'We're hoping to find any witnesses who saw William

Wellington and Ethel Tomlinson together yesterday afternoon. We'd like to put together a sequence of events.'

'Has Billy been to court yet?' asked Mrs Sixsmith.

'Later today, I believe.'

'So he's still in a cell? He won't like that. He's a very gentle boy ... normally.'

The constable looked at her. 'Perhaps what he was doing wasn't normal ... for him,' he said.

'No, I don't suppose it was. Do you think he just got, erm, over-excited?'

'Not knowing the young man, I really can't give an opinion, madam.'

'No, I don't suppose you can.'

'I'm wondering if you could help me to locate any witnesses?'

'You mean people out and about on a Sunday afternoon?' She scratched her head. 'Well, I was tryin' ter get forty winks before I got the tea ready. It's not often I get the chance, in here. You're welcome to ask among our residents but don't expect to get too much sense out of them.'

'I was thinking more of anyone outside?'

'Outside? Well, just the usual people, I suppose. There's a church at the top of the hill, but who goes to church on a Sunday afternoon? And there's the Social Club – that's open on a Sunday. Yer sometimes get blokes who're a bit the worse for drink wanderin' past.'

'What? On a Sunday afternoon?'

'Oh, yeah ... and there was that damned builder working on a wall opposite. I remember him because he never stopped singin' "How Much Is That Doggie in the bleedin' Winder"? Same soddin' song, over and over. I like me nap on a Sunday afternoon but it's not easy in this place.'

'Yes, I did see a builder working on a wall when I arrived. Anybody else?'

'That soddin' Boys' Brigade band came round. Couldn't get a wink of sleep, what with him singin' about his soddin' dog and them bangin' their drums an' blowin' their bleedin' bugles. I know where I'd like ter stick their bugles!'

'Thank you, madam. I'll have a word with the builder.'

The constable went back outside and crossed the road to where a man was working on a wall around the boundary of a four-storey block of flats. He was singing another song in his repertoire, "She Wears Red Feathers", in an out-of-tune voice. The constable had to tap him on the shoulder to attract his attention.

'Excuse me, sir, but we're investigating an incident that happened yesterday afternoon. It involved two young people from the home over there.'

'What? You mean the Loony Bin?'

'It's a home for mentally handicapped children.'

'Oh, right. Sorry, mate. What do you want to know?'

'Well, I understand you were working here yesterday afternoon.'

'I was, yeah. We're havin' ter do overtime with the job bein' behind schedule, which is not my bloody fault. I wouldn't care but I'm having ter do me own labourin' terday an' all. Lazy sod who helps me hasn't turned up. He got double time for workin' Sunday, so he's not bothered about turnin' up today. Mind you, when he's here he's

37

neither use nor ornament. Buggers off when he's supposed ter be workin' – that's the youth of today for yer.'

'You have my sympathy, sir.'

'Mind you, I were gerrin' double time meself yesterday.'

'That's good, sir. I wonder, did you see a young lady of around eighteen and a young man of a similar age, maybe a bit younger?'

'You mean, from the home?'

'I do, sir, yes.'

'What have they been doin'?'

The constable saw no reason to conceal anything that would be revealed later that day in the *Yorkshire Evening Post*.

'Well, the young lady is now dead and we think the young man might have something to do with it.'

'Bloody hell!'

The bricklayer put down his trowel and rubbed his hand across his face, ruminatively.

'Well, I were workin' round the back most of the afternoon, pointin' a wall on the main block, so I didn't really see nobody apart from me labourer ... and I didn't see too much of him, the lazy sod. He hasn't turned in today, yer know.'

'Yes, sir, you did say.'

Chapter 4

The news of Ethel's death at Billy's hands reached Lucy as soon as she got home from school on Monday afternoon. After bringing Wilf back she had set him free in nearby Adel Woods, where he'd been living since they found him four weeks previously. Lucy could do a loud and piercing whistle that Wilf recognised, knowing it signalled food, but his main source was the children's home. Lucy's mam would have noticed if anything much went missing from their pantry. It was Arnold who broke the news to the girl. He was waiting for her at the gate.

'Billy Wellington's been locked up for murderin' daft Ethel yesterday.'

'Give over. It's you that's daft, our Arnold.'

'It's right. The police took him away and he hasn't come back.'

'Honest?'

'Yeah. It'll be in the paper when it comes.'

'When's he supposed to have done this?'

'Yesterday afternoon, they reckon.'

'He was with me all yesterday afternoon.'

'Probably after he left you.'

'Well, he was with me 'til about five o'clock.'

'After that then. Look, I thought I'd catch you before you went in.'

'Why?'

'Because you'd best not tell Mam he was with you or she'll go mad. You know what she says about havin' owt ter do with kids from the home. It could've been you, y'know, instead of Ethel.'

'He's all right is Billy. Never done me no harm. I bet someone else did it and he's gerrin' the blame.'

'He's owned up to it, from what I hear.'

'Owned up? Why would he own up to something he never did?'

'Search me, but he has.'

'Oh, heck, our Arnold! What's gonna happen to him?'

'Dunno. He might get hung for murder.'

'They won't hang him, with him bein' potty.'

'It's to be hoped he doesn't tell the cops he was with you – you might end up gettin' done for lettin' them dogs out.'

'He won't. He won't drop me in it, won't Billy.' Lucy was in tears now. 'Oh , heck! I bet he's scared stiff. Poor old Billy.'

'Poor old Ethel, you mean.'

*

It never really occurred to Billy that he was being accused of killing Ethel. They just kept referring to her as 'that poor girl'. He did his best to deny that he'd hurt 'that poor girl', thinking they meant Lucy, but his attempt was feeble and dismissed as a lie by the police. It didn't occur to him to tell them that he'd been with her all that afternoon because he'd no idea what time he was supposed to have done what they said he'd done, and if he brought Lucy into it she'd get into trouble for letting the dogs out. Although how she could get into trouble when she was dead didn't occur to him. Everything was so confusing that he shut his ears to most of what was being said. He didn't argue much, except to say he didn't remember hurting anyone, but there were many things that Billy did but didn't remember doing. The police were sure he'd killed the girl because he'd already admitted to being with her. It wasn't a matter to be considered by a jury.

*

Billy's future was decided by mental health experts and magistrates. He was confined to a secure hospital near Manchester for an indefinite period. He never fully understood why he'd been sent there. Nothing made sense, so all the questioning, all the harsh words and condemnation, faded from his limited memory. It was just another chapter in his clouded world, little of which made sense, but he was potty so what more should he expect? The episode with the dogs gradually faded from his mind, but the actual murder of that poor girl didn't because it had never been there in the first place so there was nothing to fade. He knew nothing about her killing, apart from the few confusing words that had been spoken to him just after her death. Mistaken accusations that made so little sense to him that they failed to attach themselves to his fragile memory. His life was even more confused now than it had been in the home, because here they kept giving him pills and medicine that he'd never had before and he was much less aware of what was going on around him.

'It's for your own good,' he was told.

He was no longer allowed to roam the streets but was kept within the confines of a single-bed cell and allowed out in what they called 'the general population' only for meals and something called recreation. His memories of the children's home were gradually fading, but he clung to his memories of Lucy and Wilf, and wished they would come and see him. Lucy was the only friend he'd ever had. Then he remembered being told that she was dead and that made him cry. He'd cry until he was asked what he was crying for and he couldn't remember, so he told them he was crying because he was potty and they left him to it. He still wondered why he didn't have a mam or a dad. He'd once asked Missis and she'd said not everyone had a mam and a dad.

'Is that 'cos I'm not a good boy?' he'd asked.

'No, Billy, it's not that, though you are naughty some-times,' he'd been told, and never had any reason to doubt it.

Chapter 5

Helen Durkin stared at the report in the *Yorkshire Evening Post* and burst into tears. The dreadful events of seventeen years ago came flooding back into her mind. It was her son they were writing about, it couldn't be anyone else. Found in the waiting room of the Wellington Street bus station in March 1937 with a note attached: *This is William, please look after him.*

Back then she'd read about them finding the baby, which had included an 'expert' opinion that should William's mother not be found he'd most likely be adopted by a caring family. Back then this had been regarded, by both Helen and her mother, as the best solution to a dreadful problem. Helen had given birth to William at home, with her mother for midwife. Her stepfather, *the baby's father*, Maurice Bradley, was away at sea in the Merchant Navy at the time.

For the first few days William's arrival had been kept a secret from the world as Helen and her mother Doris tried to work out what best to do. Her mother pointed out a whole host of reasons why the child should be adopted: at

43

Helen's age the very existence of this child would be a blight on her whole life. Her education prospects would be ruined, as would her reputation, her marriage prospects and her happiness in general. William had been conceived very much against her will and, although she might have maternal feelings for her son, to keep him would do neither her nor him any good at all. The main problem was to keep his existence a secret until he was handed over for adoption.

Then, when Doris received a letter to say her husband would be coming home in three days, Helen took matters into her own hands. She wrapped up two-week-old William, took him into Leeds and left him in the waiting room of the bus station, wrapped in a warm blanket and fast asleep. It was by far the hardest thing she would ever do in her life.

When her stepfather came home, the first time his wife went out he tried it on with Helen again, but this time he was forcing himself on a girl who was consumed with intense hatred for him and she fought back, screaming and shouting so loudly and hysterically that the neighbours could hear. They sent for the police who arrived at the same time as Helen's mother. She took her daughter's side, confirming that this wasn't the first time Maurice had abused her. He was taken away, charged, then released on bail. He took the opportunity to sign on for another voyage and forfeited the bail. It was the last Helen had seen or heard of him, although, many years later, her mother had somehow managed to divorce him and remarry.

*

Helen's hands shook as she held the newspaper. It fell from her grip. Her eyes were streaming and her nose running as she heaved out great sobs of despair. Her son hadn't been far from her heart and mind for seventeen years. His birthday had been two months ago. It was a date she never forgot and could never celebrate: 15 March was always a painful day for her. She had nowhere to send a card or a present. She had hoped William was now a happy teenager, maybe in the sixth form in whatever school he was at. Perhaps he had a pretty girlfriend; perhaps he was a sport-loving boy who was looking forward to the start of the cricket season, or did he prefer football or rugby?

None of this. He had turned out to be a mentally retarded monster who had raped and murdered a young woman. Helen threw back her head and screamed words of hatred at her vile rapist stepfather who had created this monster child.

She was in between acting jobs and back to being a motor-cycle courier covering the West Riding of Yorkshire. Doris was now happily re-married. Neither of them had heard directly from Maurice since the day the police took him away.

Helen needed to talk to someone about what she had learned so she climbed on her Gold Star and headed out to Scarborough where her mother now lived. They went for a walk on the sea front. The holiday season had begun and they headed away from the crowded amusement arcades towards the relative quiet of the Spa, where they found an empty bench facing the sea. They sat in silence for a while, watching the sailing boats tacking across the bay, the screeching seagulls diving at the waves and the *Scarborough Belle* taking its cargo of determined holiday-makers on a bright and breezy trip around the bay. Doris finally broke the silence.

'You do know that keeping him would have been a disaster for you?'

'But perhaps if I had kept him, he wouldn't have got into trouble. The poor boy lived in homes all his life.'

'He's mentally impaired, which we didn't know back then. That could be my fault, not being a proper midwife. His birth wasn't exactly straightforward.'

'None of this was your fault, Mum.'

'Marrying that monster who abused you was my fault. I should have stayed single, me and you on our own. We'd have managed.' Helen couldn't argue with this. Her mother continued, 'And if you add William's mental health to all your other problems, your life would have been a nightmare.'

'Possibly.'

'There's nothing you can do now. You turning up in William's life isn't going to help him.'

'I'm not so sure.'

'Good God, Helen! You mustn't think like that. He's criminally insane.'

'He's my son, and your grandson.'

They continued to stare at the sea in silence. Helen resolved to see her son. Doris read her mind.

'If you must see him, leave it a while until people have forgotten about this. Give it a year.'

'Why a year? It's a long time.'

'That's how long it'll take for you to see the problem in

a clear light, because he's a massive problem, Helen. He's a burden that'll weigh you down for the rest of your life. He's not going anywhere and he won't know you. He might not even *want* to know you, and when you see him you might wish you'd never met him.'

'Sounds to me as if he's going to be locked up for the rest of his life, he's hardly going to be a burden to me.'

'Once you've seen him, he'll be in your life and in your thoughts and on your conscience a lot more than he is now. He'll be your responsibility. You'll share all his trials and tribulations. You'll feel obliged to visit him regularly, and each time you'll come away feeling sad and frustrated that you can't do anything to help him. And this is for ever, Helen.'

'I've had an image of him in my mind for seventeen years,' said Helen. 'I've thought about him a lot, especially on his birthday, and then I realise he won't even know when it is. I didn't put it on that note I left with him.'

'He'll have been given a birthday on his birth certificate.'

'Really? He'll have a birth certificate, will he?'

'I imagine so. None of us can get by without a birth certificate.'

'It won't say Bradley on it, which is a blessing. It's also a blessing that you let me keep my father's name.'

'It seemed the right thing to do at the time. William Wellington's a good strong name.'

'I know. I always thought about him as being tall and handsome and happy.'

'I've had the same image, darling, and I don't want to

47

spoil it. I think we should just hold on to our beautiful images of William and leave it at that.'

'I can't do it, Mum, not now I know the truth.'

'No, I don't suppose you can. Silly thing to say, really.'

Doris looked at her daughter's beautiful profile staring out to sea; her glossy blonde hair, styled in an urchin cut, ruffled by the breeze. All this natural beauty and never a man in her life.

'You're a good-looking young woman, Helen, but that lowlife Maurice has blighted every relationship you've never had.'

'I've never had any relationships.'

'Exactly.'

'Oh.'

'I wish you could just let go of it all.'

'I try, Mum, I do try, but it's not easy. He didn't just do it to me once, you know. It went on for over a year before . . .'

'Oh, my darling, I did suspect,' sighed her mother. 'Suspected but did nothing. My own husband doing that to my daughter . . . It was sickening. I cried every day, but I did nothing because I was a coward.'

'Mum, I never thought about it from your aspect. It must have been awful for you.'

'Oh, for God's sake, don't make it worse by feeling sorry for me, darling! I don't deserve your pity. There is one thing you might need to think about, though.'

'What's that?'

'Maurice could be dead.'

'You're just trying to cheer me up.'

For the ten thousandth time Helen thought about her

stepfather who lurked for ever in the dark recesses of her mind. She shuddered away the very thought of him and tapped the side of her head.

'He's still in here. If he was dead, I'd know.'

'I believe you,' sighed her mother.

'I sometimes think,' Helen said, 'that the only way I can purge myself of him is to track him down and kill him. I suppose that's awful?'

'Of course it's awful, but perfectly natural.'

Helen stared at the sea for a while then said, 'I tried to kill myself, you know.'

'What? When?'

'About eight years ago. I'd just missed out on that acting job with a rep company. You'd managed to divorce the monster, married Vernon and moved out here. I was really low. All I could think of was what the monster did to me and what a worthless piece of rubbish I was to let him do it. I thought about tracking him down so that I could stab him to death, but I didn't know where to start. I ended up taking about fifty Aspirin along with half a bottle of vodka. I passed out. If it hadn't been for Jilly, my flatmate, turning up and finding me, I'd be dead. She rang for an ambulance. I ended up in St James's. When they brought me round I was throwing up, had internal hemorrhaging, could hardly breathe. They gave me charcoal tablets to soak up the poison and really powerful laxatives to get rid of everything. God, I felt absolutely appalling. I wished they'd just left me to die. I wouldn't recommend pills to anyone. If you're going to top yourself, do it in style. Jump off the top of Blackpool Tower.'

'I don't think that's allowed, dear,' said her mother. 'We

do have problems here, though, with people jumping off Valley Bridge. It's becoming quite a habit.'

'I've never taken a single Aspirin since,' said Helen. 'I don't think I did my liver any good and I still suffer from gastritis.'

'Oh my God,' murmured her mother. 'And I never knew. Well done, Jilly.'

There was another silence as Doris took in what her daughter had told her. 'This killing him thing's a bit weird,' she said. 'I have exactly the same thoughts myself from time to time. Only with me it's because of guilt for not stopping him. I was such a coward.'

'He was a brute, Mum. If you'd stood up to him, he'd quite likely have killed you.'

'No, I was a coward. You stood up to him and you were just a girl.'

'And you backed me up, despite all his threats.'

'I actually did try to track him down once,' said Doris. 'I contacted that shipping company he worked for. They gave me the address of a seaman's mission in Liverpool which I gave to the police, but when they got there he was gone.'

'I wonder if he's still working the ships. Maybe we could track him down that way.'

'Do you want to have your day in court with him?'

'No, I don't want to go to all that trouble. I just want to kill him. Once he's dead I can get on with my life. Do you think I'm abnormal?'

'I don't know.'

There was a long silence now as they both stared out to sea, focussing on a point somewhere beyond the horizon.

After several minutes Doris said, 'If you thought you would never be caught, would you really kill him?'

'Yes.'

Helen said it without hesitation, still directing her gaze out to sea.

'Do you know, I think I'd help you, if only to rid myself of all this damned guilt,' said her mother thoughtfully.

'Maybe that's what we should do then, Mum. Plan it and do it – bump him off.'

'Right.'

'I mean it, Mum. While he's alive, I won't be right.'

'Nor me, darling. I often go into black depressions, which Vernon doesn't understand. I haven't told him about Maurice's vile behaviour, except to say that the marriage didn't work out.'

'So, we'll do it then?'

'It wouldn't be murder, it'd be extermination.'

'That's exactly how I see it,' said Helen.

'Best not mention any of this to Vernon, though. He might not approve of extermination, not with him being a vicar.'

'Isn't he due for retirement?'

'Next year. Why, do you think we should wait for him to leave the Church before telling him we're planning a murder?'

'Best not mention it at all,' said Helen. She got to her feet and added, 'And maybe you're right about me not seeing Billy straight away. I'll give it a year. Fancy an ice cream?'

'I don't mind if I do. I'll have a double cornet, if they do them.'

'Two double cornets it is, then. Hey, there's Max Bygraves on at the Futurist, maybe we could go and see him tonight. Does Vernon like him? He's very clean, not a bit like Max Miller.'

'Actually, Vernon likes Max Miller,' said her mother. 'He's on in Bridlington. Maybe we all could go there in the car.'

'If Vernon likes Max Miller, he might not mind us planning a murder. Not if we tell him what the evil pig did to us.'

'It's a thought,' said Doris, glad that her daughter had said 'us' and not 'me'. She'd suffered at his hands as well – but enough to kill him?

Helen was smiling as she headed for the ice-cream van. It was as if their plan to kill the monster had already lightened the immense burden he'd placed on both of them. She knew her mother didn't have it in her to harm anyone, not even Maurice Bradley.

Doris watched her walk away. She had no such reservations about her daughter.

Chapter 6

May 1955

'I wish Weary'd let me have a bike. What's the point of me being able to ride one if I haven't got a bike to ride?'

Lucy was looking out of the front-room window. With their house being on the boundary of the estate she was staring out over green fields and trees. Her hair was fair as ripening corn and she had bright hazel-coloured eyes. She was going to be pretty one day. Somehow she knew that, and over the past year had kept track of her improving looks, particularly her skin, hoping all the time that she wouldn't have to go through a spotty phase like her brother had.

Arnold looked up from his book and asked, 'Where would you go if you had one?'

'I could ride to school for a start. You've got a bike, why can't I have one?'

'Maybe because I made my bike out of bits of scrap and old Weary didn't have to fork out a penny. Everything on my bike I either scrounged, or bought with money I earned caddying up at the golf club or potato picking down at Roper's farm.'

'Or nicked.'

'I only nicked a tyre and some brake blocks.'

'That were attached to a wheel!'

'It was a rubbish old wheel.'

'A wheel's a wheel.'

'You don't know owt about wheels.'

'I know they go round and round when you pedal. What more is there to say?'

Arnold couldn't think of an answer to this.

'If I had a bike,' Lucy continued, 'I could go and see how Billy's going on. It's a year today since Ethel died.'

'Since Billy killed her, you mean?'

'He didn't kill her. He was with me when she was killed.'

'You want to stop sayin' that, Lucy. It's going to get you into trouble. The police weren't too pleased when you owned up to you an' Billy setting the dogs free.'

'They blamed Billy for that as well,' said Lucy. 'An' that was all my idea.'

'It wasn't your idea to set *all* the dogs free, just Wilf – and he buggered off.'

'That's because I couldn't give him any food. Billy used to nick it from the home. Anyway I went to Confession and told Father Mitchell about setting Wilf free and he said it probably wasn't even a sin, never mind a crime.'

'I bet you didn't mention all the other dogs.'

'If one dog's not a sin neither is twenty dogs, or a million dogs come to that. Do you think if I prayed to God, He'd get me a bike?'

'Don't be foolish. What you do is you nick a bike, go to Confession and *then* you get God's forgiveness.'

It sounded like a too-good-to-be-true idea that must have a major drawback. But Lucy couldn't see one.

'Life's all about working the angles,' her brother went on. 'What's the point of being a Catholic if you don't work the angles?'

'What do you mean?'

'Seeing things in a way that's favourable to yourself. That's what the Bible does. It gives you all the options. Very clever book, the Bible. For instance, you can turn the other cheek or you can take an eye for an eye and a tooth for a tooth, whichever suits you best.'

'Does it say anything about nicking bikes?'

'Well, I haven't read every page but it's bound to somewhere. It's a rulebook that's full of loopholes is the Bible, that's why it's so popular.'

Lucy mulled over the sense of this and asked, 'Do you think Father Mitchell'd ask me to give the bike back?'

'Prob'ly, but I wouldn't go to Father Mitchell, I'd go to Father O'Duffy. He'd just give you three Hail Marys and a Glory Be and tell you not to steal again. It's worked for me. I bet if you murdered someone, Father O'Duffy'd just give you three Hail Marys and a Glory Be and tell you not to murder anyone else.'

When the full story of how Billy was supposed to have raped and murdered Ethel came out it had shocked Lucy, especially the rape bit.

'Billy wouldn't have done it,' she had said. 'He doesn't know about stuff like that.'

She had also ascertained from Mrs Sixsmith the approximate time of the crime – between half-past three and five o'clock – and had immediately gone to Chapeltown police station to tell them that Billy had been with her up to five o'clock that day and wouldn't have been able to get back to the home until after five.

To add credence to her story she had also told them what she and Billy had been doing, which actually detracted from her credibility as a witness. She was given a caution for being involved with that particular crime and told that she must have either got her times wrong or else she was lying, and that Billy must have attacked Ethel after Lucy left him. Any other scenario would have had the police wrongly blaming a mentally deficient youth for a crime committed by a rapist who was still free to rape again.

'If we nicked a bike, would you come with me to see Billy?' she asked her brother.

'*We*? Where did this *we* come from?' said Arnold.

'Well, I can't nick it on my own, I'd most prob'ly get caught.'

'Yeah, most prob'ly – where is he?'

'He's in a mental hospital near Manchester. Is that too far on a bike?'

Arnold gave this some consideration. 'It's about forty miles. I reckon I could be there and back in a day if I set off early and got back late. You'd have no chance. You haven't ridden a bike more than a mile in your life.'

'It's only like riding a mile forty times.'

'Eighty – we have to come back, you know. Plus we'd have to ride there and back over the Pennines, which are like proper mountains.'

'I bet I could do it if I had a bike, which I never will if you don't help me nick one, which I think is a bit mean.'

'Okay, okay.' He gave the matter some thought.

'Alwoodley's our best bet. Posh houses in Alwoodley. I'll go and case the place. I've got a mate who does a paper round there. Them posh kids sometimes leave their bikes out in the street.'

'It's not really fair to nick another kid's bike.'

'Give over. Their dads have got tons of dosh. They'll most prob'ly end up with a better bike.'

'What will Mam say if I turn up with a new bike?'

'I'll tell her we found it in Adel Woods. You know how Mam always says "Finders keepers".'

'Losers weepers,' added Lucy, already wondering if Father O'Duffy would make her give the bike back. But she could always go to Confession *after* she'd been to see Billy. There was always that.

Chapter 7

'There's a sort of Community Centre place up The Avenue that's got a youth club on Friday nights. Accordin' to me mate, some kids go there on bikes and leave 'em outside chained up.'

'Chained up?' said Lucy. 'Arnold, how're we gonna nick one if it's chained up?'

'Weary's gorra pair of bolt croppers in the outhouse. They'll clip though a chain like scissors through string. I'll ride up on my bike, cut through the chain, and ride off. Then you walk up, as though you belong there, climb on the bike and ride off. Who's gonna know it's not your bike?'

It was the bolt croppers that gave the game away. Arnold had saddled his sister up to Alwoodley, with Lucy holding the cutting tool over her shoulder. Detective Inspector Daniel Earnshawe, living opposite the centre, was fixing a pelmet to his front-room window when he saw them ride past. He was still there as Arnold rode back on his own, into the centre's car park, now holding the bolt croppers in one hand. He leaned his bike up against a wall and went around the back. A minute or so later he came back, still carrying the bolt croppers, got on his bike and rode off. The policeman saw nothing amiss, and continued with his task.

It was two minutes later when Lucy came strolling down the road and walked nonchalantly into the car park. DI Daniel Earnshawe, whose mind should have been on how to fit the pelmet without its dropping to bits, was easily distracted by Lucy, whom he recognised as the boy's bicycle passenger. She went around the back of the centre and emerged, wheeling a bike. This was contrary to Arnold's instructions but the car park was bumpy with lots of potholes and she, being a novice cyclist, didn't want to fall off. Now, having put two and two together, the policeman dropped his hammer and rushed out of his house, shouting at her to stop. Lucy didn't stop. She mounted the bike and pedalled off down the street. Earnshawe had a bike of his own leaning against the house wall. He mounted that and set off in pursuit, still shouting at her to stop. Lucy was now pedalling as fast as she could, but her pursuer was gaining on her.

Arnold had stopped by the shops at the bottom of the road and saw what was happening, although he didn't know it was a copper chasing his sister, it was just a bloke wearing an old jumper and jeans. The boy got off his own bike, holding the bolt croppers, and waved his sister on. As she passed he shouted at her, 'Go through the woods!'

The policeman arrived five seconds later and was cycling straight past Arnold when he threw the bolt croppers under Earnshawe's bicycle wheels. One of the handles caught in the spokes; the front wheel stopped turning and the policeman hurtled over the handlebars and landed in a heap on the road. Arnold was back on his bike now, pedalling after his sister who had turned left on to King Lane then immediately right, heading down a path towards Adel Woods. DI Earnshawe staggered to his feet and examined his bike. The front wheel was severely buckled; his knees and elbows were grazed and his jeans badly ripped. He watched the fleeing cyclists heading for the woods and cursed both them and himself.

A bike had been stolen; he'd buggered up his own bike, plus his knees, his elbows and a pair of jeans. His ribs were killing him and he wouldn't be surprised if he'd broken some of them. He unthreaded the bolt croppers from between the mangled spokes and thought they might be some small recompense for his own loss. He'd have to put in a report now and go to the Community Centre and tell them what had happened and how he hadn't been able to apprehend the thieves, and he still had that bloody pelmet to fit! Better all round that he hadn't got involved. His life was crap enough without him chasing bicycle thieves.

As he struggled back up the street with his broken ribs and broken bike he realised he'd seen the girl before somewhere, only he couldn't remember where. Was it down at the station? Had she been in trouble before? Never mind, it'd come to him. It always did. Jesus, he was hurting and struggling to breathe.

Arnold had almost caught up with Lucy when Earnshawe collapsed. A passing motorist saw him and knocked on a nearby door for the homeowner to ring for an ambulance. For the next two hours, before coming round in a hospital bed, Daniel was in a coma, and his mind had regressed to the last time he'd been injured – Arnhem 1944.

Chapter 8

Daniel Earnshawe
Holland
Sunday 17 September 1944: 2 p.m.

The NCO, Corporal Daniel Earnshawe of the First Parachute Brigade, would be the last man to leave the aircraft. Two miles below him was the town of Arnhem on the Neder Rijn – one of the lower branches of the River Rhine before it entered the North Sea. Around him were hundreds of Allied aircraft, including Dakotas towing gliders full of other paratroops, with Spitfires and Hurricanes flying as escorts, almost wing-tip to wing-tip.

He was the only man in this aircraft to have jumped into enemy territory before; in fact he was the only man to have jumped carrying a full kit. His red beret was stuffed into his battledress. He wore a helmet instead – two miles is a long way down with only a soft cap on your head. Among his equipment was a sten gun, three spare magazines, two anti-tank mines, food rations, a grenade pouch containing six grenades, three pairs of socks and a roll of toilet paper. In the army there was always walking to be done, and walking in wet socks was no fun. He was hoping his parachute could cope with all this weight; if not he'd arrive down there a bit quicker than most. They were dispatched into the air at the rate of one man per second, giving no one any time for second thoughts.

This was Operation Market Garden; so-called because Holland was like one big market garden. The idea was to drop a large airborne force behind German lines and take all the bridges over the Rhine. This would allow the Allies to encircle Germany's industrial heartlands and thus shorten the war by several months. All Daniel knew was that they were to head for a bridge at a town called Arnhem and hold it until Allied reinforcements arrived from the south. They'd been told there'd not be too much resistance. It all seemed straightforward enough from his lowly rank.

The pathfinders, having landed first, had set off yellow smoke bombs indicating their rendezvous point to the north of the drop zone. He steered his parachute as best he could towards it. There was a wood beneath him now, just what he didn't want. The paratrooper's nightmare – having to climb down a tree you hadn't climbed up. He swung over the wood towards the smoke. Above him the sky was dotted with hundreds of parachutes, suspended from which were hundreds of men, all with the same thoughts and fears as Daniel. Their main fear was already manifested in the form of machine-gun bullets. Daniel looked around him in dismay at men jerking in agony as bullets hit their helpless bodies, some of them going completely limp and floating to earth to land lifeless on the ground. These were primarily working men trained in useful jobs, bricklayers and dock workers and plumbers and bus drivers and factory workers and the like – civilians in uniform. Few of them were fighting men by nature, only by obligation. Were their situations reversed, no way would Daniel shoot helpless, decent men in such a cowardly fashion. Bullets tore through the canopy above his head. He looked up, hoping the holes wouldn't start to rip.

He was now over a large field. Men were landing on it, releasing their parachutes and heading off to the rendezvous point. Daniel noticed a container full of explosives plummeting down about a hundred yards away. Its parachute had failed to open. It hit the ground and exploded. The blast sent his parachute into a spin. He hit the ground a lot harder than he'd hoped. He rolled, as his training had taught him, and lay there on his back with the wind knocked out of him. He moved his limbs to check for broken bones. As far as he could tell he was intact. A private from his platoon came over, a good friend from Leeds whom Daniel had known since before the war. They'd joined up together and had fought alongside each other in Tunisia and Italy. Sometimes the army kept pals together, and sometimes pals managed to keep themselves together.

'All right, Danny?'

He knew that Daniel preferred his proper name.

'Yeah, I think so, Johnny.'

His friend preferred John, but good friends take liberties under trying circumstances, to take the edge off things.

John Adamthwaite helped Daniel to his feet.

'Thanks, mate.' Daniel released his chute and checked his kit. 'I'm okay, don't wait for me. The smoke's over there.'

Private Adamthwaite set off at a low trot. He was about fifty yards away when a machine gun cut him down. Daniel flung himself flat to the ground as more rounds went over his head, one of them glancing off his helmet. From his right a Vickers machine gun opened up, firing back at the German gunner. The incoming fire stopped. Daniel called out. 'Did you get him?'

'Think so.'

There was another burst from the Vickers, then, 'Yeah, I definitely think so.'

Daniel got to his feet and ran to check on his friend whose eyes were open and full of pain and shock. His battledress was soaked in blood. Daniel screamed for a medic but there was none in the immediate vicinity. He unbuttoned John's tunic and saw intestines protruding from his pal's lacerated stomach.

'Just hang on, mate, I'll get a medic to fix you up.'

John's mouth opened and closed in an effort to speak. Daniel put an ear close to him to try and hear against the sounds of war raging all around. The dying man's voice was a barely audible croak.

'Would you ... would you keep an eye on my lad for me, please?'

'I will, John, yes. But you can keep an eye on him yourself when you get back to Blighty, mate.'

It was an optimistic comment that John didn't believe. His lips worked once again. 'And could you tell Doreen that I lo ... '

The effort of speaking and staying alive were too much for him. He died halfway through a sentence that Daniel finished for him.

'Love her. Yes, I'll tell her you love her.'

John's head fell to one side; his eyes were still open but the light had gone from them. Daniel let out a scream of rage and despair at this sudden death of his good friend, wondering if it was his fault for sending him on his way so quickly? His scream turned into a pointless shout for a medic. His shout was relayed back. A medic arrived, pronounced John dead and moved straight off, leaving Daniel kneeling there, feeling that it would be wrong to leave his friend while knowing he had no option but to carry on. He said goodbye and set off at a crouching run.

More enemy fire came his way. Mortar shells were exploding on impact with a copse of trees in between him and the rendezvous point. The urgency of what he needed to do and the danger he was in pushed the death of his friend to the back of his mind. They had been told not to expect resistance. The Allied bombers were supposed to have knocked all the fight out of the Germans. He called out to the men around him to avoid going through the trees.

'Go round . . . round!'

Most of them needed no telling but there were always a few who did. To his left was a rough farm track. A German truck pulled up and enemy soldiers spilled out. Daniel flung himself to the ground once more. Still enraged by John's death, he emptied a 32-round sten magazine in their direction.

The Germans hadn't expected such a sudden and violent attack, especially as other men in Daniel's platoon opened up as well with sten guns, Lee Enfields and grenades. The firefight lasted less than a minute before the truck exploded and the enemy stopped returning fire. Daniel signalled the men to go with him to check.

Out of eight enemy only two were alive. One of them tried to raise his weapon. A single shot from a Lee Enfield killed him. Daniel looked down at the sole survivor who had fear in his eyes lest he suffer the same fate. Daniel kicked the German's rifle away and stuck his sten gun in the terrified man's face, screaming with rage. The man brought his hands together in prayer, awaiting his final moment. Daniel pulled the trigger, knowing the magazine was empty. There was a dull click. The man fainted. Daniel withdrew his weapon. His comrades followed suit, knowing that one day soon they might find themselves in a similar position, hoping for the mercy they were showing this man. The wounded German came round and moaned in pain.

'Leave him,' Daniel said. 'I'll notify a medic to take a look at him – if he's got time. Best get to the rendezvous. Let's find out where this bloody bridge is, and watch out for more Germans!'

'Tank coming, Corp,' called a man from higher up the track.

'Shit!' said Daniel, clipping a new magazine on to his sten. He took out his anti-tank mines and handed one to a private. 'Just stick this in the middle of the track. I'll put this other one down there. They might not spot 'em if we keep 'em occupied.'

A Tiger tank came into sight, opened fire with its field gun and sent an 88mm shell screaming inches over their heads and going straight through the stone wall of a Dutch farmhouse over a mile away. The tank's machine gun opened up but Daniel and his men had by then dived off the road into a ditch and crawled through a hedge. The mines were in plain sight. An observant tank commander would have spotted them but the Paras were giving him something else to think about, firing on the tank, drawing it towards the mines. More British troops were arriving, alerted by all the gunfire, including Daniel's platoon captain. He took position on the ground beside Daniel, who apprised him of the situation.

'We've mined the track, sir but we didn't have time to cover th—'

The two mines exploded within seconds of each other. The tank slewed to a halt, its tracks and undercarriage destroyed. Daniel got to his feet and ran at the armoured vehicle, emptying his sten gun at it. The bullets bounced off the steel, but it kept the five occupants where they were. He climbed up to the turret, opened the hatch, dropped a grenade inside then leaped off, still in mid-air as the grenade exploded.

He went back to join the captain who said, 'Have you ... er ... done a lot of this sort of thing, Corporal?'

'A bit, sir. Mainly in North Africa in '42.'

'We lost a lot of men back there.'

'We did, sir. I was lucky.'

'How do you feel about it?'

'About what, sir?'

'About killing these damned Germans.'

'The first time I killed a man, I vomited, sir.'

'So did I, Corporal.'

'I'm okay with it now, sir.'

'Good. This was well done.'

Captain Morton got to his feet and looked around at the burning truck surrounded by dead enemy. He was a regular soldier in his early thirties and had only just taken command of the platoon. Daniel hardly knew him but he seemed okay as officers went.

'Was that your doing as well?'

'I had help, sir. There's one of them needs a medic when there's one spare.'

'I'll see to that. Well, carry on like this and I might have to put you up for a medal.'

'They killed a friend of mine, sir.'

'Do you have a family back home?'

'Yes, sir. I have a wife, Gloria, and two young girls, Carol and Jeanette.'

'Then they'd probably prefer you to come back in one piece. Keep your head, Corporal. Don't let your anger run away with you. We all have work to do and dead men are as useless to the army as they are to their families.' He looked at the burning tank. 'What the hell's a Tiger doing out here? Anyone'd think they were expecting us.'

*

It took them until Monday afternoon to fight their way to the bridge at Arnhem where they took up position in nearby buildings. They'd lost many men by then, Captain Morton among them. On Tuesday afternoon three Mark II Tiger tanks appeared along the Westervoortsedijk, turned the corner into Ooststraat and swung their guns round in line with the house the Paras were occupying. One of the tanks fired a shell, which came straight through the wall and hit a lance corporal from Daniel's platoon, cutting his body clean in half. They evacuated this building and took cover under the bridge only to be bombarded by German mortars. They sustained three dead and six wounded within ten minutes. Their situation was hopeless. During a lull in the firing a German voice was heard.

'Englanders ... surrender or we kill you all!'

The officer in charge, a lieutenant with a bad leg wound, looked round at his men, shrugged and asked, 'Anyone for suicide?'

No one knew a good answer to this. The officer, a young man of maybe twenty-eight, decided for them. 'Gentlemen, we're winning this war and I'd like to be around to see it won. Anyone got anything that's remotely white?'

Someone handed him a vest which might once have been white. The officer tied it to the barrel of his Lee Enfield, limped out from under the bridge and waved it in the air.

'Okay, you win,' he shouted. 'For now.'

The wounded were taken off in a truck and the others to a church where they were given soup and jars of fruit. Daniel smuggled two jars into his battledress pockets. They were marched along a corridor and up a flight of stairs, presumably to be interrogated. At the top of the stairs was a large, freestanding wooden cupboard. There was a hold-up at the front of the queue which gave Daniel time to try the cupboard door. It was open. He stepped inside and closed the door behind him. No plan in mind, it was just something to do – defy the enemy at every opportunity. He heard the queue move on. No counting of prisoners had been done, no names taken as yet. He fully expected to be caught but he might as well spin it for out as long as he could. The men would know what he'd done and it'd amuse them, which would help morale.

Daniel stayed in the cupboard all night, sustained by the two jars of fruit which served a dual purpose as receptacles for when he relieved himself, not wanting any evidence leaking outside of the cupboard.

*

The following morning he was awakened by a lot of noise outside his cupboard. Boots moving about hurriedly, clattering up and down the wooden stairs. He could hear his own men now, talking to each other, some laughing. Good for them, keep that morale up. As they passed his door someone banged on it and shouted, 'See you, Corp, we're on the move.'

He recognised the voice as that of Lance Corporal Thompson and hoped none of the Germans had seen or heard him. No chance, though. Tommo was an idiot, but a sensible idiot. He wouldn't give his corporal away. The noises subsided to nothing. Daniel stayed where he was for an hour, then pushed the door open slowly. The corridor was empty. He stepped out and stretched his cramped arms and legs. He went to the top of the stairs. No one on them and no sound coming from below. He went down as quietly as the creaking wooden steps would allow and came out beside the altar of the church. No lights were lit, not even a votive candle. Daylight streamed through stained-glass windows in coloured, dusty beams. The church was deserted. He walked up a side aisle and stood behind the main door, which was closed but not locked.

It was a Catholic church and priests never locked worshippers out, not even enemy worshippers.

Normal street sounds came from beyond. Sounds of motor vehicles, sounds of horses clattering over stone cobbles, a bicycle bell, a shout of greeting. But where the hell were the rest of the paras?

He wasn't sure if this was good or bad. It certainly meant the Allies hadn't arrived. He went back and sat in a pew to consider his options. He could be as much as forty miles behind enemy lines, depending on how far the Allies had pushed north in the last few days. He knew by now that the plan had been to hold the north side of the bridge until the Allies arrived from the south. They'd failed in their side of the plan, plus no help had arrived from the south. So how far away were they?

He went back to the door and pulled it open a crack. A column of German soldiers was marching down the street, two abreast. He counted thirty men. A tank and two armoured cars followed them. They moved out of sight. Across the street was a military motorbike, with no soldier in attendance. He stepped carefully outside and looked down the street towards the disappearing Germans. A few locals were about, no more enemy uniforms as far as he could see. He formed a vague plan that if he could steal the bike and get on to the bridge at high speed he might take the Germans by surprise and be across before they could do much about it. After that he'd head south and hope for the best – the best being that he survived. He cast out all negative thoughts such as: *Jesus, Earnshawe! Have you gone mad?*

He gave himself half a minute to summon up what

courage he could muster, then he took a deep breath, stepped out of the church and looked up and down the street. There were people about but they were locals. He put on his red beret and strolled across the street as though he had every right to be there. He certainly had more right than the Germans. One or two people looked at him, knowing he shouldn't be there, but with no inclination to hinder whatever he meant to do. He wasn't the enemy and some of them knew that a red beret meant he was a British soldier to be reckoned with – one of those mad buggers who dropped in from the sky.

He went over to the motorbike, swung his leg over the saddle and kicked it into life. He'd ridden army bikes before, never one of these, but it wasn't a problem. Daniel pulled his beret right down over his ears to keep it from getting blown off. He had a rough idea where the bridge was – somewhere south of here. He glanced up to find the sun behind the clouds and headed in that direction. He came to the river and saw the bridge away to his right. He rode towards it, trying to take in as much as he could. German vehicles were parked on the bridge – three tanks and an armoured car, along with at least two dozen soldiers. Blast! Trying to cross it would be suicide and he'd already decided that there was no future in suicide. He desperately wanted to get back home to his lovely Gloria and his daughters. Bugger the war, let someone else fight it!

He swung right, up a side road, then left, heading west. He opened up the throttle and arrived at a crossroads at high speed. To his left a group of enemy soldiers took pot shots at him but missed. To his right he saw a column of tanks heading his way. There was shouting above the roar of his engine; shouting and more shooting – much more shooting. Then pain that almost had him off the bike, careering all over the road before he got it back under control. He'd been hit in his left side and right leg.

The pain would have been atrocious had he not been partially anaesthetised by a huge adrenalin rush. His left side and his right leg weren't needed for him to ride the bike. A wound to his left leg might have been a problem with him needing it to change gear. He looked down at his right calf. The bullet looked to have come right through, probably broken a bone or two on the way, so he was now a cripple and he needed to stay on the bike as he'd never be able to remount. Using his right arm he hooked his dangling right foot over the foot rest. Thus supported it should hopefully stay where it was. He put his left hand behind him and felt liquid on his battledress. He brought it back. His hand was covered in blood and he was wondering how long he'd be able to keep going.

He passed more tanks and German troops all heading towards him and either not realising he was the enemy or leaving the job to someone else. No sign of any Paras. He looked across the river to his left and saw a row of Tigers lined up with their guns pointed back over the water, as if expecting someone.

Through Oosterbeek and scarcely slowing down, just swerving now and again to avoid slow-moving pedestrians and two horses that must have died in the earlier fighting. The sniper fire died away; he was glad of that. Dodging bullets was never any fun. A shot rang out and a bullet went clean though his beret, creasing his skull and sending blood pouring down his face. Skull wounds were notoriously bloody.

The sniper fire resumed as if the respite had been a German trick to give him false hope. The pain from his three wounds was now immense. Shots rang out continuously. Bullets whined past his head and kicked up dust from the road. Daniel battled on, seeing the road through a film of blood, all the time no more than a heartbeat away from death. His machine was weaving, uncertainly from one side of the road to the opposite, miraculously missing other road users

He was five miles west of Oosterbeek, not knowing what to expect in front of him. All he knew was that he was north of the Rhine and four hundred miles south of his beloved Gloria. She was the only thing on his mind now. Would he see her again? Probably not. Tears mingled with the blood. Keep focused, Earnshawe! Keep your mind on the job and you might get out of this in one piece. The sniper fire died down again. Another trick, maybe? Were they playing with him?

Allies were to the south of the Rhine. He was north. Maybe he might run into some helpful locals who could look after him until the Allies turned up. He was constantly wiping blood away from his eyes. Ahead he could see a military column heading towards him, taking up most of the road. Ah, well, he'd given it his best shot. There were no turn-offs between him and it. He could do an about-turn but he was feeling faint, severely weakened by his wounds and pretty much ready to give himself up. He took both hands off the handlebars and set his bloodied beret properly. If he was going to be captured, he would look the part and hold his head up with pride. Even the Germans knew what calibre of British soldier wore the red beret.

The approaching vehicles were painted in camouflage, making them difficult to identify. He pulled up in the middle of the road, just out of awkwardness, to stop the column. He closed his eyes and sat astride the bike, trying not to pass out. A soldier got out and pointed a rifle, shouting at him.

'Where did yer get that bleedin' hat, Corporal?'

Daniel sat there with his eyes closed as the words penetrated his brain. Through his pain it took him a few seconds to realise that the voice was English with a Midlands accent. He opened his eyes and peered at the British soldier who seemed amazed to see a blood-soaked para riding a motorbike behind enemy lines.

'One Para gave me it to keep my head warm. Who are you?'

'South Staffs.'

As the soldier approached him Daniel fell off the bike, his energy exhausted. The soldier stood over him. 'You wounded, mate?'

'No, I just thought I'd have a lie down.'

The soldier shook his head 'You're a Yorkshireman, aren't you?'

'Why do you ask?'

'Because I've never met a Yorkshireman yet who's right in his bleedin' head. Okay, we'd best get you seen to.'

Within a minute Daniel was on a stretcher being loaded into the back of a truck with a medic in attendance, who gave the wounded man a morphine injection before he got to work on him. Daniel drifted away on a sea of ease and comfort. His thoughts turned to Gloria, his one and only, the girl he had liked and respected more than any other before he'd realised that this was love. Now and for ever, for him there could only be Gloria.

For the next thirty-six hours he had intermittent periods of consciousness. First waking up in a field hospital, then being loaded on to a plane, then an ambulance and then waking up in an English military hospital. Twenty-four hours after that he was awakened by Gloria who had kissed him and ordered him to wake up. It was a moment of happiness that would remain forever in his memory. His previous memory was of him being resigned to certain death on a Dutch road. Such a dramatic change of fortune had him in tears.

'Why the tears, darling?' Gloria asked him.

'Just very pleased to see you,' said Daniel.

Chapter 9

'Is this Manchester?'

'I'll give you three guesses. Here's a clue. We've just passed a sign saying "Welcome to Huddersfield".'

'Aw, you've always got to be so flipping clever, you. How far is it from Huddersfield to Manchester?'

'About twenty-five miles.'

'Can we stop for a bit? I'm shattered.'

'We've stopped twice already.'

In truth, Arnold was most impressed that Lucy had only asked to stop twice. They'd done about fifteen miles, a lot of it uphill. He swung his leg over the saddle and dismounted. Lucy did the same. They stood their bikes against the kerb, each balanced by a pedal. Arnold took his road map from his saddlebag. He'd plotted out a route to the hospital where Billy was being detained. How they got inside was not Arnold's problem, that was up to Lucy. He'd made that clear from the start. They sat on a nearby wall as he perused the map.

'Right, once we get through Huddersfield it begins to get really hilly.'

'What? I thought we'd gone up enough hills already.'

'I'm talking about proper hills. We've done about fifteen

miles, which means we've got another twenty-five to go – a lot of it uphill.'

'Does this mean there's a lot of it downhill as well?'

'I hope so.'

Lucy looked at her watch. It showed 9.35. They'd been riding for almost an hour and a half.

'How long do you think it'll take us from here?'

'About three hours at this rate, maybe a bit quicker.'

'Have we been making good time?'

'Not bad. I'd have done it a lot faster on my own, though.'

'Have I done better than you thought I'd do?'

'You've done okay. We should get there about half-twelve, one o'clock. If you get to see him straight away, we might be able to set off back around two.'

'Okay.'

It occurred to Lucy that she might not be in a fit state to ride anywhere after they got to Manchester, but she'd worry about that later. Her priority was to see if Billy was okay. She'd thought about him a lot during the past year and had decided it wasn't a bad thing that he was potty. They'd locked him up for a murder he hadn't done. Had he not been potty already that would have taken care of it. Still, it was wrong he'd been locked up. When she got there she'd tell everyone she could that he'd been with her when Ethel Tomlinson was murdered. She wasn't going to mention that to Arnold, though.

'I'm just gonna get a paper from that shop,' said her brother, getting down off the wall and walking to a nearby newsagent's. Lucy thought it a bit odd. She'd rarely seen him reading a newspaper paper, unless it was the *Green*

Final – a Leeds sports paper that came out every Saturday evening. He came back with a *Yorkshire Post* and sat back on the wall.

'Nothing on the front page,' he said.

'Nothing about what?'

'That bloke I knocked off his bike. He didn't look too good. If he'd croaked it'd have been on the front page.'

'Blimey, Arnold! Yer never told me he was badly hurt.'

Arnold turned to the inner pages. 'Oh, heck!' he said.

'What?' said Lucy.

'Oh, heck, Lucy!'

'Arnold!'

'Yer know that bloke who came off his bike?'

'What? 'Course I d—'

'He's a copper. His name's Daniel Earnshawe.'

'Blimey, Arnold! I thought you were going to say he's dead.'

'Badly hurt it says here. He's in hospital with broken ribs and serious internal injuries. Oh, heck, Lucy! I didn't meant to hurt him, just slow him down a bit.'

'Does it mention us at all?' said a shocked Lucy.

'It says he recovered consciousness for long enough to tell police officers he was chasing a bicycle thief – a young girl of around fifteen with fair hair. She had an accomplice, a young man of around eighteen wearing a red woollen cap, grey sweater and blue jeans. The accomplice caused the police officer to fall from his bicycle during his pursuit of the thief. The officer has since lapsed into a coma.'

Arnold immediately took off his red woollen cap and stuffed it in his pocket. He was now wearing a brown windcheater over his grey sweater. Without the hat his luxuriant ginger hair tumbled down almost to shoulder length. Lucy went pale.

'Blimey, Arnold! What if he dies?'

'Oh, don't say that, Lucy.'

'If he dies it means we killed him.'

'It means *I* killed him,' Arnold corrected her. 'He's a detective inspector,' he added, still reading.

'How will they know it's us?' asked Lucy.

'Dunno. I'm dumping this cap. I've only had it a couple of days so it's not as though loads of people have seen me wearing it.'

'Mam has,' said Lucy.

They sat there in silence for several minutes, each young mind consumed by dreadful thoughts.

'She's not gonna shop me,' said Arnold.

'If Mam doesn't, no one else is,' said Lucy.

'What about Weary Walter?'

'Yeah, Weary might. They think I found a bike in the woods. They might think differently now.'

'If we had a phone at home I'd ring me mam,' said Arnold.

'And say what?'

'I'd tell her it wasn't us who pinched the bike.'

'You could ring Mrs Ramsden's next door – she'll get me mam round'

'Might do that.'

'Mam'll wonder why you're telling her all that. In fact, with you telling her that, she'll *know* we did it.'

'I'm scared, Lucy.'

'So am I.'

'Oh, I do hope he's all right, that copper. Do you think I should ring the hospital up and ask how he is? Maybe I could tell them I'm his brother or nephew or something.'

Lucy nodded, slowly. Knowing the copper wasn't dead would be good. But what if he *was* dead? How would her brother cope with that? She studied Arnold's pale face, remembering that he'd done all this for her.

'I'll ring, if you like,' she said. 'There's a phone box over there. I expect it's got a Leeds phone book inside. Which hospital is it?'

'Leeds Infirmary.'

'Have you got any change?'

'Yeah.'

Dismally, Arnold stuck his hand in his pocket and brought out a handful of coins. His hand was shaking so much some dropped to the pavement. Lucy picked it up and said, 'There's enough here.'

Within two minutes she was in the phone box dialling Leeds General Infirmary. The switchboard operator replied. Lucy said, 'Erm ... my name's Mary Earnshawe. I'm enquiring about my uncle Daniel Earnshawe who was brought in yesterday. We've just read about him in the paper and my mother has asked me to find out how he is.'

'Daniel Earnshawe ... let me ... Yes, he's not on a ward as yet. I'm putting you through to Casualty ...'

'Casualty ... Sister O'Brien speaking.'

Lucy repeated her lie with a little more conviction this time.

'You're his niece?'

'Yes. My mother is his sister and she's very worried so I told her I'd find out how he is. She can't come to the phone herself because she can't leave the baby. He's only a week old.'

Lucy had thought of that one on the spur of the moment and considered it a stroke of genius even as she was saying it.

'Well, you can tell your mother that her brother's condition has now stabilised. He's out of theatre and the operation was successful, but he had a very close call.'

'Oh, thank you ever so much.' Lucy wasn't faking this. Her relief at not being an accomplice to murder was immense.

'I believe he's a policeman,' said the Casualty sister.

'Yes, a detective inspector.'

'Well, I hope they catch the person responsible.'

'So do I. He's going to be all right, is he?'

'I suspect it'll be a while before he goes back to work, but if you ring tomorrow he should be on a ward and you can probably visit.'

Lucy was looking through the phone box window at Arnold whose eyes were glued to her. She stuck a thumb up, hoping he could see it, but he couldn't make out much at all through his tears.

'Thank you very much, I'll do that.'

Lucy put the phone down and heaved out a sigh of relief. Arnold got down off the wall as she approached. He was trying to read her body language. She gave him a broad smile and called out, 'He's going to be okay.'

Arnold's already misty eyes flooded with tears. Lucy went to him and gave him a hug. He clung to her like he'd never clung to anyone in his life, not even his mam.

'Thanks for that, Lucy. I couldn't have done it myself.'

'Well, we do stuff for each other, don't we, our kid?'

'Yep, it's what we do. How is he?'

'I think it was touch-and-go but he's had an operation and his condition has stabilised, whatever that means. She said he'll be on a ward tomorrow and we can visit if we like.'

'Who did you say you were?'

'I said I was his niece, Mary Earnshawe, and my mother, who is his sister, is worried about him only she can't come to the phone because of the baby.'

'Baby?'

'Yeah, she had a baby a week ago. I thought they might have a bit of sympathy for her in the circumstances.'

'If your mother is his sister you wouldn't be called Earnshawe – unless she's not married which would make you a . . .'

'I know what it would make me, clever clogs, you don't have to say it.'

Arnold managed a grin and said, 'Apart from that, you did well.' Then his grin turned sour and he squeezed his eyes tight shut.

'You okay, Arnold?'

He shook his head. 'No, not really. I've never hurt anyone before and it doesn't feel right. I know I've been in a few scraps, but that's only bloody noses and bruises – most of 'em mine. Properly hurting someone who wasn't doing anything wrong, that's not me, Lucy.'

'I know that, Arnold. You've never been a thug.'

'I feel as if I should apologise to him.'

'There's nothing to be gained by us owning up to it.'

Arnold dried his eyes on his sleeve. 'We might not have

to own up to it when Mam and Weary read about it and put two and two together. You know how strait-laced Weary is. Me nearly killing a copper isn't going to sit well with his Methodist conscience. Pity he's not a Catholic like us lot. We can always confess our biggest sins to Father O'Duffy.'

'I think I might leave it till the heat's died down before I confess to nicking the bike,' said Lucy.

'Weary's a bit of a worry.'

'There's one thing for certain,' said Lucy.

'What's that?'

'I can't keep the bike.'

'True. There's another thing for certain.'

'What's that?'

'I'm not telling me mam owt. If she finds out, she finds out. If Weary shops us, he shops us.'

'Okay. You can always ring her up to tell her we're all right and should be back around teatime. If she's read anything about the bike thieves an' thinks it's us she'll tell us then. What's Masham like anyway?'

'Why do you want to know?'

'It's where we're supposed to be going. She might ask me about it later.'

'It's just a village in the Dales. It's got a church an' stuff.'

'Is that it?'

'Yep.'

'Mam'll be really impressed with my attention to detail when I tell her about it.'

'Anyway, I think we should be makin' tracks again. How're you doin'?'

'Me legs are aching like mad.'

'You'll work through all that. We'll stop a couple of times before we get ter t' tops, then it's downhill all the way – well, mostly anyway.'

'How far till it's downhill?'

'About ten or twelve miles from here. We've got five miles of mostly flat then we'll have a break, then about seven miles mostly uphill. We'll have a break halfway up.'

'Is that when we eat our sandwiches?'

'Nope. We eat our sandwiches when we get to't top. They'll taste that much nicer.'

'I hope we can get in to see Billy.'

'I hope that's where he is,' said Arnold.

'It's where Mrs Sixsmith says he is, and she should know. They're supposed to keep her informed. That's what she told me yesterday.'

'Does she think he did it?'

'No. I told her where he was when Ethel was done in – and she believes me. She's glad I'm going because she wants to know how Billy's going on herself.'

'Have you got that letter she gave you to show 'em?'

''Course I have.'

As they walked over to their bicycles Lucy paused and said, 'What do we do if Weary Walter tells on us?'

'We deny it was us. In fact, I think I've got an idea . . .'

'What is it?'

'Gimme a chance, our lass. I haven't thought it all out yet. These things need thinking through properly. I need to cover all the angles.'

'Right.'

They mounted their bicycles and had cycled through

Huddersfield when Arnold slowed down until Lucy was alongside him.

'I think I've got it worked out,' he said. 'Just see if you can pick any bones out of this. Do you know Barry Wigglesworth's sister?'

'Eileen? 'Course I do. She's one of me pals.'

'Hasn't she got a bike a bit like that?'

'A bit like it, yeah. Same colour anyway.'

'I thought so. They're on holiday right now, aren't they?'

'Yeah, Butlin's, I think . . . why?'

'Because our shed key fits their shed door.'

For the next half-mile Arnold outlined his plan. When he came to the end of it he grinned in triumph, anticipating admiration for such a brilliant idea. Lucy shot him down in one short sentence.

'What if the copper recognises us?'

Arnold's face fell and he rode on ahead for a while, then dropped back again. 'I know this sounds rotten, but if he took a nasty knock his memory for faces might not be too good.'

'He gave that description that was in the papers.'

'Only what we were wearing. I doubt if he'd recognise me in owt else. I was wearing that red hat and he hardly looked at my face. Did he get a good look at you?'

'Dunno. He'll have seen me coming out of the car park.'

'I bet you had your head down. You always ride with your head down – never look where you're going.'

'I don't any more.'

'Mebbe not now, but you did at first. No way can he be

sure it was us. We've just got to figure out something else we were doing – but not together. We weren't together, that's what we have to say. Get thinkin', our kid.'

'Okay.'

They pedalled on in silence until the undulating road became a constant uphill grind. They cycled up it for five miles before Arnold, leading the way, swung his leg over the crossbar and cruised to a halt. A grateful Lucy did like-wise.

'Ten-minute sit down,' he instructed brusquely.

'I thought you said we could have a break *before* we started up the hill.'

'Did I really?'

'Yes. Are you okay?'

'Nope. I feel lousy. I've seriously hurt a bloke who was just doing what I'd have done in the same circumstances – or rather what I should have done. Did this woman say that he'd make a complete recovery?'

'I got that impression. She said it might be a while before he went back to work, though.'

'I'm an idiot.'

'If you hadn't been an idiot he'd have caught me and I'd have been in a lot of trouble, which would have put me in a poor position to help Billy.'

'I wish you'd drop this Billy business, Lucy. It'll get you nothing but trouble.'

'Arnold, he's a friend of mine who's locked up for an awful crime he didn't do, so how am I supposed to drop it? Okay, that copper didn't do anything wrong, but he gets a few weeks off work with his feet up. Billy didn't do anything wrong and he's locked up for life in a nuthouse, all because of coppers gettin' it wrong ... so don't ask me to feel sorry for that copper who was chasing me an' trying to get me banged up.'

Arnold nodded his head in admiration of Lucy's convenient logic. 'If you're trying to make me feel better about knocking that copper off his bike you're doing a grand job.'

'Good. Now can I have a sandwich, please?'

'Not till we get to the top. There's a sign saying Saddleworth about two miles up this hill, that's where we have a celebratory sarnie or two – and that's where we start freewheeling down the other side of these hills.'

'Two more miles?'

'About that, yeah.'

Lucy shivered and pulled up the collar of her coat as she looked at the bleak, moorland all around. Grey clouds hovered just overhead like a dirty blanket, obscuring the hilltops a mile ahead; another ten minutes and they'd be riding through fog. A pre-war Austin 7 snarled its way past them, leaving behind a cloud of blue exhaust fumes, the driver hunched over the wheel as if praying that his flimsy vehicle would make it to the top of these grim Pennines, known as the backbone of England to those who didn't have to travel up and down them too often. The arsebone to those who did.

'I'm not coming into the loony bin with you,' said Arnold. 'You know that, don't you?'

'I know, you told me.'

'Just so long as you know. You'd better hope they don't keep you in.'

'Well, I'm used to living in a nuthouse.'

They re-mounted their bikes and stood on the pedals to get them up to the foggy hilltop. Lucy's legs were aching more than she could ever remember and she knew she wouldn't be able to cycle back that same day. In fact, she'd struggle to cycle back that same week. No point telling old misery guts that, though.

Chapter 10

Norton Park was a secure psychiatric hospital a few miles
east of Manchester. Lucy and Arnold stopped their bikes
well short of the iron gate, which stood ten feet high and
was manned by a gatekeeper who stood looking at them
suspiciously through the bars. He was a tall, bulbous man
in a dark blue uniform and peaked cap. He had his own
shelter, which looked like a sentry box. On the ground
just outside were at least ten cigarette stubs. His latest cig
was still in his mouth. Arnold didn't fancy their chances of
getting past him.

'Could be you don't even get in,' he murmured.

Lucy looked beyond the gate at the hospital which had
become Billy's home. It was a sprawling brick-built building set among tidy, well-kept lawns and surrounded by a
high wall topped with barbed wire, just like the dogs'
home back in Leeds. It was to be hoped they didn't treat
Billy like a dog, Lucy thought.

'Okay, I'll come with you if you like,' Arnold offered,
surprising himself by his generosity. It had been too long
a journey for it to end in failure. Lucy took out her letter
from Mrs Sixsmith.

'It's up to you,' she said, grateful that he'd volunteered.

They got off their bikes and wheeled them towards the closed gate. The gatekeeper wore a severe expression and kept his arms folded over his chest. He took out the stub of his cigarette and dropped it to the ground along with the others, stamping on it. Lucy and Arnold smiled at him.

'We've been sent from Leeds by the guardian of one of the patients here,' said Arnold.

'Come on your bikes, have you?'

'Yes, we have,' said Lucy, holding out Mrs Sixsmith's letter. 'This is from her – it's official. She requests permission for us to visit William Wellington.'

She gave the man the letter through the bars. 'Your request should have been submitted and granted before you set off,' he said.

Lucy nodded. 'That's what she said, but we asked her to make an official request, with us riding over here anyway today – in the hope that some kind person might let us in.'

'We've actually come to see the match,' said Arnold. 'Our cousin Tommy's playin'.'

'What match would that be?'

'United are playing Chelsea. Our Tommy plays for United.'

The man looked down at the letter, which was on the Children's Home notepaper and made official by Leeds City Council's coat of arms.

I would be grateful if you would allow the bearers of this letter, Miss Lucy Bailey and her brother Arnold Bailey, to visit William Wellington who was a former resident of this home.

The guard read it and looked back at them. 'So, who's this Tommy who plays for United?'

'It's our Tommy,' said Arnold. 'His dad's married to our Auntie Violet.'

'That's me mam's sister,' added Lucy.

'Tommy Taylor,' said Arnold.

'Our Auntie Violet married Tommy's dad. That why we're called Bailey and not Taylor.'

'He comes from Yorkshire like us, y'know,' said Arnold.

'I know that, lad. So, you're Tommy Taylor's cousin?'

'We both are,' said Lucy.

'He's older than us is Tommy,' said Arnold. 'I think he's twenty-three now but we get on with him all right, don't we, Lucy?'

'We do. We're stopping at his house tonight.'

'Well, it's Auntie Violet's house. She's takin' us to Old Trafford in her car,' said Arnold, 'so we've got loads of time to visit Billy.'

'Well,' said the gatekeeper thoughtfully, 'it could be that you're spinning me a pack of lies, but with Tommy Taylor being my favourite footballer I don't want to take the risk of upsetting his family.' He pushed the letter back through the bars. 'So, I'd best not hold up Tommy Taylor's cousins.'

He opened the gate. Lucy and Arnold mounted their bikes and rode up to the hospital's front entrance.

'Are you sure Tommy Taylor comes from Yorkshire?' Lucy asked.

'Yeah, he's from Barnsley.'

'And who's Auntie Violet?'

'It's what Tommy Taylor's mam's called. I read about him once.'

'Do you remember everything you read?'

'Only stuff I'm interested in.'

Arnold tried the same story on the receptionist, who wasn't a Manchester United supporter, but she did take notice of Mrs Sixsmith's letter. She looked up at them.

'It's against regulations but I know Billy and I don't think he's had a visitor since he arrived . . .'

'He's a nice person, isn't he?' said Lucy quickly.

'He does seem to be a nice young man.'

'He's been sent here because of something he didn't do.'

'Lucy!' cautioned Arnold. 'I'm sorry, miss. My sister has got a real bee in her bonnet about Billy.'

'That's because he was with me when that girl was killed,' protested Lucy.

The receptionist looked from one teenager to the other. Arnold shook his head in despair and glowered at his sister. 'You've put her off helping us now, you idiot! She'll be worried you'll start kicking off when you get in to see Billy.'

'I just want to make sure he's okay. I'm not gonna kick off or owt.'

'If you do, they'll most likely keep you in,' warned Arnold.

The receptionist was amused by this exchange between brother and sister. 'I'll see what I can do,' she said, picking up the telephone.

She exchanged a few words with someone before saying, 'Thanks, I'm sending them over now.' She looked up at them and said, 'You can have half an hour with him before lunch. He's in Boswell Wing ... back out the way you came in, turn left, first left after that, and it's about fifty yards on your right. Tell reception who you are and they'll show you to the room he'll be in.'

They were taken to a small visiting room with three tables and twelve chairs. They were escorted by a man in a white coat who asked them to sit down and wait while he brought Billy.

As Arnold made his way across the room he noticed a door in the far corner with WC written on it.

'I'm just nipping to the bog before Billy comes.'

When he came out he selected a table beside a barred window. Lucy sat beside him. A minute later the man returned with Billy who obviously had no idea what to expect. Lucy got to her feet and went to him. He looked her up and down, confused.

'Billy, it's me, Lucy.'

He stared at her for a long moment, then blurted out, 'They said you were dead.'

'What?'

'You're dead you are.'

'No, Billy. It's Ethel who's dead.'

'I don't remember no Ethel.'

'They said you killed Ethel but you can't have because you were with me.'

The man in the white coat said, 'I'll leave you to it. I'll be right outside that door.'

'Billy, come and sit down here.'

He followed Lucy obediently and sat down in a chair opposite her and Arnold, whom he didn't remember. 'I don't know you,' he said.

'That's okay, Billy. I'm Arnold, Lucy's brother. You remember Lucy, don't you?'

'They said she was dead,' Billy repeated.

'Not Lucy. They didn't say Lucy was dead.'

Lucy reached across the table and took his hand. 'Billy, do you remember setting the dogs free?'

His face creased into a broad smile. 'Yeah, we let 'em all go. Got Wilf, didn't we?'

'So you remember Wilf, that's good,' said Lucy. 'Do you know why they brought you here?'

''Cos I'm potty.'

'But you were potty when you lived with Missis. Is this as good as living with Missis?'

'Aw, no. Missis was good. Missis didn't hurt Billy.'

'What? Billy, what are those marks on your head?'

She pointed to several pink circles on his forehead and temples.

'It's where they stick the burny things what make Billy jump.'

'I think he's being given ECT,' said Arnold, who was studying physics and knew all sorts of stuff.

'What's ECT?' Lucy asked.

'Electro Convulsive Therapy. It's supposed to alter the balance of the brain or something.'

'Doesn't seem to be doing Billy any good.'

'True – from what I've read, it's not an infallible remedy for mental illness.'

'You mean, they're using him as a guinea pig?'

'Yeah,' said Arnold, 'a human guinea pig. The next thing they do is a frontal lobotomy.'

'What's that?'

'They drill a hole in the front of your skull, right into the brain.'

'Does it work?'

'Not that I know of. It can turn people into cabbages.'

'This is nothing to joke about, Arnold. Billy is my friend.'

Arnold shrugged. 'I'm only telling you what I've read about these places.'

'He doesn't belong here,' said Lucy. 'He belongs with his mam. She lives in Middleton.'

'How do you know?'

'She went to the home to ask Mrs Sixsmith about him.'

'You never told me that. I thought she'd vanished into thin air?'

'No, she turned up at the home about three weeks ago. She had a cup of tea with Mrs Sixsmith and told her the whole story.'

'Well, that's more than you've told me.'

'Didn't think you'd be interested. You're always banging on about how I should leave the Billy thing alone before I get into trouble.'

'So, what did this woman tell Mrs Sixsmith?'

'Told her she'd been assaulted as a girl and made pregnant. She was only fourteen so she left the baby in the bus station. Mrs Sixsmith said she was a very nice person. Her name's Helen Durkin.'

'Missis,' repeated Billy, a name he remembered with affection.

Arnold was looking out of the window, deep in thought. A dustbin wagon was parked outside, with men emptying bins into it. Arnold got to his feet and studied what was going on. Then he turned back.

'Billy,' he said, 'would you like to have a go at getting out of here?'

''Course I would. It's no good in here.'

'What are you on about, Arnold?' Lucy asked. 'Is this another of your plans?'

'I'm not saying it'll work,' he said, 'but Billy's hardly got much to lose by trying.'

'What's the plan then?'

'It depends on him remembering what I say.' Arnold looked at Billy. 'I'm going to give you a few instructions, all quite simple but you must remember them.'

'I can remember stuff what I want to remember,' said Billy. 'Like I can remember settin' Wilf free and all them other dogs.'

'But you can't remember why you were sent here,' Lucy said.

'No. I don't want to, neither.'

'You've got a very selective memory, Billy,' Arnold said. 'But I want you to remember what I'm about to tell you because if you do you might be able to get out of here and then we can take you somewhere better. Are you ready to remember?'

Billy nodded eagerly. Arnold outlined his plan while Lucy listened with mounting admiration for her brother and his active brain. When he'd finished, Arnold asked Billy to repeat back the instructions. It took Billy three goes before he got it right. Arnold made him repeat it a fourth time.

'Okay,' he said. He put his hand in his pocket and

brought out some change from which he selected a few coins. 'Here's three bob. It's for your bus fare to Manchester Piccadilly station – and it's Piccadilly, not Piccalilli.'

This made Billy grin.

'It should be no more than a shilling so if you get it wrong there's money for another couple of tries.'

'I'll get it right first time, me. I remember how to go on buses. I give the man a shilling and I say Manchester Piccalilli, please. Then I ask him to tell me when we're there.'

'Piccadilly,' said Arnold, emphasising the 'd'.

'I should think Piccalilly'll get him there,' said Lucy.

'Piccadilly,' said Arnold.

He reached out and shook Billy's hand. 'Good man. Right, off you go.'

Lucy leaned over and kissed Billy on his cheek. He put his hand over his mouth in embarrassment then made his way to the toilet in the corner.

'Bolt the door behind you,' said Arnold.

'I know. Okey-dokey.'

Billy gave them a last grin and disappeared into the cubicle. He climbed through the window and jumped out. They both went to the window of the visitors' room and watched as he ran across to the bin-wagon and climbed in the back while the men were busy collecting bins.

'So far so good,' murmured Arnold.

'Is this why you went to the toilet?'

'Yeah. I always like to check everything out, just in case.'

'Just in case what?'

'Just in case I need to go for a pee or Billy wants to do a runner. I opened the window for him. I like to cover every angle, remember.'

'I can think of one angle you haven't covered.'

'What?'

'Us – aren't we going to get into big trouble for this?'

'Nothing to do with us. All we know is he went to the bog and didn't come back out. How can that be our fault? I didn't know you could get out through the bog window.'

'It's a glass door. That bloke might have seen you go in.'

'He didn't. He had his back to the door all the time. I was watching him.'

'Maybe he heard you flush it.'

'I didn't flush it. There was nothing to flush.'

'Right.'

It didn't sound like a fool-proof plan to Lucy. After a few minutes two men arrived and emptied bins into the wagon. Lucy grimaced, knowing they'd been emptied on top of Billy.

'Don't shout out, Billy,' murmured Arnold.

'I hope you're right about this being the last pick-up,' she said.

'I've been watching the direction the wagon's coming from. It's heading for the gate and there are no more buildings between here and the gate.'

'We hope,' said Lucy, 'or Billy'll be drowned in muck.'

The men got in the wagon. It moved off and turned a corner. Lucy and Arnold listened to the sound of the noisy diesel engine, which seemed to be picking up speed before dying away into the distance. It was doing no more pick-ups, as Arnold had forecast.

'Blimey, I think it's worked!' He sounded amazed.

The wagon came into view again as it neared the gate. They both almost cheered when the gate opened and the vehicle drove out. At some point it would stop at traffic lights which was when Billy had been told to get out, find a bus stop and ask someone if buses from there went to Piccadilly – not Piccalilli.

They sat in silence for five minutes then Arnold went over to the toilet door and tried it. It was locked as per his instructions. He knocked loudly, then called out Billy's name, knocking at the same time.

'Billy, are you all right?'

The door to the visitors' room opened and the man in the white coat appeared. 'Is everything all right?'

'I don't know,' said a concerned-looking Arnold. 'Billy went in here about ten minutes ago and I'm wondering if he's okay. But I can't get him to answer.'

The man joined him, as did Lucy. All of them shouted through the door.

'Oh, heck!' said Lucy. 'I hope he hasn't done anything silly.'

'The door's bolted from the inside,' said the man. 'I'm going to have to kick it open. Stand back, both of you.'

He stood back and kicked at it with the sole of his right shoe. It flew open. The man went inside, closely followed by Arnold and Lucy. Only one of them was shocked that it was empty and the window open.

'Bloody hell! He's got out.'

'Oh, Billy, you idiot!' said Lucy, convincingly. 'What's

he done that for? He can hardly get over the flipping walls.'

'No,' said the man. 'He'll not have gone far. We'll pick him up soon enough. I'm afraid your visit's over.'

'Surely there should be bars on that window,' said Arnold.

'I know, but this convenience has only just been added. The builders obviously haven't got round to it yet. We'll have to put it out-of-use until they finish. Bloody builders!'

'Oh, dear,' said Lucy, sorrowfully. 'Will Billy be in a lot of trouble when you find him? I mean, it's got to be the builders' fault really for putting temptation in his way.'

'He'll have to be severely reprimanded, I'm afraid. It seems you've had a long and wasted journey.'

'Not entirely,' said Arnold. 'We've actually come to watch United play Chelsea.'

*

Twenty minutes later Lucy and Arnold were cycling around Piccadilly Station checking all the bus stops. Billy had been instructed to get off at the station and wait by the bus stop. Trouble was, which one? They'd found eight so far but no sign of Billy. They were just setting off to do another circuit when Lucy saw a dishevelled figure sitting on a doorstep. She called out to Arnold and pulled up opposite the figure. It was Billy, much the worse for wear. He was covered in filth. They went over to him.

'All right, Billy?' called out Lucy. He looked up and grinned.

'Got kicked off two buses,' he said, 'but I got here. If I had a bike, I could have come with you.'

'Can you ride a bike?' Arnold asked.

'I don't know. I never rode one before, so I'm not sure.'

'It can be dangerous, Billy,' said Lucy. 'I know a lad who fell off his bike last week. He's got a broken leg, a broken arm and a black eye.'

'No wonder he fell off his bike,' said Billy.

Arnold cracked up. Billy laughed as well, although he didn't know why. He just liked laughing and he hadn't had much to laugh about for a long time.

'Billy,' Lucy said, 'you pong something cruel. We need to get you cleaned up.'

She tried to brush some of the dirt off him with her hand. A lot of it was stuck to his hair so she took a comb from her bag and tidied it up. 'I don't know what we're going to do about the pong, Billy. You might have to throw this jumper away.' She looked at Arnold and asked, 'How're we going to get him back to Leeds?'

'First things first,' said Arnold. 'I'll take him into the station bogs. See if I can get him cleaned up a bit more.' Then he held up a finger indicating an idea had arrived. 'No, Lucy, you stay here with him. I'm taking your bike.'

With no further explanation he mounted Lucy's stolen bike and rode back up the road. Lucy spent the next twenty minutes picking bits of rubbish off Billy and dusting him down with her hand. He complained that she was hurting him.

'Don't be so soft, Billy Wellington. It's me who's suffering here with the smell coming off you.'

'I'm hungry,' he said. 'I haven't had no dinner.'

'Right, I've got a sandwich left in my bag.'

'What sort of sandwich?'

'Lettuce and tomato.'

'Don't like lettuce and tomato.'

'You'll just have to stay hungry then.'

'All right, I'll eat it. What's it taste of?'

'Lettuce and tomato, mainly.'

She gave him the sandwich and he bit into it hungrily. She was wishing they had enough money to buy him a decent meal in the station.

'Do you know what thumbs are for?' he asked, suddenly.

'No idea.'

'Thumbs are for sandwiches.'

'Sandwiches?'

'Yeah. If you didn't have thumbs, the bottom would fall off your sandwiches.'

'I never knew that.'

'Y'see, I know some stuff you don't know.'

'Billy, you know stuff nobody knows.'

He smiled triumphantly. 'I never went to school or nowt, me, yer know. I just know stuff.'

'Self-taught lad,' said Lucy. 'Nobody ever taught you the three Rs.'

'I know what they are anyway' said Billy. 'Missis told me.'

'What are they then?'

Billy screwed up his face in order to get the three words in proper order. 'Readin', writin' and reckonin' up. I'm right, aren't I?'

'Spot on, Billy. I must remember that meself.'

103

After a while Arnold arrived back on foot, holding a bulging carrier bag

'Where's me bike?' Lucy asked.

'Sold it.'

'Sold it? What for?'

'So you and Billy can go back to Leeds on the train. Do you remember passing a second-hand shop back there, with a sign reading *We Buy Owt*?'

Lucy shook her head. 'I was concentrating on looking for Billy.'

'Well, they gave me three pounds seven and six for the bike. I think the fare to Leeds is about five bob one way, so that's ten bob for the two of you. They had some second-hand clothes there so I've got Billy some stuff – jeans and shirt and a woolly jumper, and a bar of soap, all for a quid, so there's some dosh left over.'

'For Billy,' said Lucy.

'For Billy,' agreed Arnold. 'Okay, I'll lock me bike up to that lamp post and we'll get him into the station. I reckon the people at the hospital'll still be searching the grounds. I doubt they'll believe he'll be able to make it to the station. In fact, they'll be baffled as to why they can't find him in the grounds. What are you going to do when you get him to Leeds?'

'I'll take him to his mam's in Middleton. Let her look after him.'

'Let's hope she does.'

'Mrs Sixsmith seemed to think she's okay – very concerned about her son. She didn't know anything about him until she saw the report in the paper. If I take him to her and tell her that Billy was with me when Ethel was killed, I think she'll believe me. And with her being his mam she'll take a lot better care of him than we can.'

'It took her a long time to get in touch,' Arnold commented. 'It must be a year since she read about him.'

'She had her reasons. She definitely had a good one for leaving him in a bus station when he was a baby.'

'Hmm, methinks there's more to that than meets the eye,' said Arnold, theatrically. 'Anyway, when you get back to Leeds, don't go home without seeing me first. When I get back I'm going straight there to find out how things stand with Weary. If he's shopped us to the police, I'll find out what's happening then I'm out of there. If there's a cop car outside the house, I won't be going in. Either way I'll meet you at the shops in . . .' He looked at his watch. 'It's half-past one now . . . say six o'clock to be on the safe side.'

'Can you get back by six?' Lucy asked.

'Yeah. If I make just one stop I can do it in four hours easy, but if I'm not there, wait for me. We'll need our story to be straight, not messed up by events we don't know about yet. When I meet you I hope to be fully up-to-date. But none of this will be necessary if Weary hasn't shopped us to the police.'

'I'm not holding my breath, Arnold. *We* know the copper's going to be okay, but Mam and Weary Walter might not.'

'Six o'clock at the shops then.'

'Okay, that should give me time to get Billy to his mam's. Blimey, I hope she's in.'

'Well, it's Saturday,' said Arnold, 'she probably won't be working.'

'If she's not at home I'll be outside the shops with Billy. We'll have to think of what to do with him then.'

'I'll work something out. Come on, let's get him cleaned up.'

'Before we do ... Billy, tell Arnold what thumbs are for.'

Chapter 11

Helen had no idea who the two young people standing on her step were, but they were looking at her expectantly.

'Yes?' she said.

'Mrs Durkin?' said Lucy.

'Well, it's *Miss* Durkin. What is it you want?'

'Do you have a son called Billy who's eighteen years old?'

'Do you mind if I ask why you want to know?'

'Well, erm . . . was it you who went to the children's home on Estate a few weeks ago to enquire about your son William . . . who's eighteen?'

'It was, yes.'

'I'm sorry. I thought you'd be older.'

Lucy hadn't done her sums. If she had she'd have known that fourteen years plus eighteen years was thirty-two years – Helen's age.

'Really? Why should I be older?'

'Because you've got an eighteen-year-old son and you don't look old enou— oh, sorry.'

Lucy had now done her sums.

Helen sighed.

'Look, what's this all about?'

'Well . . . this is him.'

'What?'

'This is Billy. He was locked up in a mental hospital in Manchester, but we've got him out because he didn't kill that girl. I know because he was with me at the time, miles away.'

'Billy? You mean this—'

'William, yes. This is your son who you were asking about.'

Helen was staring at Billy with tears flooding her eyes. 'You're William?'

'I'm Billy Wellington. That's me. I don't know who you are.'

'Billy,' said Lucy. 'This is your mother – your mam.'

Helen was surprised by how normal he looked. Not a bit like the violent criminal she'd imagined him to be from the newspaper reports. He was tall, strongly built, with a pleasant enough face. Only his bewildered eyes perhaps betrayed his lack of understanding of what was happening.

'I haven't got a mam,' he said.

'Billy,' said Lucy, 'I've been telling you all the way here . . . everyone's got a mam unless they're dead, and your mam's not dead. This is her.' She looked at Helen who seemed frozen to the spot. 'Look, Miss Durkin, it might be better if you invite us in. We shouldn't be standing on the step because Billy shouldn't be here really.'

'Shouldn't be . . . ? Oh, yes! Oh, my Good Lord! Come in, come in.'

The three of them went through into a comfortable living room and sat down. Billy still had no real idea what was happening to him, other than that he'd been told that this woman he'd never seen before was his mother. He'd had mothers before, but they called themselves house-mother or some other title. He couldn't see how this woman might be any different. This meeting wasn't the momentous occasion for him that it was for Helen. Lucy sensed his confusion.

'Billy, this is your real mother. She's not a house-mother or a stepmother or anything like that. She's your proper mother.'

'Well, I don't know what a proper mother is.'

'Do you like tea, Billy?' asked Helen, who was struggling to find her voice.

'Yes, please. I like tea with two spoons of sugar. They only let me have one but I sometimes put another in when they're not looking.'

'Well, I'll let you have two,' said Helen, reaching out and touching a hand she hadn't touched since he was a baby. It was a soft hand that had done no work for the past year. His face was soft too and without character or guile or humour or acne or anything that was usually visible on the face of a teenager. This surely wasn't the face of a boy who'd committed a vile crime. Helen looked at Lucy.

'You say you were with him when the murder was committed?'

'Yes, we were miles away, and the police know that, but it didn't go to court with Billy being ... you know. He was judged unfit to plead, which means he had no chance.'

Helen wiped tears away with her sleeve. 'And you say you got him out of the place in Manchester where he was locked up?'

'Yeah, today. Me and my brother. It's a long story but Billy sneaked out in the back of a bin-wagon. We've had to get him new clothes. They're not much, but he was in a bit of a smelly state when he got out. I brought him back on the train.'

'Oh, Good Lord, what am I to do with him?'

'Hide him away from the coppers. They won't know he's here. They won't know he knows about you. *They* don't know about you.'

'The woman at the children's home knows about me. She's got my address as well.'

'Oh, heck, that's right. She gave it to me.'

'So, there's no reason she shouldn't give it to the police.'

'I don't suppose you've got a telephone, have you?'

'I have, yes.'

'Well, I could ring Mrs Sixsmith at the home and tell her about what happened today. As far as me and my brother are concerned, Billy just jumped through a toilet window and was loose in the grounds when we left. If the police have contacted her already, she'll tell me.'

'Right, you must do that.'

Lucy got the number from the phone book and rang the home. 'Mrs Sixsmith? This is Lucy Bailey ... I'm fine, thank you ... Yes, we got to see him but there was a problem. He went into a toilet and jumped out of a window when we were visiting him ... No he wasn't hurt so far as we know. They were searching the grounds for him when we left. I think he'll get into trouble for it ... No, *we* weren't in trouble. Well, it was nothing to do with us. The toilet window had no bars on it so he just opened it and jumped out. Can't say I blame him. I think I'd have done the same if I'd been locked up in that horrible place for something I didn't do ... He didn't look well at all, Mrs Sixsmith. He had these little marks all over his face where they'd been electrocuting him. ECT our Arnold called it. I was wondering if they'd been in touch with you at all to tell you what was happening ... Nothing? ... No, well, I expect they'd have rung you if they didn't catch him. Maybe you could ring them ... Right. Can I call you in the morning to find out what happened to him? ... Thank you, Mrs Sixsmith.'

Lucy put the phone down and smiled at Helen. 'No coppers so far.'

'Hmm,' said Helen, '*so far* being the operative words. I think I can keep him here overnight and then I will take him to my mother's in Scarborough. No one will find him there ...ever,' she said, looking at her son with an expression that pleased Lucy no end. She spoke to Billy.

'I want you to stay with your mother now. She's going to take you to the seaside tomorrow.'

'Seaside? Oh, I've never been to the seaside. I know about it though. There's sea and water and ships and stuff.'

'That's right, Billy. You'll love it.'

'I bet I will, you know.'

Helen looked at Lucy curiously. 'How come you're such good friends with him?'

'Billy's a really nice lad when you get to know him. He's funny as well – and he wouldn't harm a fly. He might have his problems but he's a son you can be proud of.'

'And your name is Lucy, is it?'

'Lucy Bailey. I live near the children's home. I've known Billy for years.'

'Would I be right in thinking that you're his only friend?'

'I'm probably his only sane friend – that's if you can call me sane after what I've done today.'

'Lucy, I think what you've done is wonderful. Will you stay and have something to eat?'

'I'd like that, thank you, but I need to be back for six o'clock. I'm meeting Arnold at six.' She looked around the room that should have been Billy's home. It was a nice place with photos and ornaments and a clean carpet and comfy chairs.

'So,' she said to Helen, 'you don't mind looking after an escaped jailbird?'

Helen smiled. 'He's not a jailbird. The world has given him a hard life and it's my duty as his mother to protect him. I also owe him a huge debt for abandoning him as a baby, but my circumstances were such that I had no option.'

'I'm glad you're his mam, Miss Durkin,' said Lucy. 'Really glad.'

'I think you'd better call me Helen.'

'You'll get to like him, Helen. If he trusts you, he'll do what you tell him and he'll make you laugh. He's a lovely lad.'

'Make me laugh, eh? Well, I could do with a good laugh now and again.'

Chapter 12

Billy stared at the departing Lucy much as a faithful dog might stare at his owner after being ordered to stay. His every instinct told him that he wanted to go after her but she'd told him to remain with this lady who was his mam.

Helen put an arm around his shoulders. He was six inches taller than she was and a complete stranger, but she knew he was her son; she could see something of herself in his features. It wasn't his fault that he'd had a difficult birth that had probably damaged him, and it wasn't his fault that poor Ethel had died – Helen believed Lucy's story. She had to believe Lucy's story. For Billy to be a killer would be an unbearable burden for Helen to carry. Lucy turned and waved at them, her blonde hair blowing in the wind. Billy and Helen waved in reply.

'She'll be back to see you, Billy. In the meantime, I want you to stay with me.'

'My mam,' said Billy, simply.

'You can call me that.' Helen smiled. 'Or you can call me Mum or Mother or even Helen, which is my Christian name.'

'My name's Billy.'

'I know that. I gave you that name. I haven't seen you since you were a tiny baby, and look at you now.'

'Was I a baby? I didn't even know I was a baby.'

Helen led him back inside. 'Everyone starts off as a baby, even big lads like you.'

'Am I going to live here now?'

'Well, probably not. You're not actually supposed to be here. Lucy got you out of that hospital because she thinks you shouldn't have been there.'

'I didn't like it very much. Will I be able to play out here?'

'Not here, but tomorrow I'm going to take you somewhere where you can go out.'

'Is that the seaside?'

'It is, yes. I'm going to take you to your grandmother's house. She lives near the seaside. It'll be quite safe for you there.'

She was assuming that her mother and Vernon wouldn't have any objection to having a fugitive grandson living with them. It was a hell of an assumption, Helen knew that, but she also knew that Billy couldn't stay with her, for many reasons, the main one being that the police would come knocking on her door at some time. She would tell them the true story of his birth and how she had not seen her father or mother since she'd abandoned Billy in Wellington Street bus station. It was a plausible-sounding story that would sever any connection that the police might want to make between her and her mother. Their search for Billy would grind to a halt and, at some time, this Lucy girl might well prove him to be innocent.

On the other hand maybe Helen's energies might be better spent helping Lucy, rather than searching for her stepfather in order to kill him. In fact, if she told the police what he had done, they might check back in their records and find him for her.

'I've got a new television,' she told Billy. 'Have you seen a television before?'

'No, don't know what a tel – tel—'

'Television. It's like the wireless only you can see the people who are talking.'

'What about singin'? Can you see people what are singin'?'

'Yes, singing as well.'

'Can you see Ruby Murray?'

'Yes, you can see Ruby Murray.'

'Never seen Ruby Murray. I bet she's very nice.'

'Oh, she is. She's very nice is Ruby Murray.'

'Can I see Ruby Murray, then?'

'Well, not unless she's in a show. If there's a show on television with Ruby Murray in it, you'll be able to see her.'

'When's that?'

'I don't know, but I'll try and find out. There'll be all sorts of other people you can see.'

'I like Alma Cogan as well. She's a woman, yer know, not a man. I used ter think she was a man with a funny voice.'

'Why did y—? Oh, right.'

Helen looked at him and wondered just what she was taking on, but she knew the answer as soon as the thought crossed her mind. She was taking responsibility for looking after the son she'd abandoned at birth. She was filling a massive gap in her life. When she'd killed her stepfather she'd fill another gap. It was a crime against nature for that man to be left alive.

Chapter 13

'Weary's shopped us.'

These were the words that Lucy had been dreading but more than half expecting as she got off the bus at the terminus outside the shops. Arnold was sitting on his bike, smoking a Woodbine. He didn't smoke much and had probably just bought a packet of five to calm his nerves. His hunched appearance told Lucy he was a worried lad.

'What did he say?'

'Well, I walked in the house and he grabbed hold of me. Mam was there looking really worried. He said, "The police are asking for you, lad. You're in very serious trouble, as is your sister."'

'I told him to let go of me or he'd be in very serious trouble.'

'Oh, heck! What did he say to that?'

'Well, he let go. I asked Mam what was this all about. She said he thought me and you were responsible for a policeman being badly injured in Alwoodley last night. Then she asked where you were.'

'What did you say?'

'I didn't say anything. I just walked out, got on me bike and came here.'

'Blimey, Arnold. I reckon Weary'll be in Mrs Ramsden's ringing the police to tell them you're back.'

'There's nothin' surer, Lucy. We need to go through my plan again. Do you remember it?'

'I do, including the bit where the copper might recognise us.'

'That's a risk we have to take. There's risk attached to everything.'

*

They walked into the house with a belligerence befitting the falsely accused. Walter was sitting at the dining table, scrutinising them. 'I've rung the police and told them you're back. They said to hold you here until they arrived, but if you want to throw your weight about, lad, it's up to you. It'll only make things worse.'

Arnold was holding the *Yorkshire Evening Post*. He said, 'I bought this to find out what you were talking about.' He grinned and added, 'I think I've worked it out, but I can't believe you're so daft.'

'Nor me,' said Lucy. 'You're not much of a father, never have been. I wish our proper dad hadn't been killed by Hitler. I wish he'd killed you instead.'

It was cruel, but it was a truth she'd never dared tell him before for fear of upsetting her mother.

'Lucy!' she scolded. 'You mustn't talk like that to Walter. Now apologise for being so rude.'

'No apology needed,' he said. 'They'll see the error of their ways soon enough – about now if I'm not mistaken.'

A car had just pulled up outside. Walter went to the window to confirm it was a police car. Two uniformed men got out, one of them a sergeant. There was a loud knock on the door. Walter answered it and showed the two policemen inside.

'Here you are, officers,' he said. 'I think these are the kids you're looking for.'

The sergeant looked balefully at Arnold. 'You admit this, do you, lad?'

'No,' he said.

The sergeant looked at Walter. 'Can you explain why you think they committed this offence, sir?'

'Yes. You're looking for two young people fitting their description who stole a bicycle. They came home last night with a bicycle that they said they'd found in Adel Woods. I thought it was suspicious when Arnold told me that. No one leaves new bikes lying about in the woods.'

The sergeant turned his attention to Arnold. 'Is this true, young man?'

'Sort of,' said Arnold.

'How do you mean, sort of?'

'Well, I told Walter we'd found the bike in the woods – but we hadn't actually found it. I borrowed it from Barry Wigglesworth's, so me and Lucy could ride to Manchester today.'

'Manchester?' said their mother. 'You said you were going to Masham.'

'We changed our minds, didn't we, Lucy? We went to Manchester to visit Billy Wellington.'

'Billy Wellington? What do you want to go visiting Billy Wellington for?'

'Because he's in trouble for something he didn't do, just

as we would be if you believe Weary Walter,' said Lucy, heatedly. 'He's supposed to be our stepfather but he's never liked us.'

'That's not true, Lucy, and you mustn't call him that! It's very rude.'

'It is true, Mam. What sort of proper father would try and get us into trouble like this, for something we didn't do?'

'Why did you tell your stepfather that you found the bike in the woods?' asked the constable, bemused.

'Well, it was supposed to be a joke,' said Arnold, 'at least I thought it was, until I realised he'd believed me. Most people would have known I was pulling their leg, but not him.'

'And where is this bike now?'

'It's back in Barry Wigglesworth's shed,' said Lucy. 'It's his sister Eileen's but she wouldn't have minded me borrowing it.'

'And does she know you borrowed it?'

'Well, not yet. They're on holiday at Butlin's for a fortnight. Eileen said I could borrow it if I wanted. Our shed key fits their shed door.'

'So, where were you yesterday evening around seven o'clock?'

'Me and Arnold went to Roundhay Park so I could get used to ridin' a bike, I didn't actually have much experience, with no one ever buyin' me one. All my friends have got bikes but I haven't.' Lucy glanced at Walter as she said it.

'And yet you cycled all the way to Manchester and back?'

'I did, yeah. Me legs are killing me. You can ring the home if you want. They saw us turn up on bikes.'

'I had to make me own bike,' added Arnold, trying to change the subject.

'Did anyone see you in Roundhay Park?' asked the sergeant.

'I imagine so,' said Arnold. 'There were loads of people there.'

'Including a lot of young people on bikes, no doubt?'

'Oh, yeah, there were loads of kids on bikes.'

'We can take you to see Eileen's bike, if you want,' offered Lucy. 'Mam'll be able to tell it's the one we came back with last night.'

She knew her mother had scarcely glanced at the bike and probably wouldn't even remember its colour, although Eileen's bike was a pretty good match.

'As police officers, we're not allowed to use your shed key to open someone else's property,' said the sergeant starchily.

'They won't mind,' said Arnold. 'Well, Barry won't. I don't know about his mam and dad.'

'Precisely.'

'What about the injured officer?' asked Walter, in desperation. 'Wouldn't he be able to recognise them?'

'I doubt it, sir. He suffered delayed concussion, which apparently affected his memory of the incident, and there's no good reason to doubt the explanation these two have given, so, for the time being, we won't trouble you further' He gave Walter a sour look. 'In future, sir, it might be better to get your facts straight before you bother us.'

'I don't know, Walter,' said Arnold. 'I must be such a disappointment to you. No matter how hard you try, you just can't get me locked up, can you?'

'He was only trying to do the right thing, Arnold,' said his mother, caustically. Then she added, for the policemen's benefit: 'My husband is a very religious man. He doesn't like dishonesty of any sort from anyone – not even one of his own.'

Both Arnold and Lucy looked at their mother, wondering if she could see through their lies.

Chapter 14

Daniel Earnshawe was feeling drowsy from painkillers when he saw the girl appear beside his bed. For a second he thought it was someone coming to take the order for his evening meal but no, this person was too young for such a job.

'Hello, Mr Earnshawe. I read about you in the paper and I thought I'd come and visit you,' she said.

'That's very kind of you, young lady. Do you have a name?'

'I'm Lucy Bailey from Leeds 17.'

'Do you always give out your postal address?'

'What? Er, no. It's a habit I've got.'

'Right. Another question. Do you always visit people you read about in the papers?'

'No, this is my first time. When I heard about what had happened I thought you'd be dying and that made me very sad. I don't live all that far away from where it happened, you see.'

'Well, you won't if you live in Leeds 17.'

'I live on the council estate.' She said it before he asked where she lived exactly.

'It's a nice estate,' he said. 'I have a few colleagues who live there.'

'Yeah, there are two coppers living up our street. How are you?'

'I'm going to be okay, I'm pleased to report, but thank you for your concern. Is that the only reason you came?'

'Well, maybe it isn't.'

'Oh?'

'You see, I would imagine you'd have to wait until you're fully fit before they let you back to work as a policeman.'

'True. The job does require a certain level of fitness.'

'And I was wondering if you might want to take on a case of . . . erm . . . a miscarriage of justice while you wait. To keep your hand in, so to speak.'

'Miscarriage of justice? That sounds serious.'

'It is. My friend Billy Wellington was locked up in a loony bin for murdering a girl, but it couldn't have been him because he was with me when she was murdered.'

'I see . . . Billy Wellington? Rings a bell. Last year, wasn't it?'

'It was about a year ago, yes. We went to see him yesterday and he was so upset, he jumped out of a window and ran off. I expect they've found him by now but it's rotten for him to be there. He's a bit simple, see.'

'Yes, I didn't work on it but I do remember the details, which is a miracle. My memory's a bit shot right now. Open and shut case, wasn't it?'

'So the police say. There's something else I ought to tell you.'

'What's that?'

'Well, I have a stepfather called Weary Walter who doesn't like me and my brother.

124

'Why's he called Weary?'

'He never smiles. He's a lot older than our mam and he's a bit of an old woman, to be honest. He's not cruel, he's just miserable. Never goes out of his way for us, if you know what I mean. I think it's with him being a Methodist.'

'My mother was a Methodist,' said Daniel. 'She wasn't miserable.'

'He's a vegetarian as well, and that can't be normal.'

'Why are you telling me this?'

'Well, he told the police it was me and my brother who stole that bike and had you chase us when it can't have been because I was in Roundhay Park with our Arnold then. I don't think the police were too pleased with Weary Walter for wasting their time like that. I wasn't too pleased either; neither was our Arnold. I mean, if you'd died and the coppers had believed him, we'd have been locked up for murder like Billy.'

'So, you made that connection with me, and thought you'd come and ask me to help you?'

'There is another reason.'

'What's that?'

'If it really was me who nicked that bike, I'd hardly come to visit you, would I? You'd have recognised me straight away. So now I can go back and tell that to Weary Walter, to get him off our backs, because he still thinks it was us.'

'Ah, you want to get one over on old Walter, do you?'

'Something like that.'

'Well, you can certainly tell Walter that I don't recognise you as the bike thief, but I probably wouldn't have recognised you, even if you were.'

'I don't think I'll tell him that last bit.'

'But you're quite right. The girl who stole that bike would be the last person to come and visit me.'

'I'll definitely tell him that.'

Daniel Earnshawe laughed. He was warming to this cheeky, charming girl.

'So, will you help us?'

'Oh, right now, Lucy, I don't feel as if I could help anyone do anything.'

'Maybe when you're feeling a bit better?'

'Tell you what. I'll be in here for another week or so. Come back in a few days when I don't have quite so many drugs in my system. We'll talk about it then.'

'Shall I come next Thursday evening?'

'I'll look forward to it,' said Daniel.

Chapter 15

Daniel already had two visitors, the maximum allowed, so Lucy had to wait outside the ward until they left, but not before she'd asked a nurse to tell him he had someone waiting. She was there half an hour before two girls came out. They gave her a quizzical smile and the older one, a girl of around her own age, said, 'Are you Lucy?'

'Yes.'

'Thought so. He's been telling us about you. You can go in now.'

'Thank you.'

She went in and made her way over to where Daniel was sitting in a chair beside his bed. He gave her a welcoming smile. 'Ah, you've just missed my daughters.'

'I know, I saw them as I came in. They seem very nice. I've been waiting outside. The nurse said you were only allowed two visitors.'

'I know – we mustn't disobey the nurses.'

'How are you today?'

'I'm on the mend.'

'So, does that mean you'll help us prove Billy's innocent?'

He stared at her for an uncomfortable moment, then

said. 'Do you know, a funny thing happened just after I came off my bike. I was in a bit of a state, but I was perfectly conscious and trying to cart the bike back up the street and suddenly I realised that I'd seen the girl I was chasing before, and I knew exactly where I'd seen her. That was just before I passed out.'

Lucy set her face into a frown to cover her alarm.

'I thought you said you wouldn't recognise her if you saw her again?'

'Well, I don't think I would.'

Lucy's frown relaxed.

'I just remember what I remembered before I passed out,' he said. 'Does that make sense to you?'

Lucy's frown returned. Daniel went on: 'Fortunately it wouldn't be too difficult for me get her actual name. I remember the exact circumstances under which I saw her. She was in the police station about a year ago to give a statement. I can't remember what she looked like but I know she was the same girl I chased – how weird is that? Memory's a strange thing – or my memory at any rate.'

Lucy remembered exactly why she'd been in the police station: to give a statement on Billy's behalf. They had her name and address and he'd have no trouble getting it. Her heart was in her mouth when he added, 'So, what do you think I should do if I find her?'

'I dunno.'

'Nor me. You see, it wasn't she who committed the biggest crime. That was her accomplice. He caused me grievous bodily harm, which is a serious custodial offence – twelve months at least. She'd get off with a fine and twenty-four hours in a detention centre, unless she has previous. What do you think she deserves?'

'I dunno.'

'Well, she stole a bike off another girl who came by it honestly. How would you feel if someone stole your bike?'

'I haven't got a bike. And I suppose that girl's got a new one by now.'

'Really? How come?'

'Well, it's a posh street. I bet everyone who lives round there has plenty of money. I bet her dad's bought her another bike already.'

'I live round there and I can't afford to be buying bikes just like that. I've got a mortgage to pay and two girls to look after.'

'Doesn't your wife look after them?'

'My wife died four years ago.'

'Oh, I'm sorry.'

'And the girl who had her bike stolen hasn't got a dad – she hasn't got a *bike* now, and she's not likely to get another one any time soon.'

'What? Is her dad dead?'

'No, he's just gone – went off a few years ago and didn't come back. Left his wife and daughter in a financial mess too. His wife's finding it a struggle to keep her head above water.'

'I didn't know that.'

'Neither does the thief, but I expect she doesn't care a damn.'

He held Lucy with a steady gaze and she knew he'd rumbled her. She dropped her eyes, not knowing where to look.

'If I track down the girl and make a report it'll have to be filed and acted upon. What do you think I should do?'

She looked up at him, defiantly. 'Why are you asking me?'

'Because this would seriously affect the lives of both the thief and her accomplice, especially her accomplice. He'd be starting out in life with a criminal record for violence. She'd have a record for theft. No matter how many qualifications they get at school or university, that record will be staring any potential employer in the face. All criminal records have to be disclosed to employers.'

'I didn't know that.'

'Not many young people do. They should teach that in every school in the country. Get yourself a criminal record, bang go your prospects of a good job. If schools did that there might be fewer crimes committed by foolish teenagers. You see, it's within my power to ruin their future, which is a big responsibility.'

'It sounds to me as if you know who she is already.'

'I have my suspicions, and I'm beginning to think she's not the girl I thought she was.'

Lucy didn't know how to react to this. Should she simply admit it was her and Arnold? Hardly. She couldn't drop her brother in it without warning him first – warning him that she was going to get him locked up. No, she had no option but to play along with Daniel's game.

'Maybe she *is* the girl you think she is, but she stole the bike because she really needed one. And maybe the boy she was with was just trying to slow you down, not hurt you.'

'That could be true. Trouble is, I need to know that for certain.'

'So, what are you going to do?'

'Haven't decided yet. Anyway, how do you want me to help you? Do you have any plans, you and your very clever brother?'

She was wondering how he knew Arnold was very clever. She certainly hadn't mentioned it.

'Well, the thing is,' Lucy said, 'the police don't know Billy like I do. I don't think anyone knows him like I do.'

'Do you think he'd tell you if he did it?'

'He would, yes.'

'Why would he?'

'Because I'd promise never to tell anyone and he'd believe me because I've never broken a promise to him.'

'And yet you would you break that promise if he told you he'd done it?'

'I don't see how he could have done it, but if he had done it I'd have to tell on him, for Ethel's sake, because I knew her as well. But I wouldn't tell him I'd told on him – there'd be no need. He's already been locked up for murder.'

'But you'd feel guilty about breaking your promise to him?'

'I'm certain I won't have anything to feel guilty about. Billy didn't do it.'

Daniel smiled and adjusted his position in the chair with a grimace. He rubbed his bandaged ribs gently.

'The bones are healing . . . and don't they let you know it!' He opened his bedside drawer and took out a notebook.

'I've been doing some telephoning over the past twenty-four hours,' he said, 'and I've made a few notes. The way I see it is this: Billy was at the dogs' home with you at four o'clock.'

'How do you know about that?'

'From the statement you gave to the police at the time.'

'Oh,' said Lucy.

He obviously knew it was her he'd seen at the station – the same girl who'd stolen the bike. But he was doing nothing about it, so maybe he didn't want to get her and Arnold into trouble that might ruin their future.

'If Billy killed Ethel,' Daniel went on, 'it obviously had to be *after* you left him and *before* he went into the home ... and we know he went into the home at quarter-past five, a quarter of an hour late for his tea. What time did you leave him?'

'I don't know exactly,' said Lucy, 'with me not having a watch, but I know we got off the tram at ten-past four because I saw a clock, and we walked and ran all the way back to the estate so Billy wouldn't be late for his tea. I left him on Saxon Road and I went down to the woods with Wilf ... that's the dog we rescued.'

'What time would that have been?'

'Hang on ... it was three minutes to five. I definitely remember now because I asked a woman. I remember thinking Billy could just make it home for five.'

'Trouble is,' said Daniel, 'he didn't He didn't make it home until quarter-past. If we knew where he was now, we could ask him what he was doing between leaving you and getting back to the home.' His eyes were on her as he said this, as if he knew very well she knew where Billy was.

'He wouldn't remember,' she said.

'The trouble is, he could have done it, Lucy. If he did, he did it just after he left you.'

'I don't believe that!'

'Neither do I, but he needs an alibi for that fifteen minutes and I'm afraid your track record as a reliable witness isn't great after what you did at the dogs' home.'

A thought struck Lucy. 'Will I have a criminal record for what I did there?'

'No, you weren't charged with anything, just given a caution, but your caution would be brought up in Billy's court case so we can't just rely on a statement from you with nothing else to support it. A prosecuting barrister would take you apart. What I have done is check out Billy's means of getting from the dog place to the home and how quickly he could he have done it using public transport. The best way would be a tram into town and a bus out to the estate. The only bus that stops anywhere near the home is the sixty-nine, and the earliest he could have got was the ten-past four from the bus station, which would have got him back at half-four – still leaving him time to kill the girl.'

'But he went back to the estate by tram and on foot with me,' protested Lucy. 'He was with me from half-past two until three minutes to five, and we did well to get there by that time.'

'I believe you, and your word *might* carry some weight if only we could account for the missing fifteen minutes. But if *he* can't remember what he was doing, we've got no chance.'

'Maybe someone else saw him?'

'They probably did. Trouble is, because the police thought they'd got the right man they didn't do a door-to-door – asking if anyone had seen Billy around – and it's all a bit late now. It's hardly likely that anyone would be able to remember that far back and give us an exact time they saw him, which is what we'd need.'

'And it's hardly likely the coppers'll do a door-to-door after all this time,' said Lucy.

'I'm afraid that's true.'

'*We* could do a door-to-door.'

'You mean, *you* could. I've got a job I want to go back to.'

'Do you think it's worth asking people in the neighbourhood?'

'It'll do no harm, just so long as you do it properly. I'll tell you what to say – and how to say it.'

'Thank you. Can I come and see you when you get home?'

'You can. I'm guessing you know exactly where I live.'

'On The Avenue. You'd better give me the number,' said Lucy

The fact that she hadn't fallen for his little trap had Daniel smiling. Five minutes later, as he watched her leave, he asked himself for the hundredth time why he was letting her and her brother get away with doing so much damage to him. Always on his mind was his promise to John Adamthwaite who had asked him, 'Would you keep an eye on my lad for me, please?'

But he hadn't kept an eye on John's lad. He'd been to

see his wife once, said 'hello' to baby Keith, and that was about it. His own family, his career and his own wife's tragic death had kept him pre-occupied, or so he told himself. Right now he didn't even know where John's wife lived and he felt guilty about that. Maybe it was this guilt that was making him keep an eye on Lucy in place of young Keith. In any event, he would certainly need to know more about Lucy and her brother before he had a right to destroy their lives. Something that was becoming less and less likely the more he saw of Lucy.

Chapter 16

Arnold was deep in a physics textbook when Lucy got home. He had his A-levels coming up very shortly. The Bush wireless was tuned in to *Journey Into Space*, Arnold's favourite show.

'I've been to see the copper in the hosp—'

'Shhh! Jet Morgan and Doc are in trouble.'

Arnold's eyes didn't move from the book he was studying but she knew his attention was as much on Jet Morgan as on advanced physics. Lucy stood there, listening to the wireless herself, until the show finished with the usual cliffhanger and the theme music came on. Her brother sat back in his chair and looked up at her.

'So, what news? How's the copper doing?'

She knew she had to tell him what Daniel had said. She didn't confide in her brother a lot but this affected him more than her. Also, she valued Arnold's opinion.

'He's doing okay. He talked to me about how he got injured.'

'But he doesn't know it was us?'

Lucy gave him a guilty look.

'You didn't tell him, did you?'

'No, I didn't and he hasn't accused me of anything, but

he says he can find out who the girl was because she was the same one he saw in the police station a year ago, which was when I went there to give a statement about Billy. He must have seen me then.'

'A year ago? He must have a good memory.'

'He told me that just after he came off his bike he remembered he'd seen the girl before, and now he remembers where. All he has to do is check up at work and he'll get my name.'

'Funny sort of a memory. Do you believe him?'

'It doesn't matter if I believe him or nor – he's right.' She paused then added, 'I think he might have checked up already. He was telling me that the girl whose bike I stole didn't come from a well-off family and she wouldn't get another bike, and that the thief's accomplice would get done for causing grievous bodily harm and go to jail for at least a year. The thief would be fined and sent to a detention centre for a day.'

'A day? You get a day and I get a year?'

'It's 'cos of the grievous bodily harm thing.'

'So, if he's checked you out, why hasn't he had us arrested?'

'Not sure. I think maybe because he's got to know me, he's giving us a chance to prove ourselves. He's still talking about helping us with Billy.'

'By the sound of things, if you hadn't gone to see him in hospital the police would have picked us up by now.'

'I think so.'

'It shows him you're concerned about his injuries.'

'Well, I was. And so were you.'

'So he definitely knows it was us?'

'I'd say definitely's about right.'

'Do you think he knows you know he knows it was us?'

'I think so. He's not daft.'

'But you keep on pretending you're innocent, I suppose?'

'No, *we* keep on pretending.'

Arnold closed his book, the prospect of a year in prison not being conducive to study. Lucy switched off the wireless and sat down.

'I think we should go and see Billy,' she said. 'I want to have a proper talk to him.'

'To ask him if he killed Ethel?'

'No, according to the copper there's a missing fifteen minutes between when I left him and when he got back to the home that day.'

'So you do think he might have done it?'

Lucy shook her head in exasperation. 'No, I do not think he might have done it, but I'd like to know where he was for that fifteen minutes.'

'Supposing he's forgotten?'

'He only forgets the usual day-to-day stuff. There is some memorable stuff he remembers, such as the one and only time he was taken to see Father Christmas. He remembers Father Christmas.'

'And he hadn't forgotten you.'

'No, and I don't suppose I'm as memorable as what happened to Ethel – if it was Billy who did that, which it wasn't.'

'Do you want me to come with you?'

'No, I want you to stump up my train fare, which I know you've got because you didn't give Billy the rest of the bike money.'

'I know, I forgot. I've still got it. We should really send it to that girl whose bike it was.'

'That bike cost over twelve quid new,' said Lucy. 'I know because they're selling the same model at the bike shop on Harehills Lane.'

'We'll hang on to what we've still got,' decided Arnold, 'and send her the lot once we've got it.'

'Or you could buy a new bike for her and sneak it to her house at night. That'd impress Daniel no end.'

'Who's Daniel?'

'The copper.'

'Hmm. Would it impress him enough for him to let us off completely?'

'It'd do no harm. Why?'

Arnold's face took on a serious expression, as if he was about to make a momentous decision. He got to his feet and walked over to the window.

'Because I've got seventeen quid saved up. I was gonna get myself a decent bike. Jeff Bickers is selling his racing bike and I reckon I could get him down to fifteen quid. Twenty-seven-inch wheels, twelve gears, lightweight frame, racing saddle, the lot.'

'It might save you from a year in jail.'

'I know, that's what I'm thinking. Have you got this girl's name and address?'

Lucy shrugged. 'I imagine I can get it without much trouble.'

'What? From Daniel?'

'Yeah.'

'If you ask him for her name and address, he'll know who sent her it.'

'That's the idea, dummy.'

Chapter 17

It was eleven at night when Mrs Roberts heard a loud knock on the front door. With her fifteen-year-old daughter in bed and no man about the house any longer, she was apprehensive about anyone coming calling at that time of night. She went to the door and, without opening it, called out: 'Hello, who is it?'

There was no answer, which left her perturbed. Her daughter Brenda came to the top of the stairs. 'What is it, Mum?'

'Someone knocked on the door, love. It's probably kids.'

'Well, don't open it.'

'I've no intention of opening it. I'll have a look through the window.'

Mrs Roberts went into the lounge and looked through the side window of the bay. She went back into the hall where her daughter now stood, having come downstairs.

'There's something leaning against the wall.'

'What?'

'A bicycle.'

Brenda had the door open in seconds. She stepped outside in her nightgown and gave a squeal of delight. 'It's my bike!'

She wheeled it into the hall and exclaimed, 'No, it's not. It's the same as mine, only this is a new one! Mum, I've got a new bike.'

Her mother was shaking her head in amazement and surprise. 'Who the heck bought you this?'

'I don't know, Mum, but they've given it me as a present, haven't they?'

'It would seem so.'

Mrs Roberts stepped out of the house, walked to the gate and looked up and down the street. It was deserted. Arnold was already out of sight, jogging back to his own house, his mission accomplished, his conscience clear and his hopes of a jail-free future a bit higher. Mrs Roberts went back inside.

'I'll tell Mr Earnshawe in the morning. I believe he came out of hospital yesterday. He might be able to throw a bit of light on who brought this.'

'Well, it can't have been the thieves,' said Brenda. 'They don't do things like this.'

'No, I don't imagine it was the thieves, darling. Probably some well-meaning person who wants to remain anonymous.'

'Because they know you won't accept charity,' said Brenda. 'Maybe it was Dad?'

'Maybe it was, darling,' said her mother, with limited sincerity. She'd made it a rule never to bad-mouth her absent husband in front of her daughter.

Chapter 18

Billy's nose had been almost glued to the train window as the east Yorkshire countryside passed him by; occasionally he would call out points of interest, mainly cows and tunnels and chimneys. His childishness might have been an embarrassment to some, but not to Helen who saw no reason to excuse or explain his behaviour to the three other passengers in their compartment. Her son would never be the subject of any apology from her.

They got off the train in Scarborough station and Billy jumped with fright as they walked past the locomotive and the driver let off a burst of high-pressure steam with a sudden deafening hiss. Helen put her arm around her son and hurried him safely away from the frightening noise, as any mother would do to her child. For the first time in her life she felt maternal, albeit for a childlike son much bigger than she was. The thought made her smile and she knew then she'd look after this young man for as long as he needed her.

It was a taxi ride to her mother's home just outside Scarborough. She and Vernon had left the vicarage on his retirement three months previously and had moved into a cottage, half a mile from the main road and pretty much in the middle of nowhere. To Helen this was the perfect hideaway for Billy until such time as his innocence was proved. She just had to convince Doris and Vernon of this.

Doris saw the taxi coming from afar and went to the door to meet whoever their visitor was. She was hoping it might be her daughter but Helen hadn't rung to say she was coming so it probably wasn't her.

'Who is it?' called out Vernon from the kitchen.

'I don't know yet.'

The taxi drew to a halt and Helen emerged.

'It's Helen,' called out Doris.

'What, without telling us?'

'My daughter's welcome here whether she tells us she's coming or not.'

'Of course she is. I didn't mea—'

'She's got a young man with her.'

'Really? I didn't know she had a young man.'

'Not that sort of young man. This one's much too young for our Helen.'

Vernon came to his wife's side as the taxi driver unloaded a suitcase from the boot.

'Looks like they're here for a while,' said Vernon. 'I'm most surprised she didn't ring if she intends staying with us, and who's the young man?'

'I expect we're about to find out,' said Doris, as Helen and Billy walked up the garden path.

'Mum,' said Helen, 'I'd like you to meet your grand-son.'

Vernon didn't know that Billy even existed. He scratched his head. 'Grandson?' he said. 'Doris, how can he possibly be your grandson?'

She stared at Billy for a long moment, then gave him a guarded smile which he returned, saying, 'Hello, Missis. I'm Billy.'

'I, er ... we'd all better go inside,' said Doris. 'I think this is going to take some explaining – to me as well as to Vernon.'

The inside looked just as a country cottage should. The furniture was almost as old at the house itself, having been bought along with the building. There was a large kitchen with a big oak table around which they all sat, with Vernon at the head like a chairman about to open proceedings. Helen was apprehensive, Doris still dumbfounded by this strange turn of events. Her eyes were mostly on Billy in whom she could see a likeness to her daughter. She spoke first.

'Billy is Helen's son,' she declared to Vernon. Then she looked at her daughter for enlightenment. 'Will Billy be able to understand,' she said, 'if I tell Vernon the full story?'

'Perhaps he might want to go through to the lounge,' said Helen. 'He likes listening to the wireless, don't you, Billy?'

'I do like wireless, yes.'

'Then I will take you through and switch it on,' said Doris, getting to her feet.

After an awkward interval of silence between Vernon and Helen, Doris came back and sat down. 'There, he's happy enough listening to music.'

'According to Lucy he likes it,' said Helen. 'It soothes him apparently. There's nothing about music to puzzle him.'

'Who's Lucy?' asked Doris.

'She's a young girl who was with Billy when he was supposed to have attacked that other girl.'

'Really?' said Doris. 'So he didn't do it after all?'

'Not according to Lucy.'

'Could one of you tell me what all this is about?' asked Vernon.

Helen looked to her mother for help.

'All of it?' asked Doris.

'I think so, yes. Now that Billy's back, I think Vernon's entitled to know the whole story.'

'This sounds as though it might be interesting,' he said.

'It's awful, Vernon,' said Doris. 'The worst story you've ever heard.'

'Oh, dear.' He sat back and laced his fingers across his ample stomach. 'Best prepare myself to be horrified, then.'

'Yes,' said Doris, 'you better had.' She looked at Helen and added, 'If you want to sit with Billy while I tell Vernon all about it, I'll understand.'

'No. This story affects both of us. I'll stay here.'

'Oh, dear,' said Vernon.

Doris rested her elbows on the table, her forehead resting in her palms and her eyes closed.

'My second husband, Billy's father, was a vile animal,' she began. 'A Jekyll and Hyde character ... a man who could be truly charming and also immensely cruel. He was cruel to me, but even more cruel to Helen. So cruel that I still carry a burden of guilt for not protecting her better.'

'You couldn't have saved me,' she intervened.

'I should have gone to the police earlier.'

'He kept threatening to kill us both if she did,' Helen

told Vernon, who was now listening with one hand pressed over his mouth.

Doris continued the story. 'Vernon, I told you I divorced my second husband due to incompatibility. It was nothing of the sort. I eventually divorced him for desertion after he'd committed the ultimate act of vileness against his own stepdaughter. I reported him to the police. He took off and we never saw him again.'

Doris looked up at her husband to gauge his reaction so far. His face reflected only sadness for his wife and her daughter. Vernon was a kind man and not one to dwell on unpleasant details, but he needed to know one more thing.

'This cruelty,' he said. 'Was it, er, physical cruelty or mental cruelty? Because I know mental cruelty can be just as harmful as phy—'

'It was both,' said Doris, 'but mainly physical.'

Helen felt she should give her mother some help at this crucial point in the story. She looked at Vernon and placed her hand on his. 'I loathed him,' she said, then added the next bit quietly. 'But he wasn't just my stepfather . . . ' Both women's eyes were on Vernon now, awaiting his reaction to what came next. Doris finished for her. 'He's also Billy's father.'

As Vernon absorbed this information his jaw dropped in shock.

'Oh, dear. I'm feeling quite ill,' he said. 'You must excuse me.'

He got to his feet and went out of the room. They heard his footsteps ascending the stairs as he headed for the bathroom. Helen looked at her mother.

'Have we done the right thing here?'

'Time will tell,' said Doris. 'I think this is new territory for him but he needed to know the truth now that we've got Billy back.'

'He doesn't know that Billy's wanted by the police yet,' said Helen.

'What? He's still wanted? I thought you said that Lucy girl had got him off.'

'Not quite. She and her brother sprang Billy from a secure mental hospital in Manchester and brought him to me. Lucy swears it wasn't Billy who killed the girl and she's trying to prove him innocent.'

'So we're harbouring a convicted murderer?'

'He's not been convicted of anything. He was sent there by order of the court without a trial because he's mentally unfit to plead.'

'Oh, my God! We'll have to tell Vernon this.'

'What will he do?'

'I don't know, Helen. Vernon's not one of nature's law-breakers.'

'Mum, Billy's my son. He's been dealt a terrible hand in life through no fault of his own and now they've locked him up for an awful crime he didn't commit. As his mum I feel I'm doing the right thing by helping him escape. If we don't do anything he'll rot in that awful place for the rest of his life. Maybe we could get Vernon to help prove his innocence?'

Doris took her daughter in her arms. 'I'll help as well, my darling. Billy's my only grandson and he needs us.'

A few minutes later Vernon came down and resumed his seat. The shocked expression had gone from his face. He looked from one woman to the other.

'If there's more to this story, I want to hear it. It's okay, you can spare me the gory details. This former husband of yours was the spawn of the devil, take it as read. I'm impressed you've both come through such an ordeal with your sanity intact.'

'First we need to tell you more about Billy,' said Helen. 'When he was still a baby I left him in the Wellington Street bus station in Leeds. I was only fourteen and didn't know what else to do. It wasn't Mum's idea, I did it on my own.'

'Oh, you poor dear!' said Vernon.

'I knew he'd been found and I thought he'd be adopted by a caring family. Unfortunately it turned out that he was born mentally impaired. I knew nothing of this until a year ago when I read about him in the paper.'

'That could have been due to the difficult circumstances of his birth,' Doris explained. 'I acted as midwife and he was a breech baby. I had to turn him round before he came out and I didn't really know what I was doing.'

'Well, you obviously knew enough to see him born.'

'Only what I'd read in books. We kept the pregnancy a secret for obvious reasons. If we hadn't done that Helen would have had proper professional care, but I had no way of knowing Billy was breech until she was on the verge of giving birth and I saw a foot instead of a head.'

'Dear God, I shudder to imagine what you both went through.'

Vernon placed a comforting hand on Doris's shoulder. 'I think what you did was very brave, and we'll never know for sure what caused Billy's mental impairment so best not to dwell on it, I feel. Now we must do what we can to give this young grandson of ours the best life possible for him.'

Doris gave Vernon a smile and squeezed his hand. Helen was sorely tempted to leave it there but her mother caught her eyes and she knew this kind man needed to know everything.

'Vernon,' said Helen quietly, 'there's something else you need to know.'

'Oh?'

'It's, er, why I saw Billy's name in the paper a year ago.'

'Yes?'

'Well, Lucy ... the girl who brought him to me ... was with him one day while a murder was committed near the home he was living in. It obviously had nothing to do with Billy because he was miles away with Lucy at the time, but the police arrested him and he was locked away in a mental hospital without trial.'

'What? They think *he* committed murder?'

'Yes.'

'So, what's he doing here?'

Helen took up the story. 'Well, that's just it, Vernon. You see, Lucy and her brother, who also thinks Billy is innocent, went to see him hospital and helped him to run away and then Lucy brought him to me. The idea was to get him free and then prove his innocence.'

Vernon took off his spectacles, laid them on the table and rubbed his eyes with the heels of his hands.

'Billy's wanted by the police for murder?'

'Well, sort of,' Doris acknowledged.

'Doris,' he said, 'I don't think there's any "sort of" about it.'

'Okay, he's wanted for a murder he didn't commit.'

'According to Lucy,' said Vernon, 'and how well do you know this girl?' He was looking at Helen.

'Well, she brought him round yesterday afternoon right out of the blue. Never seen her before. We had tea and a nice chat and ... erm ... well, I believe the girl.'

'Of course you do. Billy's your son – why wouldn't you believe her?'

'She went to a lot of trouble for him. Why would she do that if she thought he was a murderer? And there's something else. The dead girl was raped.'

'What?'

'Billy doesn't know anything about such things. He has the mind of a child.'

'According to Lucy?' said Vernon.

'Yes.'

'How old is this girl?'

'About fifteen.'

'I really need to think about this.'

He rested his elbows on the table and sank his face into his hands. They both watched, holding their breath.

'Vernon,' said Doris, 'when you think about this, remember to think about *everything* you've just heard, not just the bit about Billy.'

He nodded, his head still in his hands.

The remainder of that day and evening passed in an atmosphere of muted goodwill with neither Helen nor Doris daring to say much for fear of lighting the fuse that made Vernon explode.

'He'll be all right eventually,' promised Doris. 'Although, I must admit, I've never seen him quite as quiet as this.'

That evening they all sat and watched *The Royal Highland Show* on BBC television followed by a one-hour play, after which Vernon decided they'd had a full day and it was time for bed.

He went first. Helen took her chance to whisper to her mother, 'When we bump Maurice off, not a word to Vernon.'

'Not a word,' Doris agreed.

Chapter 19

The following morning Billy awoke to strange noises and took some time to figure out where he was. It was the second time in two days he'd woken up in a strange bed, but this was the best bed he'd ever slept in. He went to the window, drew the curtains back and looked out over green fields. In the sky were screeching seagulls, a cockerel was crowing from somewhere nearby and a farm tractor was snarling across a field. Another sound had him looking down at a car approaching the cottage. Black with a blue flashing light on top. It pulled up at the gate and three uniformed policemen got out.

Billy, wearing a pair of Vernon's pyjamas, went downstairs to investigate. Vernon was already there, opening the door to the men who had banged on it. The noise awoke Doris who came to the top of the stairs and called down, 'What is it, Vernon?'

'It's, erm, the police,' he said, sounding embarrassed.

'Police? What are they doing here?'

Vernon didn't reply. Billy was smiling at the three policemen, one of whom had asked him, 'Are you William Wellington?'

'Billy Wellington,' he said. 'Is that your motor?'

'Yes, it is, and we'd like you to come for a ride in it.'

Doris came down, in her dressing gown, glaring at her husband. 'You traitor, Vernon! How could you do this?'

'Doris, see sense! How could I not? He's a big strong boy who's wanted for rape and murder. Supposing he attacked you or Helen, or me even?'

'He wouldn't have harmed us.'

'How could we possibly know that for certain? None of us knows him, not even his mother. He's a stranger to us all.' Vernon snapped his fingers. 'His mood could change just like that. I haven't slept a wink all night, listening out for him.'

One of the policemen, a sergeant, took control of things. 'Erm . . . I assume William has some clothes he can get into?'

'Yes, of course he has!' snapped Doris.

'One of my men will need to accompany him while he gets dressed.'

'Will he really?' said Doris.

Helen appeared and was immediately distressed. 'He's my son,' she protested. 'What are you going to do with him?'

'We'll be taking him to the station to wait for the Manchester police to come and get him. You will all be required to help us with our enquiries.'

'Really?' said Helen, angry now. 'Well, I'll be asking a lot more questions than I'll be answering. Like, why has my son been locked up without a proper trial for one?'

'I shouldn't kick up too much of a fuss if I were you, madam,' said the sergeant. 'You could be in a lot of trouble yourself over this. The fact that this gentleman handed

154

him in to us will go heavily in your favour but I recommend you all behave yourselves when questioned.'

'I'll most certainly kick up a fuss if you attempt to put handcuffs on him,' said Helen, hotly. 'He's a hospital patient who hasn't committed any crime. He ran away from people who were doing him an injustice, that's all. Billy's never committed a single violent act in his life.'

Vernon walked into the kitchen with his head hanging down. Helen gave her son a hug before he went upstairs with the constable.

'We'll do everything we can to get you back, Billy,' she said. 'We know you're a good boy.'

'I know I am,' he said, completely unruffled by his situation. 'But I haven't seen the seaside yet.'

Five people looked at him. Four of them didn't know what to say. Helen did.

'You'll be seeing the seaside soon enough, Billy, when we get the police to do their jobs properly instead of taking the easy way out all the time.'

'I'm leaving a constable here to take statements from you all,' said the sergeant, 'after which I'll send the car back to bring you all to the station for questioning.'

Chapter 20

Lucy was waiting by the gate when Arnold came home from school the following day.

'I won't be going to see Billy,' she said. 'He's been caught.'

'How do you know?'

'I rang up that place in Scarborough where his mam said she was taking him. This bloke answered and I asked if I could speak to Helen Durkin. He asked me who I was and I told him. He said, "If it's about Billy Wellington, he's been arrested by the police."'

'Blimey, Lucy! We're in trouble!'

'Ah, but we're not. Helen came on and said her mam's husband had shopped Billy to the cops, but she promised not to involve me because I'd been good to her son.'

'She sounds all right does Helen.'

'She is. I think she's in a bit of bother herself but she reckons she'll handle it without mentioning my name. But here's me, worrying about myself while Billy's banged up again.'

'Didn't you say that copper might help?'

'Daniel? Yeah, but only so far as giving advice is concerned.'

'Is he out of hospital?'

'Yeah. He came out a few days ago. You're right. I think we should go and see him.'

'We?'

'Yes, we. He'll know you gave that girl a new bike, though I still can't guarantee he won't turn you in.'

'So I become his friend, do I?'

'It'll do no harm. Better than a year in clink and a criminal record. He's all right is Daniel.'

'I suppose so.'

'Okay,' said Lucy, 'I'll give him a ring and tell him we're coming. Have you got any change for the phone box? I wish we had a phone at home.'

'If Weary put a phone in, he'd put a coin box in with it.'

*

Daniel had been staring blankly at the television screen. He was thinking of his wife, as he often did, and the man responsible for her death. His younger daughter, Jeanette, came into the room. She had answered Lucy's call earlier.

'Who was that woman on the phone?'

'What? Why do you ask? Am I not allowed calls from women?'

'Just wondered, that's all.'

Jeanette was thirteen and very protective of her father.

'It wasn't a woman, it was a girl – not much older than you. She's coming round this evening with her brother.'

Jeanette sat in another chair and asked, 'What for?'

'Oh, something and nothing . . . why?'

'Just curious.'

'It's, er, a private matter I said I'd help them with.'

'Fine.'

Daniel lapsed into a blank stare once again. His mind was back in the past; back with his darling wife; back when he'd been happy.

'Dad, are you okay? I mean, apart from your injuries.'

'Yes, I'm fine, darling.'

'Thinking about Mum?'

He looked at his daughter and gave a nod. 'Yeah – I keep having moments.'

'You know, me and Carol wouldn't mind if you did find another lady.'

'What?'

'We just want you to be happy again, that's all.'

Daniel smiled. 'And where would I find another lady?'

'I don't know. Maybe you should go out and socialise a bit more.'

'With my job? When would I get the time?'

'Maybe while you're convalescing?'

'Jeanette, do you and Carol have someone in mind?'

'No, but you're still quite young and you could be around for another fifty years if you look after yourself. We don't want you to end up a lonely old man, and if you want to get yourself someone decent you mustn't leave it too late.'

'Fifty years? I'll be eighty-seven!'

She got up, walked over to him and kissed the top of his head. 'Just thought I'd tell you, Dad. You deserve to be happy again.'

'If you want to see me happy you can make me a cup of tea and a bacon sandwich.'

She saluted. 'Your wish is my command, O Father.'

Jeanette went into the kitchen, leaving her father to consider the phone call he'd had from Lucy half an hour ago. She and her brother might well help him solve a problem he'd been wrestling with for a few days. He wouldn't ordinarily involve anyone else in his schemes, especially when they were so young, but these kids had rendered him helpless and so far he'd let them get away with it, against his better judgement. They owed him and he was about to call in that debt.

*

Daniel's elder daughter, Carol, opened the door. 'Come in, Daddy's expecting you. He's also feeling a bit sorry for himself, but don't worry, he gets like that from time to time. He's nowhere near as bad as he used to be.'

Arnold felt instantly guilty. He was the one who'd all but killed this girl's father and here she was, being bright and polite to him. If the copper suspected Arnold's involvement in his injuries, he hadn't told his daughters, which was a good sign.

'Is this because of his accident?'

'Oh, no. It's because of Mum.'

'Right.'

Arnold was now feeling guilty for being relieved that his wife's death was the cause of Daniel's gloom, and not Arnold himself.

Carol called out to her father: 'Daddy, your visitors are here. I'm going upstairs to do my homework.'

'Okay, where's Jeanette?'

'She's over at Maggie's.' To Lucy, she said, 'He's in there, drinking his whisky. It's okay, he's not drunk or anything. It just relaxes him.'

159

'Thanks.'

They went into the front room where Daniel was sitting with his feet up on a coffee table, with a glass of whisky in one hand. He turned his head without moving his body.

'Ah, the freedom fighters.' He looked at the young man beside Lucy. 'I assume you're Arnold?'

'Yes.'

'And what can I do for you? Sit down, both of you, please.'

They sat. Daniel was looking hospital pale and sitting stiffly in his chair.

'How are you doing?' Lucy asked him.

He finished his whisky off and set the glass down on the table. 'Can't complain. Shouldn't really be drinking with the medication I'm on, but I sometimes get in a bit of a stink over losing my wife and I find it helps.' He held up a forefinger. 'Most importantly, I'm getting better. Should make a full recovery. So, what brings you here?'

'Billy,' said Lucy.

'Ah, Mr Billy Wellington. I understand he escaped from the hospital and was recaptured in Scarborough yesterday.'

'How do you know that?' Lucy asked.

'I'm a copper and I have a telephone. It's my job to know stuff. I also know you two were at the hospital visiting him at the very time he escaped.'

'He jumped through a toilet window,' said Arnold.

'And you two played no part in it?'

They both stared at him, not wanting to annoy him by lying, but not wanting to own up to freeing Billy either.

'Look, I'm not going to do anything about it,' said Daniel, stubbing his cigarette out in an ashtray on the arm of his chair. 'But if we're going to work together on this Billy business we need to be absolutely honest with each other.'

'We might have helped him a bit,' admitted Lucy.

'A bit? He ended up in Scarborough with his real mother and grandmother. He'll have needed a lot of help for that.'

'We helped him a lot,' said Arnold.

'I know you did – and I applaud you for it.'

'You do?' said Lucy.

'I do. I don't believe Billy killed that girl any more than you do.'

'Then why didn't you do something about it?'

'It wasn't my case, and we don't interfere with other officers' cases unless we've got proper cause, which I haven't. The trouble is, Billy's detained under mental health legislation. Had it gone to court, I doubt he'd have been convicted. If we take it to court now, the people who put him there won't like being proved wrong, and they'll no doubt bring out all the big guns to fight us. We'd need a good barrister on our side and not a Legal Aid one who's just going through the motions to earn a crust. I know the very man, but he's expensive.'

'Well, we couldn't pay him,' said Lucy, 'so that's that.'

'I suppose it is,' said Daniel, looking from one to the other of them. 'There's a man I know who really should pay for it . . .'

'So, will he?' Lucy asked.

'Not knowingly, but he certainly deserves to pay for

161

something.' Daniel added quietly, 'You see, he killed my wife.'

Lucy and Arnold looked at each other, not knowing what to say. Daniel explained.

'He killed her in a hit-and-run. It was actually murder but he made it look like a hit-and-run accident. It's something I need to put right, but he's free and clear so far as the law is concerned.'

Daniel's face folded into a frown and tears weren't too far from the surface as he looked away from them. Lucy and her brother both felt awkward and immensely sorry for him.

'How do you know he did it?' asked Lucy, gently.

Daniel looked back at her and rubbed his eyes with his knuckles. 'Because he told me.'

'Why isn't he locked up then?'

'Because he wasn't actually driving the car, with him being already banged up at the time. He paid someone to do it, and there's no way I can get him or the actual killer. I had him put away for five years back when I was a detective sergeant. This was his revenge. He was inside four years ago when Gloria was killed. He's out now and enjoying the fruits of his criminal lifestyle.'

'So how is he going to pay for Billy's barrister?' Lucy asked.

'Well, he's not now, so I really shouldn't have mentioned it.'

'Oh.'

Daniel looked at them both, as though undecided about something. 'I'm not sure I should be telling you all this, with me being a copper. But it's not going to happen,

162

so what the hell?' He smiled to himself and shook his head. 'It's such a great plan, I've always wanted to tell someone.'

'Arnold does that,' said Lucy. 'He has these great plans and he can't wait to tell me. Sometimes they even work.'

'What was your plan?' asked Arnold, intrigued.

'It's something I've been planning for a while, just waiting for the right opportunity to put it into action. This man lives in a big house out in Bardsey, but what he doesn't know is that I have a key to that house and know the location of a secret, er, cubby hole, for want of a better word, where he hoards all the stuff he doesn't want the police, or anyone else, to find. He thinks no one in the world knows about it but him.'

'How do you know about it then?' asked Arnold.

'I have a contact, and in exchange for certain favours I've kept this contact from going to prison for many years – it's something we coppers have to do from time to time, for the greater good.'

'And this contact knows about the cubby hole?' asked Lucy.

'He does. And on top of that he hates Leonov almost as much as I do.'

'Leonov?' said Arnold.

'Peter Leonov runs the biggest criminal empire outside London. I'm the only copper ever to have put him away. My wife's death was my punishment and a warning to other coppers. Scared to death of him, some of them.'

'This secret place, is it a safe or something?'

'Oh, no. He's too clever for that. He has a safe, of

course. A very expensive safe. But he doesn't keep anything incriminating in it, just the stuff an honest businessman might keep in a safe.'

'How did this contact find out about this secret cubby hole?'

Daniel smiled. 'Oh, he has a most unusual talent for observation. It's an important part of his trade as a thief. My man had reason to suspect there must be something of that nature in Leonov's study, and when Leonov was in prison my man was in and out of the house all the time, in search of the cubby hole. Even so, it took him months to find it.

'It's a small compartment built into a wood-panelled wall behind a bookcase. There are stairs at the other end of the wall and it's somehow part of the understairs space, but you'd have to know it was there even to suspect its existence. There's a certain book in the bookcase that you have to push at quite hard until you hear a click. Then you can pull the whole bookcase open like a big door.'

'So, you plan on going into Leonov's house while he's out, and breaking into his cubby hole?' said Lucy.

'I did. Does this shock you – with me being a copper?'

'Not really,' said Arnold. 'Not after what he did to you. Especially if you can get away with it.'

'Well, I *would* have got away with it. My plan was pretty much as foolproof as you can get. The trouble is, it's too risky in my state of health and it needs to be done soon.'

'Why's that?'

'Because Leonov's gang pulled a major job in York a week ago. A man was killed but the police can't touch him for it.'

'How do you know it was him?' Arnold asked.

Daniel tapped the side of his nose with his forefinger. 'Information received, plus it had his MO all over it. He'd been planning it for months. A lot of cash was stolen and I'm betting it's all in his cubby hole.'

'So this is the opportunity you've been waiting for?'

'Yes, it's the perfect opportunity. The police can't go in without a warrant and they can't get a warrant without just cause. He knows this because he's got coppers and judges in his pocket and scared to death of him – and even if the coppers got a warrant in, they wouldn't find his cubby hole.'

'So the police don't know about this cubby hole?' Lucy said.

Daniel looked at her and shook his head, slowly and with a hint of guilt.

'No, they don't. For my wife's sake, this is something I need to do by myself.'

'You mean, steal all this man's money and keep it?'

'Well, that was my original idea,' Daniel admitted, 'but my wife wouldn't have liked that – it would have made me as dishonest as him. I just wanted to steal it to bring him down. My information is that that there's enough of value in that cubby hole to seriously damage him, maybe even destroy him financially. And if it's handed over anonymously to the police, with a message saying where it came from, it might well put him away.'

'Couldn't you use some of the money to pay for Billy's barrister?'

'I see no reason why not. My Gloria would have approved of that.'

'But you can't do it in your state of health?'

'Sadly, I'm afraid not.' Daniel looked straight at Arnold. 'And you caused my injuries.'

The sudden accusation shocked Arnold. He glanced away. 'Okay,' he admitted, 'I did it.'

'We both did,' said Lucy, glad that everything was out in the open now.

'And I'm really sorry you were hurt so badly,' Arnold said. 'I only meant to slow you down so that Lucy could get away.'

Daniel nodded. 'I was impressed that the girl was given a new bike. I assume that was you?'

'It was Arnold,' said Lucy. 'He bought it with money he'd saved to buy himself a new one.'

'What happened to the bike you stole?'

'Sold it to a second-hand shop in Manchester to pay Lucy's and Billy's train fare to Leeds.'

'So, this was all about Billy?'

'Yes,' said Lucy. 'I needed a bike to go and see him.'

'Helping him to escape was a spur-of-the-moment thing,' added Arnold.

There was a silence during which Lucy and Arnold tried to assess whether or not they'd been forgiven. Arnold decided to change the subject back to Daniel's plan.

'Even if you have a key, you couldn't just walk into his house and take his stuff.'

'I could if he's not in.'

'How would you know if he's in or not?'

'I know Leonov's comings and goings through my sources and I can tell you when he and his lady friend will be out for the evening and his house empty. His wife and family left him while he was in prison, so he lives there with his woman and a housekeeper, who lives in an annexe, and various staff who come and go during the day. So, once he's gone out for the evening with his lady friend, I'd have a key to his door, an empty house, and the exact location of his secret hiding place – every burglar's dream.'

'Don't some of these big houses have burglar alarms?' said Lucy.

'Only for people breaking in – not for people entering with a key.'

'So, you'd just walk up to his front door from the road and let yourself in?'

'No, I'd enter and leave via the back garden. There's a bridle path that goes past. I'd get there on my bike. The key is to the back door. I have the layout of the rooms plus I know how to open his cubby hole.'

'Won't your contact get the blame?'

'My contact is currently serving six months in Armley jail. He put himself there on purpose in anticipation of me making my move. He was a bit put out when I told him about my accident.'

'Wow! He got himself locked up for nothing,' said Lucy.

'He owes me a lot more than six months.'

Arnold thought for a while, then said, 'And this Leonov wouldn't suspect you of having anything to do with it, not with you being out of action with your injuries. Which means he won't take it out on your daughters.'

Daniel looked at him with admiration. 'As it happens,

yes. I had intended doing this without leaving a clue that it was me who did it. I suspect there might be an incriminating weapon or two in his cubby hole that might have put him away for life, or even hanged, but I couldn't risk him knowing it was me who put him down. On the other hand, at some time I really need to punish him so that I can get on with my life. The big problem is that word is he's leaving Leeds very shortly – moving down to London. So all this information is of no use to me unless I act very soon.'

'What sort of stuff will he have in his cubby hole?' Arnold asked.

'Oh, there'll be a lot of money, gold bars and jewels . . . all the proceeds of a security deposit box robbery in York . . . plus a very incriminating gun, if I'm not mistaken, covered in a killer's prints. I'd have taken that.'

'I bet you'd just hook your finger through the trigger guard and drop it in your bag,' guessed Arnold.

'He goes to the pictures a lot,' explained Lucy.

Daniel laughed. 'Well, he's learned how not to leave prints on a gun.'

'I bet the house has a really complicated lock,' Arnold said. 'Six levers at least.'

'Oh, you know about locks, do you?'

Arnold pulled a face. 'Not really. It's just what I've heard. Expensive locks have more levers.'

Daniel got up, went to a drawer and took out a bunch of keys and a house floor plan. He unclipped a key and handed it to Arnold along with the plan 'Here, take a look.'

He examined them with interest. The key was a lot

more complicated than the mortice lock to their council house.

'Blimey! I bet the Queen's got a key like this to lock up Buckingham Palace.' Arnold picked up the bunch of keys to clip it back on as Daniel was lighting a cigarette.

'What's the name of the book?' Lucy asked.

'What book?'

'The book that opens the bookcase.'

'Oh, it's an old dictionary of verse. The sort of book that no one would be interested in.' Daniel laughed. 'Why? Are you thinking of breaking in yourself? I wouldn't advise it.'

'You wouldn't have to,' said Lucy. 'Nicking that bike was enough for me. It scared me to death when you started chasing me.'

'So I imagine you were grateful to your brother for bringing me down.'

'When he heard what he'd done to you,' retorted Lucy, stoutly, 'our Arnold was really upset and all for handing himself in. He's never hurt anyone in his life hasn't Arnold. He made me ring up Leeds Infirmary to see how you were. I pretended you were my uncle.'

'Ah, now there's the answer to a puzzle. I was told my niece had rung to say how worried her mother – my sister – was. You see, I haven't got a sister, much less a niece.'

'Anyway,' said Lucy, 'this nurse told me you weren't goin' to die or anything so Arnold didn't have to hand himself in.'

'I'm quite glad myself that I didn't die.'

'When would you have done it?' Arnold asked.

'Done what? Had you arrested?'

'No, done the job on Leonov's house.'

'Oh, erm, tomorrow night, as it turns out. Leonov and his woman are very keen bridge players. There's a tournament in Harrogate that they've both entered. It'll keep them out of the house at least until the early hours or they might even decide to stay overnight.'

'How do you know that?'

'Oh, eyes and ears within the force. He attracts a lot of attention from the police does Mr Leonov.'

'Tomorrow? Wow!' said Lucy. 'What time?'

'After dark. I'd have gone about eleven. The housekeeper would be in bed by then, not that she'd have troubled me. Bit deaf, apparently.'

'When does Leonov move to London?'

'Couple of weeks, I think. It'll be months before I'm fit for action again.'

Chapter 21

Arnold had saddled Lucy to Daniel's house. He was doing the same on the way back when she stuck her hand in his coat pocket and pulled out a key. She reached in front of him and waved it in front of his eyes.

'I saw you drop it down your sleeve when Daniel thought you were putting it back on the bunch.'

Arnold braked to a halt and turned to look at his sister. 'What? Do you think he noticed?'

'Doubt it. He's not used to your tricks like I am. Anyway he was busy lighting a cig.'

'And he'd had a bit to drink.'

'You think he was drunk?'

'No, but he wasn't completely sober either, which is why he told us as much as he did.'

'Yeah, I know. So, what's the plan with the key?' Lucy asked.

'Dunno really. I just thought it'd do no harm for us to have it, that's all.'

'It might do you a lot of harm when he finds out you've nicked it.'

'Mebbe he let me nick it. Have you thought about that?'

'Why would he do that?'

'Why would he give us all the details about how to rob this Leonov bloke?'

'Why not? What harm could it do? He can't do the robbery now.'

'I know, but it's a bit odd how he told us exactly how to do it.'

'S'posing it was your plan and you found out you weren't able to do it, I bet you'd have told everyone about it. In fact, I know you would. Especially after you'd had a bit to drink.'

'Yeah,' conceded Arnold, 'there is that. I tell you what, though. I bet I could do it as well as him. It'd mean we'd have enough money to pay this barrister bloke ...'

'What do you think Daniel will do when he finds out you've stolen his key and all Leonov's dosh? I don't think he'll be so tolerant. He might even turn you in for knocking him off his bike.'

'Not if I give him all the stuff I nick, including the gun. We'd be even then, me and him.'

'Is that what you'd do?' asked Lucy.

'Well, I have to admit, I haven't thought it all through properly, but that might be the best thing.'

'I think you're right, and I think I'm coming with you.'

'Why?'

'Because we're in this together, Arnold, that's why.'

'Fair enough. You'd better see if Eileen Wigglesworth'll lend you her bike ... again.'

'Okay. How will you know where Leonov lives?'

'There's a tag on the key with the address on it.'

'Blimey, Arnold! I think he must want us to do it.'

*

At ten-past eleven the following evening they were sitting on their bikes on the bridle path at the bottom of Leonov's back garden. Arnold had been there earlier in the evening to figure out where to hide. They'd blackened their faces with burned cork at Lucy's insistence. The garden had a six-feet-high, solid wooden gate which was locked from the inside.

'Daniel never told us about this,' grumbled Lucy.

'Well, mebbe you're wrong about him actually wanting us to do it,' said Arnold. 'I'll give you a leg up.' He cupped his hands. 'It's probably just bolted from the inside.'

'What if it's a proper lock?'

'Lucy, it's only a flipping gate! We're not gonna let a flipping gate stop us. This is for Billy, remember?'

'Okay.'

Lucy put her right foot into Arnold's cupped hands and reached for the top of the gate. She then put her left foot on his shoulder and hoisted herself over, dropping to the ground on the other side with a thud.

'You all right?' he said in a loud whisper.

'Yeah.'

'Is it a bolt?'

There was a metallic rattling, the gate opened and she said, 'Yeah, come in.'

Arnold joined her in the garden. 'Right,' he whispered. 'You wait here. If I need help I'll give you three flashes of my torch. If you see or hear anyone coming, you come and tell me. Close the gate but don't bolt it.'

'Okay.'

Arnold was dressed in dark clothing with a black woolly hat covering his red hair. He made his way across the garden to the back door. He was carrying a large rucksack that Weary Walter had stored in the outhouse. It was a cloudy night with a half-moon showing faintly behind the clouds. He put the key in the lock, with Lucy straining her eyes to watch him. The door opened into a kitchen, as he knew it would. He flashed his torch on and off to identify the hall door and moved towards it quickly before its location had left his memory. He was now in the hall faintly illuminated by streetlights shining through a stained-glass transom window above the front door. No need for his torch. Having studied the floor plan he knew which door he wanted. The door to Leonov's study was at the end on the left; he was hoping there'd be light shining in there as well. He opened it. Yes, there was light, not much, but enough to see the bookcase on the wood-panelled wall, behind which lay the secret cubby hole. He peered at the bookshelves but it was too dark to make out any titles. He switched on his torch and shaded the light with his fingers to leave a narrow beam to see by. And there it was, at the very end of the second shelf down. An ancient volume entitled *Webster's Dictionary of Free Verse* – not the most inviting title he'd ever come across. He pushed it backwards until he heard a distinct click, releasing a lock. He pulled on the side of the bookcase. It swung open a lot more freely than he'd anticipated, causing a heavy book to fall to the floor with a loud bang.

Arnold froze for a few seconds, hoping the housekeeper hadn't heard, then he realised that her annexe was at the far side of the house. On top of which she was a bit deaf, according to Daniel. He was smiling now, the housekeeper forgotten. This was the most exciting thing he'd done in his life. Sure enough, the secret cubby hole was there and had been perfectly described by Daniel – or rather by Daniel's contact.

The loud bang hadn't woken the housekeeper but it did awaken the man in the bedroom immediately above the study. The house should be empty, apart from him. Someone was downstairs, and if it wasn't Leonov or his woman or both, it was someone who shouldn't be there. He swung his legs out of bed, put on a dressing gown, picked up a pistol from the dressing table and checked that it was loaded. He was a big man, one who had killed before and enjoyed it. He'd spent many years in prison but had only been caught for a small fraction of his crimes. Killing any witness was as good a way of protecting himself as any he knew. He was an expert in the art of disposing of bodies. Leonov paid him well for his skills and he'd be paying well for this. The hitman's name was Elias Munro.

He went out on to the landing and noticed no lights were on downstairs. No lights meant no Leonov. Good. Munro smiled. It usually meant an intruder. If it was, he'd broken into the wrong house. Munro hoped it was more than one. Two intruders meant twice the money, and so on. That was his incentive arrangement with Leonov. BCB they called it – Body Count Bonus.

It didn't occur to him to ring the police. Men like Elias Munro didn't deal with police. Whoever had broken in was as good as dead, it was simply a question of disposing of them. He'd take the body down to a factory furnace tomorrow. His van was parked in the drive. Leonov would probably moan about blood on the carpet so he'd try and keep that to a minimum. He'd order the intruders into the kitchen and let them bleed on the tiled floor. He was nodding his approval to the plan as he descended the stairs with greater stealth than many a skilled intruder.

*

As the bookcase swung open a light came on inside to reveal the contents of the cubby hole. Great, no need to bother with a torch. The space had three shelves. The top shelf was stacked with thick wads of white banknotes, the like of which Arnold had not seen before. He took a closer look and gave a low whistle at their denomination – *five pounds*. He'd never seen a white fiver before, just ten bob notes and pound notes, and not too many of them. Each wad was labelled £1,000. Arnold's hands shook with excitement as he picked the bundles up four at a time and loaded them into his rucksack, counting as he went. Four thousand, eight thousand, twelve ... He worked quickly and efficiently and had soon loaded ninety wads into his rucksack. Ninety thousand pounds! That was more than you won on the football pools. On the shelf below was a briefcase. He opened this to see it was full of assorted notes: fivers, pound notes and ten bob notes. Hundreds of them. He closed it and jammed it in the rucksack on top of the bundles of fivers. Also on the shelf were twelve gold bars, each one about eight inches long and four inches wide. He picked one up; it was very heavy. No room in the rucksack for it. Lucy had brought her school satchel. He'd need her help for this lot.

On the shelf below was a large, velvet-covered box. He opened it without picking it up and saw it was full of jewellery, mainly diamonds, some of them quite sizeable.

He picked up a ring set with an enormous stone and let it flash under the light, wondering how much it was worth.

His heart began to quicken at the enormity of this robbery he was carrying out. On the same shelf was a gun. Arnold had never touched a proper gun before. He'd fired air rifles at the fair but had never seen a real gun. It was a revolver, like cowboys used, only this was a bit more modern. He was just about to hook his finger under the trigger guard when the light went on and his heart dropped through his boots.

'Put the bag down, put your hands up and turn around.'

The voice was as cold as death. Arnold was shaking with fear. He did as he was instructed and turned around with his arms in the air, just like they did in cowboy films. A man wearing a black dressing gown and with bare feet was standing there pointing a gun at him. Not the same type of gun he'd just seen in the safe. This was a 9mm automatic, only Arnold didn't know it.

'Gimme a reason why I shouldnae shoot ye,' the man said. His accent was rough Glaswegian. When Leonov came back he'd want to know everything there was to know about this robbery. A dead body wouldn't be enough for him.

Arnold couldn't think of a reason. He went pale with fear. His eyes were fixed on the gun.

'P . . . Please don't shoot me, mister.'

'How d'ye get into this hoose?'

'Erm . . . erm . . . I just . . . erm . . . '

'I said, how d'ye get into the hoose?'

'Er, the d . . . door was open.'

The man pointed with his gun to the cubby hole. 'Oh, yeah, and how d' ye know aboot this?'

'Er . . .that . . . er . . . was already open.'

'Liar!'

Munro spat out the word with terrifying venom and pointed the gun at Arnold's face. He'd forgotten all about his kitchen plan. 'I'm countin' tae three and if ye havnae told me the truth by then I'll be pullin' this trigger and blowin' yer heid away!'

Munro looked as if he'd just risen from the dead. He had a chalk-white face, unshaven and cadaverous, with a cruel, thin-lipped mouth. His bushy eyebrows overhung cold, dead eyes, beneath which were black bags as if he hadn't slept for a year. Arnold saw no reason to disbelieve what this man was saying. Fear had completely robbed him of the power of speech and paralysed his every muscle, except the one controlling his bladder.

'One . . .two . . .thr—'

Arnold could scarcely believe what he was seeing. The man was stumbling forward. He saw Lucy in the entrance to the cubby hole. She had obviously run at the man with some force and knocked him off balance. The gun went off when it was pointing downwards. The bullet hit the man's calf just above the ankle and ended up going straight through his foot. He screamed with pain, dropping the gun which Lucy kicked away. The man fell to the floor, howling in agony. Arnold was still frozen to the spot. The anticipation of imminent death was still with him. Munro was rolling around the floor in agony, crippled and totally unable to get to his feet. How the hell had this happened? He had the reputation of being the hardest man in

Yorkshire. Leonov wouldn't be too impressed when he found him totally crippled. If he could walk, he would kill these bastards in the blink of an eye.

Lucy grabbed the heavy rucksack and heaved it on to her brother's shoulders. The two of them ran out of the back door, across the garden and through the gate. They mounted their bikes and pedalled furiously down the bridle path, away from the screams of rage and pain which had now been heard by Leonov's housekeeper, who was phoning the police to tell them about the shot she'd heard and the awful screaming coming from the main house.

There was the sound of a police siren. A police car with flashing lights approached. Lucy and Arnold expected it to screech to a stop in front of them but it went straight past. They watched it swerve into Leonov's street. Arnold turned down a side road, not wanting to risk another confrontation with a police car. Lucy understood without querying this. After a few minutes he stopped, so did Lucy. They both got off. Arnold was sick on the verge. Lucy was feeling a bit that way herself, especially after seeing her brother throw up. She followed suit.

'I peed myself back there,' he admitted.

'I'm not sure you should be telling your sister that.'

'Well, you saved my life so you're entitled to know. He said he was going to blow my head off and I believed him.'

'So did I.'

'Did you see his face?' Arnold said.

'I did. He looked like someone had just dug him up.'

'I'll have nightmares about that face for years.'

They stood there for a while, shivering with shock.

Finally Arnold said, 'This rucksack weighs a ton.' He took the briefcase out of it.

'I'll take that,' said Lucy. She slid it over her handlebars. 'It's heavy. What's in it?'

'Money. This rucksack's full of fivers.'

'Blimey!'

Arnold put the rucksack back on and mounted his bike, saying, 'Are you ready?'

'I think so.'

They'd both caught their breath and had got something out of their systems, if only vomit. Fifteen minutes later they arrived at Daniel's house. There was a light on downstairs. He must be up. They tapped on his door. He opened it looking surprised to see them, especially with blackened faces. He put a finger to his lips.

'Shhh – the girls are asleep. Come in.'

They all went through to the lounge. They dumped the rucksack and the briefcase on the floor.

'What's this?' Daniel asked them. 'Why the black faces?'

Arnold looked at Lucy, indicating she should give an explanation. The shock of being so near to death still hadn't left him.

'We robbed Leonov's house,' Lucy said, quietly.

Daniel's jaw dropped. 'You're kidding!'

'Well, no.'

'You broke into the Leonov house?'

'Erm, I took the key from you,' said Arnold. He removed it from his pocket and gave it to Daniel, who stared at it in amazement.

'Wha— how did you do that?'

'He can do magic tricks with his hands,' Lucy explained,

watching Daniel's face carefully, worried that it might tighten into anger. But he seemed more bewildered than angry.

'Arnold thought you might be hinting at us having a go, with you telling us exactly how to do it,' said Lucy. 'After, all we *are* experienced in such erm ... such things.'

Daniel smiled, 'It's a bit of a leap from nicking a bike to breaking into a gang boss's house and stealing all his loot.'

'Maybe so, but we managed it,' said Arnold.

'You did indeed, but it all could have gone tragically wrong, and that would have been my fault. In a weak moment it crossed my mind to ask you but I decided it was much too dangerous. I didn't tell you exactly how to do it ... did I?'

'You did, actually,' said Lucy, 'and we did it.'

Daniel clapped a hand to his forehead. 'Oh, God!'

'There was a man there,' Lucy went on. 'You didn't tell us about him.'

'Oh, no! I bet that was Munro. He saw you, did he?'

Arnold found his voice. 'He was going to shoot me but Lucy pushed him down. He shot himself – in the leg, I think.'

'He couldn't walk,' added Lucy.

Daniel sat down heavily in a chair. His face had gone pale. 'Oh, my God! I thought Munro might be there. He was a problem I needed to overcome, but I obviously didn't mention that to you. I never thought for one minute ... I was drinking that evening, wasn't I?'

'Yes, but you weren't drunk.'

'No, just careless in friendly company. Good grief, this is terrible!'

'It isn't actually,' said Lucy. 'Arnold got a lot of stuff.'

'I'm not sure I want to know,' Daniel moaned. I can't get over the fact that, due to my stupidity, you two almost got yourselves killed. If it was Munro, he's the one who killed my wife!'

There was a noise in the hall. The door to the sitting room opened. It was Carol in her nightie. 'I heard voices and I wondered if everything was all right.'

Daniel got to his feet and went over to her. 'Yes, everything's fine, darling. These two have had a traumatic experience.'

Carol looked at the blackened faces of the visitors. 'Is it Lucy and Arnold?'

'Er, yes,' said her father.

'Oh, right . . . er, g'night then.'

'Goodnight, darling.'

Lucy and Arnold added their goodnights as Carol left, disappointed at not being told what it was about. Daniel turned back to them. 'God knows what I'm going to tell her.'

'Not the truth, I hope,' said Lucy.

'Well, I never lie to my daughters but I might have to make an exception. Either that or tell them it's something better left unsaid.'

'That would be best.'

'I think you'd better tell me exactly what did happen.'

His face creased with concern as they each struggled to relate their part of the story, both with voices rendered feeble by their ordeal.

'Look,' said Daniel eventually, 'you're both suffering from shock. I'll make you a cup of hot sweet tea.'

'I peed myself,' said Arnold suddenly. 'My legs are chapped.'

Daniel looked at him with enormous sympathy. 'I'm really sorry about all this,' he said. 'I've got a pair of jeans that might fit you.'

With the tea drunk, Arnold in dry jeans and their thoughts collected, they managed to tell their stories. Apparently Lucy had seen a bedroom light go on and had realised Arnold might be in trouble if she didn't warn him. She ran to the house and crept in so as not to be heard by whoever was coming downstairs. She saw a man go into the room she assumed Arnold must be in and heard the one-sided conversation that ended with the man counting to three before he killed her brother. This had goaded her into charging across the room with a force she couldn't explain. She'd hit the man in the back and knocked him off balance. The gun had gone off and, as far as she knew, he'd shot himself in the leg.

'He had bare feet,' added Arnold. 'They were covered in blood. He couldn't walk or he'd have had me. Lucy kicked the gun away. After that she picked up the rucksack and put it on my shoulders, then we ran like hell. The man was screaming all the time. Terrifying he was. Telling us how he was going to kill us both.'

'Oh, there is one good thing,' Lucy remembered. 'As we were leaving we saw a cop car turning into Leonov's street. Could be his housekeeper heard all the noise and rang them.'

'Now that would be just great,' said Daniel. He looked down at the rucksack and briefcase. 'Did you, er, get everything?'

'No. There's loads left. Mainly gold bars and jewellery. There was a gun as well, I didn't get that.'

'I can't tell you how sorry I am for putting you in such danger. I apparently told you exactly how to carry out this robbery and, knowing you two like I do, I should have realised you wouldn't waste such valuable information. My stupidity almost got you killed.'

'*You* didn't put us in danger,' said Lucy. 'I never thought you wanted us to go.'

'Okay, this is all my fault,' said Arnold, 'but do you actually want to see what I got?'

'I do, yes,' said Daniel.

Arnold emptied the rucksack on the carpet to exclamations of wonder from Lucy. 'There's ninety thousand in fivers,' he said, quietly, 'and that briefcase is stuffed with more money. Like I said, there were gold bars and a box full of jewellery, and a gun, but I didn't manage to get those.'

'Don't worry about it,' said Daniel. 'You two are a couple of wonder kids. I'll pack all this stuff away. I'd like you to go home now and come back tomorrow evening. The girls are going to the pictures so we'll have the house to ourselves for a couple of hours. We have work still to do and it must be tackled carefully. The man shot himself in the leg, you say?'

'He did, yes.'

'And you left him with a bullet a hole in his leg and the cubby hole wide open, with the gold and jewels visible for the police to see?'

'And the gun,' said Arnold. 'In fact, there'll be two guns there now.'

Daniel shook his head in amazement. 'Look,' he said, 'I know you've both had a nasty shock but this has been an excellent outcome, believe me. I reckon the guns'll tell a few tales when ballistics get hold of them. By the way, you did well to get blacked up. That man'll never recognise you in a million years.'

'I'll recognise him,' said Arnold. 'I've never seen such an evil face. He had rotten teeth and cold eyes.'

'Did he have a Scottish accent?'

'Erm, yeah, he did, now I come to think of it.'

Daniel stared at him, shocked. 'Oh, hell! What did I nearly do?'

'What?' said Arnold.

'It was definitely Munro,' said Daniel. 'What you just did was miraculous.'

His hall telephone rang. Daniel got to his feet, saying, 'I hope this is who I think it is.'

He closed the door on his conversation as Lucy and Arnold stared down in silence at the fortune lying on the carpet.

'We could take some of it,' suggested Arnold eventually. 'Just a couple of hundred. Who'd know?'

'We would,' said Lucy. 'I want Daniel to use some of it to pay for Billy's solicitor.'

'It's funny that,' said Arnold.

'What's funny?'

'He hasn't asked us why we went to all the trouble of stealing it then bringing it here.'

'That was going to be my next question,' said Daniel from the doorway, smiling.

'We did it to square things between us after what I did

185

to you,' said Arnold, 'and to use some of the money to pay Billy's barrister.'

'Consider things squared and Billy's money taken care of. That phone call was from a colleague. The police went to Leonov's house in answer to a 999 from his house-keeper. They found Elias Munro badly wounded and semi-conscious, surrounded by some of the proceeds most probably from the York robbery and two guns, which will now be forensically checked. On top of which Leonov himself turned up, having had a bad night at bridge. I can safely say his night isn't getting any better.'

'So it's a good job we did it tonight,' said Lucy.

'As it turns out, yes. Are you both on bikes by the way?'

'Yes, I'm on a borrowed one.'

'In that case you can have mine, Lucy. I've had it repaired and it's obviously not a girl's bike, but if you lower the saddle it should suit you. Pick it up tomorrow if you like.'

'Wow!' said Lucy.

Chapter 22

Arnold was silent for the whole of their ride home. When they arrived and dismounted he stood by his bike as Lucy made to take hers up the path to the house. He was looking at the ground.

'You okay,' she asked.

He nodded. 'Yeah.'

She went over to him, tilting his chin up with her finger in the manner of a mother tending to an upset child.

'Hey, have you been crying?'

He shrugged. 'I thought he was going to shoot me, Lucy. I thought I was dead.'

'So did I, that's why I ran at him.'

'I was petrified. You definitely saved my life, our kid.'

'I was scared as well,' said Lucy. 'Running at him was all I could think of. It's a good job it worked. If he hadn't gone down, we'd both have had it.'

'It worked all right. You knocked him flying. Little kid like you, knocking a big bloke like him down. You came at him like a cannonball. How d'you do it?'

'Well, I think I just made him stagger a bit, then he shot himself and went down.'

'Trouble is,' said Arnold, 'we can't tell anyone how brave and brilliant you were. It'll be our secret.'

'That's good enough for me.'

Lucy stepped forward and hugged this brother she had nearly lost.

'Oh, heck!' she said, looking at the house. 'Weary Walter's up.'

They both looked at the front window where Walter was standing in the darkened room, staring at them.

'I think we've dealt with worse than old Weary tonight,' said Arnold, grinning now. Walter was an adversary he could cope with. 'We'll just tell him we've been for a moonlight ride.'

'He saw me hugging you. What's he gonna think? We've never done that before.'

'You hugged me because I bought you a bike, which is more than he ever did.'

'But this is Eileen's bike.'

'I know, but the one you're getting tomorrow from Daniel's got to come from someone, and that someone is your generous brother.'

'Generous or genius?'

'Bit of both,' Arnold said, retrieving his wet jeans from his saddlebag. 'How the heck am I gonna smuggle these past Weary?'

Lucy summoned up a giggle. 'Hey, that's your problem, our kid. You're the genius.'

Chapter 23

Daniel had left his bike leaning against the wall outside the side door. Lucy stopped to look at it.

'Do you think this is it?'

'I imagine so. Look at that, ten gears . . . that's a great bike. Better than mine.'

'You have it, then. I'll have yours. A bike's a bike to me.'

'Nope, that's your reward for saving my life. I might want to borrow it now and again though.'

Daniel opened the door before Lucy had finished knocking. He was in a good mood. 'Come in, come in, everything's good.'

'Have your daughters gone out?' asked Arnold. He'd been hoping to catch Carol, maybe say, 'Hello, what are you going to see? . . . Really? One of my favourites . . . Hey, we should go together sometime.'

But she wasn't there, so his preparations were for naught. His best pink shirt, his hair at its sleekest, his new jeans. Lucy was aware of his efforts and was amused by it all. Daniel ushered them through to the lounge.

'Would you like tea, coffee or anything else?'

'No, thanks,' they said in unison.

'Right, the girls are at the flicks so we've got bags of time.'

'What have they gone to see?' asked Arnold, who wanted to be prepared for the next time he saw Carol.

'Erm . . . *Rebel Without A Cause.*'

'James Dean, great.'

'Oh, Carol's potty about James Dean.'

Arnold made a mental note to have his hair ruffled up into the James Dean unkempt style. It probably suited his personality more than this Tony Curtis thing that needed a lot of upkeep.

'Right,' said Daniel. 'To bring you up to date, Mr Elias Munro is currently in St James's Hospital under police guard and Peter Leonov is in the cells at Millgarth police station.

'I'm as sure as I can be that Munro is the man who drove the car that killed my wife. That has yet to be proved, but the gun Arnold found last night was used in an armed robbery several months ago in which a security guard was seriously wounded. Munro's looking at a long stretch in prison for that, or he might have been, but he's taken a deal offered to him whereby if he co-operates fully, he'll be immune from prosecution on that particular charge.'

'How do you feel about that?' asked Lucy.

'Not too bad, actually. What he doesn't realise is that the police know the gun he shot himself with was used in the York robbery, which isn't part of the deal. Because of the murder committed there, the York robbery is a capital crime and he's an accessory to it at the very least.'

'So, the cops are waiting for Munro to spill the beans on Leonov, then they'll nick him on the York robbery?' said Arnold.

'Exactly.'

'Is he thick or what.'

'Yes, he's a bit thick – luckily. We often rely on villains being a bit thick and we're rarely disappointed.'

'What about Leonov?'

'Well, he had the proceeds of the York robbery in his house, minus £90,000 that Arnold took of course, but plus the murder weapon. With Munro singing like a canary, Leonov's in deep trouble.'

'Enough to hang him?' asked Arnold.

Lucy winced as Daniel gave a nod.

'I need to be careful as to how I get this money to the station.'

'Er, I thought that was to pay Billy's barrister,' said Lucy, sharply.

'Not the ninety grand. Barristers are expensive but not *that* expensive. I'm hanging on to the briefcase, which I suspect contains money that Leonov made by other means.'

'You mean, legally?' said Lucy.

'Possibly. He owns various businesses that deal in cash.'

'How much was in the briefcase?' Arnold asked.

'Four thousand three hundred and sixty-five pounds, all in used notes.'

'That's got to be enough to pay Billy's barrister,' said Lucy.

'Oh, yes – and to buy myself another bike. Yours is outside, by the way.'

'I know, I saw it. It looks brilliant. Thanks ever so much.'

'Better than mine,' said Arnold.

Daniel smiled. 'What I'll do with the remainder of the money I haven't decided, other than that I won't be keeping it. I was thinking of sending the ninety grand by post but it's a hell of a valuable parcel to be kicking about in a sorting office.'

'I'll take it to the police station, if you like,' said Arnold. 'All I need do is drop it off in the doorway and clear off on my bike.'

'That would certainly do it,' said Daniel. 'It's addressed to a DCI at Chapeltown nick along with a letter. This is a copy.'

He took a carbon copy letter from a drawer.

To Detective Chief Inspector Dransfield.
Chapeltown Police Station
Leeds

Dear Sir,
I am the person who broke into Peter Leonov's house last Tuesday night. This parcel contains all the money I took. I did it to incriminate him because he is an evil man who has made my life a misery. The man with a bullet hole in his leg was about to kill me when my associate came to my aid. He shot himself, I had nothing to do with it. It is my dearest wish that this stuff will send Leonov to the gallows.
That is all,
Me

*

Arnold watched from the saddle of his bike. The parcel was in the small lobby of the police station. There was a door that opened from the lobby into reception. No one had come out or gone in for five minutes. Then he saw a pair of uniforms walking up the footpath. He watched as they paused in the lobby and looked down, reading DCI Dransfield's name. One of them picked up the heavy parcel and went inside. Arnold pushed himself off and stepped on the pedals. Everything was done. No one would ever know by whom. Not the police, not Leonov, not Munro, no one. They'd done all this and they couldn't tell a soul. Then he smiled as a thought struck him.

Maybe one day they might be able to tell their great story – he could certainly prove it. He'd got a ring in his pocket – the one with the enormous diamond. He hadn't purposely stolen it, he'd forgotten he'd put it there – just before he'd almost been killed putting some major villains in jail. He'd earned it, surely. No point telling Lucy, she'd give him an argument he didn't need.

Chapter 24

Maurice Bradley
1944

Able Seaman Maurice Bradley was on the deck of the *SS Empire Maclean* when German U-boat U-49 fired the torpedo that struck it amidships and broke it in two. They were off the south-west coast of Ireland at the time. Bradley was thrown into the sea by the blast. He was knocked momentarily unconscious and came to his senses when he hit the cold water.

The ship was carrying a cargo of oranges from Florida to Liverpool; the first such cargo for three years after the U-boat threat had subsided somewhat. All merchant ships were now travelling in large convoys protected by Allied destroyers and frigates all equipped with Asdic sonar devices, which enabled them to detect submarines up to a mile away. The weather had taken a turn for the worse, causing the *Empire Maclean* to be trailing at the back of the convoy. The U-49 had spotted it ploughing a lonely furrow through the rough sea. One torpedo was all it needed. The explosion ripped open the hold and tore hundreds of orange crates to matchwood. The convoy and the escort ships were a good two miles away by now.

Maurice Bradley was flapping about in the water; swimming wasn't one of his strong suits.

The ship had a crew of twenty-three. Many of them had been killed instantaneously, others were wounded. The sea was rough and full of debris; bobbing heads and oranges and floating bodies. Bradley had no life jacket on. He kicked himself back to the surface and managed to tread water as he watched the remains of the ship disappear beneath the waves, but he knew he wouldn't last long in this cold and turbulent water. Then he saw an intact crate, tossing about on the waves. He swam clumsily towards it and, with a monumental effort, pulled himself on top. He lay on it, face down, clinging to the slats and listening to the cries of fear and pain and the appeals for help all around, with no intention of helping anyone. As far as he was concerned this was a one-man crate. No passengers allowed.

'Hey there! I need a hand.'

The shout came from nearby. Bradley looked up and saw the first mate waving at him; disappearing behind a swelling wave then reappearing, shouting.

'Room for two on there?'

It was obvious the officer fully expected him to help but Bradley figured that two on board this crate would cut his chances of survival by fifty per cent. But the man was a senior officer, one of his many superiors. He had to think of that. Then he thought: I haven't got a boss out here. I haven't even got a bloody ship under me.

The first mate, who was injured, managed to swim with one arm alongside Bradley's crate, expecting a helping hand to fish him out of the water. Bradley raised his knee and kicked the officer in the face with the heel of his boot, knocking him unconscious. The exhausted man sank beneath the waves. Bradley looked around to see if anyone had seen him, but the rough sea had concealed his murderous act.

He was picked up by an escort frigate forty minutes later, one of six survivors. The first mate wasn't one of them.

Maurice Bradley would tell his heroic story for many years to come, leaving out the bit about the first mate. He'd even tell the story to his cell mate in Walton Prison eleven years later.

*

'Mo, what's yer real name?'

'It's Mo – what's it supposed ter be?'

'I thought it might be somethin' longer than Mo. I mean, who calls a little baby Mo?'

'The same sort of people who call their baby Joe.'

'Yeah, but Joe's short for Joseph. At least that's what it says on me charge sheet.'

'All right, me name's Maurice. Now, will yer please shut up? I'm still half asleep.' He looked at his watch – 7.15 a.m. 'It's not unlock fer half an hour.'

Bradley turned his face to the wall. Joe shrugged and went back to his *Liverpool Echo*. It was a two-day-old paper – the same day's newspaper was rarely available in Walton Gaol.

'*Maurice Bradley*,' he read, out loud. '*If anyone knows the whereabouts of Maurice Bradley who lived in Ashley Avenue, Leeds, in 1937, please contact Box Number 374D as soon as possible. It will be to their advantage.*'

196

'Here, give me that!' shouted Bradley, swinging his legs off the bunk and dropping to the floor. He grabbed the paper and tried to find the notice. 'Where is it?' he yelled.

Joe pointed out the relevant place. Bradley read it, then got to his feet and started pacing up and down the cell.

'It's got ter be that bitch of a wife o' mine!'

'Wife? I didn't know you were married.'

'I don't know if I still am. It were a long time ago, she might have divorced me for all I know.'

'You mean yer might be married but yer not sure?'

'Marriage is for mugs. I won't make the same mistake again, so why should I be interested?'

'Mebbe she's popped her clogs and you're her next-of-kin. You get all her money.'

'She never had any.'

'Back then she had no money. There's been a war and all sorts of stuff since then.'

'I did me bleedin' bit in the war. Four years in the Merchant Navy. Torpedoed in the mid–Atlantic an' bugger all ter show for it. Get back into civvy street and every time I turn round there's a copper waitin' ter bang me up fer the slightest bleedin' thing. Spent half me time in civvy street banged up.'

'And while you spent half yer time in civvy street bein' banged up, she might well have got her hands on a great big pile o' dosh. Yer could be a rich widower. Pound to a pinch, this is some solicitor tryin' ter settle a will.'

'She won't have left me nowt in her will.'

'That's if she left a will. If she didn't, yer'll be next-of-kin.'

'She had a girl – wouldn't she be next-of-kin?'

'No idea,' said Joe. 'Mebbe she's popped her clogs as well. Would that bother yer?'

'Not one bit.'

'So, do no harm ter tell 'em where you are.'

'What? With me banged up doin' a five stretch for givin' a whore a bit of a slap.'

'Bit of a slap? She's in a wheelchair now, isn't she?'

'Yeah, and that's not gonna impress 'em.'

'Mo, they're not lookin' ter be impressed. They're just tryin' ter find yer.'

'Mebbe.'

'Yer'll be out in four months if you behave yersen. If it were me, I'd lerrem know where I am, mate. What harm can it do? Yer can hardly be worse off than you are now, can yer?'

Maurice Bradley read the notice again. 'Information that will be to his advantage,' he read. 'What information?'

'You won't know unless you ask.'

Bradley climbed back into his bunk and gave the matter half an hour's thought before the cells were unlocked at 7.45.

*

Helen stood at the advertising counter of the *Liverpool Echo* and handed over the receipt she'd been given two weeks previously.

'Could you check to see if there have been any replies to this?'

'Certainly, Madam. You do know we can send all replies to you by post at no extra charge?'

'I do, but this is quite convenient. I work nearby.'

It was as far from convenient as it was from the truth. She had assumed that Bradley would be living in or near a busy seaport, and Liverpool was at the top of her list. Two weeks previously, in order to maintain her anonymity, she'd travelled to and from Liverpool by train to place the advertisement, paying for it in cash. She'd made the same journey to pick up replies. What she didn't want was to leave any trace of who had placed this advert, just in case it formed part of the police investigation into her stepfather's murder. If she drew a blank her mother was going to do the same in Hull, then Helen had volunteered to try Glasgow.

The young man returned with a brown envelope and handed it to Helen. 'This is what's been received so far. We may get more, so perhaps you can pop in next week.'

Helen, who was wearing a blonde wig and heavy-rimmed glasses, smiled and said thank you, yes, she'd do that. She left the building and went to a nearby café to check the contents.

The envelope contained just two replies. One from a Liverpool woman who had known a Leeds man of that name five years ago but said she knew he'd been sent to prison for a vicious attack on a street worker. The use of the innocuous term 'street worker', and the general tone of the letter, gave Helen the impression that the sender was, in fact, that very prostitute. The description she had given matched Maurice Bradley in age, general appearance and demeanour, albeit he must have lost a lot of hair since she'd last seen him. There was no address given.

The second letter was much more interesting. Helen gave a shudder when she recognised her stepfather's writing. Maurice Bradley had been grammar school-educated, with a certain amount of shallow charm, which had once fooled her mother.

27 June 1955
Bairstow M. F   29306
HM Prison Walton
Liverpool
To whom it may concern,
   I am the Maurice Bradley who lived at that address in Leeds in 1937. At the moment I am incarcerated in Walton Prison in Liverpool due to a miscarriage of justice. However, I am due to be released in four months' time, when I will be fighting to clear my name. You can reach me at this address and explain why you need to contact me.
   Yours faithfully,
   Maurice Bradley

*

Helen sipped her tea and allowed herself a small smile of triumph at this early success. What she needed now was to get the address he was being released to. This would be difficult without giving away her own whereabouts or those of her mother. However, it would seem they had time to plan this – four months, apparently.

Once again she thought about the act of murder and it made her sick to her stomach and she hated her stepfather even more – for he would have caused her to become a murderess. Would she feel guilty afterwards? Who cared?

The only feeling she could anticipate was the sensation of a gigantic burden being lifted from her. For that to happen, *she* had to be the instrument of his death and to hell with guilt. If that was the price, she had to pay it.

If he died tomorrow under the wheels of a bus the burden would be eased but the sin not fully absolved. Only his death at her hands would provide proper retribution. For absolution Bradley would have to answer to a higher power once she'd seen him off.

Then she thought of her son and how she had four months to help Lucy prove his innocence before she went to work on her stepfather. She was in trouble with the police for harbouring Billy but her solicitor reckoned that, under the circumstances, he could get her off with a slap on the wrist. It would be more than a slap on the wrist if they caught her killing Maurice Bradley. She was also having second thoughts about involving her mother. No way would Vernon ever condone such a thing, and to keep it from him would be an added difficulty. Plus, Helen wasn't sure that she'd forgiven him for turning Billy in. She had a lot to do to switch her life around but at least she could see a light at the end of the tunnel. The trouble was, it was a dangerous tunnel with quite a few unknowns waiting for her. Mind you, Maurice Bradley had a bit of an unknown waiting for him too. Just the thought of that eased Helen's mind somewhat.

Chapter 25

Mrs Sixsmith opened the door to Lucy and stepped back, allowing her through. 'I expect you've come to ask about Billy.'

'Well, I was wondering if he got into much trouble for running away.'

'He did, actually. I got a letter saying that because he was a person considered to be a danger to society, he's been moved to a more secure place.'

'Danger to society, Billy? He's more of a danger to himself.'

'Lucy, we mustn't forget that he's there because of what happened to Ethel.'

Lucy sighed. 'I know, I know – where's he been moved to?'

'He's down in Nottinghamshire – a place called Rampton. He'll never escape from there but they will treat him properly, so I'm told. What worries me is that there's a lot of violent criminals in Rampton.'

'Billy's not violent, and he's not a criminal either,' said Lucy. 'Do *you* think he killed Ethel, Mrs Sixsmith?'

'Well, he admitted to doing something bad that afternoon, and there was a girl involved. I was there when the police questioned him.'

'He *did* do something bad – he was with me, letting the dogs out of a dogs' home. I'm a girl and I was involved! In fact, it was all my idea. I bet you never heard him say he killed Ethel.'

Mrs Sixsmith gave this some thought, then nodded slowly as she said, 'No, I don't think he actually said that. In fact, I'm sure he didn't. The trouble is, when he was asked about Ethel, he didn't deny it.'

'Mrs Sixsmith, Billy never denies anything, because he's never sure if he did stuff or he didn't.'

'I know that.'

'There's a police inspector,' said Lucy, 'who knows the coppers involved in Billy's arrest, and he thinks they're the type to settle for an easy capture rather than do the job properly.'

Lucy was almost quoting Daniel verbatim. She chose not to mention his name lest Mrs Sixsmith repeated this to anyone and got him into trouble.

'Why doesn't he do something about Billy then?'

'Because it wasn't his case and he can't go interfering with other coppers' cases.'

'Well, that doesn't make much sense to me,' said Mrs Sixsmith.

'No, nor me neither.'

They were standing in the hallway. A man came down the stairs and walked past them.

'Morning, Mr Sixsmith,' called out Lucy.

He grunted a reply but didn't turn round.

'Pay no mind to him,' said his wife. 'He's a bit grumpy at the moment. He's just been made redundant after thirty-two years at McLaren's. I married him for better or for worse but not for lunch. I hope he gets another job. I can't do with him getting under my feet around here.'

'He might be able to help you run this place,' suggested Lucy.

'Him? Help out here? I don't think so. He doesn't fully understand the residents, if you get my drift. Doesn't suffer fools gladly doesn't my husband.'

'Oh, heck!' said Lucy.

*

Billy had been given a room of his own until he became acclimatised to the Rampton regime. He stared out of the window and wondered if Lucy might come to visit him again. Doris and Vernon were fading blurs in his memory. Running away from the last place was also a blur, so he couldn't have implicated Lucy and Arnold even if he'd wanted to. He'd forgotten they were involved; in fact, he'd almost forgotten that *he'd* been involved. He didn't really know what he was doing here among all these people he didn't recognise. He remembered being in a place where he did know people, such as Missis and Lucy and Wilf the big dog.

One other person did cling to his spongy memory – Helen. She stood out because Lucy had told him Helen was his proper mam. He didn't fully understand how this could be – what he did know was that Lucy always told him the truth, which meant Helen must be his mam. He also knew that he liked Helen because of the way she talked to him and the way she treated him and the warmth that seemed to come from her. He'd liked it when she'd kissed him on his cheek because he knew for certain that no one had ever kissed him before, not even Lucy. So

Helen was there, in his thoughts, along with Lucy and Wilf and Missis. They were all his mind could cope with. His memory of Arnold came and went. Mostly he remembered Arnold's hair, which he really liked. Billy would like his own hair to be like that one day.

Chapter 26

Arnold leaned his bike against a lamp post outside Copley's Café on the shopping parade. His A-levels were over and he had time to spare. There was a girl he had his eye on who went there on a Sunday afternoon with her friends, to drink coffee and talk nonsense. He'd teased his Tony Curtis quiff to perfection and was wearing his Wrangler jeans and a lumberjack shirt; enough to turn any girl's eye.

He sat at a table next to the three girls, pretending not to notice them at first, then he affected a theatrical double-take and said, 'Hiya – didn't see you lot there.'

'You must need your eyes testing,' said Sandra Chillington, the one he fancied.

He turned and looked at her, face on, his eyes crossed, and said, 'There's nothing wrong with my eyes, young man.'

Sandra laughed and patted the vacant seat beside her, saying, 'Wanna sit with us?'

'Only if you promise not to poke fun at me. My mother warned me about girls like you.'

He sat beside Sandra and ordered a coffee from Mrs Copley, who was just bringing it to him when Mr Copley, the proprietor, came in through the front door. He spotted Arnold and hovered nearby uncertainly before coming over to him.

'You're Lucy's brother, aren't you?'

'I am, yes.'

'I wonder if I can have a word over here.' He inclined his head towards an empty table in the corner. Intrigued, Arnold excused himself from the girls and joined Copley at the table.

'What is it, Mr Copley?'

'Arnold . . . look, I've had your Lucy in here banging on about Bootsie—'

'I know,' said Arnold, 'she won't give up on him. She's got me convinced he didn't do it.'

'Erm, not only you, Arnold.'

'Eh?'

'Well, she was giving me chapter and verse about what happened that day and I swear to God I've only just remembered something I should have told the police. I mean, it happened, Billy was arrested, and as far as anyone knew he'd owned up to it, so I suppose I let it slip from my mind – thought no more about it. No copper ever came to question me, otherwise I'd have put them straight then.'

'What are you talking about, Mr Copley?'

He rubbed his chin nervously, as if knowing what he was about to say wouldn't make him very popular with Arnold. 'Well, that afternoon when young Ethel was killed, Bootsie came in here.'

'I wish you'd call him Billy, Mr Copley. I never call him Bootsie, nor does Lucy.'

'I'm sorry – I mean Billy. He came in here for a cup of tea. Now, according to your Lucy he was with her going on for five o'clock and I know for a fact he was in here from five to nearly quarter-past because I couldn't get shut of him. It wasn't 'til I remembered they had their tea up at the home at five that I thought to tell him that, and he shot out of here without paying.'

Arnold's eyes opened wide. 'He was definitely here from five to nearly quarter-past?'

'He was.'

'And he was back at the home at quarter-past, according to Mrs Sixsmith.'

'So I'm told.'

'That's it then, Mr Copley! That's the only time he can't account for. That's the time the police think he did it.'

'I know, lad, and I wish to God I'd come forward sooner. I feel a right idiot. If it hadn't been for Lucy coming in and telling me the tale, I'd still be none the wiser. Honestly, I could kick meself.'

'Have you told the police yet?'

'I haven't, lad, no. I've only put two and two together this morning, but I'll go down now if you think it'll do any good.'

Arnold suddenly lost his temper. 'Do any good? Bloody hell, Mr Copley, if you'd come forward when Billy was first arrested, he'd never have been locked up for it!'

Arnold turned and looked at Sandra and her friends. 'Have you heard this? Billy Wellington was in here when the police say he killed Ethel Tomlinson. This feller knew and he didn't come forward.'

Copley's face went bright red as all the girls stared at him. 'Look, I . . . I'm going to the p . . . police station right now,' he stuttered, nervously.

'I should bloody well think so!' said Arnold, not even trying to hide the disgust he felt. He sat down with the girls as Copley went back out.

'Poor man,' said Sandra. 'I don't suppose he meant Billy any harm. He's harmless is old Copley.' The other girls murmured their agreement. Arnold looked at Sandra in amazement.

'What? He's not all right, he's an idiot!'

But Arnold decided against giving her any further argument. 'Look,' he said, getting to his feet, 'I really need to tell my sister. I'll, er, see you later.'

In seconds he was racing home to give Lucy the news. An hour later he was still at home talking to her about how and when they could get Billy free when the police knocked on the door. Walter answered. Two uniformed policemen were on the doorstep.

'Is Arnold Bailey here?'

'Arnold . . . why do you want him?'

'Are you his father?'

'Stepfather.'

'Is your stepson at home?'

'He is, yes.'

'We need to speak to him.'

They pushed their way past. Arnold came through from the front room with Lucy close behind him. One of the policemen confronted him.

'Are you Arnold Bailey?'

'Er, yes, why?'

'Do you have a bicycle on these premises?'

'My bike? Yes, it's in the outhouse.'

'We'd like to see it.'

'Sure. I don't know why, though.'

'Is the outhouse open?'

'Er, yes. What's this all about?'

'That's what I'd like to know,' said Walter.

His wife came into the room from upstairs. 'What's happening, Walter?'

'No idea, love. They want to see Arnold's bike.'

'What on earth do you want to see his bike for? It isn't stolen or anything. He made it himself.'

The two policemen went out of the house and into the brick shed in the garden and wheeled out the bike. Arnold had come out of the house along with Walter, his mother and his sister. One of the policemen undid the straps on the saddlebag. Before he opened it he said to Arnold, 'We have received information that you were involved in the murder last year of Ethel Tomlinson and that there is evidence in this saddlebag to confirm that. Do you have anything to say before I open it?'

'What?' said Arnold, shocked.

His mother, Lucy and Walter stood there with mouths agape.

'There's only my toolbag in there,' said Arnold.

'Just a toolbag, nothing else?'

'No.'

The policeman opened the saddlebag, reached inside and withdrew a pair of knickers, which he held up for everyone to see. 'Our information is that this garment belonged to the murdered woman.'

'I . . . I . . . I didn't put it there!' protested Arnold.

'Arnold Bailey, I'm arresting you for the murder of Ethel Tomlinson. You are not obliged to say anything unless you wish to do so, but whatever you say will be taken down in writing and may be given in evidence.'

Arnold clasped his hands to his head. One of the policemen forced them back down and slapped handcuffs on him. Tears were streaming from Lucy's eyes. Her mother was pale with shock, unable to protest.

'Mam!' said Arnold. 'I haven't done anything!'

'I know you haven't, Arnold.'

Walter took a step forward, his face clouded with anger. 'I don't know what's happening here but I do know you people are making a stupid mistake! The lad can be a bit daft but he's not a rapist or a murderer!'

'Stand aside, sir.'

'No, I damned well won't stand aside! You've already charged one innocent lad for this. What are you going to do, charge all the lads on the estate until you think you might have the right one? Someone's obviously played a prank on Arnold and you're treating him as a murder suspect. My God! No wonder crime's on the increase if you're typical of the policemen we've got nowadays.'

The officer pushed Walter aside. Walter, who was slightly built, fell to the ground. He sprang to his feet and waved a fist at his assailant. 'I have your number, you damned thug! Striking old men is probably all you're fit for!'

'Mam!' shouted Lucy. 'They're taking Arnold away. Why are they taking him away? He hasn't done anything!'

Arnold was led to the waiting police car which drove

away, leaving his bereft family standing on the footpath. In the space of a few minutes their lives had been turned upside down. Neighbours appeared on the street asking what was happening and receiving no reply. It was just too embarrassing and awful to talk about. The three of them went back inside the house and shut out the curious world, not having a clue what to do to help Arnold.

Chapter 27

Lucy rode to Daniel's on the bicycle he'd given her. Arnold's bike had been confiscated by the police as 'evidence'. Their mam had been most irate with the constable who came to collect it.

'What're you going to do, put the bike in the bloody witness box to give evidence against our Arnold?'

'I'm not sure why they want it, Mrs Bailey.'

'They've got two innocent lads locked up for that murder now, and the real killer's still running around free. You bloody lot must be real proud of yerselves!'

Lucy had by then convinced her mother that Billy was innocent, especially now that they had Mr Copley's testimony to help his case. The constable said nothing in reply. He just wheeled the bicycle out to the police van and drove off, glad to be clear of Mrs Bailey's venom. It was two hours after Arnold's arrest when Lucy knocked on Daniel's door. Carol answered.

'Hiya, Carol, is your dad in?'

'Erm, yes, he is. I'll get him.'

Lucy waited at the door for Daniel, who was mildly impatient with his older daughter. 'Carol, Lucy's a friend. When she comes to our door, you invite her in. We don't keep friends waiting on the doorstep.'

For the first time Lucy looked at him in a new light. Daniel was a handsome man: tall, neither fat nor thin, with dark brown hair that didn't need artificial styling – unlike her brother's. He also had kindly brown eyes and a friendly voice. Up until then she'd looked upon him as a figure of authority who could get both her and her brother into trouble, but that was no longer the case, especially after the Leonov caper. He was over twenty years older than she, but that didn't make him any less attractive to her. William Holden, one of her favourite film stars, was probably older that Daniel and no more handsome.

'Sorry, Daddy. I didn't realise she was one of our friends.'

'Hey, don't have a go at Carol!' said Lucy. 'I'm not sure *I'd* have let me in the house if I was her.'

This forestalled any resentment Carol might have felt and it also amused Daniel. 'Come through, Lucy,' he said. 'Is this a private matter or can the girls hear what you have to say?'

'It's about Ethel Tomlinson's murder.'

'Ah, that.'

'Dad, we both know all about it, and that Lucy thinks Billy Wellington is innocent.'

'I, erm, told them some stuff,' said Daniel. 'My girls are curious about the comings and goings of you and your brother. They don't know anything that might get you into trouble.'

'It wouldn't make any difference if we did,' said Carol, stoutly. 'We certainly wouldn't make a fuss.'

214

You might if you knew it was us who had caused your dad's injuries, Lucy thought. What she said was, 'Arnold's been arrested for Ethel's murder.'

There was a shocked silence from both Daniel and Carol. They all went into the lounge where Jeanette was sitting. She looked up and said, 'I heard what Lucy said about Arnold and I don't think he did it.'

'You're right – our Arnold's no more guilty than Billy Wellington is.'

'On what grounds has he been arrested?' Daniel asked, sitting down and gesturing with his hand for Lucy to do the same.

'They found Ethel's knickers in his saddlebag. They came to the house and knew exactly where to look – as if someone had told them. Well, I bet that person was anonymous, and I bet he was the killer, and he put them in Arnold's saddlebag so as to point the finger of blame at him.'

'That's quite possible,' said Daniel, 'but under the cir-cumstances the police would have had no option other than to arrest Arnold. It's material evidence – as damning as a smoking gun. Does Arnold have an alibi for the time Ethel was killed?'

'I don't know what he was doing. I was too busy sort-ing out Billy's alibi – not that it did him much good. Although just before he got arrested, Arnold came up with proof that Billy couldn't have killed Ethel. He was at Copley's Café during the time he was supposed to have done it. Mr Copley told our Arnold that. So, the minute we get Billy in the clear, they lock our Arnold up.'

'Billy won't be in the clear yet,' said Daniel. 'Mr

Copley's evidence might be crucial but it'll have to be presented at a trial. The prosecution still have the victim's statement, brief as it was, plus Billy's so-called confession. I think he'll be found not guilty but they'll have to go through the motions to justify locking him up in a mental hospital for so long.'

'Ethel said it was someone called Bill,' said Lucy.

'Yes, and that will go in Arnold's favour.'

'Won't they let him out on bail or something?'

'Not for a capital crime. You don't get bail for murder.'

'So, they'll keep them both locked up for the same crime?'

'It won't be the first time the law has held two suspects in custody. The prosecution might well say that Arnold and Billy were in it together.'

'They didn't even know each other back then. When they got Billy for it, if our Arnold had been involved too he'd have been worried sick. Did he look worried to you?'

'I don't know, Lucy, although I must admit doing such a thing is hardly Arnold's style – what happened to Ethel was the work of a sadistic pervert.'

'I'll tell you what's occurred to me,' said Carol.

'What's that, darling?'

'I've heard you say that when Ethel was asked who did it, she just said Bill and then she died.'

'Yes, that's true.'

'No one ever called him Bill,' Lucy intervened.

'Maybe she died before she got the whole name out,' Daniel pointed out.

'If it *had* been Billy, she'd have said Bootsie,' argued

Lucy. 'All the kids at the home called him Bootsie, and Ethel was from the home.'

'But suppose she wasn't giving you a first name,' Carol said. 'Supposing she was trying to say Billingham or Billings or some name like that. Might she know someone with that sort of name? Has anyone asked at the home?'

'Or builder?' suggested Lucy. 'Was there a builder she might have known? Maybe someone working on the estate. There's still a lot of building going on there.'

'Blimey!' said Daniel. 'I've got a couple of real sleuths here.' He looked at Jeanette. 'Do you have anything to add to all this?'

'Yes,' she said. 'The day after it happened me and a couple of friends went there on our bikes. We couldn't get near the scene of the crime because of all the policemen, but I did notice one thing.'

'What was that?'

'There was a builder working on a wall, bang opposite the home – well, two of them, actually.'

'Could have been a bricklayer and his labourer.'

'Ethel will only have known them as *bill*...ders,' said Lucy, emphasising the first syllable.

'Hey, that's right!' chorused the sisters.

'It would seem there's a lot to work on,' conceded Daniel, 'and I've still got a way to go with my recovery before I'm any real use to anyone.'

'You look okay to me,' said Lucy.

'Thank you, Lucy, but my doctors might give you an argument. There's a lot of internal healing to take place before I can exert any pressure on my battered body.'

'I wish I could get my hands on those people who did it to you,' said Carol.

Lucy looked at her and tried to assess what damage Carol might be able to inflict on her. Not much. She was a year younger, three inches shorter and many pounds lighter than Lucy, who could handle herself in a fight against most girls of her own size. Arnold had taught her a few moves over the years and he was no mug when it came to a fight.

*

Arnold was being treated badly. On arrival at Chapeltown police station his personal possessions had been taken from him, he'd been photographed, finger-printed and thrown bodily into a cell that stank of disinfectant. In the cell was a bench with a thin mattress on it, and a bucket. He lay down on the mattress and stared at the ceiling, trying not to blame Lucy for all this. She, via Billy Wellington, was his only connection to the Ethel Tomlinson murder and he knew that this was the reason he was in this cell accused of murder. He wondered if Billy might be released, now they'd got another suspect, and also how wise he had been in going along with his sister's argument that Billy was innocent. Although Mr Copley had confirmed that.

Arnold hadn't heard about the murder until the day after it had happened and was now struggling to remember what he'd been doing when it had taken place. He'd known Lucy would be going to the dog place to free Wilf, but what had he been doing himself? She'd asked him if he'd go with her and he'd said no because he had better things to do that day. It had probably been a lie because he hadn't wanted to get involved, but what *had* he been doing?

*

In the interview room Arnold sat opposite Inspector Goodfellow and a sergeant. A thought struck him.

'Aren't I allowed a phone call to my solicitor or something?'

'Oh, yes, and who's your solicitor?' sneered the sergeant. He was a very big man with a jowly face, close-cropped hair like an old tennis ball, and a walrus moustache.

'I thought you supplied one,' said Arnold, uncertainly.

'You'll be allocated a solicitor in due course,' said the inspector. 'In the meantime I must ask you where you were on the afternoon of Sunday May the twenty-third 1954.'

'I've been trying to remember, but I can't. I can tell you where I was on May the twenty-fourth when I found out about the murder, but I'm blowed if I can remember where I was the day before. Blimey, it's over a year ago!'

'So, you've got no alibi for the time Ethel Tomlinson was murdered?'

'I might have, I've no idea. I don't keep a diary or anything, and nothing happened on that day to make me remember it.'

'Nothing happened?' snarled the sergeant. 'You think the rape and murder of a young woman is nothing, do you?'

'No, but I didn't know about it until the day after, so it wasn't a significant day to me. Who's gonna know what they were doing on a random day a year ago? Most people don't know what they were doing on a random day a week ago.'

219

The sergeant leaned across the table and punched Arnold on his jaw, knocking him out of his chair, on to the floor.

'What was that for?' he mumbled, rubbing his face.

The sergeant screamed at him, 'For being a filthy dirty rapist bastard who killed a mentally deficient girl just to satisfy your filthy lust!'

'I'm not. I didn't do it.'

The sergeant walked over to him and slapped him across the face.

'Do we look like idiots, lad?' he yelled. 'We know you did it, you scum! The only hope you've got is to confess here and now, then we just might request a more lenient sentence. You might get away with life instead of having your scrawny neck stretched by a hangman's noose ... and don't believe all you hear about hanging being quick and painless. Some murderers take ten minutes to stop kicking their feet. It's a bad way to die, scum, so do yourself a favour and confess.'

Blood was pouring from Arnold's nose. He was crying now. All he could think of to say was the truth. 'I didn't do it. I didn't kill her.'

'Get back in the chair, scum!' ordered the sergeant.

Arnold summoned up the courage to be defiant. 'What, so you can knock me to the floor again? I might as well stay here.'

'Get back in the chair,' said Goodfellow.

Arnold didn't move. The sergeant dragged him to his feet and flung him into the chair.

'Why was the murdered girl's underwear in your saddlebag?' asked the inspector. He spoke as though there had been no act of violence between his last question and this.

'I don't know,' Arnold muttered, holding his jaw. 'I assume someone put it there. It wasn't me.'

'And why would anyone do that?'

'I don't know. How do you even know those knickers were Ethel's?'

'Because they had her name on a tag sewn into them.'

'Oh,' said Arnold. 'I think he might have broken my jaw.' Arnold tried to work his jaw up and down. 'I really need to see a doctor to have it checked.'

'I'll ask you again,' said the inspector. 'Why was her underwear in your saddlebag?'

Arnold had obviously given the question some thought. 'Well, your guess is as good as mine, but I know what my guess would be.'

'Do tell me.'

'A lot of people know that my sister doesn't believe for one minute that Billy Wellington killed Ethel because he was with her most of that afternoon. I'm guessing the killer's getting a bit nervous that she'll find out the truth. In fact, only today I found out something that should prove Billy can't have done it. So at some stage the killer, who still had Ethel's knickers, decided to give my sister something else to think about by framing me and ringing you up, anonymously, to tell you where the evidence was.'

'You've a lot to say for a man with a broken jaw,' said Goodfellow.

'I still need to have it checked out. When the doctor

asks me how it happened, shall I tell him the truth or would you prefer me to tell a lie?'

'I believe lying comes naturally to you.'

Arnold looked Inspector Goodfellow in the eye and shook his head, defiantly. There were tears in his eyes and his jaw was still hurting but he needed to defend himself against this injustice.

'You already know that some of what I've just told you is true. The bit about him ringing you anonymously and telling you where to find the knickers. I mean, even if it was me who attacked Erhel, which it wasn't, how would anybody else know I had a pair of her knickers in my saddlebag?'

The sergeant leaned across the table until his face was inches away from Arnold's. 'Maybe he was a witness to the murder and saw you put them there, you filthy scumbag!'

Arnold sat back in his chair to avoid the spray of spittle that had accompanied the sergeant's outburst. He composed himself before replying. 'What? And he waited a whole year to tell you – obviously hoping I hadn't taken them out of my saddlebag during the interim. I mean, how likely is that?'

Goodfellow leaned on the table and said, menacingly, 'We don't know where this person got his information from, and we don't need to know. All we care about is that it was accurate.'

'Of course it was accurate. It was always bound to be accurate if he put them there! I only ever go into my saddlebag to get my toolkit.'

'So, when was the last time you went into your saddlebag?'

Arnold thought for a moment, back to the time he'd put his wet jeans there. No advantage in telling them about that. A believable lie would be better. 'I had a puncture a couple of weeks ago,' he said. 'I'll have needed my tyre irons and my puncture outfit. There were no knickers in it then. I mean, why would I even keep a girl's knickers?'

'Once again, I don't need to know the answer to that,' said the inspector.

'You know I didn't do it,' protested Arnold.

'If I knew that,' Goodfellow said, 'I wouldn't be formally charging you with her murder . . . which I'm about to do right now.'

The sergeant grinned and mimed a noose tied around his neck. 'You'll hang, lad. We've got you.'

'I won't hang,' said Arnold, 'because I didn't do it, and in any case I was only seventeen when it happened. They don't hang seventeen years olds – especially for murders they didn't commit.'

The sergeant looked as though he was about to hit Arnold again. Goodfellow put a restraining hand on his arm. The sergeant scowled. Arnold looked away, not wanting them to see the tears rolling down his face. He knew that he was innocent, but that might not be enough to ensure he wouldn't end up doing life. It seemed the police had a way of twisting the truth to suit themselves.

Chapter 28

Lucy's life had taken a massive downturn. Not only was Billy locked up for a crime of which he was innocent, but her brother too was locked up for the same crime – one so bad that she and her family had been pretty well ostracised from local society. She'd become the butt of jokes at school, which had led to her almost being expelled for punching Moira Dickinson in the face. Moira had made a cruel joke about her brother the rapist. A joke which neither she nor any other girl would dare to repeat, given the violent reaction it provoked. Lucy had been called into the headmistress's study to face both her and Moira's irate mother.

'Bailey, Mrs Dickinson is insisting that I expel you and I'm trying to persuade her not to report your assault on her daughter to the police.'

'I've already done that, Mrs Crabtree,' said Lucy, truthfully. 'I reported it last night to Detective Inspector Earnshawe of Chapeltown police.'

The two women were taken aback by this. 'And, er, what did the detective inspector say?' asked Mrs Crabtree.

'He said I had mitigating circumstances insofar as I was first the victim of a cruel verbal assault by Moira. He said

224

the magistrates would have to take that into account. I told him that I only hit her once, whereas she'd been verbally assaulting me all day and it seemed to me that physical retaliation was the only way to shut her up.'

'I've never heard anything so ridiculous in my life!' snorted Mrs Dickinson.

'She may have a point,' said Mrs Crabtree.

'She's a very unpleasant girl is Moira,' said Lucy. 'Nobody likes her. With my brother being in jail for a terrible crime he definitely didn't commit, a lot of girls stopped talking to me. After I hit Moira some of them are talking to me again. Some of them even said she had it coming.'

Mrs Crabtree knew that Moira wasn't a popular girl, unlike Lucy who was. She looked at Mrs Dickinson and said, 'If this were a boys' school it would be dealt with by a caning and the incident would be forgotten. At this school we don't cane our girls, but I do think five nights' detention would do Bailey no harm and it would show the other girls that we don't condone physical violence, no matter what the provocation.'

'So, you believe this liar's story about Moira provoking her?' seethed Mrs Dickinson.

'I do, actually. I've had several independent reports as to what had been going on that day and your daughter was indeed taunting Bailey about her brother.'

Mrs Dickinson spun on her heel and stormed out of the room. Mrs Crabtree glared at Lucy. 'I'm giving you one hour's detention for the next five school nights, starting tomorrow. Inform your parents that you'll be late home and tell them why. If Mrs Dickinson reports you to the police we must hope your policeman friend was right in his assessment.'

Lucy almost asked how she knew Daniel was her friend but decided against it.

'May I be excused, Mrs Crabtree?'

'You may.'

As Lucy turned to go she missed the glint of admiration in Mrs Crabtree's eyes.

Chapter 29

When the phone rang Daniel was standing at the kitchen window, contemplating whether or not he should attempt mowing the lawn. His daughters had been tending the garden but he thought a little exercise might do him no harm. Up until now his only exercise had been walking, which he did every day. It was a woman's voice that greeted him when he answered the phone: youngish, well-spoken, pleasant.

'Am I speaking to Detective Inspector Daniel Earnshawe?'

'You are.'

'My name is Helen Durkin. I was given your number by Lucy Bailey, with whom I believe you're acquainted.'

'Yes, I know Lucy.'

'Well, I'm William Wellington's mother and I understand from Lucy that you're helping her to prove my son's innocent of this awful murder he's supposed to have committed?'

'Ah, yes, I know who you are now. You do realise I'm not on duty at the moment due to injury.'

'I do, yes. How are you, Mr Earnshawe?'

'To outward appearaces I'm well, albeit a bit slow on

my feet, but there are a few internal complications.' Diplomatically, he chose not to ask if she knew who had been the cause of his injuries. 'How can I help you?'

'Well, I don't want to leave all of this up to Lucy, especially now she has the added burden of her brother being on remand for the same crime. I thought I might come and see you, to discuss the best way to approach things.'

'I imagine that might be useful,' he said, curious to meet this motorbike courier and occasional actress.

'Am I to gather that you think my son is innocent?'

'I think there's every chance he is and, while I'm convalescing, I told Lucy that I'd help out unofficially with advice only. I can't use my official status in any of this.'

'So, when can I come and see you? I have my own transport.'

'Now's as good a time as any for me.'

'Now it is then. I have your address I should be there in half an hour or so.'

Half an hour later she was standing at his door, wearing a worn leather flying jacket, jeans and leather boots. Her goggles were up on the brow of her black crash helmet, which she removed to allow a cascade of blonde hair to fall about her shoulders. He'd hoped she might be good-looking and he wasn't disappointed. She took off a leather gauntlet and held out her right hand.

'Thank you for seeing me, Mr Earnshawe.'

'Not at all. Please come in.'

She looked down at the walking stick he was leaning on. He stood back, indicating that Helen should follow him. He looked at the stick and grinned. 'Oh, don't feel any sympathy for me because of this. It's mainly for show nowadays. People give way to me in the street and in shops and when I'm crossing the road. I just try and milk it for all it's worth. My daughters have rumbled me, of course. I'm receiving a diminishing amount of sympathy from them.'

'Really? How old are they?'

'Carol's fifteen and Jeanette's thirteen.'

'A difficult age for girls.'

'It's a more difficult age for their father! But we've sat down and they've told me all they know, which was more than I knew, so that part of it's not a problem.'

She smiled. 'Your wife died, I understand?'

'She did, yes.'

He chose not to elaborate and Helen chose not to press him. She took her flying jacket off to reveal a checked shirt covering what he couldn't help but notice was a very shapely body. He took her coat and crash helmet and hung them on a coatstand. They went through to the lounge where they sat in chairs facing each other.

'Do you want to know about me?' asked Helen.

'Well, it'd do no harm.'

'Such as why I abandoned my baby?'

'That's entirely up to you. Can I get you a coffee or anything?'

'In a minute, thank you. I need to get this off my chest first. I've asked you to help me with William and it's only right that you should know his story.'

'Do you smoke? I do.'

She accepted a cigarette, which he lit for her. He settled back to listen to her story.

'I'm going to make this brief and to the point,' said Helen, closing her eyes and bowing her head as if to summon up the strength to begin.

'My stepfather's name is Maurice Bradley and he ... er ... he sexually abused me as a child.' She avoided looking at Daniel and took a deep breath before continuing. The words tumbled out this time. 'This resulted in me becoming pregnant with William. I was thirteen years old at the time. Bradley was a sailor who had recently gone away on a voyage. I left school at Christmas 1936, just after I reached the age of fourteen, and Billy was born the following March. My mother delivered my baby and we intended having him adopted before Bradley, who knew nothing about the pregnancy, returned. When William was two weeks old we received a letter saying my stepfather would be home in three days' time. I took matters into my own hands and left William at the bus station on Wellington Street, which is where he got his surname from.'

Daniel watched her face as she told her story. He looked away when he saw tears welling in her eyes and left it a while before asking: 'Has your stepfather ever been punished for his actions?'

It was a copper's question. If a man commits a heinous crime he should never get away with it.

'No. When he got home he tried it on again. This time I was ready for him and screamed blue murder. The neighbours called the police, my stepfather was arrested and bailed. He did a bunk, and was never seen by my mother or myself again.'

Daniel's face showed great sympathy. 'I can't imagine what your life's been like.'

'It hasn't been great. I've spent a lot of it trying to blot out what he did to me – not with any great success, I might add.'

'My God! If ever a man needed stringing up . . .'

Helen wiped away her tears, thinking, *Does this mean he'll approve of me murdering my stepfather?* It was a thought she kept to herself.

'How has this affected your relationships with men?' Daniel enquired.

It seemed an impertinent question to be asking such a beautiful woman, who would normally be able to wrap men around her little finger. She smiled.

'Well, it's kept me single up to now.'

He nodded. 'Okay, that's all I need to know about you. You're obviously a good woman who's done nothing wrong. You're a victim, as is your son. I take it you want Billy back, despite his disability?'

'I do.'

Daniel thought she'd had enough of telling her tragic life story and it would do no harm to lighten the conversation up a bit. 'Out of curiosity, what sort of bike have you got? I heard it coming up the street and I thought I recognised it.'

She grinned. 'I've got a 1948 BSA Gold Star.'

'That's what it sounded like . . . 500 at a guess?'

'Yeah.'

'I had a 1939 Gold Star 500.'

'Classic,' she said. 'What happened to it?'

'The war. I got my call-up up in nineteen forty-one, didn't fancy putting it in wraps, so I sold it. Daftest thing I've ever done. I took a couple of bullets six months before

231

the war ended. It was a bit painful but at least it got me home in double-quick time. I was out of action for five months after that. In fact, I never went back on active service. After being demobbed I came back to my wife and girls. To be honest I couldn't afford any bike, never mind a Gold Star. On top of which I was on a motorbike when I got shot. I think it must have put me off them – never ridden a bike since. I travel by car and pushbike now.'

This was small talk but Helen felt comfortable in his company. He was a genuine type . . . and he was interested in her Gold Star.

'So you had a painful war.'

'It was certainly eventful. I rose to the dizzy heights of corporal in the Paras. Ended up with two bullet holes and five campaign medals. Never been back, not many of us have – bad memories, you see. Friends died while I lived. There was something unfair about it all.' He looked at her and smiled. 'Right, I'll make you that coffee and then we'll talk about your son.'

Along with the coffee he brought a slim manila file, which he set down on the coffee table along with the cups. 'I've made a few notes about Billy's case.'

He opened the file. 'Erm, right. The case against him is twofold. One, the evidence given by the dying witness; and two, the confession he made soon after his arrest. The first piece of evidence is tenuous in so far as the victim's dying word was "Bill". Although at the time this was taken to refer to your son's Christian name, it could have been a reference to a profession, i.e. builder, or part of a surname, i.e. Billington. On top of this we know that your son was known as Bootsie to many of his friends including the victim, so why would she say Bill when she knew him as Bootsie?

'The spoken testimony is tenuous as it wasn't recorded – no contemporaneous notes were taken. We also have Lucy's evidence that she was with Billy for all of that afternoon except between five and five-fifteen, during which time he was in a café or walking from the café to the home.'

'So it should be easy to get William out of that mental asylum?'

'You would think so, but it might not happen speedily. He's detained there under the Mental Health Act, so we've got a combination of barriers to overcome: first the health authorities and then the Director of Public Prosecutions. The best way to do all that is to hire a top barrister and get the thing into court.'

'Which I assume costs a lot of money.'

'That's been taken care of.' Daniel eyed her closely and added, 'Don't ask.'

'I won't. I suppose Lucy's brother being accused of the same crime won't harm William much.'

'I don't know. I've heard it mentioned that they might both have been involved.'

'What?'

'I don't believe it either, but it'd get the police off a couple of very awkward hooks.'

The front door opened and shut then. Daniel cocked an ear. 'That's one or more of my daughters home from school. If they think I've got company they'll be in here within seconds.' The words had scarcely left his lips when the girls came into the room. They both looked curiously at Helen.

'These two reprobates are my daughters,' said Daniel, 'Carol and Jeanette.'

He identified each girl with a sweep of his arm. 'And this is Helen Durkin, who's a motorbike courier, an actress, and William Wellington's mother.'

'An actress?' said Jeanette. 'What have you been in? Anything on the telly?'

Helen smiled. 'No, I'm mainly a stage actress, when I'm in work.'

'Are you in work now?'

'No, that's my bike parked outside.'

'Oh, so you're delivering something to Dad?' Carol sounded disappointed.

'William Wellington's mother!' exclaimed Jeanette, realising what her dad had said. 'You're here to talk about Billy?'

'Yes,' said Helen.

'Well, none of us think he did it,' said Carol. 'We don't think Arnold did it either. Since my dad went on sick leave the police force has gone to pot.'

'Are you going to be in anything soon?' Jeanette asked.

Helen was taken aback by the fluctuating questions. 'What? Oh, actually, yes. I've just got a part in a fit up that's touring around Yorkshire and Lancashire for a couple of months.'

'What's a fit up?'

'Oh, it's a type of theatre production where the company carries all its own props and scenery and fits them together, sometimes even the stage too, wherever they perform. Everybody has to muck in. It's quite good fun, really.'

'Will you be coming to Leeds?'

'No, but we're in Harrogate and York in September.'

'What's the play?'

'It's called *True North*. I play a northern girl who falls in love with an aristocrat whose family thinks I've married above my station.'

'You don't sound very northern.'

Helen slipped into a Leeds accent. 'Yer wot? I were born an' bred round 'ere. Brought up on fish'n'chips an' rabbit stew.'

The girls laughed, as did Daniel.

'Will you be staying for tea?' asked Jeanette.

'Well, no, I actually came to talk to your father about getting Billy free.'

'Which is her polite way of saying scram, both of you,' said Daniel.

'I didn't mean that at all,' Helen protested.

'No, but I did,' said Daniel.

As they left the room Helen distinctly heard Jeanette say, 'She'll do.' Daniel heard it too, and was forced to explain. 'Take no notice, they're constantly match-making.'

'Oh,' said Helen, secretly pleased that at least she met with the girls' approval. 'So, what we're waiting for now is the barrister to get a hearing date?'

'That's pretty much it. And with the summer recess very near it won't be until the autumn. October or November probably.'

'That's disgusting.'

'The wheels of the law grind very slowly.'

'Will Billy be given any compensation for all this wrongful imprisonment?'

'I don't know ... quite possibly.'

'It'd be good to think that he would. I could take him on a really nice holiday – abroad somewhere, in an aeroplane.'

Daniel thought of the cash he still had from the raid on Leonov's house – four thousand three hundred and sixty-five pounds. Enough to pay the barrister, send Billy and Helen on holiday *and* buy them a house to live in. His wife would have approved of that. His daughters certainly would. Maybe when the right time came he would ask their opinion.

'I'm sure Billy will enjoy that,' he said, 'especially with his mum. I'm sorry I can't be of more immediate help, but unless the real killer is found soon I suspect both Billy and Arnold are going to be banged up pending their hearings. And I have to say that, as things stand, William's got a much better chance of being found not guilty than young Arnold has.'

'Poor lad,' said Helen. 'And I suspect he somehow became involved because of trying to help William.'

'I'm sure that's what's happened,' said Daniel. 'Someone's trying to cover his tracks at Arnold's expense.'

'And you're on his side?'

'Unofficially, yes.'

'Then I suspect he's in safe hands.'

'I wish I had your faith.'

'I've got every faith in you, Mr Earnshawe.'

Helen's eyes were fixed on his as she said it and it

seemed to him that there was more in her gaze than faith. Or was that just wishful thinking?

'Thank you,' he said.

'Er . . . I understand that when he was locked up in the Manchester hospital, Billy was subjected to Electro Convulsive Therapy.'

'Who told you that?'

'Lucy . . . he still had the marks all over his head. Arnold knows about such things, apparently. I've checked and it's a procedure that's very much in its infancy – in fact, it's known that it can do more harm than good. It wouldn't surprise me if he was being sedated with drugs he didn't need at his children's home.'

'It's quite possible,' said Daniel.

'According to Arnold, it's also quite possible that this new place might try and give him a frontal lobotomy, which could destroy what mind he has.'

Daniel said nothing. He wouldn't put anything past those mental hospitals.

'I've written a letter to the governor of Rampton,' Helen said. 'I thought I'd run it past you before I sent it.'

'Fire away.'

She took a letter from her bag, unfolded it and passed it over.

To the governor of Rampton Hospital,

Sirs,
My name is Helen Durkin. My son is William Wellington who is incarcerated in your institution having been accused of murder

and found unfit to plead. In other words, he has not been proved guilty and therefore, in accordance with British law, is innocent until proved otherwise. I wish him to be treated as such. It is our intention to have him properly tried in court in the near future.

In his last place of incarceration he was subjected, without my knowledge or permission, to Electro Convulsive Therapy which, I suspect, may well have further damaged his mind. I wish to make clear my objection to any further treatment of this nature, or to any medication other than for routine physical ailments. In particular I would strongly object to his being subjected to any extreme surgical treatment such as frontal lobotomy.

We have every confidence in proving Billy's innocence, and when we do we will expect him to be released in the same state of mind as when he was wrongfully imprisoned. His story will appear in a national newspaper, which will receive a copy of this letter.

She looked at Daniel and said, 'What do you think?'

'Well, if he was my responsibility, I'd wrap him up in cotton wool.'

'That was the idea.'

'Which newspaper is it?'

'Ah, that was a lie.'

'You had me convinced. I'd send it.'

Chapter 30

Arnold's address was now cell B2 19, HM Prison Armley, Leeds. It was a remand prison where Arnold would remain until he was either sentenced or released. Either way he knew he'd be there for a while as he'd been given a date for his hearing of Monday, 14 November and it was now the middle of July – almost four months of worry to endure. His main concern was that he might be on the same wing as Peter Leonov. Not that Leonov would know him from Adam, but if he ever did find out that Arnold had robbed his house then Arnold's life would be in serious danger.

He was sharing a cell with a man called Russell Brown who was accused of sexually assaulting a young boy. Arnold hadn't had to ask him why he was here, he hadn't needed to. The rest of the inmates had made him aware of his cell mate's history as a nonce, especially Abe Doyle who was up for a charge of attempted murder that he didn't expect to beat. With his record, he'd go down for a ten stretch at least.

Abe was a hulking, violent bully who constantly tormented Russell, the 'kiddie fiddler' as he called him. Russell was a social misfit who spent most nights weeping himself to sleep in his bunk, the one above Arnold, who was half sorry for him and half exasperated by him.

'Russell, can you stop all that crying? *I'm* not crying, am I? And I might get hanged for doing nowt.'

'They won't hang you. You're much too young.'

'I don't know. They hanged Ruth Ellis yesterday and no one expected that.'

The execution of Ruth Ellis for the murder of her abusive lover had shocked the whole of Britain. Everyone had expected her sentence to be commuted to life imprisonment.

'That was awful. Sorry, Arnie.'

'My name's Arnold.'

'I'm just frightened all the time. Abe hurts me every day, and he smells horrible.'

'Well, I can't argue with that,' said Arnold. 'I don't know why they let him get away with smelling so bad.'

'I think he's in league with one or two officers, bringing in drugs and stuff and selling them to the prisoners.'

'We should have a whip-round and buy him half a ton of Lifebuoy. He's got body odour that could strip pine has Abe.'

'I think he might kill me before my trial comes up,' Russell confided.

'Why not ask to be put in solitary?'

'*He's* the one who should be in solitary. They should lock him up in a pig sty.'

'That wouldn't be fair to the pigs,' said Arnold, raising half a smile from Russell.

'I didn't do what they said I did to that boy. I didn't even know him. It's only because I'm different that the police came after me. People have always been cruel to me and told horrible lies about me. Someone will have put them up to it. They do that, you know – when you're different.'

'Well, you're different all right,' said Arnold, stuffing a blanket into his ears.

*

Arnold had been inside a week when Abe cornered him in the prison yard. 'I heard yer raped a barmy lass and murdered her,' the bully accosted him.

'You heard wrong,' said Arnold. 'I was fitted up.'

Abe grabbed him by the scruff of his neck and almost choked him to death. 'Don't you tell me I'm wrong!' Then he let go and his manner changed completely, as is the way with psychopaths. 'I'm here to do yer a favour, lad. To mek yer life in 'ere a bit sweeter. Smoke, do yer?'

Arnold turned his head to one side in an attempt to breathe air uncontaminated by Abe's virulent stink.

'Now and again – can't really afford to.'

'Yer'll have people outside who can put money your way?'

'Not really.'

'Look at me when I'm talkin' to yer!'

Arnold looked back, trying to breathe just through his mouth.

Listen, pal,' snarled Abe, 'I'm offering yer a bargain here. Special baccy, if yer know what I mean. Makes yer life pleasant. I can get yer a nice smoke for a bob.'

'A shilling for a cigarette? You can nearly buy a packet of ten for that.'

'Not these ciggies, pal.'

'You mean, drugs?'

241

"Course I mean drugs, yer thick pillock!'

'Like cannabis?' It was a drug Arnold had only just heard of.

'Not *like* cannabis, it *is* cannabis. The finest money can buy.'

It seemed to Arnold that to comply might give him an easier life. He knew enough to realise that going up against the prison hard men held no future.

'My wages in the laundry are only five bob a week.'

'That's five smokes.'

'I don't want to spend all my money on smoking ... maybe two, eh?'

'Maybe three,' said Abe. He stuck his hand in his top pocket and drew out a fat roll-up. 'Here, this is a free sample. Pay me Friday.'

Arnold stuck the free sample in his shirt pocket. He scarcely smoked ordinary cigarettes so he was a bit wary of these. A middle-aged fellow prisoner, who had seen him talking to Abe, stopped him in the yard.

'Got yer doin' drugs, has he?'

'He's got me buying them.'

'Wise boy. Yer can allus sell 'em on, so long as he doesn't hear about it.'

'Who to?'

'Me. I'll give yer a tanner each for 'em.'

'He's charging a shilling.'

'I know. I'm payin' a tanner.'

'Right ... how does he get the stuff in here?'

'One o' the screws.' The man nodded towards a tall, thin prison officer leaning against a wall. 'That big long streak o' piss – Gladbury 'is name is.'

'Do you think we could persuade him to sell Abe some soap?'

The other man grinned. 'I think Abe's allergic to soap and water. Never see him in the showers.'

'I think I'm allergic to Abe.'

'Gladbury keeps the stuff in his locker by all accounts. Him and Abe split the profits.'

'I'm amazed that no one's ever reported them,' said Arnold.

'It's been done, son. Don't ask me how, but they got away with it. I think the wing governor might have been in on it. He's the one it was reported to. The lad who squealed on 'em got ghosted ter Wakefield. Word followed him there that he were a grass and he were given a terrible hard time. Topped himself, so I heard. In here you just keep yerself ter yerself, lad. There's no way of knowin' who's on your side. Just don't make any waves.'

*

Abe was relieving himself in the toilet. After he finished he popped his head into the shower area to see who he could torment next. Half a dozen men, including Arnold, were taking showers. Abe's eyes lit up when he saw the skinny form of Russell drying himself off.

Abe shouted for all to hear: 'Watch yer arses, lads, there's a bumboy about!'

He walked over to Russell, snatched the towel from him and whirled it into a tight knot, with which he began to whip the weeping and terrified Russell. Arnold watched from under a shower, wanting to intervene but knowing he'd only end up as one of Abe's victims himself if he did. Russell screamed in pain and fear and dropped to the floor, curling up like a foetus. Then, with a courage Arnold was later to admire, he shouted at Abe, 'You rotten bully! You stink. You should take a shower yourself, you stinking pig!'

The veins stood out on Abe's neck like ropes as anger raged within him. His face went puce. He looped the twisted towel around Russell's skinny neck and dragged him to his feet. One of Abe's cronies arrived to see what was going on. He grinned and gave his friend shouts of encouragement. He and the other men in the showers knew that Russell was going to die. Only Arnold said anything.

'Leave him, Abe! He's scared to death. He doesn't know what he's saying.'

But Abe didn't seem to hear. He just tightened the towel until he'd cut off Russell's breath. Arnold stepped out of the shower, wanting to go to his cell mate's aid, but self-preservation told him not to – or was it cowardice? He would no doubt have suffered the same fate as Russell, especially with Abe having a crony with him, but it didn't make Arnold feel any better about himself. He stood there and watched his cell mate turn blue in the face. He watched Russell's eyes bulge until the life went out of them, and he watched as Abe let go of the towel and allowed the body to drop to the floor where the bully added to its indignity by kicking it in the naked buttocks. He then looked round at all the naked men watching him.

'See him?' he said. 'That'll be you if you say a word about this to the screws or anyone else. He was lying there when you came in, right?'

'Right,' mumbled five of the six men. Arnold couldn't

bring himself to say the word. He just looked down at Russell who had been locked up for a crime he said he didn't commit. Right then Arnold believed him. After Abe and his crony had left he said to anyone who might be listening, 'Someone fitted him up for assaulting a kiddie. I thought he was a good bloke.'

It was all he could offer Russell in recompense for not going to his assistance. One of the men came over to him.

'If yer thinking of shoppin' Abe to the governor, it'll be your word against ours. None of us are goin' up against Abe and his crew. We value our lives too much.'

Arnold nodded. He could see the sense in this but he could also see the grave injustice. He simply shrugged and got dressed and left before any prison officers arrived on the scene.

When questioned about it later he told the governor that the last time he'd seen Russell he was alive and just going in to the shower as Arnold was leaving. He was asked who else was in the shower and Arnold said he didn't know. He never looked at anyone when he went for a shower in case they took exception to it. The governor looked at him closely, and said, 'I understand you're pleading not guilty to this murder you're accused of?'

'I *am* not guilty, sir.'

'Tell me, if the jury find you not guilty, would it encourage you to change your statement about Russell Brown's murder?'

'Possibly, sir.'

'I see. Thank you, Bailey. You may go.'

Chapter 31

The dark blue Rover 90 pulled up outside Lucy's house and sounded its horn. She was out before the sound had died away, waving at the driver. Daniel acknowledged this with a raised hand. She jumped into the passenger seat, asking, 'Where are we going first?'

The excursion had been arranged over the phone a week previously. The idea was to work through all the knowledge they'd accumulated about Billy – and now Arnold.

'We're going to pick up Helen Durkin. She obviously wants to be involved.'

'I thought she was touring with a play?'

'That's right, she's in Harrogate right now, but today's a day off in between productions or something so she's asked to come with us.'

'Good, I like Helen.'

'Yeah, so do I – I like her a lot.'

Lucy felt a sudden pang of jealousy at this, then dismissed it as nonsense.

'Have you thought any more about our Arnold?'

'Well, he's to be defended by Mr Barrington-Smythe, who's also defending Billy, so he'll have every chance.'

'What does Mr Barrington-Smythe think of my brother's chances?'

'He thinks he'll need to be on top form to persuade a jury that the evidence was planted in Arnold's saddlebag, but if anyone can do that it's Mr Barrington-Smythe.'

'And will we still be paying him out of the Leonov money?'

'Of course. It's all part of the same thing. The money was ill gained so must redeem itself by going to a good cause.'

Lucy gave this some thought, then nodded her appreciation of Daniel's thinking. 'That sounds very fair,' she said. 'So, what's happening to Leonov?'

'At the moment he's being held on remand, charged with theft and money laundering, until such time as the police get all the more serious charges made watertight. Elias Munro, the man who attacked Arnold, is being charged with the murder of a security guard at York. Once he's found guilty and sentenced to hang, I'm hoping he'll own up to killing my wife on Leonov's orders.'

'Would he do that?'

'A man condemned to death has nothing to lose. He'll probably tell us all we want to know in the hope of a reprieve, which he won't get, but no one's going to tell him that now.'

'You said Leonov's being held on remand. Whereabouts is he?'

'Oh, hell!' said Daniel. 'He's in Armley, on the remand wing, but he won't know anything about Arnold being involved in the robbery at his house – or you, for that matter.'

'What about the other bloke? He'd recognise Arnold.'

'Would he?'

'Well . . . he might not,' Lucy conceded. 'Arnold had his hair covered in a black woolly hat and we'd blacked our faces.'

'At the moment Munro's on the hospital wing so he won't come into contact with Arnold.'

'I think I should tell him, all the same.'

Daniel was quiet for a while as he headed the car towards Leeds centre, then he said, 'The prosecution in Arnold's case have brought up something that might be tricky – if it's true.'

'What's that?'

'They're under the impression that he might have a nickname. Are you aware of one?'

'Not really. I've heard him called Silly Billy Bailey sometimes, in fact I've called him that myself, but it's not a proper nickname.'

'So, no one ever calls him Bill Bailey, because of the song?'

'You mean, "Won't You Come Home, Bill Bailey"?'

'Yeah, or simply because the two names begin with the same letter. I used to get Ernie Earnshawe all the time when I was a kid.'

'Yeah, I think Arnold's been called Bill, but not often. Like you say, it's because the two names begin with the same letter. I've been called Bessie Bailey before now.'

'Alliteration,' said Daniel.

'I know,' said Lucy.

'So, my question is, would Ethel ever have called him Bill?'

'Oh, I don't know. I don't think she even knew him. Why?'

'It seems the prosecution has found someone who has heard him referred to as Bill Bailey, which certainly won't help his defence.'

'That's just not fair,' said Lucy.

'No one's ever accused justice of being fair,' said Daniel, wryly.

'The copper who nearly broke Arnold's jaw certainly wasn't being fair. He called my brother "scum" and all sorts of other horrible names. Told him he was going to hang and that it takes ten minutes to die when they string you up.'

'I didn't know about that,' said Daniel quietly. 'Did Arnold tell you who the copper was?'

'He was a sergeant in uniform. Great big bloke with more hair in his moustache than on his head. The other copper was an inspector called Goodfellow.'

'Ah, that'll have been Goodfellow and Wallace doing their good cop/bad cop routine.'

'I don't think Arnold noticed the good cop bit. He thinks they should lock Wallace up for assault.'

'Well, your brother certainly has the right to make a complaint. I'll show you what to do, but the most urgent thing is to get him out of prison . . . and in order to do that we need to find Ethel's real killer.'

*

When Helen emerged from her front door in response to Daniel hooting his horn she was looking radiant – too radiant for Lucy's liking. Lucy knew many things about herself and one of them was that she'd never been called radiant – that day would come, she wasn't short of self-confidence in that respect. Right now she had a pleasant enough face, no real sign of a bust as yet, and legs that were too skinny for her liking.

Helen was once again wearing jeans and Lucy secretly hoped this was because her legs weren't much to look at. Trouble was, the rest of her looked pretty shapely. Her hair looked glorious, beautiful and blonde and glinting in the morning sun. She sat in the front next to Daniel. Lucy, feeling like a spare part, sat in the back

'Hi, Lucy,' said Helen.

'Hello.'

'You okay?'

'Yeah – just worried about Arnold, that's all.'

'Why? Has something new cropped up?'

'Daniel thinks the prosecution have someone who's heard Arnold being called Bill, which is who Ethel said had done it.'

'Oh, no!'

'It might be nothing,' said Daniel. 'At least our barrister's forewarned and will be ready with an answer.'

'What answer?' asked Lucy.

'I imagine he'll have a go at this new witness and make him sound unreliable. That's what barristers do.'

'So, this witness . . . it's a him, is it?' said Lucy.

'I believe so.'

'You don't know his name, do you?'

'If I did I certainly wouldn't tell you, Lucy. Intimidating witnesses is a serious crime.'

'How can I intimidate anyone? I'm a fifteen-year-old girl.'

'You're Lucy Bailey.'

'So?'

'So I've had to tell Helen about the Leonov thing, with her wondering where we got the barrister's fee from. I've also told her about your part in it.'

'Well, that's only fair,' conceded Lucy. 'With us all being in it together.'

'What you did was incredibly brave and resourceful,' said Helen. She turned round in her seat to look at Lucy. 'Had it not been for you, Billy would be locked up for life with no prospect of ever getting out. You've given my boy a chance, for which I'm very grateful.'

Lucy now felt guilty for harbouring unkind thoughts about Helen. Maybe Daniel wasn't ready for another woman yet, with him still grieving over his dead wife. And maybe in two or three years he would be, by which time she'd have filled out, had her crooked tooth fixed, her hair permed and possibly dyed blonde, and her legs would have filled out and be as shapely as film star Betty Grable's that were insured for a million dollars.

'I did it because he's my pal and he never touched Ethel. He's a big softy is Billy.'

'I suspect the barrister will ask you to be a defence witness,' said Daniel.

'I'd like to see him try and stop me!'

Chapter 32

September

Arnold was in the dinner queue holding his tin tray; the aroma reminded him of school dinners on a swede and cabbage day, but it was an aroma that was soon to take a turn for the worse. The dining room was rowdy as usual with just two bored-looking officers overseeing proceedings, both of them standing by the door and smoking. Abe pushed into the queue and was now right behind Arnold, who didn't need to turn round to know he was there. Abe's pungent body odour told him all he needed to know. In any case, experience had taught him not to look round in a crowded room as the person behind might well ask him who the hell he thought he was looking at? Such bullies had been few and far between at his school but not in prison, which was a dog-eat-dog society with a hierarchy based on fear and strength. Arnold wasn't at the bottom of this hierarchy but he wasn't far off. Abe Doyle was the top man on Arnold's wing. He put one meaty hand on Arnold's shoulder.

'Undercutting me, are yer, lad?'

Arnold turned round. Abe didn't look pleased.

'How d'you mean?'

'I'm sellin' spliffs fer a bob and you're sellin' 'em for a tanner.'

'Yeah, but I'm buyin' them off you first.'

It was a reasonable argument that might have carried weight anywhere but inside a prison. As it was Arnold felt his legs being swiped from under him. He fell to the floor and many feet began to kick him, not just Abe's but at least four more. Life was cheap in such places, especially someone else's life. The perpetrators of prison violence assumed they would get away with it and were often proved to be correct. Abe wasn't particularly worried about Arnold selling on his drugs, but regarded him as the most unreliable link in the list of witnesses to the murder of Russell Brown. Disposing of Arnold would remove him as a potential witness, plus terrify the rest into a permanent and reliable silence.

No words were spoken to accompany the extreme violence that would end in Arnold's death if no one intervened. Everyone in the queue knew what was happening but they tried to look nonchalant. It was his cries of pain that drew the attention of the two POs, neither of whom approached the queue with any show of urgency. They both hoped that whatever was going on would have stopped by the time they got there, thus making their lives easier.

They arrived to find Arnold on the floor, unconscious and covered in blood. All his attackers had backed away very quickly. One of the officers ran to raise an alarm and within a minute twenty more men arrived in the room, swinging their truncheons at anyone who got in their way. Innocent men left in Arnold's immediate vicinity were herded into a corner for interrogation. His attackers were among the group who were ordered out of the dining hall and back to their cells. A doctor arrived. He called for a stretcher and Arnold was taken to the hospital wing then rushed straight to the Intensive Care Unit at Leeds General Infirmary. He stayed there for five days before being returned to the hospital wing and put in the next-bed-but-one from Elias Munro, who was still nursing a bullet hole in his foot.

Chapter 33

Daniel drew his car to a halt outside a site hut on the Moortown Estate. There were three or four building contractors involved in building the estate and Daniel was hoping he'd picked the right one – J. J. Richards Ltd. A site foreman was standing at a table examining a large architectural plan when Daniel knocked on the open door. The foreman looked on as Daniel got out his warrant card to identify himself as a policeman. He was now back on the job and had asked for, and been given, the task of investigating Ethel Tomlinson's murder. His chief inspector was fairly certain this would be a fruitless task, but suitable for easing Daniel back into the job without putting too much pressure on him.

'What can I do for you?' The foreman walked up to the warrant card and peered at it. 'Detective Inspector.'

'I'm trying to track down a man who was working on a wall on Cranmer Bank opposite the children's home in May last year.'

'May last year? Bloody hell, I don't know! I weren't workin' here last year.'

Daniel glanced down at the plan and saw it was a layout of the estate. He pointed to where the wall in question was represented.

'The wall's here. Would your firm have built it?'

'Yeah – mind you, you might have a job finding out who the brickie was. They come and go on this job, sub-bies most of 'em.'

'Is there anyone around who might remember? I gather he sang a lot while he worked. Got on people's nerves, so I hear.'

The foreman smiled. 'Singin' brickie, eh? Well, there's plenty o' them, but we do have one who never shuts up, an' he gets on my nerves right enough. But whether he built that wall or not, yer'll have to ask him.'

'Is he around?'

'No, we've got no work for brickies right now but I think he's working over at Seacroft. His name's Kevin Brad-shawe. Just hang on, I'll check where he is.'

As the foreman went outside Daniel was disappointed that the brickie's name wasn't Billy, but him being a builder might be enough. The foreman came back and confirmed that Kevin was definitely working at their Seacroft site and gave Daniel the address.

'Hey! Is this ter do with that lass what were murdered here?'

'It is,' said Daniel. 'We hope Kevin might remember something, or somebody.'

'I thought they'd got the feller what did that.'

'This is just a follow-up investigation.'

'Well, if yer think Bradshawe had owt ter do with that, I wouldn't blame yer.'

Daniel, who was just leaving, stopped in his tracks and turned round.

'Wouldn't you? Why not?'

'He'd shag owt that moves, him. He's got kids all over Yorkshire who've never laid eyes on him. Bloody good brickie though, to be fair. But I wouldn't trust him with my daughter, if yer get my drift.'

'Really? Is he a violent man, would you say?'

'I've heard he's handy with his fists. Mind you, if he ever raises 'em ter me he's out of a job like a shot.'

'Thank you.'

Daniel was deep in thought as he got back in the car.

'Well?' said Helen.

'His name's Kevin Bradshawe and he's working on the Seacroft Estate – that's if he's the one who was working on the wall last year. It sounds like the description we had – sings a lot and gets on people's nerves.' He started the car.

'What else?' asked Lucy, who sensed he hadn't told them everything.

'Well, he's handy with his fists and, erm, he puts it about a bit.'

'Puts what about?'

'Well, to quote the foreman: he's got kids all over Yorkshire who have never laid eyes on him.'

'Ah, puts *that* about,' said Lucy. 'Well, Billy never put it about, I can tell you that for nowt.'

'He could be our man,' said Helen.

'Could be,' Daniel agreed. 'But I'll have to play this very carefully and not let him know I suspect him.'

'How do you do that?' asked Lucy.

'No idea. I just hope one comes to me.'

'Is that how you got to be a detective inspector?'

'Pretty much, yeah.'

He smiled at her in the driver's mirror. Lucy smiled back and stored a pleasant thought in her memory. *I bet he never smiles at Helen like that.*

*

Daniel drove on to the Seacroft site and parked by a similar-looking hut to the Moortown one – painted dark blue with a waterproof felt roof and a sign on the door reading *Site Office*. He knocked and opened the door, with his warrant card at the ready. Helen and Lucy stayed in the car, wondering why they'd been asked along.

'Men's work, obviously,' said Helen. 'Us weak woman aren't capable of asking questions, we'd only get in the way.'

Lucy was pleased that she was being antagonistic towards Daniel. It meant she didn't fancy him to death, as Lucy realised she herself did. If only he wasn't so much older. But women do get married to older men. She was trying to think of an example among the film stars she knew of.

'I think they'd take more notice of a policeman,' she said.

'You really like him, don't you?'

Lucy blushed. 'He's all right.'

'I mean, you've got a crush on him.'

'Crush? Give over. He's much too old for me.'

'But he's very good-looking and he has a way with him, don't you think?'

Helen was teasing, but she was too near the mark

for Lucy to realise this. 'I haven't noticed,' she said, sharply.

'Ah, methinks the lady doth protest too much.' Helen smiled.

'Is that a saying you got from the theatre?'

'It's from *Hamlet*.'

'How's it going, the theatre?'

'Oh, quite good. In fact I've got a casting call for a part in *The Makepeace Story* tomorrow morning.'

Lucy was impressed despite herself. 'Wow! I watch that. It's brilliant! What part will you be playing?'

'Hey, I haven't got it yet but I'm hopeful. Being seen on TV's a big help to any acting career. I'd be playing a mill girl, but I get quite a few lines and I'll be in three episodes if I'm picked.'

'Oh, I hope you get it. I'll be able to tell everybody I know a famous actress.'

The car door opened and Daniel got in. 'He's left town.'

'What?' said Helen and Lucy simultaneously.

'I've just spoken to the site agent. Kevin Bradshawe hasn't been to work for three days. The foreman went round to his address yesterday and his landlord reckons he's done a bunk. Apparently the police came round looking for him while he was out. As soon as the landlord told him that, Bradshawe packed his bags and left before they could come back. I'm going to check and find out what he was wanted for.'

'I bet it's nothing savoury,' said Helen.

'Could be he's attacked another woman,' added Lucy.

'Don't think so. If it'd been anything so serious the

police would have left men waiting for him. Apparently he's had bailiffs chasing him as well.'

'Sounds like a man who doesn't want to be found,' said Helen.

'Could be anywhere in the country,' said Daniel. 'Good building workers can walk into jobs with no references and not even a fixed abode. All he has to do is show he can lay bricks, and he's earning. In fact he's not even forced to stay in this country. There's plenty of work abroad for good tradesmen. He might even get his fare paid.'

'Does this mean we'll never find him?' Lucy asked.

Daniel gave it some thought then said, 'If this was an official police investigation we'd struggle to find him without using Wanted posters and maybe putting his photo in the papers. Even then he could give us the slip by going abroad.'

'But this isn't an official investigation,' remarked Helen.

'No, it's not, but I'll find out why the police were looking for him. My guess is he's failed to show up in court for something and there's a warrant out for his arrest.'

'We're not going to track him down are we?' said Helen.

'It's not looking good.'

'Then we must hope he had nothing to do with Ethel's murder,' Lucy said.

Helen and Daniel turned in their seats to look at her. 'We only *think* it's him,' Lucy said. 'And you know what thought did.'

'What did thought do?' Helen asked.

'Followed a muck cart and thought it was a wedding,'

said Daniel. He sensed the other two looking at him. 'It's my job,' he said. 'I need to know such things.'

'I often wondered what coppers did,' said Lucy. Her remark earned her another smile from Daniel in the driver's mirror.

Chapter 34

Mickey Mossop was looking out at the dismal September weather beyond his bedroom window and thinking that he'd had better days. His girlfriend had just packed him in for a more likely prospect who was at university and presumably more intelligent and with better prospects than Mickey, an apprentice fitter at the West Yorkshire Engine Company.

Wedged into the frame of his dressing-table mirror there was a photograph taken in the spring of the previous year. Glimpsing it made him smile. It had been taken in a seaside photo booth and had cost him a shilling for three prints – one each for him and his two pals, who all featured in the tiny, cardboard-framed picture. He picked it up and took a closer look at it, just to bring back a happy memory.

They'd been on a day trip to Bridlington on the east coast of Yorkshire. Just after the photograph was taken they went into a pub and each drank six pints of Tetley's Bitter which, when you're seventeen and not used to such quantities, leaves you quite drunk. He laughed as he remembered their antics on leaving the pub and making their way to the station, almost missing the last train back to Leeds. At one point Mickey had fallen on to the line and had to be rescued by his two pals. The last train back was a non-corridor train, which meant there was no access to toilets. Luckily they had a compartment to themselves and had frequently emptied their bladders through the open window into the dark East Yorkshire night. It had been a great day out with great mates, one of whom was now in prison accused of a crime Mickey knew he wouldn't have committed. Definitely not Arnold.

He looked closely at the photograph and noticed something he hadn't seen before. All he'd noticed previously were three daft lads all grinning like monkeys, nothing more. He sat thinking for a while then cursed himself loudly.

'Aw, hell, Mossop! You bloody great plonker!'

He ran downstairs, grabbed his coat and shouted to his mam that he was going round to Tony Rowlands's house.

*

Remand Wing: Armley Prison, Leeds

Arnold trudged into the visitors' room. His face was pale, bruised and bandaged; he kept his eyes trained towards the floor, feeling slightly embarrassed. He looked up and spotted Lucy and didn't want her to see him like this: a third-class citizen, a young man not allowed his freedom, an inferior person who was now a victim rather than a free man. His beating at the hands of Abe and his cronies had taken a severe toll of Arnold's self-confidence. He was aware that they'd tried to kill him but he'd been too scared to tell anyone who had done it to him.

'They attacked me from behind, sir,' he told the governor. 'I was on the floor before I knew anything and they were kicking me, then I blacked out. I didn't see any of their faces.'

What he didn't describe was the loathsome smell that had hung over him while he was being attacked. A smell that that could only have come from Abe Doyle. Lucy was smiling and waving. Arnold smiled back to acknowledge that he'd seen her but his smile was not as broad as it usually was.

He'd been on remand for two months and, so far, Lucy had been his only visitor. This was at his request. He needed her to tell him how things were progressing on the outside. He knew she was working with Daniel to try and prove his innocence. Arnold had sent word for his mam not to come and suffer the humiliation of visiting him in prison, but she had insisted and was due to come next week. He was dreading that – having to reassure her that he really wasn't a rapist and a murderer. Any talk of sex was taboo in their Catholic household, so his being accused of rape and murder must be a horrendous stigma for the Bailey family to bear. He sat down opposite Lucy, who was still smiling. Arnold felt like crying with the shame of it all. This was his kid sister who had always looked up to him. He wasn't much to look up to now.

'Hiya, Lucy. Thanks for coming. It can't be very pleasant for you to visit this place.'

'It's an experience,' she said.

'Yeah, it's a bit of an experience for me as well.'

'You're not looking so good. How are you doing?'

Arnold's head was still bandaged. What she could see of

his face was dark with bruising. His left arm was in a sling and he was using a walking stick due to his severely beaten legs.

'Couldn't be better,' he said. Then he leaned towards her and said confidentially, 'Guess who's in the next bed but one to me?'

'How should I know?'

'Well, he's a big rough Scottish bloke with a bullet hole in his foot.'

Lucy stared at him as her mouth opened slowly in realisation.

'No!'

'Yes.'

'The bloke from Strav—'

Her brother shushed her into silence. 'He hasn't recognised me yet because of my bandages and bruises and stuff. And we were blacked up that night and I had me hair covered with that woolly hat.'

Lucy clapped a hand to her mouth. 'Blimey, Arnold!'

'I know.'

Then she surprised him with, 'Well, you've only got yourself to blame.'

'What?'

Lucy was smiling at him. 'You heard.'

'You don't think I killed Ethel, do you?'

''Course I don't. I mean, if you'd used that great big brain of yours things wouldn't have got this flipping far.'

Arnold shook his head. 'Lucy, you've got me beat. How can all this be my fault?'

She looked at him and said, 'Mickey Mossop and Tony Rowlands came round last night. They couldn't stop apologising for not coming sooner, but it's like me mam said: it's more your fault than theirs. And with it being a year ago now it's barely even anyone's fault . . .'

'Lucy,' her brother said firmly, 'you'd better explain exactly what you mean.'

'Well,' she said, 'think back to the day when Ethel was killed.'

'I can't think back to that day because I don't remember it.'

'Yes, you do.'

'Lucy, I don't.'

'Well, you must remember telling me all about that dogs' home and how we could get Wilf out. You must remember 'cos you'd been there yourself to check the place out.'

'Okay, yes, I do remember that. So what?'

'And when I asked if you would come with me to get Wilf, you said no because you had better things to do.'

'Did I? I don't remember.'

'Well, you did. That's why I took Billy with me. I never did ask you what you were doing that day that was so important.'

'Prob'ly nothing,' said Arnold.

'That's not what Mickey Mossop and Tony Rowlands said. They came round to say you'd all gone to Bridlington that day and didn't get back until about midnight.'

Arnold stared at her. He felt as if a great weight had been lifted from his shoulders. 'That was the day Ethel died, was it?'

'Yes. Sunday May the twenty-third, nineteen fifty-four.'

'I remember going to Brid but I thought it was ... blimey! I don't know when I thought it was. Lucy, are you sure?'

'Yes.'

'Then how come I didn't remember? How come *you* didn't remember?'

'I didn't know you'd been to Brid that day, and at the time I didn't even think about what you were doing. I just knew you wouldn't come with me to the dog place.'

'I should have remembered going to Brid.'

'Arnold, you're always gettin' mixed up about the days stuff happens. Remember us arguing about what day it was Mam and Weary got married? You said it was a Cup Final Saturday in April and I said it was on Valentine's Day, which is February the fourteenth, and it was a Friday. I was right then, wasn't I?'

'Yeah, I know. I've got that sort of brain. Are you absolutely sure it was that day? I'm not. It definitely was a Sunday, though, because Mickey works half-day on Saturdays.'

Lucy put her hand in her pocket and brought out a small photograph in a white cardboard mount. It showed three youths all with silly grins on their faces. The one in the middle was Arnold. On top of the mount was printed *HAVING A GREAT TIME IN BRID*, and on the bottom the date: 23.5.1954.

Arnold looked at it. His face cracked into a wide grin. 'That's right! That's where I was! We had it done in a photo booth. It cost a shilling and we got three copies, one each. I completely forgot we did that. Arnold, you bloody idiot!'

'I have to agree with you,' said Lucy. 'Anyway, Mickey and Tony have both taken a day off and gone down to see your solicitor and make statements. They've taken their photos with 'em. Tony's still got a train ticket with the date on it.'

'Yeah, he saves stuff like that does Tony – mementoes he calls them.'

'I expect you'll be hearing from your solicitor today.'

'I've got my copy of this photo somewhere . . .'

I know, you daft ha'porth – this is it. I found it in your room among all your other photos and mucky magazines – which I've chucked, by the way.'

Arnold gave an embarrassed smile as Lucy continued: 'Mickey was looking at his photo yesterday and he realised the date might be the same as when Ethel was killed so he went straight round to Tony's. They came round to our house and asked me if I knew the date it happened. Well, of course I did. But they were like you. It's so long ago they didn't put two and two together.'

'I don't believe this,' said Arnold, kissing the photograph. 'I don't think I ever told me mam where I'd been. Can't remember why not.'

'For someone who's supposed to be clever, you forget all the most important things. If you'd told me where you'd gone, I'd have definitely remembered.'

*

An hour later Arnold was in the governor's office, sitting listening to his solicitor on the phone giving assurances that all charges against Arnold had been dropped by the police and the court would shortly order his release.

The governor put the phone down and smiled at

Arnold. 'Congratulations. It seems you've been done a grave injustice.'

'It seems I've been fitted up, sir, by the person who planted evidence on me. Whoever that is, he isn't banged up anywhere, like me and Billy Wellington are. I hope he ends up in here before too long.'

'Quite. So, regarding the murder of Russell Brown and the assault on yourself. Has this turn of events refreshed your memory?'

'It might have, sir. Although it does worry me that Abe Doyle may have friends on the outside who could get to me there.'

'Abraham Doyle? Yes, we pretty much assumed it was him. But if that were your objection to helping us, I would tell you that, despite the influence he manages to wield in here, outside prison Doyle's guilty mainly of crimes of violence committed single-handed. He has no money or gang of men to do his bidding. His influence is contained within these walls. Of this I can assure you, as will the police when they ask you to give evidence against him.'

Arnold remembered Russell Brown's terrible death. 'It'll be a pleasure, sir. I don't think Russell was any more guilty that I am.'

The governor sighed and looked down at his desk top.

'Recent events have proved you correct, Arnold. Russell Brown's accuser has retracted his statement. It seems he was in the habit of making false accusations.'

He got up from his chair and reached out to shake Arnold's hand. 'I expect that your solicitor will see you are properly compensated for wrongful imprisonment and the injuries you suffered, for which I apologise. For your last night with us, I will arrange for you to be given a single room in the hospital wing.'

'Thank you, sir. May I ask a favour?'

'What would that be?'

'When I'm being escorted to the hospital wing, could I be taken via the canteen?'

'Not necessary, your meals will be brought to you.'

'No, but the remand prisoners will be dining right now, will they not? I just want to see the look on Abe's face when I tell him I'm being released.'

The governor stared at him, not answering immediately. Arnold pressed, 'If I'm to give evidence, it's my one and only condition.'

The governor nodded and said, 'Right, okay. In fact, I think I'll tag along, just to make sure you don't cause too much mayhem.'

Arnold and the governor entered the canteen along with a small posse of prison officers. All heads turned in their direction as they headed towards the table where Abe was sitting. Arnold tapped him on the shoulder. Abe turned to glare at him.

'I'm being released, Abe,' he said. 'I'm an innocent man. They've asked me to give evidence about when you murdered Russell Brown. It's the gallows for you, Abe lad.'

If Arnold had told the governor in advance what he was going to say, he wouldn't have been allowed anywhere near the canteen. This was very much a taunt too far for Abraham Doyle, and it wasn't the only taunt Arnold had planned. Abe made a grab for him but three officers intervened, all of them wrinkling their noses in disgust at Abe's pungent body odour.

'Hey,' said Arnold, loudly now, 'I've asked them to hose you down as well. There's not a man in this room who won't be glad of that. You stink like a sewer, Abe. Oh, and I've told them about your little drugs racket with Mr Gladbury too. They should be searching his locker about now, plus your cell of course.'

He looked around the room and saw many faces that did not look displeased by this turn of events.

'See, Abe? Everybody's happy that I've stuffed you. Good riddance to a bad smell is what everyone's thinking.'

Abe roared and cursed, lashing out at the officers trying to restrain him.

'Take him to the block,' ordered the governor. 'It may be the best place for him until his trial comes up.'

'You can't do this to me!' roared Abe.

'Of course they can,' said Arnold, milking his moment for all he was worth. 'Outside this prison you're a big nothing. Just a stinking tosspot who never gets washed!'

Abe's rage sent adrenaline rushing through his body. He threw off the officers and launched himself at Arnold, grabbing him by the throat, choking him with his huge hands. Arnold blacked out as the officers pounded Abe's skull with their truncheons until he too was unconscious. He released Arnold, who dropped to the floor.

The governor looked down at his motionless body and said, 'Oh, Jesus ... please, no!'

Chapter 35

Lucy was in the front room watching the family's new television when she heard a knock at the door. Her mam had persuaded Walter to take her out to celebrate Arnold's imminent release from prison but Lucy had homework to do, a job she intended starting as soon as this new comedy programme, *The Benny Hill Show*, had finished. She was laughing when she peeped through the curtains and saw Daniel's car there. *Great,* she thought. *He'll know about Arnold being let out. We can discuss what to do about Billy now.* But Daniel's expression was serious when she opened the door. Maybe he hadn't heard about Arnold.

'Have you heard the great news? Two of Arnold's pals have—'

Daniel interrupted her. 'It's, er, your brother I've come to see you about.'

She frowned. Why was he looking so serious? 'You mean about him being released tomorrow?'

'No, the station rang me because they know I'm in touch with both you and Arnold and thought this would be better coming from me.'

'What are you talking about?'

'There was an incident at the prison. Arnold was attacked by the man who injured him last time.'

'But he's all right, isn't he?'

'He's in a coma, Lucy. They've taken him to Leeds Infirmary. I don't know the precise details of what happened but this attack has apparently exacerbated his previous injuries.'

'How could they let this other bloke anywhere near him?'

'I asked the same question. Apparently Arnold asked to be taken to see this Abe Doyle so he could tell him he was going to give evidence about Doyle murdering Arnold's cell mate. I've no idea why he thought he needed to do that, or why they let him. What I do know is that Doyle got very angry and attacked Arnold before the officers could stop him. Doyle himself took quite a beating and is also in a coma.'

'I hope he dies. How bad is Arnold?'

'They don't know. Apparently he was choked, which can cut off the blood supply to the brain and heart. He might have had a heart attack. They don't really know yet.'

'Heart attack?'

Lucy's face folded up with anguish. She was crying now. 'Oh, Daniel, tell me he's all right.'

'Lucy, I don't know. Are your parents in?'

'No, they're out – to celebrate Arnold being released.'

'Do you want to me come in and sit with you until they get back?'

Under any other circumstances she'd have jumped at this offer, but right now she had other priorities. 'I think I'd like to go and see my brother.'

'Right now?'

'Yes, please. I can leave Mam and Weary Walter a note telling them what's happened and where I am and that I'm with you.'

'Do you call him Weary Walter to his face?'

'I think he might have heard us call him that, why?'

'Well, you might get on better with him if you cut out the "Weary" bit.'

'Yes, you're prob'ly right. He really stuck up for Arnold when the coppers came to arrest him. Nearly got *him*self arrested too.'

'I heard. He made a complaint. The copper got a reprimand.'

'Good.'

'Do the note, I'll be in in the car.'

'Daniel, Arnold's not going to die, is he?'

Experience had told Daniel never to give people false hope. It always made things worse if that hope was misplaced. Better by far to prepare them for the worst and hope for the best.

'I honestly don't know, Lucy. He was in a bad way when they took him in, but there might have been some improvement since then.'

Tears were streaming down her face and Daniel felt a surge of real affection for this extraordinary girl. He put has arms around her and let her sob on his shoulder. 'Look,' he said, 'let's get ourselves down there and see exactly how he is.'

'Thanks, Daniel.'

Of all the people in the world, he was the one Lucy most needed then.

Chapter 36

Arnold was in a side room in the Casualty Department of Leeds General Infirmary. He had a mask over his mouth, helping him to breathe, and tubes running to and fro, facilitating the entry and exit of all necessary fluids. His left arm, broken in the first assault, was suspended from a sling and his head still heavily bandaged, as it had been when Lucy had seen him earlier that day. A doctor joined her and Daniel as they entered the room.

'We've stabilised him. His heart rate is low but he can breathe without assistance. The oxygen is just to make life easier for him.'

'Has he woken up at all?'

'I'm afraid not but it's early days yet.' The doctor looked at his watch. 'He's been in a coma for just over five hours, which is no cause for alarm.'

'Did he have a heart attack?' Daniel asked.

'A cardiac specialist has had a good look at him and doesn't think so. However, a neurosurgeon examined him and suspects the attacker put pressure on his carotid arteries, which has caused this condition.'

'What are they?' Lucy asked.

The doctor placed his forefingers to either side of his

neck. 'They're the two large blood vessels that supply oxy-genated blood to the brain. We're thinking Arnold might have had a stroke but we won't know until he wakes up.'

'Are you saying his brain could be damaged?' Lucy asked.

'I'm afraid we don't know.'

'But he's definitely not going to die?'

'I'm hopeful. His chance of survival is certainly better than it was when he arrived, but I can't offer any guaran-tees. This young man has suffered serious trauma.'

'The bloke who did it's in a coma as well.'

'Yes, we have him here.'

'I shouldn't waste too much time on him,' she said. 'They're going to hang him anyway.'

The doctor shrugged. 'I can't really comment on that. To me he's just another patient.'

Lucy began to say something but Daniel stayed her with a warning finger. Arnold's eyes were closed and Lucy wondered if he could hear them talking. She leaned over him and said, 'Do you hear that, our kid? The doc says he can't offer any guarantees that you'll survive. I bet you could offer us a guarantee, now you've heard him say that.'

She spoke to the doctor while still looking at her brother. 'Arnold never likes being told what he can or can't do.'

The doctor smiled and said, 'All we can do is wait for him to wake up.'

'Oh, heck! You could wait for ever for our Arnold to wake up. He could sleep for England could ... our Arnold.'

The last two words came out through tears that dripped on to her brother's bruised cheek, which she kissed.

'There,' she said. 'If you don't wake up soon, I'm going to do that again and again. So don't say I haven't warned you.'

Lucy wiped away the tears with her sleeve and gave a loud sniff. 'I've never kissed him before. He'll hate that, will Arnold.' She looked at the doctor and asked, 'Can I stay here with him? I think me mam'll be here soon.'

'Yes, that'll be fine. Just don't get in the way of the nurses.'

Chapter 37

Walton Prison, Liverpool

Maurice Bradley glared at the letter he'd just received. His irritation was directed at the address it was sent from – Box 374D *Liverpool Echo*.

> *Dear Mr Bradley,*
> *We are satisfied you are the gentleman we have been looking for and would be obliged if you would let us know your release date and the address where you will be living. Please reply to the above box number and excuse our need for anonymity. This is a delicate matter, which will be very much to your advantage. We will contact you again at the address you give us.*
> *We thank you for your co-operation.*

That was all. No name, no indication at all as to the identity of the sender, other than that it had been posted in Manchester. All Helen had needed to do was use a postmark that didn't give away her Leeds location to either

Bradley or the police who would investigate his forth-coming murder. It had been a simple return train journey to Manchester Piccadilly. Step outside the station, stick the letter in a nearby letter box and back on the train. Job done. This part of her plan had been easy to carry out. It was the next part that she hadn't yet planned. Nor had she mentioned it to her mother since the day they'd planned it on the seafront in Scarborough. Doris would have for-gotten about it by now, Helen hoped.

She did wonder if she'd be able to go through with it. Murder was such a horrendous crime and the recent hanging of Ruth Ellis had given her nightmares. She had even signed a petition for the abolition of capital punish-ment. Then she thought about what her vile stepfather had done to her. He had destroyed a vital part of her exis-tence. The thought of having sex with any man again was, to her, disgusting. She would never be able to do it. She would never be able to take a husband even if she felt she loved him. She would have to tell him, and that would be that.

Daniel the copper might have been a likely candidate otherwise. He was single, owned his own house, was kind, amusing, good-looking, the right age, he had a good job, and Helen was certain he liked her. Her stop/go occupa-tion as an actress meant she had to keep herself looking presentable, so when the inevitable happened and he asked her out she would have to turn him down ... and he wouldn't be the first by a long way. There would be no love life for her. Maurice Bradley had seen to that. Such thoughts stirred up Helen's hatred of him and deter-mination to kill him. Maybe killing him might release something within her. Might it kill her abhorrence of having sex with a man? Might it give her the love life taken from her by her stepfather? Her monstrous stepfather who surely deserved to die, and the instrument of his death must surely be her. It was her destiny.

Maurice Bradley passed the letter to Joe, his cell mate. 'What d'yer make o' that?'

Joe's lips moved as he read it. He handed it back Bradley. 'Well, it's from a solicitor, innit, Mo? Solicitors allus say "we" a lot. An' they don't like ter give stuff away in case it gets 'em into bother. That's why they won't let on who they are.'

'Hmm, I was thinking the same thing. Or else it could be someone trying to set me up for something.'

'It's obviously someone intelligent,' said Joe. 'How many intelligent people d'yer know?'

Bradley gave it a moment's thought. 'Can't think of too many offhand – not anyone who might want to set me up for something anyway.'

'So, just be on yer guard and go along with it.'

'Oh, I'll be on me guard all right.'

Chapter 38

Lucy was sitting by Arnold's bed. He'd been moved out of casualty into a single-bed ward in the Brotherton wing of Leeds Infirmary. She'd visited every day after school and sat reading to him for an hour. His favourite author was Damon Runyon and Lucy had perfected American accents to fit all of Runyon's gangster characters. She personally had only met one gangster, Elias Munro, and he wouldn't have fitted anywhere in a Runyon story. Arnold had been unconscious for nine days. Abe Doyle had woken up two days ago, which didn't seem fair.

Abe had recovered consciousness but many of his faculties were impaired. It was suspected he'd suffered severe brain damage. A sympathetic nurse had brought Lucy the up-to-date news about him. Lucy thought that brain damage was no more than Doyle deserved but it made her worry even more about Arnold. Would he end up the same? The thought reduced her to tears. The nurse realised what she'd done and tried to make amends.

'Hey, we had a man in here recently who'd been in a coma for three weeks. He walked out a week later as if nothing had happened.'

'Thanks,' said Lucy, drying her tears. Daniel had told

her about the severe beating Abe had taken and that his skull had been shattered by several truncheon blows. She glanced at her brother. Much of his bruising had gone and the bandages were due to come off that day. However, an X-ray had showed that strangulation had exacerbated his head injury and he now had a subdural haematoma which was pressing on his brain. They'd had to drill into his skull to release the pressure. The surgeon had told Lucy he thought he'd got it in time, whatever that meant.

'Come on, Arnold. You've had enough sleep. Wake up, you lazy monkey!'

'Not . . . until you . . . finish the . . . the story.'

Arnold's speech was slurred and it took him a full ten seconds to say this. But Lucy screamed with delight and hugged him.

'Arnold, you're awake!'

'I . . . I'll go back to, er . . . to sleep if you . . .don't, er, let go of . . . of me.'

The nurse smiled and said, 'He seems to have his wits about him. I'll get a doctor.'

*

The desk sergeant looked up as Lucy entered the police station. 'How can I help you?' he asked her.

'I need to speak to Sergeant Wallace.'

'In what connection?'

'I have important information about a person he arrested for murder . . . Arnold Bailey.'

'And your name is?'

'Lucy Bailey, I'm his sister.'

The sergeant stared at her for a long moment then lifted up a flap in the counter. 'You'd better come in then.'

He took her through the door behind him, down a short corridor then into a large room occupied by six uniformed policemen. He called out to one man who had his back to them.

'Sergeant Wallace, there's someone here to talk to you about the Ethel Tomlinson murder. It's Arnold Bailey's sister.'

Wallace turned round. He was just as Arnold had described him: tall and overweight, with short hair and a bushy moustache. Lucy walked over to him.

'So,' said Wallace. 'What do you want to see me about? And I hope for your sake you're not going to give me a false alibi for your brother.'

'Well, he's certainly got an alibi. It turns out he was in Bridlington with two friends on the day of Ethel's murder, and he's got proof of it. In fact, he's already been released from prison. The trouble is he's now in hospital because one of the prisoners beat him up so badly that he nearly died. And the only reason he was in prison in the first place is because people like *you* put him there.'

The other officers were taking an interest in this. They all stopped what they were doing to listen closely.

'What do you need to speak to me for?' said Wallace, uneasily.

'Well, it wasn't only the man in jail who beat him up, you did as well. I gather that beating people up is part of your interviewing technique. To me that makes you as bad as the thug in the prison, only he's going to hang because Arnold saw him murder someone.' Lucy looked at the policeman coldly and added, 'Pity they can't hang you, really.'

One of the other policemen sniggered. Wallace glared at him.

'I don't know what you're talking about,' he said.

'Oh, I think you do. Anyway, Arnold will be making an official complaint about you and Inspector Goodfellow. It'll be in the papers as well – I'll make sure of that. It's a great story, don't you think?'

'You can tell your brother that if he tells any lies about me, I'll sue the pants off him!' roared Wallace.

Lucy laughed. 'Sue our Arnold? Blimey! You really are as stupid as he said. Sergeant, you can sue our Arnold for every penny he's got and he won't be any worse off.'

There was more sniggering. Wallace went red in the face. He took a step towards Lucy, who stood her ground. 'If you lay a finger on me,' she said, 'you'll be occupying the cell recently vacated by my brother. Anyway, I won't keep you. You've probably got some innocent prisoners to beat up.'

She turned to go, leaving Wallace embarrassed and enraged. Lucy had a smile on her face that was still there when she got home. The confrontation was something to tell Arnold about, that and the prospect of putting the story in the papers. It was something she'd thought up on the spur of the moment, but it wasn't a bad idea. She'd see what her brother thought about it.

Chapter 39

Rampton Secure Hospital, Nottinghamshire
September 1955

Billy was scrubbing a stone floor on the refractory ward. He had been scrubbing it since 8.30 that morning and it was now 2 p.m. He was due to finish at 6 p.m. In his working day he'd have two half-hour breaks for meals. His task was to clean the floor of a corridor seven yards long and two yards wide. He had become so efficient at this repetitive work that he could scrub the whole floor in well under two hours. When he'd finished a nurse would kick his bucket over and tell him to start again, which he did. In a working day he would scrub the same floor five times. After two weeks of this he'd be allowed out in the afternoons for normal exercise, scrubbing the floor for four hours in the morning only. Then after two weeks he'd be back to full-time floor scrubbing for another fort-night.

Billy was classed as a Criminal Defective and this was the only work for which he was deemed suitable. It had been his sole occupation since he'd arrived at Rampton three months previously. His hands and knees were red raw. He wasn't given a job that required tools, because most tools could be used as weapons. The idea was for him to gain satisfaction from doing an honest day's work, but it did little to help his self-esteem, which was very limited to start with. This harsh treatment couldn't have been more damaging to him

Until this day no one had been to see him at Rampton. Helen couldn't bring herself to visit this son who seemed destined to spend his whole life locked up as a murderer of the worst kind. She hated herself for this, and hatred of herself made her hate Bradley even more. He was the cause of everything bad in her life. It was Lucy who eventually persuaded her to visit Billy.

'I applied to visit him but I'm not allowed because I'm too young. I've got to be accompanied by an adult,' Lucy told her.

'How did you propose getting yourself there on your own?'

'I don't know. Arnold can't help me, with him still being in hospital.'

'How is he doing?'

'Okay. He can't walk properly yet but he's not been paralysed or anything – just broken bones an' stuff.'

'That's good. Oh, I'm not saying broken bones are good, it's—'

Lucy interrupted her. 'The good news is that the murder charge has been dropped. As soon as he's up and about he's free to come home.'

'That's great.'

'Shall we go and visit Billy together?' Lucy asked.

Helen's theatre tour had finished, she'd got the TV part and done the job, and was now back to being a courier until her next acting break turned up. She looked at this young girl who had done more for Billy than anyone, including his own mother.

'Yes,' she said. 'I think we should. We can go there on my motorbike.'

'Really? Oh, that's brilliant. I've never been on a motorbike.'

'You'll have to clear it with your mum and Walter.'

'They won't mind,' lied Lucy, who had no intention of asking them. She knew their answer already.

*

Billy was on his knees, scrubbing away when an orderly appeared and leaned over him. 'Come with me, you've got visitors.'

Billy looked up at him and said, 'Got ter finish me work or Mr Harris'll go mad with me.'

'No, he won't. Come with me.'

'He might,' said Billy. 'He wants it to be nice and clean. He told me.'

The orderly looked at the stretch of floor which was clean enough to eat off, and smooth enough to be dangerous to anyone unsteady on their feet. He didn't agree with this method of keeping the inmates subjugated.

'Bloody hell, Billy! It'll never be any cleaner than it is now. Just come with me.'

'Okay. I'll come with you then.'

'Good.'

'What shall I do with me bucket?'

'Just leave it where it is. It'll still be here when you come back.'

'What shall I do with me brush?'

'Billy, leave it in the bloody bucket and come with me.'

'Okay, I'll come with you then.'

Billy followed the orderly back to the ward and into an ante-room where Helen and Lucy were waiting. Upon seeing Lucy his face cracked into a beaming smile and he said, 'Helloey, Lucy.'

It was a joke he'd made up himself.

'Helloey, Billy.'

Then he looked at Helen and knew he'd seen her before but couldn't remember where. Lucy saw this uncertainty. 'Me and your mam have come to see you,' she said.

'Hello, Billy,' said Helen, wanting to hug him but thinking it might not be reciprocated, plus hugging inmates might be against the rules.

'Hello, Missis.'

'This isn't Missis,' said Lucy. 'This is your mam.'

Billy stared at Helen and said, 'I don't know me mam.'

'Don't you remember, Billy?' said Helen. 'You came to stay with us at that nice house in the country only some men came to take you away. I didn't want them to do that.'

Billy stared at her, then narrowed his eyes as her words tweaked a distant memory.

'Was it at the seaside?'

'It was, yes.'

'I didn't see no sea.'

'No, but you will next time we take you there.'

'Are yer gonna take me there now?'

'Not right now, Billy,' said Helen, 'but soon.'

He was looking dishevelled from his work. Lucy took hold of his hands. 'What have you been doing, Billy?'

He looked at his hands and said, 'I've been doin' me work.'

'What work's that?' asked Helen.

'Scrubbin' floors.'

'You must do a lot of floor scrubbing to get hands like that. How long have you been scrubbing floors?

'All day. I scrub floors all day. It's me job ... I'm a scrubber, me.'

Lucy looked at the orderly who was standing by the door, listening to their conversation. 'Is that what he does all day?' she asked.

'It is, yes. The same floor, all day and every day. When he's finished he starts again.'

'Why?' asked Helen.

'I don't know. I suppose it's something he can do without having to think about it too much.'

'It sounds like hard work. How long does he do it for?'

'Half-past eight in the morning 'til six o'clock. Six days a week.'

The orderly knew the hospital wouldn't want this broadcast to all and sundry, but it was the truth so why shouldn't they be told?

'Scrubbing the same floor? Is he being punished for something?' asked Lucy.

'No. It's just their way of keeping him occupied.'

'Isn't this supposed to be a hospital?' Helen asked.

'So I'm told. Look, I just work here. It doesn't mean to say I agree with what goes on.'

'Is there someone senior I might have a word with?' asked Helen.

The orderly looked relieved. 'I'll see who I can find.'

Five minutes later a middle-aged woman came into the room and introduced herself. 'I'm Senior Staff Nurse Wilby, can I help you?'

'Yes,' said Helen, summoning up her acting ability to more than match Nurse Wilby's stern demeanour. 'My name is Helen Durkin, I'm William's mother and I want to know why he spends his days scrubbing the same piece of floor over and over again. And before you answer, please take into consideration that my son did not commit the crime he's been accused of, nor has he been convicted of any crime in a court of law.'

'He's been given a job that's not too taxing for his mind,' replied Wilby.

Helen glared at her. 'My son,' she said, 'has an underdeveloped mind that needs taxing now and again, the same as you tax underdeveloped muscles. Would you not agree? What you've given him is a job that's very taxing for his body but which must further confuse his mind with its uselessness. He must surely wonder why he's achieving nothing for all his hard work. I bet you have a treadmill in this place as well. This is a hospital, isn't it?'

'It is indeed, madam.'

'And isn't it the sole purpose of hospitals to cure people, rather than to make them worse?'

Nurse Wilby didn't answer. The floor scrubbing wasn't her idea and she wasn't going to defend it.

Helen looked at her with fire in her eyes. 'I'd like you to take him off this work and help him with his mental problems without exacerbating them. At no point in his life has anyone ever attempted to do this.'

'I don't have the authority to do that, madam.'

'Then you'd better find me someone who has. My guess is that it'll be some man in a suit who has never clapped eyes on my son.'

'I'll see if the manager's available.'

'Good.'

Nurse Wilby left to find the manager. Billy had been sitting in a chair looking animatedly from the nurse to Lucy to Helen throughout the conversation.

'Hey,' he said, grinning, 'yer told her where ter gerroff.'

'I only hoped I haven't overstepped the mark,' said Helen.

The orderly came back into the room and said, 'Do me a favour. Don't say it was me who told you about all this floor scrubbing or I'll get a right roasting.'

'I'll say it was Billy who told us all about it,' said Lucy. 'He has moments when he makes sense.'

'Does he?' said the orderly. 'I haven't noticed.'

'He didn't do what they said he did,' Lucy told the man.

'Oh, I can believe that.'

'Who's this manager she's bringing? What's he like?'

'Ex-army major,' said the orderly. 'Bit bombastic but I think he's as thick as two short planks – only don't say I told you that either.'

After he left, Lucy looked at Helen and grimaced. 'Ex-army? Are you going to be all right?'

'Well, forewarned is forearmed,' she said, taking a deep breath and thinking quickly.

The manager arrived a few minutes later. He was tall, erect and every inch the ex-soldier. He introduced himself brusquely.

'My name is Claybourne, I'm the manager of this wing. How can I help you?'

Helen looked him up and down and said, 'I'm guessing ex-army. High-ranking officer. Am I right?'

'I was a major, yes. How did you know?'

'From your manner and bearing. My father was army – lieutenant colonel.'

'Really? What regiment?'

'King's Royal Lancers. He was killed in North Africa in 1942.'

'I'm sorry to hear that. El Alamein, by any chance?' said Claybourne.

'Yes. Why, were you there?'

'No, no, I was in Europe for much of the war.'

Lucy was impressed that Helen had immediately established an affinity with this man who was bombastic but as thick as two short planks.

'So,' he said. 'What is it you want?'

'Well, I'm not too happy with the treatment my son is receiving. He's in here accused of a crime I'm certain he didn't commit and he's being made to scrub the same patch of floor, day in, day out.'

'I'm aware of the letter you sent the hospital, madam.'

'Good. There will come a time in the very near future, I hope, when Billy's innocence is established and his story will receive maximum publicity ... with him being the grandson of a war hero. Now I know you're not responsible for his being incarcerated here, but you are responsible for his treatment.'

'War hero? Who exactly was he?'

'Lieutenant Colonel Harry Durkin, DCM, MC – he was awarded his DCM posthumously.'

'Brave man.'

'Yes, he was.'

Lucy was even more impressed. Not only was Helen's fictional father a hero, but a hero who had outranked Claybourne. Helen pressed home her advantage.

'My son's birth was a result of my being sexually assaulted. His birth was difficult, resulting in his being brain damaged. My father was already away in the army and I was forced to give Billy up for adoption. All the publicity surrounding his arrest brought him to my attention once more so I tracked him down. This young lady here assures me that he had nothing to do with the crime he's been accused of.'

'This animal who assaulted you ... was he ever brought to justice?' The major's handlebar moustache quivered as she spoke. He was a jowly man with bushy eyebrows and a wealth of greying hair which he parted down the middle.

'No, he wasn't. Look, I realise you've only got my word that Billy didn't commit this crime and I don't expect anything from you other than to treat him humanely.'

'We treat all our patients humanely.'

'Well, I doubt if his grandfather would have agreed with that, nor will people who read in the newspapers about the terrible injustice that's been done to my son. Surely you don't want to be seen as part of that injustice.'

Claybourne was lost for words. Helen softened her voice and Lucy could see what a talented actress she was.

'All I ask is for my son to be treated like a patient and

293

not like one of the many convicted criminals you have in here. Just speak to him, compare him to these people and form your own opinion. I'm sure you'll see he's just an ordinary, polite young man who wouldn't harm a fly.'

'He was my friend before they locked him up,' added Lucy. 'He was with me at the time of the murder he's supposed to have done but I can't stand up and tell them that because he hasn't even been to court.'

Claybourne looked at Billy, who was unconsciously playing his part by smiling politely as this conversation went on around him. He certainly didn't look like someone who had raped and murdered a young woman.

'He was considered unfit to plead,' explained Helen, 'but we're applying to the court to hear his case properly.'

'We have a barrister called Mr Barrington-Smythe who's confident that when Billy goes to court he'll be found not guilty,' added Lucy.

'I'll see what I can do,' Claybourne told them.

'We'd be most grateful,' said Helen.

'So will Billy,' said Lucy, 'because he remembers things, you know. He just told us all about how he has to scrub the same floor, time and time again, every day from half-past eight in the morning until six at night. There are things he remembers and things he doesn't. So if I tell him things are going to be easier from now on, he'll take my word for it and play pop with me if I turn out to be wrong. So don't let us down, will you, Major Claybourne?'

The latent threat in her words didn't escape Claybourne.

'I'll have him taken off floor-cleaning duty.'

'Thank you,' said Helen, 'and please find him something more challenging and less demeaning.'

Lucy looked at her and realised that it wasn't just her silver tongue that had impressed the manager, but her looks as well. She was dazzling him, just as she probably dazzled Daniel. After Claybourne had left, Helen gave Lucy a broad wink.

'We make a good team. I think we just hung him out to dry.'

'I've got to get back to me work,' said Billy.

'Your work's finished,' said Helen. 'That man said you haven't to do it any more.'

'Not no more?'

'No.'

His face dropped. 'What will I do then? I haven't got no job no more.'

'Billy,' said Lucy, 'they're going to find you a more important one.'

*

An hour later they were leaving the hospital when a worrying thought hit Lucy. 'I'm guessing you were making it up about your father being a war hero.'

'More or less.'

'But what if Claybourne checks up? I mean, he was in the army too, I bet he could check the records.'

'If he does,' said Helen, 'he'll find that Lieutenant Colonel Harry Durkin, DCM, MC, was killed at El Alamein in 1942. He was my father's cousin.'

'And you thought all that up in a few minutes?'

'Less than that, it's called improvisation.'

'Wow!' said Lucy. 'So who was your father, then?'

Helen had wondered whether or not to tell Lucy about Bradley. It wasn't something she wanted too many people to know, but somehow she felt it was right to tell Lucy.

'This is highly confidential. In fact, I don't know why I'm telling you, other than that I think you have a right to know exactly who and what I am.'

'If it's a secret, I'm good at secrets.'

'This is very much a secret. My mother and her husband know, and so does Daniel. No one else.'

'Wow!' said Lucy.

'My father died when I was three years old. I scarcely remember him, but I'm told he was a kind man who loved me dearly. The secret, as you call it, is about my stepfather, Maurice Bradley.' Helen stopped talking as they reached her motorbike. She took two crash helmets out of the side panniers. Then she looked across the bike at Lucy as she handed her a helmet.

'He's not just my stepfather,' she said quietly. 'He's also my son's father.'

Lucy took a few moments to absorb what she'd just heard.

'You mean Billy?'

'I mean Billy.'

'You mean . . . Bradley's the one who . . . er . . . assaulted you?'

'Yes. I was thirteen.'

Lucy clapped her hand across her mouth. 'Oh, heck! I . . . er . . . I don't suppose Billy knows.'

'Good heavens, no! And even if he did, he wouldn't understand. He must never be told such a dreadful thing.'

'Oh, blimey, Helen!'

'It's why I couldn't keep him.'

'I've never heard anything so rotten in me life.'

'Do you understand why I couldn't keep him?'

'Well, no ... I mean, yes ... I ... I don't think I understand anything, Helen.'

'Please don't tell anyone, not even Arnold.'

'No, I won't. Honest I won't.'

In fact Lucy would rather Helen hadn't told her. It was something too awful for her to comprehend. The sixty-mile return trip was done without a break, with Lucy on the pillion, clinging on to Helen, this woman who'd experienced the most horrendous thing she could imagine. When they got back to Lucy's house she dismounted and just stood there, taking off her helmet and handing it over wordlessly.

'Still shocked?' Helen asked.

'Helen, I know none of this is your fault, and it's not Billy's fault either. I just can't think what to say about it.'

Because she didn't know what else to do, Lucy leaned forward and gave Helen a hug, knowing, in the same instant, that if this damaged woman wanted Daniel then Lucy must not try and stand in her way. This woman deserved all the happiness she could get, and Lucy must try even harder to get Billy back for her. The injustice of it all was almost too much to bear. This world was far more cruel than she had ever imagined. She went to bed that night and thanked God for setting Arnold free and keeping him alive.

Chapter 40

It was Saturday. Walter answered the door to Daniel's knock. He introduced himself.

'Ah,' said Walter. 'Detective Inspector Earnshawe. What can we do for you?'

'Well, I heard that Arnold was out of hospital and thought I might pop in and see him.'

'That's very good of you, come in. He's in the front room listening to his records. We're glad to have him back, I can tell you – after what he's been through.'

'Yes, I imagine you are.'

'In fact I've just been talking to him about applying for compensation for wrongful imprisonment. What do you think?'

'I suspect he's entitled to something,' said Daniel, following Walter through to the front room.

'I would think he's entitled to at least five thousand, considering the injury he sustained while he was in custody.'

'I don't really know, Mr Bailey.'

'It's Entwhistle,' said Walter. 'The children are still Baileys but me and the wife are Entwhistles. I know it's a bit confusing but Mrs Bailey as was insisted on leaving the children with their original names. Bereavement's bad enough as it is without having to change your name.'

Arnold was sitting next to an RCA Victor record player on which Bill Haley and His Comets were belting out 'Rock Around the Clock', the record that had heralded the rock 'n' roll era.

'Arnold, how're you doing?' Daniel said.

Arnold lifted up the record player's arm and dropped it in the rest. The record came to a halt.

'Thank God for that,' muttered Walter. 'He's been playin' it all damned day.'

'I have not!' protested Arnold. 'I've been playing "Shake, Rattle and Roll" as well.'

'Same rubbish,' said Walter. 'Anyroad, lad, the inspector's been good enough to pay you a visit. I'll make us all a cup o' tea.' He left them to it.

'Pleased to see you, Daniel,' said Arnold. 'Weary's just been telling me I might get around five thousand for my trouble. What do you think?'

'I've got no idea, Arnold.'

'Nor me. I'm just glad to be alive and out of prison. Abe Doyle's gone permanently nutty, did you know that?'

'I heard as much, yes. Word is he'll be sent to Broadmoor. Probably end his days there.'

'I saw him murder my cell mate. I'm supposed to be a witness at his trial.'

'Yes, I heard that as well. There won't be a trial now, but even if there was it seems several other witnesses have come out of the woodwork, now they know he can't do them any harm.'

'Pity,' said Arnold, 'I'd have liked to have seen him sentenced. Judge with his black cap and all that.'

Daniel raised his eyebrows. Arnold explained himself. 'Doyle was within a whisker of killing me.'

'The governor got the sack, did you know?' Daniel said.

'Oh, heck! Because of what happened to me?'

'Because he took you to see Doyle at your insistence.'

'I said I'd give evidence against Doyle if I was taken to see him.'

'To gloat?'

'Okay, to gloat. People like Doyle need a bit of gloating over, to take them down.'

'Arnold, you shouldn't have made it a condition and the governor shouldn't have agreed. Almost got you killed, that did.'

'I know. It does get a bit wearing – people trying to kill you.'

Daniel grinned. 'Yes, it's a habit you need to break.'

'One of your sergeants assaulted me when I was being questioned. He knocked me out of my chair. I thought he'd broken my jaw.'

'I know, Lucy told me. You should make a formal complaint. I'll show you how to do it. Your word should carry weight, in the circumstances.'

'Thanks,' said Arnold. 'Lucy's out with me mam shopping if it's her yer wanted ter talk to.'

Daniel sat down. 'No, it's you I came to see. I assumed you wouldn't be out.'

'I'll not be stuck in for long. I need to get back to school to do an A-level resit.'

'Really? Lucy gave me the impression that you were a genius.'

'I wish! I blame it on everything that's been going on. I failed phsyics! Couldn't believe it. Turns out I read a question wrong that counted for forty per cent of the marks.'

'Oh, dear. When do you do the resits?'

'Back end of November. I had a place at Durham lined up as well. Still have, I think. So, from one invalid to another, how are you doing?'

'Not bad at all,' said Daniel. 'Fully mended, back in harness. They've let me loose on the Ethel Tomlinson job, thinking I can't do much damage.'

'How's it going?'

'A bloke I suspect might be in the frame has done a bunk.'

'The builder?'

'The bricklayer, yes.'

'What about his labourer?'

'What?'

'I heard he had a labourer working with him. Have you checked on him?'

Daniel stared at Arnold and said, 'No, we damned well haven't! God! No wonder they're not in a rush to have me back full-time.'

'Well, it could just as easily have been him,' said Arnold.

'Yes, I know it could!' Daniel was annoyed at himself. 'My daughter reckoned she saw a labourer with the brick-layer, although that was the day after the murder. Blast! How the hell did I miss following up on that?'

'That could be my fault,' said Arnold. 'You were still injured and your mind wasn't right.'

'Good idea. I'll blame you.'

'Happy to be of assistance.'

Daniel smiled then his expression faded, as though he'd thought of something.

'What's up?' asked Arnold.

'Elias Munro,' said Daniel. 'He got off the York murder charge on some legal technicality. It'll never even get mentioned at his trial. They can still nail him on some other stuff, though not the murder.'

'So, no vengeance for your wife's death?'

'None whatsoever. The evidence is too flimsy and if he's found not guilty at the trial he can't be re-tried for the same crime. I was hoping for a bit of poetic justice from the York murder. I need to see him hanged, Arnold. A man does that to someone you love, it's hard to think he's still alive.'

'I saw him inside, you know. Now there's a face you can't easily forget – and his voice. Jesus! It was head under the bedclothes for me when I heard that voice again.'

'Good job he didn't recognise you.'

'I doubt if *you'd* have recognised me, the way my face was bashed about.'

'Did he say anything to you?'

'No, I was in the next bed but one, wrapped up like a mummy. He never spoke to me. Mind you, he never stopped talking to the bloke in the bed in between us. He had a lot to say for a man up for murder. I got the impression he knew he'd get away with it.'

'Really? What did they talk about?'

'Oh, I don't know. Football, women, rubbish jokes, jobs they'd done.'

'I see. Anything interesting?'

'Dunno,' said Arnold. 'Why?'

'Because he'll have been completely off his guard. He might have let something slip about the York murder that'll change the DPP's mind about adding it to his charges.'

'Right.'

'So?'

'I'm trying to think.' Arnold considered for a while than slapped his head in self-recrimination. 'Damn! You're right!'

'Right about what?'

'About ... about him being off his guard.'

'What have you remembered?'

'Well, it might be nothing, but I heard Munro talking about a car, a 1949 Lagonda – my favourite cars, which is why I remember it. He was talking about how he'd got it hidden away in a lock-up garage, which is a crime in itself for a car like that.'

'Did he say where?'

'In ... er ... in Beeston somewhere. He hasn't gone near it since.'

'Did he say why?'

Arnold closed his eyes as he searched his memory. 'Erm ... something about not wanting anyone to see him with it in case a connection was made – something like that.'

'Connection? What sort of connection?'

'I don't know. He reckons he's gonna burn it as soon as

he gets out. I remember that because I thought he was a bit confident about getting out for a man up on a murder charge.'

'And what else was said?'

'The other bloke was saying not to burn it because he knew a firm that'd give a nice price for it, but Munro didn't want to know. I think he said it'd been there for years.' He looked at Daniel. 'You said your wife was killed by a car, didn't you?'

'She was, yes. No idea what make. Did he say whereabouts in Beeston?'

'He did actually, because they were laughing about the name of the road ... What do they call it now?'

Daniel was trying to control his impatience. 'It'll help if you remember. I could get a street map and read out all the roads, to try and jog your memory.'

Arnold held up a hand with one finger outstretched. 'No, no ... it's on the tip of my tongue. Damn! Funny name, to do with ... erm ... dead people ... graves ... erm ...'

'Cemetery Road?' suggested Daniel

'Cemetery Road, that's it! This car's in a lock-up garage just off Cemetery Road. Is that in Beeston?'

'It is, yes.'

'It could be the car that killed your wife.'

'It'll do no harm to check it out,' said Daniel, who was feeling a surge of excitement. 'No harm at all.'

Walter appeared with three cups of tea on a tray together with a plate of biscuits. He forced his face into his version of a smile; the end result was more of a grimace. 'So,' he said, 'have you two put the world to rights?'

'Not yet,' said Daniel. 'But Arnold has given me information that might well bring a murderer to justice. He's a lad to be proud of is Arnold.'

'Yes, he's not a bad lad.'

Arnold looked up at his stepfather with raised eyebrows. Walter treated him to one of his grimace-smiles and went back into the kitchen.

'Not a bad lad?' said Arnold. 'That's going way over the top for Weary. I've never had such praise from him.'

'Does he treat you all right?'

'Well, he's not exactly a barrel of laughs but he's never treated us badly.'

Daniel thought about Helen's stepfather. 'There's a lot of kids in this world who'd love to have a stepfather like that.'

*

The following day Daniel called in to see Arnold again. Lucy opened the door and beamed at him. Daniel was looking so much better now that he was back to his old self. Colour in his cheeks, a light in his eyes, even his hair seemed to have a glow to it. A really handsome man. She thought about the promise she'd made to herself about leaving him to Helen and wondered at the wisdom of it. The words 'All's fair in love and war' came to mind.

'Have you tracked down that labourer?' she asked.

'Labourer? Ah, er, no. He's the very next thing on my list. I came to tell Arnold something. In fact, I can tell both of you.'

'Come in. Mam and Walter have gone to Mass.'

'I thought Walter was a Methodist.'

'He likes to keep his options open.'

'Don't you go with them?'

'I went to the eight o'clock. No sermon, church half empty. You're in and out in half an hour.'

'I see.'

He followed her through to the front room. *Two Way Family Favourites* was coming from the wireless. Alma Cogan was singing 'Dreamboat' and Arnold didn't appear to be a fan.

'This is the rubbish Lucy listens to,' he said, looking longingly at the record player on which sat a silent 'Rock Island Line', the record that had just shot Lonnie Donegan to fame. Daniel read the title approvingly.

'Good taste, young man. Best record for years.'

'See,' said Arnold to Lucy.

'I never said I didn't like it,' she protested. 'It's just that I don't like to hear it a hundred times a day.'

'Mam only bought me it yesterday.'

'Yes, and I've already heard it a hundred times. Same with "Rock Around the flipping Clock".'

Daniel held both his hands up to stop the argument. 'Peace, children,' he said. 'I bring news.'

'About who killed Ethel?' asked Lucy.

'No, about the man who killed my wife.'

'You found the lock-up?' said Arnold.

'We did, and there was Lagonda inside. It was under a canvas cover, which kept it free from dust and has helped a lot with the fingerprinting.'

Arnold frowned. 'How would fingerprinting help? If it has Munro's prints on, all it proves is that he was driving it.'

'True, but there was a dent in the front grille and a clear

handprint on the roof that wasn't Munro's. The sort of print you'd find if someone had been struck by the car, tossed into the air and was instinctively sticking out a hand to save herself.'

'*Herself?*' said Lucy. 'You mean ... is it your wife's print?'

Daniel looked at her and nodded, frowning away a tear. 'It's Gloria's print, yes.'

'How awful,' said Lucy, touching his arm in sympathy.

Daniel blew out a long sigh. 'Yes, it sickened me when I found out, but I tell myself that Gloria did it to leave me a clue. The tyres match the marks left by the vehicle that killed her. It was a wet day, there was mud all over the place, including on the car tyres. It's still there.'

'So you've got him?' said Arnold.

'Oh, yes. Sticking her hand out didn't save Gloria, but she managed to leave enough evidence to send her killer to the gallows.' Daniel looked at Lucy and Arnold, who were transfixed by his news. 'The Lagonda was registered to Peter Leonov, but Munro's fingerprints are all over it. Leonov's given him up to us already and Munro's saying he did it on Leonov's orders, so they both swing for it.'

'That's brilliant!' said Arnold.

'Yes, it is,' said Daniel, then he sighed. 'I didn't realise my colleagues had taken Gloria's prints, which they had apparently – post mortem.'

'I don't suppose they wanted to trouble you with that information,' said Lucy.

'That's exactly right.'

'So, me being locked up and in the next-bed-but-one to Munro was a good thing, in the long run,' said Arnold.

'You knocking me off my bike was a good thing, in the long run,' agreed Daniel. 'Strange how things can work out for the best. Had you not done that, none of this would have come about.'

'Wow!' said Lucy. 'That's right. It's like it was all meant to be.'

'Well, that's how it's all worked out,' said Daniel. 'And I'm most grateful to you both. I'm also in the high ups' good books at work.'

'So they're still going to let you track down Ethel's killer?' said Lucy.

'Oh, yes. I'm insisting on that, and they're not quite as sceptical as they once were.'

Chapter 41

When Daniel telephoned Helen to tell her about Munro he took the opportunity to ask her out for Sunday lunch, which she happily accepted. To her, Daniel was a man who got things done. He'd sorted out the man who had killed his wife, and Helen was sure he was equally capable of setting her son free. What she was most anxious about was his actual motive for asking her to lunch. He'd taken her to a country hotel near Wetherby and had selected a table in a quiet corner. With their meal finished they were having coffee when he unexpectedly reached over and took her hand.

'It's over four years since Gloria died,' he said, 'and in that time I haven't even thought about another woman, much less asked one out on a date.'

'Is that what this is – a date?' said Helen. 'I thought it was a celebratory lunch.'

'Well, it's as near as I've got to a date in four years. Look, we don't know each other very well but I thought I might as well let you know that you're the only woman I've felt any affection for since my wife died.'

'I see,' said Helen, uncomfortable now.

'And when I say affection, I would add that I know

exactly what it feels like to love a woman because I loved Gloria and I was sure I'd never feel that way about a woman again – but it seems I was wrong.'

'Oh, dear,' said Helen.

Those two words spoke volumes to Daniel. 'Ah, say no more,' he said. 'Sounds like I've put my foot in it. Look, sorry. I just needed to get it out in the open in case you might feel the same way.'

'Daniel, I don't know what it feels like to love anyone like you loved Gloria. What my stepfather did to me has deadened all such emotions in me, possibly for good. He filled me full of awful demons that won't go away. I'm really flattered that a good man such as yourself has feelings for me but I'm afraid I can't return those feelings. I'm thirty-two years old and I've never had a relationship with a man. In fact, I've ruined quite a few perfectly good friendships by turning men down.'

He took his hand off hers and thought about what she'd said.

'You know, it could be that you feel like that because he's got clean away with it. You may still harbour a sense of injustice and think you would be betraying yourself by giving yourself freely to another man before your stepfather's been punished for what he did.'

She shook her head and gave him a dazzling smile. 'That's me well and truly psychoanalysed. Have you studied psychiatry or something?'

'No, I went to a lot of counselling sessions to cope with the loss of Gloria. I was a real mess.'

'And you haven't had a relationship with a woman since then?'

'No.'

Helen held his gaze for a few seconds as a mischievous thought crossed her mind. 'You're a very good-looking man, Daniel,' she said, 'and a very kind and decent man.'

'What are you getting at?'

'I'm just thinking how stupid I am for turning you down simply because I don't know if I can ever have a physical relationship with a man.'

'And ... ?'

'And I'm wondering if we should give it a try.'

He froze with his glass held in mid-air.

'You mean ... ?'

She smiled. 'Yes. This is a residential hotel. Why don't we book a room?'

It was more of a challenge than a proposition, and he knew it. 'I'm tempted to scare you to death and say "yes".'

'Say it then.'

As he looked at her, many conflicting thoughts raced across his mind. He hadn't been with a woman since Gloria and here was a beautiful one, to whom he was seriously attracted, handing sex to him on a plate. And suddenly he couldn't get his lovely Gloria out of his mind. He felt himself blushing with embarrassment. A minute went by with Helen's eyes fixed firmly on him, waiting for his answer.

'Maybe not right now,' he said, eventually.

'Why not?'

He looked at her and gave a wry smile. 'Because you've set a test for me and I've just failed.'

'Your love for Gloria is holding you back, the same as my hatred of Maurice Bradley is handicapping me.'

Daniel shrugged. 'What's holding me back is that I feel I might be a disappointment to you. I'm very much attracted to you.'

'Do you love me?'

'I think it's too powerful a word for me to use right now. If I hadn't once loved Gloria, though, I'd say "yes". I went through some serious stuff in the war and came out reasonably sane because I still had everything that was important to me – my wife and my girls – and I was pretty much in one piece myself, which was a miracle.'

'And are you over all that now?'

He smiled and shook his head. 'No, I'm not over Gloria, never will be, but I think my asking you out is a good sign.'

'It probably is and I'm glad I was able to help.'

'I might be able to help you, if you'd let me.'

'How?' she asked.

'Well, the burden of grief and loss was lifted from my shoulders somewhat when I knew for certain I'd nailed Munro, and I know it'll be completely gone when he's been hanged as punishment for my wife's murder. It wasn't just her death that was making me suffer, but the complete injustice of it all. It's that same deeply ingrained sense of injustice that kicks off family feuds, even wars.'

'What you're saying is, if I get justice, I'll be able to cope with relationships better.'

'Yes, that's exactly what I'm saying.'

'And how am I supposed to get justice for something that happened all those years ago? Something that destroyed my life, but which I have no way of proving?'

Daniel sat back in his chair and shook his head. 'I didn't

say it would be easy . . . just that the main thing lacking in your life is justice for the atrocious thing he did to you. Do you know where he is now?'

'Yes, he's in Walton Prison for sexually assaulting women.'

'Really?'

'Yes. Due out shortly.'

'Well, with his criminal record it might be possible for you to nail him in court, especially if your mother backs you up. Something like that would put him away for ten years at least.'

'Daniel, ten years wouldn't do it. I'd need to see him swinging alongside Munro and I'd want to be the one who puts the rope around his neck; the one who pulls the lever to open the trapdoor under his feet. And then I'd like to go and swing on his feet, to make sure he's dead.'

'That's a lot of hatred.'

'Wouldn't you like to do the same with Munro and Leonov?'

'Yes, I would.'

Helen took a sip of her coffee, placed the cup back on the saucer and signalled a waitress.

'Would you like another coffee?' she asked Daniel. 'By the way, you're looking very beautiful tonight.'

'Thank you.'

He was wearing his one and only decent suit, dark grey single-breasted with a faint stripe, and a dark blue silk tie. This was as good as he ever looked.

'No, I think I'm ready for something stronger. A large whisky I think.'

Helen smiled and said she'd join him. To the waitress she said, 'Two large whiskies, please.'

Daniel looked at her and thought he'd never seen her looking quite so beautiful. She was wearing what looked like a new dress. Light blue with a low neck and a gold necklace holding a locket.

'You're looking pretty good yourself. What's in the locket?'

'A photo of the only man I ever loved.'

'I'm guessing that's your real father.'

'It's certainly not my stepfather.'

Helen leaned forward and spoke quietly. 'Suppose I just went and stabbed him through the heart. Do you think that would chase the demons away?'

Daniel leaned forward as well and spoke very quietly. 'I imagine so, but I couldn't recommend it.'

'Why not?'

'Because, for all your talk, you're a good woman.'

'I'm actually a good woman who's making plans to kill my rapist.'

'I assume you're joking.'

'Then you assume wrongly.'

Daniel sat back again, nor believing her. Then he thought some more about what she'd said. It was outrageous but not totally unbelievable. Her stepfather's death might well give her a fresh start.

'What plans?' he asked.

'Not finalised yet, and I'm now relying on the affection you say you feel for me to prevent you from ever telling a soul about this conversation.'

'Well, you have my word for that, if not my approval.'

'I'm not asking for your approval.'

Helen told him then about how she'd been in contact

with Bradley anonymously, and how she had plans to meet him once he was out, and to kill him then.

'And how do you propose killing him?'

'I haven't thought about that bit yet.'

'So, you're planning the perfect murder but you don't know how as yet?'

'That's right.'

'It's been tried many times by much more ruthless killers than you.'

'Daniel, I'm not a ruthless killer, that's the beauty of it. Who'd suspect me?'

Daniel shook his head and smiled at her. 'Please don't try anything without running it past me first.'

'So you don't disapprove?'

'Helen, of course I bloody disapprove! By the way, would you have gone to bed with me?'

'No,' she said. 'I couldn't. As you guessed, I was just testing you.' She smiled at him, realising that, without this big black bogeyman looming over her, she might get to like this man a whole lot more.

Chapter 42

Daniel was in his office when Mrs Sixsmith rang. 'Am I speaking to Mr Daniel Earnshawe?'

It wasn't the form of address he was used to at work, but he let it go. 'You are, yes. Who is this?'

It was a woman's voice and, with it being a bad line, it crossed his mind that it might be Helen. He was to be disappointed on this point.

'My name is Mrs Sixsmith. I'm the house-mother at the Archbishop Cranmer Children's Home.'

'Yes, I know it. What can I do for you, Mrs Sixsmith?'

'Billy Wellington was one of my boys and I understand that you're still investigating the case.'

'That's correct.'

'Well,' she said, 'I've just had Lucy Bailey round. I gather you know her?'

'Yes, I know Lucy.'

'We've just been having a really good talk about what happened on the day Ethel was murdered and something's occurred to me that the police have got wrong.'

'What's that, Mrs Sixsmith?'

'Well, I remember it being said in the papers that Billy

confessed to the murder when he was first questioned.'

'I believe he did, yes.'

'Then I'm afraid you believe wrong, Mr Earnshawe. I was there and Billy did no such thing. In fact, it's only after talking to Lucy just now that I've realised where the mistake came from.'

'What mistake is that?'

'Well, I was as bad as you police, to tell the truth, because I got hold of the wrong end of the stick as well. I thought he was talking about Ethel, just the same as the policemen did, only he wasn't, was he? Billy never mentioned being with Ethel, I'm sure he didn't. It's one of them times you remember. I was so shocked, I swear I can remember every word he said.'

'I'm not really following you, Mrs Sixsmith.'

'Billy was with Lucy that afternoon and they set the dogs free at the dogs' home in Crossgates. *That's* what Billy thought the police were talking about. He never mentioned Lucy's name because he thought he would get her into trouble. I remember him saying he did it on his own. The police thought he was admitting to the murder, but he wasn't. He was admitting to setting the dogs free! If Lucy had been at that interview, she'd have put the copper straight about that.'

The woman's words tumbled out quickly and Daniel tried to take in what he'd just been told. He knew that Billy's incarceration had been because of his confession. He'd later denied harming Ethel, but his first confession was what the police took to be the truth. Many confessions are retracted by criminals who decide they've acted too hastily. But now here was a witness contesting the police's interpretation, and convincingly.

'So you're saying the police and Billy were talking at cross-purposes, and what sounded like a confession to murder was really nothing of the sort?'

'That's right. I only wish I'd come forward then. If it'd gone to court I might have done, but to be honest I never made the connection with him being with Lucy until she came round just now.'

'Hmm, I believe it was an informal interview and no notes were taken, so it's hard to prove what was said one way or the other.'

'Well I don't remember anyone taking notes and I was sitting right with 'em.'

'Right.'

Daniel was aware that, with Billy being mentally subnormal, the interview was more of chat, to see what should be done with him rather than to charge him with anything. He knew his boss, Harry Bradford, was uncomfortable with such people. He also knew his own detective sergeant, Charlie Boddy, had been in on the interview. Boddy shared an office with Daniel and was sitting there right now.

'Mrs Sixsmith,' said Daniel, 'thanks for this. I'll get back to you.'

He put the phone down and looked at Charlie, who was laboriously typing up a report.

'Charlie,' he said.

'Yes?'

'When you and the DCI interviewed Billy Wellington last year, were any notes taken?'

Charlie gave the question a moment's thought, then said, 'I don't think so, sir. The boss considered the interview to be informal as we weren't sure what to do with the lad. In fact he stopped it short so that Wellington could be interviewed by medical experts.'

'So there's no record of his confession?'

'No, sir. Just three witnesses.'

'Two witnesses, Charlie. That was the third one, Mrs Sixsmith, on the phone. She reckons you and the DCI and Billy were talking at cross-purposes about who he was with that afternoon. You thought he was admitting to being with Ethel whereas Mrs Sixsmith is now sure he was talking about being with a girl called Lucy Bailey. Did he actually mention the name Ethel?'

Charlie stared at him. 'To be honest, I don't remember, sir. I think we just took it as read that he was talking about the dead girl. I mean, that's what the interview was about.'

'Not to Billy it wasn't. He thought you were talking about him letting dogs out of a dogs' home in Crossgates and Lucy Bailey will back him up on that if it ever gets to court.'

'Well, he *might* have said Ethel's name, I can't remember.'

'Which is what you will have to tell the court when the case comes up. In fact, it would be more honest if you told the court what you first told me – that you can't remember him saying Ethel's name and that you took it as read that he was talking about the dead girl. That's what you must tell the court, Charlie.'

'Must I, sir?'

'Yes, you must, because if you don't, I will tell the court that that's what you just said to me. In fact, as things stand, it wouldn't even get to court. The DPP would drop it like a hot brick due to lack of evidence.'

He was thinking about the case against Elias Munro.

'Look, sir. I know you think he didn't do it, but must we admit to making such an almighty cock-up? The DCI won't thank me for it.'

'No, I don't suppose he will. The alternative is for you to let Billy spend the rest of his life locked up for a crime he didn't commit. It all depends on what sort of copper you are, Charlie.' Daniel gave the matter a moment's thought, then said, 'Besides, this wasn't your cock-up. We should blame it on the medical experts and the magistrates who made the decision to lock him up and throw away the key.'

Daniel looked at Charlie's downcast face and said, 'Don't worry, I'll tell the DCI.'

*

DCI Bradford was absorbed in an article in the *Yorkshire Post* when Daniel knocked on his door and looked in.

'Ah, Daniel, come in. There's an article in here about police brutality to prisoners in the cells. I've a mind to invite this damned reporter to come and spend a week helping us out with our charming prisoners. I'd have him spend his first day on light duties such as vomit-cleaning and have him work his way down from there.'

Daniel sat down as his boss folded his newspaper and asked him what he wanted.

'I've had a disturbing telephone call from a Mrs Sixsmith about the interview you and DS Boddy held of Billy Wellington, last year.'

He went on to summarise the whole situation, including the fact that notes hadn't been taken at the interview.

'Well, it didn't reach the stage of being a formal interview. I soon realised we were out of our depth with young Wellington's mental situation and passed him over to the medical experts. Whatever decision was made about him didn't come from this station.'

'That's what I thought, sir, which is why I consider it best that we should nip it in the bud before we're obliged to pass this new information over to the DPP.' Daniel looked at the newspaper on the desk and added, 'Mrs Sixsmith is the type of person who might well go to the papers, and I'm afraid Lucy Bailey would back her up.'

'You know this Lucy Bailey well, do you not?'

'I do, sir.'

'And it's she who's encouraged you to follow up on the Ethel Tomlinson murder?'

'More or less, yes. She's absolutely convinced Wellington couldn't possibly have done it, sir, and I think she'd make a most plausible witness in court.'

Bradford sat back in his chair and nodded to himself. 'It seems our medical experts have made an almighty cock-up, Daniel.'

'Better them than us, sir.'

'Hmm, so I need to tell the Director of Public Prosecutions, and I must word this very carefully.'

'It's what you're good at, sir.'

'Yes, quite, thank you, Daniel. Excellent forward thinking. Glad to have you back with us. I'll put wheels in motion right away. Inform Mrs Sixsmith before she does anything rash.'

'I'll do that, sir.'

*

Charlie was out of the office when Daniel got back. He duly rang Mrs Sixsmith and told her that her phone call had had the desired effect and that Billy would be freed soon. She was quite amazed that she'd made such a dramatic and sudden change in Billy's circumstances.

'It seems,' Daniel had said, 'that neither of the two police officers could swear on oath that Billy did indeed say he'd been with Ethel that afternoon. It was actually quite unfortunate that he'd gone off with Lucy Bailey that day.'

'Really? And will you be telling Lucy that?'

'No, I wouldn't dare.'

After he put the phone down Daniel stared at it for a few seconds wondering if passing the good news on to Billy's mother might increase his chances with her. He decided it would do no harm so he dialled Helen's number, hoping she might be in. She was.

'Ah, you're at home. I thought you might be out on your bike or something.'

'No, I'm taking the day off. I've got an audition this afternoon.'

'You mean for a part in a play?'

'No, a part in a TV serial. My bit part in *The Makepeace Story* is paying dividends.'

'What's the serial?'

'Oh, it's a period thing called *Robin Hood*. I'm up for Maid Marian. Personally I think I'm too old but the actress I'm up against – Bernadette O'Farrell – is only a year younger than me.'

'I think I've heard of her.'

'Yes, you will have. That's why she'll probably get it. Still, I might end up with something.'

'Well, I wish you the best of luck. And while I'm talking about luck, I think I should tell you that Billy will be freed quite soon.'

He heard a gasp at the other end of the line, then, 'Honestly?'

'Yes. I've just had a word with my DCI about the strength of the evidence against Billy, or lack of it, and he's going to advise the DPP to drop the case.'

Although he hadn't lied to her, Daniel had made it sound as if he was totally responsible for Billy's being freed. Being in Helen's good books, no matter how briefly, was a step in the right direction, he decided. She wouldn't completely replace Gloria in his affections, no one would ever do that, but he felt he'd never find anyone else he wanted quite so much as he wanted Helen.

'And is this all your doing, Daniel?'

He felt that becoming modesty was called for now. 'I played a part,' he said.

'Oh, Daniel. I don't know how I'm going to be able to thank you.'

He could have given her a few ideas but it would be wrong to take too much advantage of the situation.

'Billy being freed will be thanks enough. It still leaves me with a killer to find, though.'

'You're a good man, Daniel Earnshawe.'

'I trust you've got no further with the plan we discussed the other day?'

'What? No, no. It seems I'm going to have other things on my mind for the foreseeable future.'

'I'm glad to hear that.'

323

'The day will come, Daniel. It's what keeps me ticking.'

'Just tell me when you're ready to act is all I ask.'

'I'll do that. Do you know when Billy will be free?'

'Not sure, but I know the DPP will drop the case like a hot brick when they hear from my DCI. Billy should be home within a week, I imagine.'

'What do I do? Should I get in touch with Rampton?'

Daniel saw a good way of keeping in touch with her and took it. 'I'll monitor the situation and get back to you. Any hold-ups and I'll try and hurry things along.'

'Thank you so much, Daniel.'

'That's okay. As I say, I'll keep in touch.'

He put the phone down and ran her final words through his mind. *Thank you so much, Daniel.* Had he detected a note of affection there or was it just wishful thinking?

Chapter 43

The one person who hadn't been told about Billy's impending change of fortunes was Lucy. Daniel was working, Helen was preparing for her forthcoming audition and Lucy was at school. On top of which, their house, like the vast majority of houses on the estate, had no telephone. But by the time Lucy got home from school Billy's fortunes had undergone a swift about turn.

Daniel had been out of the station for a couple of hours, visiting Henry Barrington-Smythe, Billy's barrister, to discuss what best to do next. By the time he got back, events had overtaken him. Charlie Boddy was at his desk, nervously twiddling a pencil in his fingers and avoiding Daniel's gaze.

'Problems?' asked Daniel, who could read Charlie like a book.

His sergeant looked up at him and stopped twiddling. 'Erm, it's about this Billy Wellington thing. The more I think about it, the more I'm sure Billy confessed to it.'

Daniel half-turned his head, without taking his eyes off Charlie. 'Am I missing something here?'

'How d'you mean?'

'Am I missing the fact that DCI Bradford's had a persuasive word in your ear?'

'Well, he came down and we had a good chat about it.'

'And he persuaded you to stick to your guns and tell the court that Billy confessed?'

Charlie nodded, dismally.

'Bloody hell! And how are you going to explain this when we prove Billy innocent? It's the case we're working on, remember?'

'The DCI's taken me off it,' said Charlie. 'Sorry, boss.'

'And replaced you with whom?'

'I don't know.'

Daniel stormed out and barged into the DCI's office without knocking. 'I gather you've browbeaten Charlie into telling the court that Billy Wellington confessed. Are you going to say the same, sir?'

'Calm down, Daniel. I didn't browbeat anyone. I was probably a bit hasty when I told you I'd contact the DPP to get the charge dropped.'

'I don't think you were being hasty, sir. I think you were being fair to the boy.'

Bradford was obviously uncomfortable about the whole thing. 'Look,' he said, 'during the original interview I was of the firm opinion that he did confess, as were DS Boddy and Mrs Sixsmith. It's ridiculous to change our minds after all this time.'

'Did this come from the DPP, sir?'

'In a roundabout way, yes. I sounded out an acquaintance of mine who works there and it was his opinion that prosecuting counsel would tear us to pieces if we changed our story at this late stage. Time distorts memory, Daniel. We must go with what we thought at the time.'

'I prefer to go with what's right, sir,' he answered. 'Does this mean I'm being taken off the Ethel Tomlinson murder?'

'Yes, it does, I'm afraid, and I don't want you compromising the police by pursuing the case in your own time.' He handed Daniel a file. 'This is an arson attack I want you have a look at. Two people died and another is seriously injured in hospital. No suspect as yet.'

Daniel took the file with no enthusiasm and went back to his office, deep in thought. He became aware of Charlie looking at him. He picked up the arson file.

'Charlie,' he said, caustically. 'I want you to take this file and find out who the arsonist is. When you've found him, bring him in.'

Charlie took the file and left Daniel cursing his own stupidity. Damn! He should have waited until the decision to free Billy had been officially approved. Why the hell had he been so quick to tell Helen the good news? He knew the answer. He'd just wanted to hear her delighted voice. He'd wanted her to have a reason to really like him and admire him. Now what was she going to think of him? He looked at the telephone and wondered whether or not to get it over with.

Then he told himself she was probably out, and if she was in, such news wouldn't put her in a great mood for her audition. Ring her tonight, Earnshawe. He'd call in and see Lucy when she got home from school and tell her what had happened. See her reaction when the good news turned back to bad. Would *she* think badly of him?

Jesus! What was it about that girl? Here he was, a grown man in his prime, a ranking police officer, seeking the approval of a fifteen year old. He glanced across at Charlie's desk and remembered his earlier conversation with his sergeant.

'Well, he might have said Ethel's name, I can't remember.'

'Which is what you will have to tell the court . . .'

'Must I, sir?'

'Yes, you must, because if you don't, I will tell the court that that's what you just said to me.'

He'd just told Henry Barrington-Smythe about this conversation and he knew the barrister would insist on using it in Billy's defence. Giving evidence against his own colleagues wouldn't do Daniel's career prospects much good, but it might help his prospects with Helen.

*

Daniel's call was the second Helen received that evening in the space of ten minutes. The first was from her theatrical agent to tell her that her audition had been unsuccessful. It wasn't entirely unexpected but she had hoped to pick up another role in the same series. No such luck.

She listened to what Daniel had to say in complete silence. Not getting the part was a disappointment but not unexpected; just part and parcel of the acting profession She'd been lucky to get down to the last two for a major part like that. But having her hopes about her son raised so high, then dashed almost immediately, was almost unbearable.

When Daniel finished she made no comment. She put down the phone and stood there in desolation, eyes wide and watery as silent tears rolled down her face. This was a time of great sorrow and even greater hatred – hatred towards her stepfather. She opened a drawer in the hall cabinet and took out the knife she'd bought to kill him with. It had an elaborate, carved bone handle and a six-inch blade ending in the needle-sharp point that she would, one day soon, plunge deep into his putrid heart. It was this thought that eventually dried her tears. Kill him she must, even if they hanged her for it.

She grasped the knife with both hands, raised it above her head, and thrust it, with all her might, into the top of the cabinet where it stuck, an inch deep, into the mahogany top. When she plunged it into Bradley's soft body it would go many times deeper, right up to the hilt. She looked at the knife and pictured it sticking out of her stepfather's chest. His poisonous blood would quickly stain his whole shirt and he would sink to his knees in horror as she told him that he was dying because he wasn't fit to live.

Then she shuddered at the conflicting emotions she felt. This repulsive man, who had done her so much damage, was about to turn her, who had never harmed anyone in her life, into a murderer. She left the knife where it was, until the day arrived when she must use it for its appointed purpose. Seeing it there in the meantime would be a constant reminder.

*

Daniel stared at the phone, now buzzing out the dial tone, wishing she'd said something, if only to scream her rage at him. Rage he could cope with, maybe even counter in time. He had an ache inside his chest, caused by the possibility that she was now out of his reach. He didn't want that. It was the ache he'd last felt when he lost Gloria.

Maybe he should go round, tell Helen how he'd stand up in court and give evidence against his own colleagues. His evidence plus that of Mrs Sixsmith might sway things Billy's way. And it might not do any harm to find out who it was at the DPP Bradford had spoken to about changing his story. If he got this man's name, Barrington-Smythe wouldn't hesitate to subpoena him.

With this in mind Daniel made his way to the telephone switchboard where Diane was on duty, answering calls and plugging in connections. He waited until she had a spare moment. She turned in her chair and smiled at him. Daniel knew she had a soft spot for him. He returned her smile.

'Diane, I wonder if you could do me a small favour?'

'If I can, sir.'

'Erm, earlier today DCI Bradford put a call through to the DPP. I'm supposed to remember who he spoke to but it's gone completely out of my head and I don't want him to think I'm an idiot and stick me back on sick leave. Can you remind me who it was?'

She looked at a notepad she had on her desk, ran her finger down a list and said, 'Is that the Director of Public Prosecutions?'

'That's it.'

'Yes, it was a Mr Elliot Hazelhurst.'

'Elliot Hazelhurst. That's him! I knew it was a mouthful. No wonder I forgot it.'

'Do you want me to write it down for you?'

'Erm, yeah, I think you'd better, and his number if you would.'

She wrote it all down and handed it to Daniel. He put a finger to his lips. 'Mum's the word, by the way.'

She mimed a zipping of her lips.

'Thanks, Diane, you're a life-saver.'

Leaving her basking in his approval he went back to his office, wondering if he had enough ammunition to convince Helen that he was on her side and her only hope of setting her son free. Then he asked himself: would he go to these lengths to help Billy if Helen wasn't in the picture – risking his career to keep in her good books? He very much doubted it. He realised that his feelings for her far outweighed any allegiance he had to his colleagues or his job. These were powerful feelings he'd thought he'd never know again. He rang Barrington-Smythe to appraise him of the latest events and tell him that he was prepared to give evidence contradicting that of the DCI and DS Boddy.

'You're putting your job at risk, Daniel.'

'I know.'

'Which is why I must ask if you have an ulterior motive?'

'What ulterior motive?'

'I don't know. Perhaps the delectable Helen Durkin. I have met her, you know.'

'I know you have.'

'Well?'

'Okay, perhaps she might be an ulterior motive. Right now she must hate me.'

'The prosecution mustn't find out about this ulterior motive. Have you mentioned her to your sergeant?'

331

'No – there's actually nothing to mention.'

'That's good. You must keep it that way until we get to court. I was given a date yesterday – Monday the fourteenth of November. I'll leave it until the last minute before I subpoena Mr Hazelhurst. In the meantime you must get on with whatever cases you're given and ignore this one, unless something falls into your lap.'

'Yes, I will.'

Daniel put the phone down and realised that he was in danger of losing both his career and Helen if things didn't go well. The ache inside his chest was still there and it wasn't caused by the prospect of forfeiting his career. It was an ache that needed curing as soon as possible. He left his office, got into his car and headed for Helen's house.

*

She greeted him with, 'Oh, it's you,' turned her back on him and went into the front room. He followed her.

'Okay,' he said. 'You almost had Billy back and now you've lost him again. I shouldn't have said anything until it was all official, but I didn't expect my DCI and my sergeant to chicken out the way they did. Neither of them heard him properly confess, but to admit it now would put my DCI in a bad light.'

Helen said nothing. She sat down and lit a cigarette, not looking at Daniel. He continued:

'I've had a word with Barrington-Smythe and told him I'm prepared to give evidence against DCI Bradford and DS Boddy.'

'Won't this affect your career?'

'I don't suppose it'll do me any good. Barrington-Smythe's also issuing a subpoena against a man from the

DPP whom Bradford consulted about what would happen if he went back on his word about the confession. This man will have to tell the truth, confirming that DCI Bradford and DS Boddy were unsure about what was said. On the other hand, Mrs Sixsmith is absolutely sure.' Daniel hesitated then added, 'I'm sorry for jumping the gun, but I'm doing my best for you, Helen.'

She glanced at him and said, 'Yes, I know you are, and I wonder why.'

'Well, maybe I got swept away by Lucy's enthusiasm.'

'Yes, she is an enthusiastic girl. You do know she's in love with you, don't you?'

'What? Come off it.'

'She is.'

'Well, no doubt it'll wear off when she meets someone half my age, who's as new to life as she is. Great age, that – fifteen to eighteen. It's full of new experiences which we oldies all take for granted.'

'Such as?'

'Oh, being allowed out late, learning to drive, drinking in pubs and getting drunk for the first time, smoking, rock and roll, and of course all the boy/girl stuff. That's the big one.'

'You mean sex?'

'Well, yes. It's kind of ... inevitable when you're young.'

'It certainly was for me. Although I never experienced this sex for pleasure thing.'

'I'm sorry, that was clumsy of me.'

'Don't apologise. I'm damaged goods. Nothing you or anyone can do about it.'

'Except convince you there's nothing wrong with being a late starter. It's like keeping the best for last.'

Helen smiled and shook her head. 'You said for me to keep you up-to-date with my plan to kill my stepfather.'

'And?' he said, hesitantly.

'Did you see the knife in the hall, the one sticking in the cabinet?'

'Yes, I did, actually.'

'Well, that'll be the murder weapon.'

'It'll certainly do the job.'

'You don't think I'm serious, do you?'

'Yes, I think you're serious, but I also think that when push comes to shove you won't be able to do it. At least, I hope you won't.'

'Would you turn me in if I killed him?'

'No.'

She examined her cigarette, thoughtfully. 'Daniel, are you in love with me?'

She'd mentioned that word again. He was surer of his answer this time.

'Unfortunately, yes.'

'So, why hadn't you told me?'

'Because . . . what good would that do?'

'Well, I've never had anyone in love with me before.'

'I find that hard to believe.'

'What's it like, being in love with someone?'

'If they love you back it's great. No better feeling.'

'And if they don't?'

'Well, if they love someone else I imagine it's unbearable, but if they're friendly with you but not in love with anyone else it's more or less bearable, I suppose.'

'So, I'm bearable?'

'Oh, you're extremely bearable.'

'I don't mind being your friend, Daniel, but I can't promise anything else.'

'I value you as a friend, Helen.'

'Do you know when Billy's case gets to court?'

'Yes, I found out today – November the fourteenth.'

* * *

Cisko Courier Service had a phone call regarding a delivery to St Helens. Helen was in the depot and heard the dispatcher tell the caller that it was out of their area. On impulse she called out that she'd do it.

'Just a moment, please,' said the dispatcher. He put his hand over the mouthpiece.

'Are you sure? You know where St Helens is, don't you?'

'I do,' said Helen. 'It's near Liverpool. That's like four deliveries all in one run. I assume I'll be paid accordingly?'

'Helen, are you sure?'

'Why wouldn't I be sure?'

'Well, you haven't been yourself lately.'

'Say we'll do it.'

He put the phone to his ear again. 'Yes, we can do it. The cost may be quite high but we can have it there by close of business this afternoon.'

After he put the receiver down he said to Helen, 'They're dropping the parcel off in an hour. You'd better grab a bite to eat and get straight off.'

'I need to go home first, but I'll be back and fed by the time the parcel arrives.'

* * *

The knife was in a leather sheath looped into her belt. Her parcel had been delivered and her time was her own. A woman with murder on her mind needs to have plenty of time to herself. Since she'd heard the good/bad news about Billy depression had crushed her. Daniel's words had fallen on deaf ears. Helen knew the court would find her son guilty. It was the way of things. When Billy was sent down for a murder he hadn't committed, she needed to balance things out a bit by giving them a murder of which she was guilty – a murder that meted out the justice the law had overlooked. It was her way of justifying what she was about to do. A good person cannot commit a murder without proper justification.

Killing her stepfather had become a burning obsession with Helen, a force that was driving her towards him. It seemed to her that this courier delivery was the work of fate, and fate had decreed that Bradley must die today.

After she'd done her delivery, finding the bail hostel was not a problem to a professional courier with a street map of Liverpool. She drove along a grimy street and pulled up beside a sign reading: *Dublin Street Bail Hostel*. In the air was the smell of the Irish Sea mixed with various nearby industrial emissions. It wasn't a healthy smell. Most of the other buildings seemed to be of the commercial variety: garages, workshops, storehouses and an uninviting pub on the corner called the Howard Arms. She looked up at the crumbling brick walls of the dilapidated three-storey bail hostel and thought it a more than fitting habitat for her stepfather.

She drove round the corner and left her machine outside Batty's Brush Works, which seemed to be disused.

She didn't want her bike to be associated with the hostel by any witnesses questioned by the police. She dismounted, put her crash helmet in the side pannier, swapped her leather motorcycle jacket for a more businesslike grey coat, put on a pair of gloves and walked back down Dublin Street. It was fairly empty, which suited her. A banging sound came from a nearby workshop. A car and a van were parked higher up; a man came out of the pub and headed off round the corner. She looked at her watch. It was almost half-past five. Would he be in? Did he have a job? Was he still living there? Would she even recognise him after all these years?

As she walked she reached her right hand beneath her coat and felt the handle of her knife by her left hip, running it up and down in the sheath a few inches to check its ease of removal. She had no plan other than to knock on his door, stab him with every ounce of her strength and run away. It was a simple plan but she could find no flaw in it. Her blonde hair was disguised by a dark brown wig. From her pocket she took a pair of horn-rimmed spectacles with plain glass lenses. They had been a prop in one of her plays. She'd checked this image in a mirror and knew it made her look totally different. It probably wasn't the perfect murder, but any murder that sent Bradley screaming down to Hell was perfect enough for her.

The front door of the hostel was large and arched and had once been painted blue, and prior to that dark red. Both colours were evident, but the more recent blue somewhat more so. She tried the door and it opened on to a large hallway with a staircase, three doors and a passage leading from it. It was a dark place lit only by a single, dirty window beside the door. There was no sign of life and Helen wondered if anyone actually lived there. If they did it was probably worse than the prison they'd just come from.

'Hello?' she shouted.

A door along the passage opened. Footsteps echoed towards her. They belonged to an elderly man who wore a stained apron and an equally stained flat cap.

'Can I help yer, love? I'm the warden here.'

His accent was broad Liverpool, Scouse through and through. Helen's plan was to be as straightforward as possible. She took an official-looking manila file from her shoulder bag and opened it.

'Am I right in thinking Maurice Bradley lives here?' she asked, using a voice that wasn't entirely her own. It was an Irish accent that she'd used in the same play as her spectacles.

'Are you from Probation?'

'Yes,' she said, happy with the help he'd just given her subterfuge. She had been going to claim to be a solicitor, but a probation officer was much better.

'Haven't seen you before.'

'That's because I haven't been here before. Is he still in room eight?'

'That's right. First floor, down to your right.'

'And is he in?'

'I think so, unless he's gone to the pub.'

'The one on the corner?'

'That's right. God knows where he gets his money from. He never does a day's work that feller.' The old man looked at his watch. 'Mind you, it's a bit early fer the pub, even fer him.'

'I'll try his room,' said Helen.

'Right yer are,' said the warden, walking back down the passage.

Helen waited until he'd closed his door before she made her way up the stairs. Her heart was pounding and she kept a picture in the forefront of her mind of the times she'd been assaulted. It was that picture that drew her on. She turned right on the first landing. Room eight was two doors down on the left. Her hands were balled into tight fists with her fingernails biting into her palms, drawing blood but causing no pain that she noticed.

Loud wireless music was coming from the other side of the door. A big band sound – Glenn Miller possibly. She had no memory of him liking any kind of music, but her memories of him were restricted to what he'd done to her, nothing more. But at least it told her he was in and not in the pub, which was good. Doing this in the pub would have been well-nigh impossible. She'd have had to wait for him to come home. But he was here, just a few feet away. Behind this door was the man who had all but destroyed her life and she had a knife in her hand, ready to destroy his. Her chance had come at last. She was clutching the knife beneath her coat, still in its sheath, easy to draw, easy to stab him with. This man whom she desperately needed to kill.

She stood there for a full minute, summoning all her hatred of him. Reminding herself of what he'd done to her. This stepfather who was also the father of her mentally impaired son. Her heart rate subsided a little. Now she was ready.

*

Maurice Bradley was lying on his bed, staring at the ceiling and listening to the wireless, wondering when this solicitor person would get in touch again. He'd been out of prison a fortnight. When he was arrested he'd had a hundred pounds seaman's wages on him. It had been given back to him. That plus his dole money was enough for him to live on until he got another ship, but he had to report to the probation office once a week for three months before that could happen. Even then he'd have to apply for special permission to leave the country. If he didn't get that permission he'd go anyway. Sod 'em, he had to earn a crust. If he'd been left money by that bitch of an ex-wife of his that might not need to happen, of course. He didn't go to sea because he enjoyed the life, he did it because it was the only job he knew.

Footsteps in the corridor outside had him swinging his legs off the bed just in case it was someone coming to see him. Maybe a solicitor with a fat cheque. The footsteps stopped. There was a long silence then a knock on the door.

'Who is it?' he called out.

Just three words but she recognised his voice. The voice of her abuser. Helen drew in a slow breath and called out, 'Probation Service,' taking her lead from the man downstairs.

She could hear him grumbling. She unsheathed the knife and held it behind her back in readiness as the door opened and Maurice Bradley stood before her.

He hadn't aged well. His face was lined, his hair much

340

thinner, but she remembered those cruel eyes. The evil eyes that had stared down at her as he'd thrust himself inside her all those year ago. Hatred surged through her. Before he could say anything Helen drew back the knife brought it up towards his heart with all the speed and strength she could muster. Instinctively he turned to one side, taking the blow in the upper right side of his chest.

His eyes opened wide with pain and shock. Helen let go of the knife, which was lodged in his body. He looked down at it and pulled it out with his left hand, staggering as blood poured from the wound. Helen stood there, watching him do this, hoping her job was done. One blow to his heart was all she'd planned but he was still on his feet. Why was this? The knife was now in his hand. Just before he sank to the floor he slashed at her. Her coat was open, offering no protection. Razor sharp, the knife cut into her stomach. She gasped with pain and looked down at him writhing on the floor. The knife had fallen from his grasp. He wasn't dead but it would have been easy to finish him off. Blood was everywhere, some of it hers.

Horrified by what she'd done, she ran down the stairs and out of the building. As she reached the street the effects of her wound began to take their toll. No one was around to see the injured woman staggering up the street, her coat darkened with blood. She reached her bike and took the coat off. Then, almost weeping with pain, she managed to get her leather jacket out from her pannier, put her bloodied coat in its place, put on her jacket and crash helmet, and started up the bike.

Blood was seeping down Helen's jeans as she rode through the streets of Liverpool. She was feeling faint but knew she must fight it. Her journey to Leeds would take her almost three hours. No way could she manage that. She knew that about four miles to the east was stretch of open countryside with a hedge by the side of the road. She could maybe get herself and her bike to the other side of that hedge, out of sight of the road, where she could tend to her wound with the first-aid kit she had in her bike's saddlebag.

Her vision was faint as she made her way to the A57, the road to St Helens. The pain was now unbearable. She passed by a council estate into which she turned in her agony. At the end of the road was a field bounded by a hedge; in the hedge was a gap to which she pointed her machine. Once through the hedge she swung the bike to the right, switched off the ignition and fell off, unconscious.

*

Maurice Bradley lay on the floor screaming in agony and anger, but not in mortal danger. Three of his neighbours came out to look at him, none came to help. Blood and screams of agony didn't impress them. They didn't like this man and maybe he was doing this to draw attention himself. Two of them went back into their rooms, the third went downstairs to alert the hostel warden, who called the police and an ambulance. The police arrived first and took advantage of this to approach the injured felon, who was well known to them and should be made to answer a few questions.

'Did you know your assailant, sir?'

'What? No, she said she was Probation. Then she stabbed me.'

'Is this the knife, sir?'

'I think so. I stabbed her back, if you must know.'

'Really? So she's injured, is she?'

'Well, yeah.'

'So your fingerprints will be on this knife, will they? And there's a woman with a knife injury caused by this weapon.'

'What?'

'Mr Bradley, I understand you were imprisoned for sexual assault. Might this have been one of your victims?'

'How the hell would I know who it was?'

The police turned their attention to the hostel warden. 'Could you describe this woman, sir?'

'Well, she was from the Probation.'

'Yes, but what did she look like?'

'Irish . . . she was Irish.'

'She had an Irish accent, did she?'

'That's what I said.'

'Could you give us a description, sir?'

'Not a bad looker. Dark hair, glasses. Irish.'

'How old would you say she was?'

'Oh, I don't know. Twenty odd, I should think.'

'A young woman then?'

'Yeah, real looker. I did wonder when she said she was Probation. Never knew them have any lookers before this. You wouldn't expect it, would you?'

'No, and I still don't, sir. Nor do I think Probation Service employees go round stabbing people.'

'It wouldn't bother me if they did, some of the low-life buggers you get in here.'

'Are you sure you're suited to your job, sir?'

'You tell me. Part of it is having to live in this shit 'ole.'

'I take your point, sir. Did anyone see where this woman went? Was she in a car?'

'No idea. Yer'd better ask up and down the street.'

'Our plain clothes people will no doubt attend to that, sir.'

CID made enquiries locally and no one had seen anything. Her motorbike hadn't aroused any suspicion, nor had it been noticed, so far from the scene. They checked through the records for names of any Irish girls who might have been victims of Bradley, The enquiry was short-lived. An attack on a known sex offender wasn't worth too much police time. Maybe if he'd died they'd have spent an extra day or two.

*

Helen woke up some time later and looked into the dark sky. The pain in her stomach was so excruciating that she wished she hadn't woken. Streetlights cast enough illumination for her to see by. She unbuttoned her bloodied shirt to take a look at the damage.

'Good God!' she murmured.

The bleeding had mercifully stopped, but the cut was deep and perhaps four inches long. In her first-aid kit she had bandages, a tin of Germolene, a packet of Elastoplast and a bottle of Codeine tablets. She took out the kit and began her treatment by swallowing six tablets – three times the recommended dose. After half an hour the pain had eased so she began to patch herself up. As she worked she wondered if she'd succeeded in her task. Her stepfather had been bleeding profusely, in far worse shape than she was.

It took her another half hour before she felt she'd done all she could. This had included a liberal pasting of Germolene over the whole wound and looping the bandage around her stomach, which involved several shouts of pain she hoped hadn't alerted anyone. She fixed the bandage firmly in place with the plasters and, with a monumental effort, heaved her bike back up, kicked it into life and rode out of the field. The pain was still acute but bearable. She'd put the tablets in her pocket with the intention of taking more if it became acute. But she knew there was a balance to be drawn between pain and drugging herself into a state that made riding her bike too dangerous. She looked at the milometer and mentally added ninety miles. She'd try to do the journey in half-hour stretches. At a steady speed, five of these should see her home. As she rode she felt that the spectre of her stepfather was travelling with her. Was he dead and haunting her or, worse still, alive?

Three stops and nine Codeine talets later she was at the other side of the Pennines, dropping down towards Huddersfield, when the pain and too many tablets began to take their toll of her senses. She blacked out for a few seconds. A car horn woke her up. She was on the wrong side of the road with a wobbling front wheel. The car was heading straight for her, with headlights shining into her eyes. She brought her machine under control and steered it back across the road. The car went past with the driver shouting an obscenity through the window. She brought the bike to a halt and sat with her legs astride it, knowing she couldn't make it home. The pain was crippling her. So, what to do? If she was found on the road from Liverpool with a knife wound in her stomach a couple of hours after a man had been knifed to death in that same city by a woman, how would she explain that?

Oh, give it a go, Helen. See how far you get, she decided. It took all her remaining strength to kick the bike back into life. She'd been going for a few minutes at no more than twenty miles an hour when she saw a pub, or was it some sort of mirage in her delirium of pain? It was a cold night and she was right at the end of her tether once again. Inside the pub would be warmth and chairs and a telephone. Was this a good idea? Did she actually have an alternative? Inside her head she had two telephone numbers – Cisko Couriers' and Daniel's.

Cisko would be shut but would Daniel be at home? God, she hoped so. Helen pulled into the pub car park, which was almost empty. She switched off and sat there for a while, gathering whatever strength she could muster. It wasn't much but it should be enough to take her inside without passing out, and she could ask if there was a phone there she could use. Then she saw a street phone box on the other side of the road. All the better. She could speak in privacy. All she had to do was get to that phone box without being run down.

*

Daniel's younger daughter, Jeanette, answered the phone. Helen could only gasp a few words. 'It's Helen . . . is your father there?'

'Helen, how nice to hear from you.'

'Your father. Is he there?'

'Yes, I'll get him.'

Jeanette popped her head into the living room. 'Dad, it's Helen. She sounds a bit annoyed.'

'Oh, great.'

He went into the hall, took a deep breath and said, 'What is it, Helen?'

'Daniel ... I need you to come and get me.'

'What? Why? Where are you?'

'I'm on the A62 about five or so miles west of Huddersfield ... could be ten, not too sure. I've been injured, Daniel ... Not thinking straight.'

'Helen, I need to know exactly where you are.'

She looked across the road at the pub. 'I'll be in a pub called the ... er ... ' she peered through the phone box window at the pub sign ' ... Horse and Groom.'

'Why can't you call an ambulance?'

'Because I was injured while dealing with my stepfather. Please don't ask any more questions. Come and get me ... please.'

'I'm on my way.'

There was a light in the phone box, which would have been a novelty in Leeds. She checked her clothing for blood. Her leather jacket was clear but there was blood on her jeans, to halfway down the front of her thighs. Hopefully no one would notice. She made sure no traffic was within two hundred yards of her, either way. She needed crawling time just in case she collapsed while crossing the road. She was still on her feet when she entered the pub. The landlord was attending to a customer and didn't see her come in and stagger to the bar, leaning on it for support. He turned and welcomed her. Her bloodied jeans were hidden from his view.

'Evening, madam, what can I get you?'

She placed a two shilling piece on the bar. 'I'd like a large glass of orange, please.'

'Pint?'

'Yes, and a packet of crisps.'

'Take a seat, I'll bring them over.'

These were welcome words. Helen hadn't been sure if she could manage to carry a pint of orange juice to a table without spilling half of it and drawing attention to herself. She looked round. There were half a dozen people in the bar, none of them showing any interest in her or her bloodied jeans. There was a table about ten feet away. If she could get there without staggering and put the table between her and the room, she should be safe until Daniel got there, providing she didn't pass out.

She achieved this and made herself comfortable in a chair with arms that would help to keep her upright, but she was breathing like someone who had just run a fast hundred yards. A man nearby looked at her and passed a comment to his female companion. Helen smiled at them both and controlled her breathing. *Get a grip, Helen. All you have to do is wait an hour and you're home and dry.*

Her drink and crisps arrived. She was tempted to take more Codeine, then she added up what she'd taken so far – fifteen. *Bloody hell! It's a wonder you're conscious, Helen. Leave it until Daniel gets here and take a few then. You can sleep all the way back if you want.*

*

Daniel took a few minutes to get the number of the pub and ring them to find out exactly where it was. He was tempted to ask if a very pretty blonde woman had just

348

come in, but decided against it. He got in his car and headed west, flat out, his warrant card at the ready in case he was stopped for speeding. It took him thirty-nine minutes to get to the Horse and Groom. Helen was halfway through her orange juice. She was still wearing her wig. He did a double take and sat down opposite her.

'You look awful,' he said. 'What happened?'

She kept her voice low. 'I went for him ... stabbed him. He stabbed me back ... Slashed me across the stomach. I've patched myself up but I really need stitches. Riding a bike with a big gash in the belly is no fun.'

'Believe it or not, I had a similar bike ride about eleven years ago and you're right. It's no fun at all.'

'That's right. You were on a bike when you got shot. Well, I hope this doesn't put me off doing my job.'

'I very much doubt that. I think you're made of sterner stuff. By the way, you were going to let me know before you did anything.'

'Sorry ... acted on impulse.'

Daniel hesitated before he asked the next question. 'What about him? How is he?'

'Well, I stabbed him but he pulled the knife out ... got me back. Then he fell to the floor.'

'Alive?' asked Daniel, hopefully.

'I don't know. Daniel ... I'm in terrible pain and I don't want anyone in here to know. Can you get me out?'

'Can you walk okay?'

'If you give me your arm, I should be able to.'

'What about your bike?'

'It's in the car park. I'll worry about that later.'

He got to his feet. 'Okay, off we go.'

With his help she left the pub without drawing any real attention to herself. Daniel sat her in the car and said, 'Wait one minute.'

He went back inside and showed his police identification to the landlord. 'The young lady I escorted out left a motorbike in your car park. Do you have anywhere where it can be kept safely until I arrange to have it picked up?'

'What? You've arrested her, what for?'

'No, I haven't arrested her. Quite the opposite.'

'I have a garage, sir. I'll put it in there.'

'Thank you. I'll have it picked up within a few days.'

He got back in the car. Helen lay slumped in the front passenger seat. She was allowing herself to relax completely and it was an amazing relief, despite the pain. He started the car, her eyes flickered open.

'Daniel, I'm bleeding again. I really need stitching up.'

'I'll take you to Huddersfield Infirmary.'

'Won't they need to inform the police?'

'I am the police.'

'Don't you have to be the Huddersfield Police?'

'I don't think doctors are that fussy. I'm a bona-fide copper with a warrant card. You've been stabbed and you're in my care. I'll stay with you until you're patched up.'

'What if they want to keep me in for observation?'

'You have the right to discharge yourself. It's a hospital, not a prison.'

'I hope it's that simple.'

'We have no option but to get you attended to. That's the priority. The rest will have to take care of itself.'

'I'm your priority? I'm flattered.'

'Just close your eyes. We'll be there in a few minutes.'

Huddersfield Royal Infirmary's Casualty Department was having a busy night. Helen wasn't the only stabbing victim and Daniel wasn't the only copper in attendance. The fact that she'd arrived accompanied by her own detective inspector moved her up the Casualty queue. It was assumed that she'd been involved in the same fracas as the other injured people and few questions were asked. An hour after Daniel had taken her in she was back in his car, heading to Leeds, with twenty very neat stitches across her stomach. She was clutching a note for her doctor requiring that she be given an appointment at a Leeds hospital to have her stitches removed.

'Is that the end of it?' she asked Daniel.

'It depends what the Liverpool police come up with. Are you sure Bradley didn't recognise you?'

'Don't think so. I was wearing a dark wig and glasses, and he hasn't seen me for eighteen years. I was with him for about thirty seconds during which time I think he had other things on his mind than trying to figure out who I was.'

'Did anyone see you leaving on your motorbike?'

'Doubt it. I left it quite some distance from the hostel.'

'I'll make some discreet enquiries tomorrow.'

'Will you find out if he's dead?'

'Yes.'

'Tomorrow might well be the first day of the rest of my life.'

'My mother used to say that, or was it today?'

'It's tomorrow with me. I need him to be dead, Daniel.'

He made no comment. He was in love with this lady

who had more important things than him on her mind. He needed to keep her safe. That was all he knew.

'Thank you for helping me,' she said.

'Any time,' said Daniel.

She looked at him, knowing he meant it. She also knew that tomorrow she'd find out if her stepfather was still alive – if all this pain had been worth it.

Chapter 44

Billy's case began as scheduled on 14 November. The first day was spent with barristers and solicitors discussing procedure with the judge. Billy had been allowed to sit in the dock. He asked to go to the lavatory after an hour and soon latched on to the ruse that it was a good excuse to get out of this place and go for a walk accompanied by a policeman. He knew they'd let him go whenever he asked because he was potty. The one thing he'd learned in his confused life was that being potty had certain advantages. One was that people didn't know what to make of him.

Helen was there, of course, as was Daniel. When the court broke for lunch they didn't come back. No point. Nothing of interest would start until tomorrow. They went for a drink in the Victoria Hotel at the back of the Town Hall where the courts were.

There was no romantic relationship between them. Maurice Bradley had survived and had left hospital after a week. He was now back in the bail hostel. Helen's stitches had been removed at Leeds Infirmary the day before; she

353

was still on painkillers but the pain was lessening daily. She asked Daniel for a glass of wine. He had a beer and took both drinks to a table.

'What's the scar situation?' he asked her.

'Not too bad. The nurse who took the stitches out reckoned they did a neat job in Huddersfield. Just a fine line about four inches long. No one will ever see it but me.'

She said it pointedly. He took her meaning but pretended not to notice its significance.

'Why do you ask?' she pressed.

'Well, you're a woman and women don't like blemishes on their skin, no matter where.'

'And men don't mind?'

He shrugged. 'Not really. I got a couple of beauties in the war.'

'Ah, you were shot, weren't you?'

'I look upon it as the price I paid for avoiding six months in a POW camp. I was invalided out on VE Day, otherwise I might not have got a demob until 'forty-six. A lot didn't – held back looking after displaced persons. I was in police college a month after VE Day.'

'Did you get a medal for being wounded?'

'No – only the Yanks got medals for that. I got the usual campaign medals. I've five of them. Just an ordinary soldier, although I ended up a corporal. How did you spend the war?'

'I joined the Wrens in nineteen forty-two – ended up as a dispatch rider.'

'Hence the job as a courier?'

'That's right, although I always had an ambition to

become an actress. Maybe, with my background, I wanted to live in a make-believe world.'

'And what sort of medals did they give you Wrens?'

'A couple of service medals.' She hesitated then added, 'I got a BEM as well.'

'British Empire Medal? Now I'm impressed. They don't give them away just for turning up. What did you do?'

'Oh, I was out on the bike and I saw one of our aircraft crash on a beach up in Scotland. It was a biplane— Fairey Swordfish. I went down and pulled three men out before it went up in smoke.'

'Sounds like a very brave thing to do.'

Helen looked at him. 'Maybe ... maybe not. I've never placed a high value on my life, Daniel.'

'Well, I place a high value on it. I do hope you haven't got a death wish.'

She didn't respond to this. 'I got the gong from the King. He was really nice.'

'At the palace?'

'Yes. They gave me a brand new uniform, made-to-measure.'

'Made-to-measure uniform? I never aspired to any such thing.'

It was more interesting than the average small-talk, but small-talk nevertheless. A silence followed. Helen was thinking about Billy; Daniel was wondering if she intended having another go at her stepfather. He was also wondering if she could ever rid herself of the crushing effect her stepfather's very existence had on her love-life. He was thinking it might have been better all round if she had killed him. Get a grip, Earnshawe! That was ridiculous thinking.

He broke the silence with, 'I think we'll have a good idea of the outcome when the DCI and Charlie give their evidence. They should be up first.'

'Have the defence got Mrs Sixsmith lined up?' she asked.

'Yes, and raring to go.'

'And this bloke at the DPP?'

He grimaced. 'That's got very political. He's claiming some sort of immunity from giving evidence, due to where he works. It's the DPP who are bringing the prosecution so it's going to look strange if one of their own people is a witness for the defence. I think the bloke's in trouble with his bosses. Even if he does give evidence he might not make a good witness.'

'So it's the word of the two coppers against Mrs Sixsmith?' said Helen.

'Not entirely. We've got the evidence of the café owner who reckons Billy was in his place when the murder is supposed to have been committed.'

'But that depends on whether Lucy's version of the time they got back is believed.'

'Lucy'll make a good defence witness,' he assured her.

'I'm worried, Daniel.'

He put his hand on hers. Helen took her hand away and picked up her glass. Daniel pretended it didn't matter, but it still hurt. Maybe he was making a fool of himself.

*

The prosecution evidence was short but solid. It was based on the single dying word of Ethel, the murdered girl. It was *Bill* who'd killed her. It was damning evidence against Billy Wellington – the only Bill she knew. No notes had been taken at the original police interview but both DCI Bradford and DS Boddy were convincing witnesses. Billy had confessed, they had no doubt about it. Mrs Sixsmith wasn't called as a witness for the prosecution. Her change of tune wouldn't help them.

The prosecution case lasted just two days, during which time the defence counsel, Henry Barrington-Smythe, asked if he might be allowed a late witness. Prosecution argued against this, as was their duty, but the judge allowed it, as was his.

Chapter 45

It was the first day of the trial when Lucy called in to see Mrs Sixsmith at the children's home. She'd been to Lucy's house earlier in the day and asked if she could pop round when she got home from school. The house-mother came to the door when Lucy called and took her to the Sixsmiths' private rooms. 'I tried to get hold of Mr Earnshawe but they said he wouldn't be in. He's not at home either,' she said.

'What did you want him for?' Lucy enquired.

'Well, I know he couldn't find that bricklayer . . .'

'No, unfortunately.'

'But the bloke who was with him's come back. He's over there now.'

'What?'

'He's over there now, working.'

Lucy went back to the front door and looked across the road. A young man was working behind the wall. Only his head and shoulders were visible. He was thin-faced and had greasy unkempt hair. He had a long nose surrounded by a tangle of beard.

'I don't like the look of him,' said Lucy, over her shoulder.

'Face like a rat looking through a lavatory brush,' agreed Mrs Sixsmith. 'Types like him might have to force themselves on women.'

'Ah,' said Lucy. 'I see what you mean. If I have a word with him, I might get a better idea of what he's like.'

'I should leave this to the coppers, love.'

'I think I can talk to him without raising suspicion.'

Before Mrs Sixsmith could stop her Lucy was crossing the road. 'Excuse me,' she called out, poking her head over the wall. The labourer was pushing a wheelbarrow full of builder's rubbish along a path. He lowered the wheelbarrow to the ground. He didn't look any better in close proximity: tall and angular, with huge boots and filthy work trousers that were much too short for him, displaying three inches of thin white shin between boot and trouser.

'What is it, love?'

He sounded okay, even chose to smile at her, which wasn't a good look for him. His teeth were what Arnold would call dustbin teeth – one in every yard – but Lucy felt safe enough. If he was a murderer, having a wall between them would do no harm, and Mrs Sixsmith was standing at the other side of the road, watching closely.

'I was wondering if you knew the police were looking for the man who built this wall.'

'What? Kevin?'

'That's him. Yes.'

'Why? It's not such a bad wall, surely? Hey, I bet it's his singing. He's a criminal singer is Kevin.'

'I think it was something to do with the girl who was murdered.'

The man's grin disappeared. 'Oh, right.' He nodded in the direction of the home. 'She was from over there, wasn't she?'

'That's right. Her name was Ethel.'

'What? And they think it was Kev who did her in? Give over, that's not Kev's style.'

'Well, he's done a bunk so it looks a bit suspicious,' said Lucy.

'I thought they'd got someone for it.'

'They have. Do you know who it is?'

'How would I know?' said the labourer.

'It was in the papers.'

'If it wasn't in the sports pages I don't know about it, love. Mind you, I could take a guess who they got for it.'

'Really? Who's that?'

Chapter 46

Opening for the defence, Henry Barrington-Smythe, QC, called for Lucy to give evidence. He smiled at her when she arrived in the witness box and took the oath.

'Would you give the court your full name and address?'

Lucy did as he asked.

'Thank you. Tell me, Lucy, were you with William Wellington on the afternoon of the twenty-third of May nineteen fifty-four?'

'I was, yes.'

'Have you ever had cause to be frightened of William Wellington?'

'Frightened? Why should I be frightened of him? He's a big soft lump is Billy. Nobody's frightened of Billy.'

'So, he's never frightened you in any way?'

'No, never.'

'And could you tell the court what you and William Wellington were doing that afternoon?'

'We'd gone to rescue Wilf from the dogs' home at Crossgates or he'd have been put down.'

'I assume Wilf is a dog.'

'Yes, he is. I'd been looking after him, but the dog people picked him up and took him away to kill him, most prob'ly because he's a bit ugly and he slobbers a lot and never does as he's told, which I didn't think was fair.'

'And was your mission successful?'

'Er, do you mean, did we get him out?'

'That's what I meant.'

'Yes, we did. In fact, Billy let all the dogs out which was maybe a bit naughty, but Billy knows no better and he never means any harm. Not to anybody.'

She looked across at Billy and smiled at him. He smiled back and stuck one thumb up. Barrington-Smythe addressed the judge.

'My Lord, we'll be bringing a witness from the dogs' home to confirm that the accused and Miss Bailey were there at four p.m. that day.'

The judge nodded and wrote something down. Barrington-Smythe returned his attention to Lucy. 'Could you tell the court how you got back home that afternoon?'

'Well, we jumped on a tram at first but you're not allowed to take dogs and we hadn't the fare so we got off after one stop.'

'Where did you get off?'

'On York Road, opposite Dalton's cornflake factory.'

'And after that?'

'After that we walked home.'

'You walked from there to the Moortown Estate?'

'Well, we walked a bit and ran a bit or Billy would have been late for his tea at five o'clock.'

'My Lord, the walking distance from that particular tram stop to the Moortown Estate is over four miles. For them to have covered that distance in an hour they would most certainly have had to walk a bit and run a bit.'

'Yes, I agree with you, Mr Barrington-Smythe. A forced march in the army required us to cover four miles in an hour.'

'Exactly, My Lord. Although in the army you'd have had a pack on your back'

'We would indeed, Mr Barrington-Smythe.'

'But you were trained soldiers, these two are not.'

'Quite so.'

Buttering up a judge never did any harm. Buttering done, Barrington-Smythe returned his attention to Lucy. 'Do you know what time you got back?'

'Yes, I left Billy at about five o'clock. I know this because I asked a lady for the time.'

'And did Billy go straight back to his home?'

'I thought he did but he didn't, he went to the café.'

'Why would he go to the café if it made him late for his tea?'

Mr Newcombe, the prosecuting counsel, got to his feet. 'My Lord, the witness can't possibly know what goes on in the defendant's mind.'

Lucy looked at the judge. 'He's dead right, sir. I don't know what Billy's thinking most of the time, but he is a lovely lad, anyone will tell you that. Wouldn't hurt a fly wouldn't Billy.'

'M'Lord,' protested Newcombe.

'Yes, yes. Just answer the questions, Miss Bailey.'

'I thought that's what I was doing, sir.'

'I have no further questions for this witness,' said Barrington-Smythe before the judge could reprimand her.

Newcombe got to his feet and glared at her. 'Miss Bailey, this escapade of yours to rescue the dog ... How did you manage to persuade the lady in charge of the centre to allow you and William Wellington inside unaccompanied?'

'Well, I told her we'd come to look for a dog, which was the truth.'

'And did you tell her you'd come to look for a particular dog ... that is, the dog you call Wilf?'

'Erm, no. I just said I wanted to look at all the dogs to see if there was one I liked, and if I did my dad would come in his van and he'd buy it for me.'

'Which was a lie.'

'I s'pose so, bu—'

'And was your father going to buy you one of these dogs?'

'My father's dead. He died in the war.'

'I'm sorry to hear that, but I believe you have a stepfather. So presumably it was he who said you could have a dog?'

'Erm, no.'

'So that was another lie. Does your stepfather have a van in which to transport a dog?'

'No.'

'Lie number three. So, none of what you said to the lady at the dog centre was true, was it?'

'Er, no, I don't suppose it was.'

'It was all a pack of lies. Just like the lie you told about what time you got back to the Moortown Estate.'

'No, it was definitely five o'clock. A woman told me what time it was.'

'So you say. But how do we know you didn't travel back by public transport and arrive back at, say, four-thirty?'

'We didn't have any money for the fare.'

'Miss Bailey, we've established that you tell lies. Why should we believe this?'

Lucy was confused. 'I'm just telling you the truth. I didn't tell the woman in the dog place the truth or our plan wouldn't have worked.'

'By the same token, your plan to get your friend Billy off this charge won't work if you tell the truth.'

Barrington-Smythe got to his feet. 'Might I suggest, My Lord, that this witness was just employing clever subterfuge in order to help her achieve her aim of releasing the dog?'

'I fail to see the difference, Mr Barrington-Smythe,' said the judge. 'The better the liar, the more successful the subterfuge.'

'And this subterfuge was extremely successful,' added Newcombe. 'The lady at the dog centre was completely taken in by this witness's ability to lie convincingly. I have no further questions, My Lord.'

'You may stand down, Miss Bailey,' said the judge.

Barrington-Smythe got to his feet. 'M'Lord, I'd like to call Mr Augustus Copley.'

The call went out for Copley to come to the witness box. He was dressed in a smart three-piece suit, Montague Burton's finest, and he'd had his hair cut for the occasion.

'Mr Copley,' said Barrington-Smythe, 'you are the proprietor of Copley's Café on the Moortown Estate, are you not?'

'That's right. Me and my wife run it.'

'Are you acquainted with the accused, William Wellington?'

'Billy, yes. He comes in the café quite a lot.'

'And did he come into your café on the afternoon of May the twenty-third last year?'

'He did, yes. Obviously I remember that day because of what happened to young Ethel.'

'Quite. So you remember him being there?'

'I do.'

'And can you tell us approximately what time he was in?'

'I can tell you exactly. He came in at five o'clock, all flustered like he'd been running, and he left at quarter-past when I told him he'd be late for his tea at the home. Shot off like a rat up a drainpipe he did. Never paid me for his cup of tea.'

'So he was with you between five and quarter-past?'

'He was, yes.'

'As a matter of interest, were you in the café all afternoon, without a break?'

'Is this relevant, Mr Barrington-Smythe?' enquired the judge.

'I'm simply establishing who was where on that fateful afternoon, My Lord.'

'Really? Then you must answer the question,' the judge said to Copley.

'Yes, I was there all afternoon without a break,' he said. 'Busy time at my café, Sunday afternoons. I get a lot of young people in.'

'Yes, I understand it's very popular with teenagers.' Barrington-Smythe smiled. 'I have no further questions for this witness, My Lord.'

'Mr Newcombe?'

'Yes, My Lord. I have just one question. Mr Copley, you say the accused was looking flustered when he came into your café?'

'He was, yes.'

'Out of breath?'

'Yes.'

'As if he'd been engaged in strenuous activity, such as raping and killing a young girl?'

'This is preposterous, My Lord!' called out Barrington-Smythe.

'I have no more questions, My Lord,' said Newcombe, smirking.

Barrington-Smythe glared at him and announced, 'I would like to call Arnold Bailey.'

Arnold hobbled up to the witness box, using a crutch. 'Would you be more comfortable sitting down after you've taken the oath?' asked the judge.

'I would, thank you.'

Arnold took the oath, gave his name and address and sat down.

'Mr Bailey,' said Barrington-Smythe. 'These injuries, which must be more than apparent to the jury, occurred in prison, did they not?'

'They did, yes.'

'Could you tell the court why you were there?'

'I'd been accused of murdering Ethel Tomlinson.'

'On what grounds had you been accused?'

'The police came to our house and found a pair of Ethel's knickers in my saddlebag.'

'The saddlebag of your bicycle?'

'That's right.'

Barrington-Smythe looked at the judge. 'My Lord, I will in due course present a police witness who will say this was as a result of an anonymous tip-off they received by telephone.'

Barrington-Smythe looked at Arnold. 'How do you think the garment got into your saddlebag?'

'Well, someone put them there.'

'Why do you think that was?'

Newcombe was on his feet. 'My Lord, supposition.'

'I appreciate that, Mr Newcombe, but after what this young man's been through I think we should allow him to express an opinion.'

'I think someone tried to frame me,' said Arnold. 'If my pals hadn't come forward to tell the police I'd been with them in Bridlington that day, it'd have been me standing over there where Billy is.'

'Well, it couldn't have been Wellington who tried to frame you as he was in custody,' said Barrington-Smythe. 'Nor is he the type to have friends who might take such a risk on his behalf, so who do you suppose it might have been?'

'I think it was the killer. Stands to reason.'

'I really must object, My Lord!' protested Newcombe.

'Must you?' said the judge. 'Hmm. Mr Barrington-Smythe, please confine your questions to the matter we have before us.'

'I do apologise, My Lord, but what happened to this witness has a major bearing on this case as he was held in custody for several months on the very same charge as my client and I'm at a loss to know who placed the evidence in his possession. It certainly wasn't my client. The item in question was missing from the crime scene, so it's not unreasonable to suppose it was the killer who put it in this witness's saddlebag.'

'Nonetheless,' said the judge, 'we are here to try William Wellington on the evidence put before us. If that evidence is insufficient for a guilty verdict then no doubt the police will follow up on your theory. But right now a theory is all that it is.' He turned to the jury. 'You will disregard all talk about another killer.'

'I have no further questions,' said Barrington-Smythe, satisfied that Arnold had balanced the damage done to the case by his sister.

Newcombe got to his feet. 'Mr Bailey,' he said, 'are you a friend of William Wellington?'

'Not really. It's our Lucy who's friendly with him.'

Barrington-Smythe was on his feet. 'Relevance, My Lord?'

'I'm not sure,' said the judge. 'Mr Newcombe?'

'I'm proposing an alternative theory, My Lord. Simply wondering if the accused had an opportunity to hand the item to a friend before he was arrested, and for that friend to put it in Mr Bailey's saddlebag.'

Barrington-Smythe sprang to his feet, genuinely angry. 'My Lord, such an action would require quick thinking and opportunism. Faculties sadly denied my client by Mother Nature.'

'Might I suggest, My Lord,' said Newcombe, 'that where Mother Nature denies certain faculties, she occasionally increases the power of other faculties to extraordinary levels.

369

For all we know this may be the case with Mr Wellington. I'm led to believe that he has unusual talent as a singer, for example.'

Helen glanced across at the jury to see their reaction to this. One or two of them were nodding.

'Do you have any evidence to support this theory, Mr Newcombe?' enquired the judge.

'I'm afraid we haven't sought such evidence, but who's to say it doesn't exist?'

Barrington-Smythe was on his feet again. 'My Lord, I do hope my learned friend is not trying to imply that the undoubted singing talent of my client afflicts him with an unquenchable desire to commit rape and murder. In fact, I do believe my learned friend is a chorister himself. Perhaps we should alert the court of the danger *he* poses.'

'Quite,' said the judge, glancing at Newcombe, who sang bass in the Harrogate Male Voice choir. The prosecutor made no answering comment.

'Would you like my opinion of Billy?' asked Arnold, unexpectedly. 'I know him better than anyone in here, apart from our Lucy.'

'You're here to answer questions, young man,' said the judge, sternly, 'not to ask them.'

Barrington-Smythe got to his feet. 'It's certainly a question I should like to hear the answer to . . . and I'm sure the jury would too.'

Newcombe got to his feet to protest. 'My Lord—' was as far as he got before the judge waved him back down, saying, 'Very well. Give us your opinion of the accused, Mr Bailey, and please make it brief.'

'Quite simple really,' said Arnold. 'The closest person to me in this world is my sister Lucy, and it never bothered me that she befriended Billy and spent time in his company. Billy Wellington is a completely harmless and defenceless person and presents no threat to anyone. Never has, never will.'

Lucy, having given her evidence, was sitting in the public seats and was astounded to hear her brother speak about her in such affectionate terms. There was a tense silence throughout the court, broken eventually by Newcombe. 'I have no further questions, My Lord.'

'Who is your next witness, Mr Barrington-Smythe?' asked the judge.

'He's Mr David Henderson, My Lord.'

'Is he the late addition to your list?'

'He is indeed, my lord. His evidence is crucial to this case and was only brought to my attention after these proceedings began.'

'Please call the witness, Usher.'

The labourer whom Lucy had approached came into the court. He had changed to better trousers for the occasion and was now wearing dirty jeans and a woollen sweater. Barrington-Smythe was wishing he'd shaved off his beard and brushed the dried mud off his jeans. Newcombe folded his arms, totally confident that no evidence given by this atrocious individual was going to put a dent in the prosecution's cast-iron case, which was based on Ethel's dying word and Billy's confession; a confession that had been verified under oath by two experienced police officers. Henderson gave his name and address and took the oath.

'Mr Henderson, are you chewing something?' enquired the judge.

'What? Oh, yeah. Bit o' chewin' gum, that's all.'

'Remove it, and do not stick it on the side of the witness box.'

Henderson removed his gum and held it in his hand, not knowing what to do with it.

'I assume you have a pocket about your person,' said the judge.

'What? Oh, right.'

He rolled the gum into a ball and put it in his breast pocket. Newcombe smirked and sat back in his seat. Barrington-Smythe stood there patiently, awaiting his turn to question this witness. He spoke with a measure of respect Henderson's appearance didn't seem to merit.

'Mr Henderson, you are a workman employed by J. J. Richards Limited?'

'I am, yes.'

'Could you tell me what you were doing on the afternoon of May the twenty-third last year?'

'That's the day that young lass got murdered, isn't it?'

'It is.'

'Well, I were labourin' for a brickie. We were buildin' a wall opposite the 'ome where she lived.'

'Did you know the dead girl?'

'Only by sight. I knew she were called Ethel. She were watching us workin' on that same afternoon she were killed.'

'Mr Henderson, I'd like you to cast your mind back to that day. Did you see Ethel talking to anyone?'

'Oh, yeah. She went off down t' path with 'im.'

'Which path's that?'

'That path what leads ter them woods behind the 'ome.'

'What time was this approximately?'

'Well, we packed up at four, with it being Sunday, and it wasn't too long before that – quarter to four mebbe.'

'And did you see them come back up the path?'

'Well, no. I mean like I said, we packed up just after that.'

'This man she was with . . . do you know him?'

'Not personally, but I know who he is, yeah.'

He now had the undivided attention of everyone in the court except Billy, who was finding his evidence boring and was studying the Leeds coat-of-arms on the wall behind the judge. He was wondering if, when all these people had stopped talking, he'd be going back to the home or would he be going to the seaside? He wouldn't mind a sherbet lemon and he wondered if Lucy had any she might give him. He wasn't allowed sweets any more and that wasn't right.

'And this man she was with,' the barrister continued, 'did he see you?'

'Well, I doubt it. I saw him talkin' to Ethel, and next thing I know they're off down that path wi' their backs to me. So he probably wouldn't have noticed me.'

'And . . . will he have seen the bricklayer?'

'Kev? No. He were workin' round t' back by that time, doin' some pointing.'

'So this man wasn't aware that anyone had seen him go off with Ethel?'

'Erm, no, I don't suppose he was.'

'But you got a good look him, this man who went off with the girl?'

'Yeah. I was as close to him as I am to you.'

'Could you tell the court who he is?'

'Yeah, well, I thought yer'd never ask. It were that bloke from t'caff – Bill Copley. We sometimes go there for a bite to eat. He's a bit topside with his prices but he does a decent bacon sarnie for a tanner.'

There was a general gasp from the crowded courtroom. Copley wasn't there but his wife was. Her face looked pale and fixed like a stone mask. Her eyes came alive with rage as Barrington-Smythe addressed the judge.

'My Lord, the witness known to this court as Augustus Copley is in fact Augustus William Copley, better known as . . . Bill.'

He left a dramatic pause before he said the name so that the jury would have no doubt as to its significance. Then he quashed any remaining doubt by adding, 'The very name on Ethel Tomlinson's lips when she was asked who did this to her. The last thing she said before she died . . . Bill. Not Billy, not Bootsie . . . Bill.'

Mrs Copley got to her feet, screaming with rage. 'He bloody wasn't there all afternoon! He were lying!'

The judge banged his gavel and glared at her. 'What exactly do you mean by this, madam?'

'Well, I'm his wife.'

'Whose wife?'

'His . . . Bill bloody Copley's wife. He buggered off for a good hour that afternoon. I wondered why he was lying. Now I know. The lousy murdering bastard! He'll have done it all right. Ethel used ter come in t'café. He told her ter call him Bill, the seedy bastard! He's allus knocking me about and I've never been able to trust him wi' women. And I've been living with him all this time and him a murderer! Sharing his bed! Oh my God!'

She broke down in tears; Helen sat there with her mouth open wide, feeling a bizarre combination of shock and delight; reporters scribbled furiously; a police constable left the court to relay events to his sergeant, who would no doubt wish to apprehend Copley before he left the building.

Billy, frightened by all the shouting, began to sing his favourite psalm:

> 'The Lord's my shepherd, I'll not want,
> He makes me down to lie
> In pastures green; he leadeth me
> The quiet waters by . . . '

The judge clutched his gavel and did nothing but stare at Billy in amazement. His counter tenor voice, the highest of all male singing voices, was pure and beautiful and echoing around the courtroom. It was the voice of an angel, coming from this sturdy young man who was standing trial for a murder it would seem he did not commit. The lawyers and court officials turned to look at him, enchanted by his voice and not wanting him to stop. The jury and the people in the public seats sat in entranced silence at this unexpected treat. If this young man was innocent, he was surely entitled to do what he did best. What right did anyone have to stop him?

> *'My soul he doth restore again,*
> *And me to walk doth make*
> *Within the paths of righteousness*
> *E'en for his own name's sake.'*

As he paused for a breath between verses Lucy called out to him: 'Billy!'

He recognised her voice and turned round to her. She put a finger to her lips indicating that he should stop singing. 'That's enough, Billy. It was really lovely.'

The judge banged his gavel three times. Order was restored, silence prevailed. All eyes were now on His Lordship, awaiting his comment on what had just happened. He allowed a long moment to pass before he spoke.

'Thank you, young lady,' he said. 'It was possibly remiss of me not to restore order sooner, but I feel that a power much greater than I was at work here today. The court is adjourned pending further investigations into this matter. I trust you have no objections, Mr Newcombe?'

'Er, no, My Lord.'

'Mr Barrington-Smythe?'

'None at all, My Lord.'

'Er, what about me?' asked Henderson, who was totally bewildered by what was going on around him.

'Oh, yes. Thank you, Mr Henderson. You may stand down,' said the judge.

Chapter 47

Daniel was at work when the call from Helen came through. To say she was over-excited would have been an understatement.

'The judge has adjourned the hearing. They've found out who did it and it wasn't my Billy!'

'What?'

'Lucy got hold of this new witness who actually saw a man go into the woods with the girl.'

'What man?'

'Copley, that man from the café.'

'I thought he was a defence witness?'

'He thought so as well, but they brought another chap in who actually saw him with the girl.'

'What man?'

'He's a builder's labourer. He was working opposite the home on that day, along with the singing bricklayer.'

'I've been trying to track him down myself.'

'It was Mrs Sixsmith who spotted he was back again. She told Lucy . . . and you know what she's like. She shot across the road and had a word with the labourer. He told her he'd seen Copley go off with Ethel, so she told Barrington-Smythe. I don't know why she didn't tell you.'

'I imagine she tried but couldn't get hold of me. I've had a busy twenty-four hours chasing an arsonist that no one else had a clue about.' Daniel raised his voice to say that last bit so that Charlie could hear him.

Helen went on, 'Copley's wife made a right scene in court. She reckons her husband did it ... he was lying about where he was that afternoon apparently. I've spoken to Arnold and he reckons Copley must have planted the knickers in his saddlebag one day when he called in at the café. Apparently there's a girl called Sandra Chillington who'll remember Arnold chatting her up and Copley coming through the door. It was the time he told Arnold about Billy being there from five to quarter-past. I wonder why he did that?'

'To deflect attention from himself – make people think he was one of the good guys. He'll have found out the case was going to be heard in court and he knew Billy wasn't the killer so there was a good chance he'd be found innocent and the police would start looking for the real murderer. Best get himself in place as a valuable witness straight away.'

'Anyway they've just arrested him. He was still in the town hall, having a cup of tea, when they got him. I'm going to get my boy back, Daniel. Hey, you'll never guess what he did in court! He started to sing a psalm. Honestly, I was in tears. Have you ever heard Billy sing?'

'What? He started singing in court?'

'He did. He has a fabulous voice.'

'I don't know what to say.'

'You don't have to say anything, Daniel. You and those two kids have been such a help to him.'

'Thanks. I imagine they'll have Copley in the town hall bridewell, but he'll be brought here when they're through with him. I'd like to have a word with him myself.'

'I was wondering if you fancied having a drink to celebrate?' asked Helen.

He was wondering if this might be jumping the gun once again, but he wasn't going to turn down such an invitation, not from her.

'I've got a couple of things I need to tie up but I'll be in the Victoria in half an hour.'

'I'll be there.'

She sounded as buoyant as he'd ever known her. Could this development affect her outlook on life? Her feelings towards him? Daniel put down the receiver and stared hard at Charlie's back until his sergeant turned round to face him.

'That was Billy Wellington's mother. It seems the real killer has just sprung from the woodwork. He's been arrested at the town hall. This is going to make your confession evidence sound a bit suspect.'

Before Charlie could reply Daniel had gone. He went to the DCI's office, tapped on the door and went in. Bradford was just hanging up the receiver.

'I've heard,' he said.

'About Copley being the killer?'

'Yes, he's just confessed to the boys at the bridewell.'

'That was quick.'

'When he heard about the new witness and his wife's outburst, he folded completely. Told them how the girl had led him on and how he didn't intend hurting her and she was alive when he left her, and all that nonsense.'

'We must hope it's a signed confession made in front of witnesses . . . unlike Billy's.'

Bradford looked at him warningly. 'I hope you're not here to gloat, Daniel.'

'Gloat's not the word I'd use. I just thought I'd do you the courtesy of warning you, sir.'

'About what?'

'You gave evidence that could have ruined Billy's life more than it's been ruined already, and that evidence was false. I intend submitting a report to the chief superintendent giving my view of the whole matter, including Mrs Sixsmith's statement and your phone call to Elliot Hazelhurst of the DPP, who will also have a few questions to answer.'

'I'm sorry, Daniel, I thought we were doing the right thing.'

'Yes, sir, and I believe I'm also doing the right thing in explaining why there was never a real case against Billy Wellington. I think his barrister might have a few choice words to say as well. I'm guessing he'll be asking for costs at least, and Billy should get a nice few quid for wrongful imprisonment.'

'I'd have preferred it if you'd come to gloat. These things happen in police work, Daniel.'

'You mean things that lead to innocent people being locked up, sir?'

The DCI made no comment. Daniel left his office.

Chapter 48

Billy's story made the national newspapers. It did little credit to the courts or to Leeds police, especially with its being a fifteen-year-old girl who had unearthed the vital witness. It was the story of an unmarried mother who had been forced to abandon her illegitimate child at birth and had discovered him in later life, locked up for a crime he hadn't committed. Helen's being an actress who had appeared in *The Makepeace Story* on TV added further spice to the story. It would have been a much more prurient tale had the reporters known that her stepfather was also her son's father.

Maurice Bradley, still living in the bail hostel, read the story and studied the photograph of Helen on the front page. It was a publicity photo they'd got from her theatrical agent. Agents never shy away from publicity on behalf of their clients. He didn't recognise her as his stepdaughter at first, but he recognised the name and he recognised her as the woman who had tried to kill him. Why was that? Should he go to the police? If he did she'd have quite a tale of her own to tell. He also wondered who the father of the boy was. Then he noticed Billy's age and realised who it might be.

'Bloody hell!'

Even by his own low standards this was a crime that made him shudder. Then, as he sat on his bed, he decided he needed to know certain things. He needed to know who the father was; he needed to know if it was Helen who had been sending him the letters that had got his hopes up; he needed to know why she had tried to kill him; and he needed to know where she lived. Middleton, it said in the paper. Well, he knew where Middleton was. It wasn't a big place. All he had to do was ask around in a pub or two as to the whereabouts of their local celebrity, maybe even check her out in the phone book. Shouldn't be too difficult.

*

Two days later, at six o'clock in the evening, Maurice Bradley came knocking at Helen's door. He was as tidy as he could make himself. At fifty-five years old he looked nearer seventy. He'd still retained his prison pallor but sadly not much of his hair. Helen recognised his familiar face instantly. The publicity surrounding the case had taken her by surprise and she'd been worried that he'd find out about her.

She tried to slam the door in his face but he was ready for her and put his foot out. Then he heaved the door open, forcing her back into the small hallway. He came inside, pushing her in front of him, right into the living room where she fell backwards into a chair. He sat down opposite. The sight of him brought back all her old fears and she was wishing that she'd killed him when she had the opportunity. Such was her shock that she was finding it difficult to breathe. Tears trickled down her cheeks.

'Where's this bastard son of yours?'

His voice was just as evil as ever. It brought back awful memories. It never once crossed her mind to tell him that Billy was his son as well. Billy had enough problems in his life without knowing that this monster was his father.

'He's upstairs.'

'Who's his father?'

'A boy I knew.'

'You mean a boy you opened your legs for, you filthy girl!'

She said nothing.

'And you left the child in a bus station. How could you leave a baby in a bus station? What sort of person are you? Leaving a baby in a bus station, you worthless little bitch!'

Still she said nothing. His words polluted the air like poison. She was feeling sickened by the sight and sound of him.

'Please go away,' she murmured.

He took out the anonymous letters she'd sent him and threw them at her.

'Did you send these, you bitch?'

She looked at them and said, 'No.'

She knew things might get worse if she admitted to sending them, and besides, creatures like him weren't entitled to the truth.

'You tried to kill me.'

'Oh, yes.'

'Why did you do that?'

She had to summon up courage to tell him the truth, but tell him she must. 'Because of what you did to me when I was a girl.'

'Is that all?'

He said it as if it was trivial. This sowed the seed of anger within her. 'What do you mean, is that all? You raped your own stepdaughter, time and time again, and you expect me to live with that, do you?'

He leered at her. 'You liked it, girl. Don't tell me you didn't enjoy every minute of it.'

'Yes, I liked it so much I wanted to kill you to drive away the memory of it, and I wish I *had* killed you. Why have you come here?'

'Same reason as you came to see me. I came ter kill yer before yer kill me. I've killed before and got away with it.'

Her eyes moved around the room to see if there was a suitable weapon to hand. Just a poker lying by the fire. That would do if she could get to it in time. His eyes followed hers and he leered again.

'Fancy having another go, do yer, girl? But if I grab it first I'll stick it up inside yer, right where yer used ter like me stickin' things.' His eyes took on a licentious glaze at the thought of it. 'In fact, that's just what I'll do ter yer.'

He made to pick up the poker. She flung herself at him, hammering her fists into him, but he warded them off with his forearms, laughing at her screams. He grabbed her by the throat and flung her to the floor, picking up the poker and ripping at her skirt. She continued to fight and scream. Then Billy came into the room and stood there for a second or two, wondering what was happening. Helen saw him.

'He's hurting me, Billy. Help me!'

Billy grabbed Bradley by the throat and dragged him off her.

'Get him out of the house!' Helen yelled.

With the older man wheezing and choking, Billy dragged him backwards out of the house and threw him down the steps. He lay there for a while, breathing heavily, with Billy and Helen standing over him.

'If I tell the police what you've done they'll put you straight back in jail, won't they?' Helen taunted him.

He pushed himself to his hands and knees and gasped, 'They'll put *you* in jail if I tell them what you've done.'

'Doubt it,' said Helen. 'I'll just deny it. I'm not a criminal with a record like yours. Go away and don't come back.'

Bradley got to his feet and faced them both. 'This isn't over,' he said. 'I'll get you for this, you bitch!'

*

Daniel was sitting in the chair Maurice Bradley had occupied fifty minutes previously. He was there in response to a panicky phone call from Helen. She'd told him everything that had been said by her stepfather, Bradley, and her replies, such as they were. After the violent interlude Billy had gone back upstairs where he had his own television.

'He'd come to kill me, Daniel. He said he'd killed before. He told me exactly how he was going to kill me. He was going to rape me with the poker.'

Daniel grimaced at the thought but admired her for being cool-headed enough to be able to tell him such a detail. Most women would have been desperate to expunge that memory from their thoughts.

'Strictly speaking,' he said, 'this is a police matter. I should contact the Liverpool police and tell them to arrest him and hold him until I get there.'

'I know, but he'd tell them about me trying to kill him.'

'Which you'd deny.'

'Yes, but there was another man at the hostel who saw me. He might remember me, despite the fact I was wearing a wig and talking in an Irish accent.'

'True.'

'And I've got a scar on my stomach where he stabbed me back.'

'Ah, yes. And that could lead to added complications.'

'Such as you helping me?'

'Exactly.'

'I thought when I got Billy back I'd get my life on track, but I haven't. I'll never be right while Maurice Bradley lives.'

'Helen, I do hope you're not going to have another go at him.'

'If I don't, he'll have another go at me. I could easily have finished him off last time, Daniel. I wish I had.'

'But you didn't because you're hampered by humanity.'

'What?'

'It's why you didn't finish him off. You couldn't bring yourself to do it.'

'I think I might, given another chance. I just can't let him live, Daniel. He's like an evil disease I need to rid myself of.'

He got to his feet and put his hands on her shoulders. 'Helen, I want you to promise not to do anything without telling me first, and I want you to keep that promise this time.'

'No,' she said

'What do you mean, no?'

'Daniel, this visit of his has made me feel worse than ever. It's taken me right back to when I was fourteen and leaving my baby at the bus station. I can't shut my mind against it. The fact that he's walking around somewhere and liable to come for me at any time is too much for me to bear. I just want to live my life in peace and bring up my son as best I can.'

'Remember, you won't be able to bring him up if you're locked up for life ... or worse.'

'They wouldn't hang me for killing scum like that.'

'Helen, four months ago they hanged Ruth Ellis. No one expected that.'

'Well, I won't be caught. I'll plan it more carefully.'

Daniel sat back down and said, 'If you were married to a copper, Bradley'd think twice about bothering you.'

She looked up at him, amazed. 'What?'

'I think you heard me.'

'So you'd marry me to keep me safe?'

'Well, that wouldn't be my principle motive. There is another reason.'

'You mean because you love me?'

'Yes, and I'd take a chance on you falling in love with me.'

'Right now I can't see me falling in love with anyone. I'm all empty inside here.' She tapped her chest. 'There's no room for any feelings except love for my son and loathing for my stepfather.'

Daniel sat down, defeated. He'd now had two great loves in his life. One was dead and the other beyond his reach. The sensible thing to do would be to walk away and leave Helen to lead her own life. She'd got her son back.

Perhaps Daniel could warn her stepfather off. Maybe have the Liverpool police pay him a call. It'd do no harm. Another idea occurred to him.

'Would your mother and Vernon take the two of you in, now they know Billy's not a killer?'

'That had crossed my mind. It'd be an upheaval but Cisco Couriers have an East Riding branch so I might get some work from there.'

'Why not give it a try.'

'It'd mean he's directing my life. Every time I woke up at my mother's I'd know I was there because of him. I need to be able to live my own life. I can't let him beat me. I've got to beat him. He's always there, always hurting . . .'

'And you think you can heal that wound by killing him?'

'Only then can I stop being afraid of him coming to kill me. He has no right to be alive, Daniel.'

'I think I need a drink,' he said.

'Well, I won't marry you but I will let you take me for a drink. Billy'll have to come with us. I'm trying to keep him close.'

'Billy will be most welcome. I hear he can be entertaining company.'

'He's a lovely lad. You must hear him sing.'

Chapter 49

The man calling at the bail hostel was asking after Maurice Bradley. He looked official in his grey suit and carrying a briefcase. He said he was a solicitor and had shown the warden a business card. The warden said Maurice Bradley wasn't in; he'd gone to the pub on the corner.

Bradley was in the Howard Arms. His knife wound was itching annoyingly as it often did, as if to remind him of its existence. It was the only wound he'd ever had. The war had left him unscathed, despite his being torpedoed in the Atlantic. He'd been dangerously cold then but otherwise uninjured. He hadn't been scratched by the Germans, just by his stepdaughter – the evil little bitch. He was drinking alone as usual, reading a newspaper, but his mind dwelt more on the anonymous letters and if the bitch been telling the truth when she'd said she hadn't sent them?

The man from the hostel went to the pub and looked around. There were six customers in the place. Only one of them answered Bradley's description. He sat on his own at a corner table, unshaven, with a half-full pint of beer in front of him and a cigarette in his mouth. The man walked over to his table and sat down.

'Excuse me, but are you Mr Maurice Bradley?' He

spoke in an educated Liverpool accent and wore a neatly clipped moustache.

'Who's asking?'

'Oh, sorry.' The man removed a leather glove from his right hand. He shook Bradley's hand and replaced his glove. 'My name is Paul Anderson. I'm a solicitor with Anderson, Peebles and Bates of Manchester. I was told you might be here by the warden of the hostel.'

'What do you want?'

'We've been writing to you on a rather delicate matter.'

'Oh, that was you? I wondered about that. I thought it was someone else but it was you, was it?' It pleased Maurice that it hadn't been Helen who'd sent the letters. There might be something in this for him after all.

'Erm, yes, I'm sorry about the cloak-and-dagger stuff but this is a most delicate matter which involves your, er, recent conviction. Please don't worry, this will be to your advantage.'

'You mean my financial advantage?'

'I believe so, yes. Can I get you a whisky to chase that pint down?'

'Yeah, why not?'

The man went to the bar and came back with two whiskies. He slid one over the table to Bradley. 'There you go,' he said.

Bradley picked up the glass and held it up in salutation, saying, 'Cheers.'

The man clinked his own glass against Bradley's.

'Cheers.'

They both swallowed their drinks in one.

So,' said Bradley, 'what's all this about?'

'It's about your stepdaughter, Helen.'

'Eh? What about her?'

The man in the grey suit leaned over the table and spoke in a quiet voice.

'She tried to stab you, didn't she?'

Bradley was amazed that the man knew this. 'Yes, she bloody did!'

'Well, she's sorry for what she did and she's sent me to put it right.'

'What? By giving me money to keep me quiet?'

'No, she wants to put it right by having me do the job properly.'

Bradley stiffened, fists clenched, aggressive now. 'Oh yeah? And what're you gonna do?'

'Actually, I've just done it.'

'Done what?'

'Well,' said the man, reasonably, 'it's only right that I explain exactly why this is happening. You raped her when she was a young girl and she wants reparation.'

'How d'yer mean, reparation?'

'I mean the sort you get when you put cyanide in a rapist's whisky.'

Bradley's eyes opened wide. He gasped, 'That little bitch—'

'Ah,' said the man, wincing sympathetically. 'Quicker than I thought.'

Bradley clutched his hand to his throat and began to breathe rapidly, unable to speak now. His pallid skin began to turn cherry red.

The man leaned towards him and said softly, 'Your stepdaughter's just had you killed, Maurice. Goodbye.'

Bradley's eyes widened in terror, then they half closed as he slumped into a coma. The man got up to leave. He was already outside the pub when Maurice Bradley keeled over and fell to the floor, quite dead.

The man mounted a bicycle that was leaning against the pub wall and cycled off. He stopped at a letter box and posted a letter addressed to the Liverpool police:

To whom it may concern.
I am the person who poisoned the vile creature Maurice Bradley in the Howard Arms. I did it because he raped a good friend of mine here in Liverpool, one of many such crimes he hasn't been punished for (including murder) ... until now. There is nothing to be gained by punishing me. I don't make a habit of this sort of thing. Our city needs to be rid of such men.

He knew the police would appreciate this. It was always good to know exactly why a murder had been committed, even the murder of a lowlife such as Bradley. The last sentence would indicate that the killer was local, as would the rape victim also mentioned in the letter, and that would be the course their investigation would take. Three minutes and a mile later he rode into a public car park, where he dismounted and loaded the bike on to the back seat of a car. He then removed his spectacles and his false moustache. As far as he was concerned he'd left no fingerprints and no car number plate to be recognised. It was unlikely that anyone would make a connection between him and the late Maurice Bradley. If they did, he had an alibi.

*

Two days later Daniel met Helen in the Victoria Hotel. He was carrying the folded front pages of two newspapers. She was sitting in one of the smaller rooms, somewhat bemused as to why she was meeting him.

'Is this something urgent?' she asked.

'I've got some news for you.'

'What news?'

He handed her the newspapers – two copies of the *Liverpool Echo*.

'Read these. One's today's, one's yesterday's.'

She read the earlier one first. There was a paragraph on the front page about a man who had collapsed and died in the Howard Arms. Police were treating it as a suspicious death. She looked up at Daniel, who said, 'Now look at today's front page.'

The story was featured under a bold headline:

SEX OFFENDER FOUND POISONED IN PUB

Recently released serial sex offender, Maurice Bradley, collapsed and died in the Howard Arms on Tuesday evening. It is suspected that his drink was poisoned by a man who entered the bar and bought Bradley a whisky, which the police say was poisoned with potassium cyanide. The suspect left just before Bradley collapsed. He was described as being between 30 and 40 years old with a moustache and spectacles, possibly a disguise. He was wearing a dark suit, and spoke with a local accent.

393

Helen looked up at Daniel once again and said, 'He's dead?'

'Yes.'

'Maurice Bradley is definitely dead?'

'That's what it says.'

She read more of the article, then asked, curiously, 'Daniel, is this in the national papers as well?'

'Not that I know of.'

'Then how did you get to know about it?'

'I'm a copper.'

'So, coppers know about every murder committed all over the country?'

'I've been keeping my eye on Liverpool, what with your stepfather being there.'

Helen went quiet, then she asked, 'Did you do this?'

'The report said the man had a local accent,' Daniel pointed out.

'I can do a Scouse accent, I bet you can as well.'

'You're making me sound like a criminal. I'm a police-man, Helen.'

'Daniel, I don't want it to be you, because the police have a habit of catching killers and I wouldn't want them having to catch you.'

'They have no reason to come after me.'

'Good, my mother will be relieved.'

'Your mother? She doesn't know me.'

'No, she'll be relieved Maurice is dead. She thought I was going to bump him off. In fact, she volunteered to help me.'

'I think a lot of his other victims will be relieved when they hear about his death.'

'Whoever did this did us all a big favour,' Helen agreed, looking at him with curiosity.

He smiled back, blandly.

*

The following day Daniel rang an old associate in the Liverpool police on a matter not connected with Bradley's murder. He skilfully manoeuvred the conversation around to a point where it was his associate who mentioned the pub killing. Daniel was told they had drawn a complete blank but weren't going to waste too much time checking on any of Bradley's victims who might have sought retribution. His contact also mentioned an anonymous letter that was pointing them to a particular villain who had a sound alibi, but he would, wouldn't he? It was a delicate area, with potential press repercussions they could do without. This was what the police privately called a GRC – a good riddance case.

A happy Helen invited Daniel out to dinner. During the meal there had been no talk of her stepfather's death. Daniel certainly didn't want to bring up the subject – he had another one entirely in mind. They were having coffee when she looked at him and said, 'I still have a problem, Daniel.'

'Your stepfather's memory troubling you?'

'No. He's gone and so have all the horrors that he brought me. I feel free of him and I thank you dearly for making that happen. My problem is confusion.'

'So is mine at this moment in time.'

'I'm sorry. I need to explain myself better but I don't want to hurt you.'

Daniel's heart sank. He could see what was coming and thought he might as well beat her to it.

'You don't love me?'

'Well . . . it's not quite as simple as that. My problem is that with the enormous thing you've done for me, I feel as if I'm obliged to fall in love with you.'

'What enormous thing would that be?'

'I think we both know what I'm talking about.'

'Ah, you're on about that again, are you? I hope Chief Inspector Bradford doesn't get wind of your suspicion. I'm not his favourite copper as it is. He's been moved over to uniform for what he almost did to Billy.'

'Serves him right. I'm surprised they didn't sack him.'

'He's not a bad copper. Just one who likes to get quick results.'

'I can't fall in love with you to order, Daniel.'

'Well, it would be handy if you could, but I can hardly force it on you. I'm sorry I turned down your kind offer, by the way.'

'You turned me down because you thought you might be a disappointment to me.'

'Possibly, but I know you wouldn't have been a disap-pointment to me.'

Helen smiled. 'What I'm trying to say is that it if you asked me to marry you, I would say yes simply because I'm so beholden to you. You've given me my life back.'

'That's not a good basis for a marriage.'

'I agree. So, are you going to ask me to marry you?'

'Erm, possibly not, under the circumstances. In fact, definitely not.'

'I'd be obliged if you didn't . . . I'm so sorry.'

He sighed. 'Don't be. You've had a rough time and your happiness is my chief concern.'

'Oh, God! Why must you be so bloody noble? I'm not sure what I did to deserve the risk you took for me.'

'Well, if you change your mind about this you must propose to me immediately, don't wait for a leap year. I'm not on the open market for a wife so I should still be available, unless of course Doris Day takes a shine to me. Mind you, even Doris would have to pass muster with my daughters and they already approve of you.'

Daniel's manner was humorous but it cloaked a deep inner despair. Was there nothing he could do to win this woman over?

Chapter 50

Helen smiled at the young man who was just leaving by the gate as she called at Lucy's house. She had no specific reason to go there other than to share her latest good news with this girl who had made such a difference to her life. It was Lucy who had fought to set Billy free, and Lucy who had brought Daniel into Helen's life. She was as sure as she could be that it was Daniel who had killed her step-father, and she felt guilty about turning down his unspoken proposal. Lucy answered her knock at the door.

'Oh, it's you. I thought it was Tony coming back for something.'

'That was Tony?' asked Helen.

'Yeah, he's a pal of Arnold's but he's just asked me out to the pictures.'

'I do hope you said yes. He's very good-looking.'

'He is, and he's really nice as well. Trouble is, he's one of Arnold's pals – one of them who got him out of prison.'

'Is that a problem?'

'Well, I'm not sure if going out with one of your brother's best pals is a good idea. A few years ago they had belching competitions. It's hard to admire a boy who used to go in for belching competitions.'

'I see your point.'

Helen was in her riding leathers, holding her crash helmet under her arm. 'It's not a problem I could advise you on, never having been in that situation myself.'

'Come in, Helen. Don't stand on the step. Everyone's out. I'll make us a cup of tea.'

'Well, I've just popped in for a natter, to tell you how Billy's getting on and one or two other things. I've got him a job at the courier depot. Just fetching and carrying, but they all like him and he's a good worker.'

'I bet it's a doddle after what they had him doing in Rampton.' Lucy filled the kettle from the tap and put it on the gas cooker as Helen sat down at the kitchen table. 'I'd love to come over and see him. That day in court when they found out it was Copley who killed Ethel was brilliant. I was looking at Billy. He'd no idea what was going on.'

'Of course you knew what David Henderson was going to say, didn't you?'

'I did. When he told me he'd seen Copley with Ethel, I went mad with him for not coming forward. I told him how he could have prevented both Billy and our Arnold from being locked up ... Honest, Helen, I could have really slapped him, the dozy sod.'

'I've got some other news as well,' said Helen.

'What's that?'

'Well, you remember when I told you about my step-father ...'

'Er, yeah. How could I forget?'

'Well, you can forget him now. He's dead. Somebody murdered him.'

'Wow! Who?'

'They don't know.'

'Do *you* know?'

Helen was taken aback. Did she know? Of course she knew. Or did she?

'No, I don't. It was a man who went into a pub and poisoned his drink. The police think he was connected with one of my stepfather's victims. He'd just done five years in prison for a sexual assault.'

'Sounds like someone did you a favour.'

'A massive favour, Lucy. As big a favour as you did when you got Henderson to give evidence.'

'Well, that wasn't just me.'

'In my eyes it was. And my life's beginning to take a turn for the better now.'

'Does this mean you and Daniel might get together? You should, you know.'

Helen looked at Lucy, trying to gauge her sincerity. 'I thought you had a crush on him.'

Lucy blushed slightly. To her it hadn't been a crush and it wasn't in the past tense. 'He's too old for me, Helen. Much too old.'

'So, what about handsome Tony? Are you going to the pictures with him?'

'I said I would but only because it's a picture I want to see.'

'Is he working?'

'No, he's at Leeds University studying English Literature.'

'Handsome and clever, eh?'

'I suppose so.'

'And how old . . . eighteen?'

'Same age as Arnold, yeah.'

'Not too old then. When you go out with someone your own age you get to enjoy life's new experiences together. An older man's seen it all, done it all. What's new to you isn't new to him.'

'With respect, Helen, how would you know that?'

'I read, Lucy. And I read about everything I've missed out on. For me it's all too late, but not for you.'

'Are you trying to put me off Daniel because you want him for yourself, because if you are I can tell you, he's not interested in me.'

'No, it's not that. And there's no romance between me and Daniel.'

'That won't be any of his doing. He's nuts about you and you should be nuts about him if you've any sense.'

Lucy was pouring hot water into the teapot. 'Do you take sugar?'

'No, thanks, just a drop of milk. I'm afraid my recovery hasn't arrived at the point where I can manage romantic feelings towards any man. I sometimes wonder if I might be a lesbian.'

Lucy paused for thought. 'Blimey, Helen! If you're one of them you are in trouble. They lock you up for that, don't they? They lock fellers up anyway. Look at that Lord Montagu who got put away last year.'

'You can't help what you are, Lucy. Anyway, I didn't say I *was* one I just said it might explain the way I feel about men.'

'Isn't it more to do with the way you feel about women?'

Helen laughed. 'Okay, I give in. I don't feel romantically attracted to women either.'

'I should think what your stepfather did is explanation enough,' said Lucy.

'Yes, you're probably right,' sighed Helen. 'I just hope he hasn't killed my romantic inclinations stone dead. I really wish I could feel the same way as you do about Daniel.'

'This is a very weird conversation, Helen. Can we talk about Billy?'

Chapter 51

Daniel was reading a file on a robbery case that had been passed to him. He sensed Charlie looking at him from his desk at the other side of the room. The atmosphere between them had been strained since the Billy Wellington trial. Charlie had been suspended pending investigation of his conduct in court but had been restored to his job with no loss of rank or pay. He was now standing in front of Daniel's desk, forcing his boss to look up at him.

'What is it, Charlie?'

'I, er, I understand you spoke up for me, boss . . . and I'd like to say thank you.'

'Boss now, is it? I used to be sir, now I'm boss.'

'Well, that's what you are, and you acted like a boss when you told me to tell the truth in court.'

'You shouldn't have needed me to tell you that, Charlie. An innocent young man's life was at stake. You can't play around with the truth under such circumstances.'

'I was influenced by the DCI, boss.'

'I know that, Charlie, that's why you got away so lightly. In my book you both committed perjury. I'm amazed the DCI didn't drop a rank.'

'I don't imagine I've done my promotion prospects any good, boss.'

'Will you stop calling me boss! I'm sir to you. And, yes, you did set yourself back quite a bit. Just keep your nose clean from now on, Charlie.'

'Sir.'

Charlie turned to go back to his desk then paused mid-stride. 'Is it true that you've taken up running, sir?'

'Well, I wouldn't call it running. We athletes call it jogging. Yes, I do three five-mile runs a week to get myself back in shape. Does you no harm to take some exercise.'

Daniel was actually into his second week of running and was just beginning to feel the benefit. His daughters had encouraged him to take it up and had gone with him to town to buy a tracksuit and suitable running shoes. He had no fixed schedule, just ran when he could fit it in. The man in the Austin 12 who had been watching his house from a distance found this most inconvenient.

Daniel was home that afternoon and decided to take advantage of the empty roads before the rush-hour traffic arrived. He jogged down The Avenue and swung right up King Lane, a narrow hill leading out to the country. The man in the Austin already knew Daniel's preferred route and drove up a side road to head him off. When Daniel was halfway up the hill the Austin was already at the top, heading his way. Daniel was at the opposite side of the road from the car, unaware of the danger it posed.

When he was no more than five yards from Daniel the driver swung the wheel to the right and hit the jogging policeman full on at forty miles an hour, knocking him clean over the bonnet, banging his head against the windscreen and sending him spinning sideways on to the road. He looked in his mirror and saw Daniel lying in a heap, not moving. Another car appeared at the bottom of the hill, coming his way. He put his foot down and carried on, his work done.

The other driver would tell the police he'd seen a black car pass him. He might even remember the make, but definitely not the registration number. The police would check all such Austins as best they could, but their checks wouldn't extend as far as Newcastle where that car was from.

Daniel was rushed by ambulance to St James's Hospital. He had nothing to identify him on him and it wasn't until his daughters got worried that he hadn't returned from his run that they rang his colleagues at the police station. It took Charlie just a few minutes to track his boss down to St James's, where he had been in surgery for over an hour.

'I think he's one of ours – Detective Inspector Daniel Earnshawe. I'm on my way down.'

An hour later Daniel was still in surgery. Charlie, Jeanette and Carol were waiting outside the theatre in worried silence. All they knew was that he was very poorly.

'Do you think I should ring Helen?' said Carol, eventually. She was feeling so helpless she felt she had to do something.

'I think she'd want to know,' agreed Jeanette. 'I've got her number in my diary.'

She took a small book from her bag, opened it and gave it to her sister.

'There's a public phone down there,' said Charlie. 'Do you need any change?' He felt he needed to make a contribution.

'No, I've got some pennies, thanks.'

Carol got up and went to the phone. Tears were beginning to roll down her face as she picked up the receiver. She had to tell someone that her dad was in hospital and she didn't know if he was going to live. She put the receiver down again and tried to pull herself together but it was no use, she couldn't manage to make the call. She went back to the waiting area, still in tears.

'All right?' said Jeanette.

'No, I couldn't do it.'

'Would you like me to?' asked Charlie.

'Yes, please. This is the number.'

Charlie took a deep breath and picked up the phone. He knew who Helen was, and that his boss had a thing for her that hadn't amounted to anything. He didn't know how she would take this news.

'Hello, Leeds 703056.'

'Is that Helen Durkin?'

'Yes, who's this?'

'My name's Charlie Boddy. I work with Detective Inspector Earnshawe.'

'Ah, yes. I've heard him talk about you. What is it?'

'He's been involved in a road accident and is in St James's Hospital.'

There was a short silence as Helen took in what he'd told her, then she asked, 'How is he? Is he all right?'

'He's been quite badly injured and is in theatre right now.'

'Charlie, is he going to be okay?'

'I don't know, Helen. I'm sorry. I'm down here with his daughters waiting to hear.'

'I'm coming.'

Helen felt a dark sickness surge through her body. Daniel might die, that was pretty much what Charlie had just told her. Whatever latent feelings she'd had for Daniel came surging to the surface, but it was too late. She knew it would be too late.

She got on her bike and thought of Lucy, who wouldn't know. She wasn't on the phone so unless someone went round to tell her, Daniel might die without Lucy being aware he was injured. Helen pointed her machine towards north Leeds and Lucy's house. Forty-five minutes later they joined the gloomy trio in the waiting area outside the operating theatre.

'Any news?' asked Lucy.

Three heads shook simultaneously.

'He's been in there for three hours,' said Charlie. 'We don't really know anything.'

'How did it happen?'

'Hit and run, apparently.'

'Just like Mum,' said Jeanette, who had obviously been crying.

'We should ring Gran and Granddad,' said Carol, who was fighting back her own tears for Jeanette's sake.

'Oh, heck, we should, shouldn't we?' said Jeanette helplessly.

'Do you want me to do that?' said Charlie.

The girls looked at each other and nodded. 'I've got their number,' said Jeanette. 'They live in Bournemouth. They retired there a few years ago.'

'I bet they'll come straight up,' said Carol.

Jeanette nodded, in floods by now. Lucy looked away

from her, trying to fight her own tears. It was a losing battle. Soon everyone was in tears except Charlie, who was on the verge and blinking rapidly. He put an arm around Lucy and she took comfort from it. A man in a green surgical gown arrived. They all looked at his face in anticipation. His expression was serious.

'To whom am I speaking?' he asked politely.

'We're his daughters' said Carol, indicating herself and Jeanette.

'Right, your father has sustained multiple injuries. We've patched him up internally. We've removed his spleen, which isn't vital to his existence although he might be more susceptible to infections as a result; he had a punctured lung which we've repaired; he had damage to his kidneys and a nasty knock on the head that fractured his skull. Apart from that he's sustained many broken bones which are now being fixed by an orthopaedic surgeon. The good news, if we can call it that, is that there's no apparent damage to his spinal column, which is something of a miracle, considering what else was broken.'

'Which bones are broken?' asked Charlie, still with his arm around Lucy.

'Three in his left leg, including his femur – his right leg survived unscathed. Then three ribs, his left shoulder, his left arm and wrist and, erm . . . his left ankle, I think. He's also sustained extensive abrasions and may need plastic surgery.'

'Please, not to his face!' said Carol who, like Jeanette, had listened to their father's list of injuries in mounting dismay.

'No, his face is unscathed. His right arm may need a skin graft. It all depends how well it heals on its own.'

'Is he out of danger?' Helen asked.

'Not yet, I'm afraid. But I would never say that until I'm one hundred per cent sure.'

'How sure are you?' Lucy asked.

'Probably about seventy-five per cent at the moment, but I've always been very conservative about these things. If he's still with us after our bone doctor's finished, I'll stick another ten per cent on that.'

'How long will that take?' asked Helen.

'Oh, another couple of hours. We've got our top man working on him and he does like to take his time, especially on policemen. He's never lost a copper yet, so he tells me.'

'When can we see him?' asked Carol and Jeanette simultaneously.

The surgeon rubbed his chin. 'I suppose I'd be wasting my time advising you all to go home and come back in the morning.'

'Yes, you would,' said Lucy.

'Right ... well.' He looked at his watch. 'A couple more hours in surgery, then we have to give him time to wake up and to stabilise his pain, which will be considerable. I'd say midnight at the very earliest, and even then it would only be close relatives allowed in.'

'That's us,' said Carol. Jeanette nodded her agreement.

'I'll stay anyway,' said Lucy.

'And me,' added Helen.

Charlie said nothing. It had occurred to him that this might be a hit and run in retribution by someone Daniel had offended. If so, the hitman needed to be caught before he had another go at the boss. Charlie realised he still had his arm around Lucy and she'd still made no attempt to move away. It was Lucy he spoke to.

'I need to go. There's something I've got to do.'

She turned and smiled at him.

'Thanks for being here, Charlie. My dad thinks a lot of you.'

'Does he? I haven't noticed.'

'Better not tell him I told you, then.'

'I wouldn't dare tell him that.'

Chapter 52

At 10.30 the orthopaedic surgeon came to say he'd done as much as he could for the time being, and that the patient was no longer critical. He also confirmed that Daniel did not have a spinal injury.

'Does this mean he'll definitely get better?' asked Jeanette.

'The signs are positive, but ask me again in twelve hours. I can be more definite then.'

*

Charlie had gone to the police station to report his suspicions to Detective Superintendent Foulds, the senior officer on duty.

'I'm thinking it could be Leonov's doing, sir. Hit and run. It's his MO. I imagine his man'll try again when he finds out DI Earnshawe's not dead.'

Foulds nodded. 'The first car on the scene passed a big black Austin, pre-war, probably an Austin Twelve, maybe a Ten. I'm putting a dozen CID in and around the Casualty entrance and parking areas. They won't go for him tonight, with him being pretty much out of their reach, but when he goes on to a ward we'll leave no uniforms guarding it and tempt them to go for him there.'

'You mean, use the DI as bait, sir?'

'I'm guessing it's what he'd have done himself. If this hitman's working for Leonov he won't want to leave the job half done.'

'I'd like to be one of the bodyguards, sir.'

The superintendent looked him up and down. 'I think I've got a job you can do, DS Boddy.'

*

It was three o'clock the following afternoon when Daniel was taken from ICU to an emergency ward. He'd been in and out of consciousness, only waking up properly when he was transferred from a trolley to a bed. His daughters were with him. He recognised them for the first time.

'Carol, Jeanette, what's happening?' His voice was hoarse.

'You've been in an accident, Dad. You're in St James's.'

'What sort of accident?'

'A car ran you down.'

'A car? Where was I?'

'King Lane. You were out for a run.'

'Why can't I move anything?'

'You're mostly in pot. You're okay. No spinal injury. You'll make a full recovery.'

'Okay? Is this what you call okay? I'm glad I'm not ill or anything.'

Carol and Jeanette smiled. They were going to get their dad back.

*

At six o'clock the man parked his Austin on Stanley Road, a good quarter of a mile away from the hospital. Leonov still had people in his pay everywhere, including a woman in the bed allocation office who, for the odd tenner, more than her week's wages, was willing to give out information regarding patients. She didn't see what harm it could do when she told Leonov's man that patient Daniel Earnshawe was due to be transferred to Ward 26, bed 7.

The man entered the hospital dressed in a white coat. He had a stethoscope around his neck and a six-inch dagger in his pocket. He walked with a confident air, pausing only to glance at the noticeboards directing him to Ward 26. The CID people didn't spot him, some of them being preoccupied with the two Austin Tens and an Austin Twelve that had entered the hospital grounds.

The man went up in the lift to the second floor and got out. He turned right, as directed by the sign in front of him. There were no visitors at this hour, just hospital staff about their own business, as was he. It was a big hospital and not every doctor was known. An unknown man in a white coat might be given a respectful nod by a passing nurse or porter, no more.

Just outside Ward 26 a porter approached, pushing an empty wheelchair. He scarcely glanced up at the man, who really appreciated his anonymity in such circumstances. He would enter the ward, check that bed 7 was unattended, walk up to it quickly, kill the hopefully sleeping patient and walk away. If the patient was awake he would pretend to listen to his heart with his stethoscope and, instead, thrust the knife into it. The patient would be dead before he could make a sound and would probably not be discovered for several minutes.

The fake doctor was within six feet of the bed when his right arm was grabbed and twisted up behind his back. His whole body was forced forward, his feet kicked out from under him, ending with him flat on his face on the floor with a porter lying on top of him. The porter whom the man had just passed looked up at the faces of two nurses peering down at him and said, 'If I've made a mistake, I'll apologise to him but I don't think this is a doctor. Anyone recognise him?'

He pulled the man's head to one side so that they could see him. The nurses shook their heads, as did a ward sister who appeared on the scene.

'What is this?' she demanded.

'I'm a police officer,' said Charlie. 'I think this man came to kill the patient in bed seven.'

*

Daniel was awake enough to realise the danger he'd just been in. The hitman had been taken away by other officers called to the scene. Charlie stopped to chat to his boss and bask in a rare moment of glory.

'Okay,' said Daniel. 'I give in. Who's idea was it that this wasn't a normal hit-and-run accident?'

'Well, I didn't know for certain,' said Charlie, 'but the hit-and-run is Leonov's MO as you well know, sir. So, if it *wasn't* an accident the odds were that it was Leonov's doing.'

'So it was your idea?'

'Well, yes. I suppose it was. I told the super what I thought and he agreed with me and set everything up.'

'With you as a porter?'

'Right, that was his idea. He said I had the look of a hospital porter.'

'So ... and I'm trying to get my mind around this ... you see this bloke in a white coat come into the ward and you just set about him What made you so sure he wasn't a doctor?'

'Well, of course I wasn't a hundred per cent sure, but I'd clocked all the doctors who've been in and out of here and he wasn't one of them, so I thought, *Hello, is he kosher?*'

'He might have just come on shift.'

'Ah, but he was also wearing boots.'

'Boots?'

That's right. Have you ever seen a self-respecting doctor wearing boots? Being a doctor's a job for shoes.'

'Is it? I didn't know that.'

'Good job I knew then . . . sir.'

*

Helen was unaware of what had happened when she called to see Daniel that same evening.

'Just a flying visit,' she said. 'The last time I was here you were almost at death's door.'

'I was at death's door an hour ago.'

'Oh?'

He told her the story of the recent attempt on his life. Her face was a mask of concern, which pleased him to the extent that he exaggerated the drama of it all. Helen held his hand.

'I, er, I've come to ask you something and I'd like you to tell me the truth, Daniel, because it's important to me.'

'I always tell you the truth.'

'I don't think you do. You see, I don't think I've properly laid the ghost of my stepfather.' She tapped her chest. 'He's still in here, gloating.'

'Well, he won't have much to gloat about.'

'I needed him to know that I was the cause of his death.

415

I needed him to know that I'd got him back for what he did. As it is, I feel he died thinking he got away with it, and that's not a good feeling. I know I must sound weird but I can't help it.'

He looked up at her. The look of concern was still on her face but the reason for it was now different. It made her even more appealing – irresistible even. He held her gaze and knew she'd won this battle. She needed to hear the truth.

'Oh, he knew all right.' Daniel spoke in a low voice. 'The reason he was dying was made abundantly clear to him. He had only a minute to think about it but it will have been the very last thing on his mind. He knew you'd got him.'

Helen's expression lifted. 'You're not just saying this?'

He crossed his heart. 'No, Scout's honour. When a man dies he's entitled to know why, and Maurice Bradley knew exactly why he was dying – and he wasn't too pleased with you. Called you a nasty name. Last word on his lips.'

'I bet it began with a B.'

'Bitch.'

'That's the one.'

Helen smiled and hung her head down, shaking it. Then she looked up at Daniel with tearful eyes.

'Is this it then, Daniel? Is it all over for me? Is this as good as I'm going to feel?'

'I doubt if you know how you're going to feel until it's all sunk in.'

'Could you tell me any more about what happened? I think I need to know as much as I can.'

'There wasn't much to it really.' He indicated that she should bring her head closer to his. 'I found the hostel easily enough and had a word with the warden, who told me Bradley'd be in a pub called the Howard Arms. This made things a bit easier although I had a half bottle of whisky in my pocket just in case the deed had to be done in his room.'

'Would the warden recognise you?'

'Doubt it. I was wearing a false moustache and horn-rimmed glasses and I spoke with a Scouse accent.'

'I knew you'd be able to do Scouse.'

'Anyway I went to the pub, which was nearly empty, and recognised your stepfather immediately. He was sitting at a table on his own, reading a paper. I went over to him and introduced myself as the solicitor who'd been sending him letters. I asked did he want a whisky? He said yes. I bought him one and laced it with potassium cyanide that I'd got from the police evidence room. He drank it straight down and died within a minute. I got up and left before anyone noticed they had a dead man in the room. I had a bike outside that I rode to where I'd parked my car, just in case anyone took the number. Stuck the bike in the car and drove home.'

She shook her head in amazement, saying, 'Easy as that, eh?'

'Not really. I've killed in the war so I've got over the shock of taking another man's life, but killing's never easy.'

'Even a creature like my stepfather?'

'I must admit I felt worse about killing Germans than I did about him.' Daniel put a finger to his lips and said, 'My life is now in your hands.'

She kissed him on his forehead and said, 'Daniel, your secret couldn't be safer.'

Chapter 53

St James's Hospital, Leeds
January 1956

Daniel had been there for five weeks and was fed up of being hospitalised. He was spending much of his day with the physiotherapists. His main injury was the broken femur in his left leg, and his physiotherapy was hampered by his broken left arm and wrist, and his left shoulder. These had more or less healed and he was now able to support himself on crutches. All his pot had been removed except for the one on his left leg. His internal injuries gave him little pain and he was constantly pestering his doctor to discharge him.

'Your blood pressure's still too high, Daniel, just give it another few days and allow us to be fully satisfied with your progress.'

He was under the impression that his superiors in the police force had issued instructions for him not to be discharged a minute before the hospital needed to.

'Have you been talking to my bosses?'

'We're just looking after your welfare, that's our job. If you have a relapse you won't thank us for letting you go.'

'Look, even my visitors are getting brassed off. They

have much better things to do than trek out to this place. Hospital visiting's as big a pain in the arse as being a patient is. I need to be at home.'

'You need daily physio using our equipment. How are you going to do that at home?'

Daniel couldn't argue with this one. Then he had a thought. 'I was reading in the paper yesterday about a young lad who might never walk again if he doesn't get an operation that they can only do in America.'

'Yes, I've heard about him – there's a fundraiser for him but I think the cost is going to be too much.'

'Do you know him?'

'No, he's in the paediatric ward.'

'According to the paper his name's Keith Adamthwaite. I was wondering if I might have known his dad.'

'Well, I believe his father died in the war.'

'Yes, that's what it said in the paper. If it's the bloke I think it is, I was with him when he died. I visited his wife and son afterwards but lost touch. John was a good friend.'

'I see.'

'I wonder if you could do me a favour, Doctor. Could you find out if his mother's name's Doreen, and is the boy is about twelve years old, and where they live?'

'Shouldn't be a problem.'

The doctor returned an hour later with enough information to confirm that the boy was the son of Daniel's pal, John Adamthwaite. The boy he'd promised to 'keep an eye on'. The boy he hadn't seen for eleven years.

'I would add,' said the doctor, 'that you're going to make a full and complete recovery, so don't give us any more aggravation. Young Keith will never walk again unless his mother can raise five thousand pounds to send him to a specialist in America, and he's giving us no aggravation at all.'

'How much has she raised so far?'

'Five hundred maybe, which is quite a lot considering, but it'll never be enough. Pity — there's a specialist over there who's a genius and he works in a hospital with amazing facilities, so I'm told.'

Daniel gave this some thought. 'Who's doing the collecting for him?'

'His family mainly, although his school's got a fundraiser going. His mother's here every day, sitting by his bed, hoping for a miracle.' He raised an eyebrow as he looked down at Daniel. 'You've already had your miracle.'

'Okay, okay, consider me told off. I'll give you no more trouble.'

The doctor left a chastened Daniel, who picked up his crutches and hobbled off to the telephone to ring home.

'Jeanette, it's Dad.'

'Hiya, Dad.'

'Are you coming this evening?'

'No, it's Carol's turn this evening.'

'What? You're taking it in turns, are you?'

'We do have other things to do on an evening, Dad.'

'There's something I'd like her to bring me.'

*

That evening his daughter had just left when another visitor came into the ward. She looked at the name on the foot of his bed and said, 'Daniel?'

He looked up. He knew who she was but eleven years and worry had changed her quite a lot.

'Hello, Doreen.'

'Long time no see,' she said.

'I know. My fault.'

'Too busy chasing the baddies, eh?'

'Something like that.'

'I heard about your wife,' she said, 'I was really sorry. I wish I'd met her.'

'You'd have liked her, Doreen. How are you?'

'Oh, struggling on. Never got married again.'

'I imagine John was a hard act to follow.'

'Well, he was no Errol Flynn but he made me laugh. You know about our Keith, I suppose?'

'Yes, I read about him in the paper. Wasn't exactly sure it was your lad until I checked. What's his problem?'

'Well, without going into all the technical details, which I don't fully understand myself, he's got a muscular wasting disease and he can't walk. If he's not treated soon, he'll spend the rest of his life in a wheelchair.'

'I understand you're trying to raise money to send him to America for specialist care?'

'I am, yes, but I think it's going to be a bit too expensive, what with me having to go with him. I can't just send him on his own.'

'Of course not. I understand you're trying to raise five thousand pounds.'

'*Trying's* the word – it's not going too well.'

She was a woman of around his own age, with long-term sadness visible in her eyes. Daniel gave what he was about to do some deep thought.

'Doreen,' he said, 'just before John died he asked me to tell you he loved you.'

'Yes, I believe you told me that.'

'But just before that, he asked me to keep an eye on his lad.'

'I didn't know that.'

'He went very quickly. Our gunner killed the man who shot him.'

'Good. John died in your arms, didn't he?'

'He did. He wasn't frightened and he showed no sign of being in pain. He spoke to me for a few seconds, then he went – quick as that. I had to leave him with a medic, with me having a job to do.'

'He thought the world of you, Daniel.'

'We were good pals. Look, going back to the promise I made John. I'd really like to help Keith, but I need to you to place a lot of trust in me and to keep this strictly between us.'

'Keep what between us?'

'I've been given some money to give to you by a donor who wishes to remain anonymous, and I don't want anyone to know it came to you via me because then people will start asking me who he is, and I could do without all that.'

'I see.' She sounded uncertain.

'Doreen, you can trust me.'

'I do trust you.'

'Not a word to anyone?'

'No,' she said. 'Not a word. But I don't see why you should worry about me telling anyone.'

'You might when you know how much it is.' He kept his voice low.

'Oh, how much is it?' Her voice was equally low.

'It's in a briefcase in my cupboard. Could you take it out and put it on the bed?'

She opened his cupboard and took out a leather brief-case.

'Okay, take a look inside.'

She did as he asked and gave a gasp. The case was full of used notes. She looked up at him.

'Daniel, h . . . how much is there?'

He leaned forward and said, so that only she could hear. 'Four thousand three hundred and sixty-five pounds.'

'What?'

'I think you heard me.'

'And a man's given me all that?'

'He has, yes, but he doesn't want you to know who he is. So, as far as you're concerned, it was given by a gener-ous donor who wishes to remain anonymous. Can you remember that?'

'What?' She clasped a hand over her mouth. 'Of course I can, yes.'

'That's all we ask, Doreen. Me and the generous donor, that is. I hope it's enough to get Keith to America.'

'Oh, it is, it will be. We've already got nearly six hun-dred pounds.' She was in tears now and leaning forward in an attempt to hug him.

'Hey! I'm a bit fragile, Doreen.'

'Oh, right, sorry, Daniel. Oh, dear. I never thought anything like this would happen.'

'Good things sometimes happen to good people, Doreen. I'll keep in touch to see how Keith's going on and report back to my, er, generous friend.'

'Oh, please thank him for me, Daniel. Thank him from

the bottom of my heart. I'll take this to the bank first thing tomorrow. They'll be so amazed.'

'Remember to tell them the donor was anonymous, that's most important.'

'I'll do that, Daniel.' She leaned towards him again and asked, 'How much did you say there was?'

'Four thousand three hundred and sixty-five pounds.'

'Oh, my Good Lord! You could nearly buy our street with that sort of money.'

'Keith's health is worth more than any street. I should stick that briefcase in your shopping bag ... and don't leave it on the tram. In fact, I suggest you use some of it for a taxi.'

'Taxi?'

'Safest way, Doreen. John would have put you in a taxi.'

'God bless you, Daniel, and God bless your friend too.'

*

Two days later Daniel had an unexpected visitor, Arnold, who brought him four bottles of beer in a carrier bag.

'I'm hoping you've brought a bottle opener,' said Daniel.

'Hey, I'm eighteen not eighty.'

Arnold produced one from his pocket. He looked around to see if any nurses were looking and opened two of the bottles.

'So, they're not all for me then?' commented Daniel, taking one.

'I'm being sociable for your benefit.'

'What brings you here?'

'Well, something I read in tonight's paper,' said Arnold. 'Something that made me a bit curious.'

'Go on.'

'There's an article about a woman who's raising money for her very poorly son to go to America.'

'Really?' said Daniel.

'That's right. It says that some generous donor has come up with a load of money in cash. It was the headline on page two.'

'Did it say who the generous donor was?'

'No, only that he had a connection with St James's Hospital where her son currently is . . . and where you are, for that matter.'

'Well, I'm definitely here and no mistake.'

'You see, it was the exact sum that I found curious. It wasn't a round number like you'd expect a donor to give. It was exactly the amount of money that was left in that briefcase we were going to use to pay Mr Barrington-Smythe. Only of course we didn't need to, what with Billy suffering a miscarriage of justice and all his fees being settled for him.'

Daniel looked at Arnold, knowing he'd been rumbled. But no one else was in a position to do so, except maybe Lucy.

'Does your sister know?'

'I haven't mentioned it to her. I thought I'd come and see you first. I assume this was your doing?'

'Well . . . it was, yes. I know young Keith. I was with his father in France when he died. I promised to keep an eye on the lad. I wasn't going to keep the money for myself and I certainly wasn't going to give it back to Leonov. I came across a worthy cause and handed it over – in very strict confidence, I hasten to add. I hope you don't mind?'

'Er, no. It was never my money and it's gone to a good cause by the sound of it.'

He sounded hesitant . . . uncomfortable. Daniel noticed this. Copper's instinct told him there was something on his mind other than the money.

'What is it, Arnold?'

'What's what?'

'I don't know, but there's something you're not telling me.'

Arnold stood there for a while in deep thought, then he sat down on the bedside chair.

'So?' said Daniel.

'Can you read people's minds or something?'

'Some people, yeah.'

'All right, erm . . . look, when we broke into Leonov's house and Munro jumped me, I was looking at a diamond ring.'

'One of the jewels in the cupboard?'

'Yeah. I was looking at it when he came up behind me.'

'And . . . ?'

'And when I got home, I found it in my pocket. I must have put it there without thinking.'

'Probably a normal reaction,' said Daniel.

'And I didn't tell you because I didn't realise I had it until I got home.'

'So you've still got it?'

'Yeah.'

Arnold took the ring from his pocket and gave it to Daniel, who blew a low whistle of amazement.

'Wow! This is some ring.'

'I know,' said Arnold, 'but I don't want it and I daren't

426

sell it. We should have handed it in with the rest of the stuff . . . I thought you might have a use for it one day.'

Daniel wiggled his fingers. 'Me? No, diamond rings don't suit me.'

'I mean for if you ever get engaged or anything . . . to Helen or somebody.'

Daniel sighed. 'I'd gladly keep this ring if I could put it on Helen's finger but she doesn't want to marry me, I'm afraid.'

'Oh, I thought . . . '

'Helen's had massive problems in her life and marrying me isn't going to solve anything for her. There are some things you just have to accept.'

'I want you to have it anyway. I don't want it because I've got no right to it and it reminds me of . . . ' His voice tailed off before he shuddered and added, 'You know.'

'I know, but you've probably got more right to it than I have.'

'Should we hand it in or something?'

'Probably, but to whom? I think it's legally Peter Leonov's and I don't think he'll need it where he's going.'

'Not from the York robbery then?'

'No, none of the money in the briefcase was either. I checked the serial numbers. It could be that one day you'll have a young lady friend who might appreciate a beautiful engagement ring. Are there any contenders?'

'You mean, girlfriends?'

'Why not? You're a good-looking lad.'

'You're right about me being a lad. I'm ten years off getting married.'

'So you don't have a girlfriend?'

'There's a girl called Sandra Chillington. I've taken her out a few times. She's all right but I don't think I'd want to spend the next sixty years with her. I think she'd drive me mad. We don't seem to like the same things.'

'Ah, now there's a recipe for disaster,' agreed Daniel.

'So what's the secret to it? How do I avoid this disaster?'

Daniel rubbed his chin and said, 'You fall in love with a good friend.'

'That's it?'

'Yeah. If you fall in love with a good friend and she with you, that's it, game over, stop looking. Rare creatures, though, the ones you both like and love.'

'Can you love someone you don't like?'

'It happens, but such relationships always break down, which is not good, especially when there are children involved. Be very careful who you fall for.'

'Are you speaking from experience?'

'Only from experience as a copper attending domestic disturbances. My personal romantic experience was with one woman. I was lucky enough to get it right first time.'

'So you missed out on all the fun?'

'I didn't miss out on anything. When you meet someone you think you can spend sixty years with you'll know it, and she'll be the one and only. All you've got to do is hope she thinks the same way about you.'

'Point taken. In the meantime I'll have fun looking for her among all the contenders.'

'I wish you every success, Arnold.'

'Knowing you has been good for me, and for Lucy.'

'Really? I thought I'd caused you no end of trouble?'

'Well, having Elias Munro threatening to blow my head

off wasn't pleasant, but on balance you've been a pretty good influence.'

'I thank you for that,' said Daniel. He looked at the ring again. 'Like I said, this didn't come from the York robbery. Every jewel that was stolen then was recovered, plus a few pieces that have never been reported as stolen from anywhere. This is probably one of those.'

'You mean, it's not stolen or anything?'

'I would say not. I would say its rightful owner is Peter Leonov. Legitimate jewels are sometimes used as currency by criminals – far less incriminating than big bags of cash. You can get dirty money that needs laundering but jewels are just jewels – beautiful and blameless.'

'In that case you should definitely have it. Leonov owes you a lot more than it's worth, for the damage he did to you.'

'There's not enough money in the world to compensate me for the damage Leonov did me.'

'Then you should keep the blameless ring.'

Daniel was still studying it as he sipped his beer. 'You know,' he said, 'maybe I will. Maybe I am entitled to some damages from Leonov. You've most certainly paid me back for the damage you did to me, why shouldn't he pay something? I might hang on to it for a while.'

'I wish you good luck with it, Daniel.'

'Thank you, Arnold. I think we should finish off the other two bottles now. How did you go on with your resits by the way?'

'Oh, I got through okay, thanks. The trick is to understand the question.'

'Motto for life, that. Always understand the question.'

Chapter 54

The following day Daniel was sitting on his bed in the ward, reading a *Sunday People* that he'd found lying around. Two o'clock came, visiting time. He heard the click-clack of approaching high heels but he never had any high-heeled visitors so didn't look up. He just kept on reading the sports pages. Leeds United were vying with Sheffield Wednesday and Liverpool for the Second Division Championship and Leeds had just dropped an away point against West Ham.

'Hello, Daniel.'

He knew she'd been there on the night of his accident, but she hadn't visited him since. He'd been hoping his confession about her stepfather's death might have altered her feelings towards him. Another visit wouldn't have done her any harm, surely – no strings attached and all that. He'd have liked to have seen her. She was constantly in his thoughts.

'Hello,' he said, guardedly.

She looked great. Helen was a good-looking woman but today she looked spectacular.

'Hello, Daniel.'

'Long time no see,' he said.

'Which is my fault. You could hardly come and visit me.'

'True. They won't let me out.'

She sat in the chair beside his bed and took a bunch of grapes from a shopping bag she'd brought.

'Standard hospital visitor's gift,' she said. 'I've brought you a book as well. I've just read it, thought you might like it.'

She handed him a book. He read the cover. '*The Ginger Man*, J. P. Donleavy. Any good?'

'He's an acquired taste – a bit like you.'

'Thank you.' Daniel put the book in his drawer.

'I gather the man who tried to kill you was working for Leonov,' she said.

'Yes, my sergeant figured that out and saved my life.'

'So I heard.'

'Charlie'll be getting a commendation, which will wipe out the black mark he got for his performance in court when your Billy was on trial.'

'Good for him,' she said. 'Oh, I suppose you know about his new girlfriend?'

'Why should I know?'

She hesitated before telling him. 'Because it's Lucy.'

'No!'

'That's what I thought.'

'She's only fifteen.'

'Sixteen next month, apparently.'

'Charlie's twenty-six. He's the youngest detective sergeant in Leeds but he's much too old for Lucy.'

'He's eleven years younger than you.'

'How do you know how old I am?'

431

'I take an interest in people I like. At least Lucy's finally setting her sights on a younger man.'

'Oh.'

'Yes . . . oh indeed. She fancied you, remember?'

'No?'

'She did.'

'Well, if she did it was an infatuation at the most, and she'll run rings round Charlie. I wonder why he never told me about her?'

'Because he's afraid of what you might say, with you being a friend of hers.'

'Hmm.'

They both sat in silence for a moment then Helen said, 'Leonov's had his appeal turned down.'

'I know. Being involved in Gloria's murder and my attempted murder hardly went in his favour. Munro's due for the drop as well. Next month, both of them.'

'You believe in a life for a life, then?'

'I believe there are some people who are so evil and cause so much misery that they shouldn't be on this earth.'

'Like Maurice Bradley.'

'Absolutely. The scales of justice need a nudge now and again, but they've swung in our favour at long last. The bloke who knocked me down'll get life for attempted murder.'

'And Billy's home with me.'

'All done and dusted, then.'

'Not quite,' said Helen.

'Why?'

'You mean, who.'

'Who?'

'Doris Day.'

'What?'

'Has she made a play for you yet?'

'Well, she hasn't been to visit me. Which is something of a disappointment.'

'So, have you given up on her?'

'Probably. I think this *Calamity Jane* film went to her head.'

'And does that leave the way clear for me?'

'For you to do what?' said Daniel.

'To propose to you.'

'You're proposing to me?'

'Yes.'

'But ... what about the problem with your stepfather?'

She looked down at her hands as she gathered her thoughts, then back up at him. 'Actually, most of that fell into perspective the night you were injured.'

'And what I told you about his death, er, did that help at all?'

'Oh, don't get me wrong. My life has been relieved of an intolerable burden. The wrong done to me has now been put right. I can finally move on.'

'Well, I'm so pleased it wasn't all a waste of time.'

'I couldn't live with my stepfather in this world, but now I realise I can't live without you.'

'If it's not one thing, it's another.'

'Don't be facetious, Earnshawe! For a while I thought you were going to die and I had a serious pain inside me, thinking I was going to lose you. Never felt anything like that before.'

'Really?' he said. 'That's good. Talk about every cloud

having a silver lining. My cloud must have been lined with pure gold.

'I had genuine heartache, would you believe?'

'I had years of that when Gloria died. Not sure it's gone away even now.'

'Are you still in love with her?'

He nodded. 'Yes, I am. To say I'm not would be an insult to my memory of her.'

'Does this mean there's no room for another love?'

'Not at all. I've got two girls. I love them both. If I had ten I'd love them all just as much as I love Carol and Jeanette.'

'But that's a different kind of love.'

'I know that. But I think most men can only manage to love one wife at a time. Anything beyond that's got to be very complicated.'

'I wouldn't know,' said Helen. 'When it became clear you were going to survive, the pain more or less went away, but the longing didn't. It was like a door inside me had been kicked open and all this ... this damned longing stuff came in.'

'Damned longing stuff? Not sure I like the sound of that.'

'Well, I suppose you people who know about such things would call it love. To me it was just an alien feeling that I didn't fully understand.'

'Are you telling me you love me?'

'I just told you I'll struggle to live without you, so yes, what else can it be? I've left it this long to see if it might go away. I certainly didn't want to make the mistake of rushing here and declaring my undying love for you when all I had was dyspepsia, which I suffer from, by the way.'

'Why? What have you been eating?'

'Daniel, this is not dyspepsia! Look, I've just proposed to you. Aren't you supposed to say yes or something?'

Daniel looked around the ward. Other visitors were arriving. No one was taking any notice of them.

'Helen, we haven't even kissed or anything,' he whispered.

'I've never kissed any man.'

'Well, I think we should get that bit over with before we take it any further.'

'Okay, shove over.'

She got on the bed beside him, he moved to one side. She put her arms around him and kissed him on the lips. It was his first kiss since Gloria had died; Helen's first real kiss ever. But it was a new experience for both of them – a surreal experience for both of them. Whatever they had between them, they knew it was right.

'Wow!' he said.

'Wow? Is that the same as a yes?'

'It was me saying, Bugger Doris Day, she had her chance.'

She kissed him again. Having practised, Daniel noticed she was getting better. A thought struck him. He broke off first.

'Ah, I've got something for you,' he said.

He opened his bedside drawer with his one good arm and took out the ring. Helen looked at it in amazement. He tried it on her ring finger. It slid on easily, a bit too large.

'Good God, Daniel! I didn't expect this. Is it a real diamond?'

'I hope so. Two or three carats, I should think.'

'And the rest.'

'Look,' said Daniel, 'its provenance is a bit ...' he searched for the right word ' ... cloudy, but it's morally mine to give.'

'Provenance?'

'Er, yes. I'd better explain, then you can make your own decision. If you don't want it, I'll get you another one.'

She held it up so the light reflected off its many facets. 'Oh, Daniel. I do hope I decide to want it.'

In a low voice he explained the ring's recent history and how Arnold had given it to him in the hope he might want it to give to Helen. She already knew the story of how Lucy and Arnold had broken into Leonov's house.

'Nobody will know of its existence,' he said, 'probably not even Leonov. He'll have other things to worry about.'

'So this is really Leonov's ring?'

'It was one of his many possessions,' said Daniel.

She studied the diamond. 'Leonov, eh? The man who all but ruined your life.'

'He did, but we can't blame the ring for that.'

'Oh, no, I don't blame the ring. I love the ring. It's an antique so it'll have far more romantic memories attached to it than merely sitting in Leonov's hidey hole.'

'And we could be its most recent romantic memory,' said Daniel, warming to her theme.

'That's right,' she said. 'This ring is all part and parcel of how we got to know each other.'

'So you'll keep it?'

'I most certainly will,' she said. 'It's now a happy ring. I'll keep it as a memento of the happiest day of my life.'

436

'So far,' he said.

'So far sounds good to me.' Helen leaned over and kissed him again. 'I love you, Daniel Earnshawe, and I'd be delighted to become Mrs Earnshawe as soon as possible.'

'Excuse me,' he said. 'I haven't said "yes" to your proposal yet.'

'Haven't you?'

'No . . . I mean, yes. But I'd be delighted to marry you, Miss Durkin.'

'Are you sure?'

'Quite sure, thank you.'

'That's settled then.' She looked at the ring again and said, 'I'll need to have it re-sized.'

'I think it might do no harm to have it, er, personalised as well. Maybe a couple of rubies, one either side of the diamond.'

'You mean, disguised?'

'That as well.'

'Sapphires,' she said. 'I prefer sapphires.'

They hugged for a while, then Helen said, 'Oh, heck, I forgot! I brought Billy with me but I told him to wait outside until I got this sorted out.'

'So you were confident I'd say yes?'

'Not really. I've never been confident about anything that might bring me happiness.' She looked at him consideringly. 'Of course, I should have mentioned that if you get me, you get Billy and a motorbike as well.'

'And you get Carol and Jeanette and a mortgage.'

'Fine by me.'

'I'll do my very best to bring you and Billy every happiness.'

'Shall I get him now?'

'Yes, wheel him in.'

By now they'd attracted the attention of several people. As Helen left to fetch Billy, Daniel felt he needed to explain himself.

'She just proposed to me,' he announced. 'I said yes.'

There was a murmur of approval and a ripple of applause from both patients and visitors. Helen came back with Billy to shouts of, 'Congratulations!'

'I've announced our engagement,' explained Daniel. 'Hello, Billy.'

'Hello, mister,' said Billy, uncertainly.

'Billy, this is Daniel,' said Helen. 'He's going to be your new dad.'

Billy stared at him with curious eyes. 'Are you going to be my new dad?'

'I certainly am,' said Daniel, still somewhat stunned by this amazing turn of events. 'You'll get me and two sisters.'

'I don't know nothing about no sisters. Are they nice like Lucy?'

'Yes, they are.'

Billy gave the matter some consideration then said, 'How can yer be me dad when yer in bed all the time?'

'I'll be out of this bed very shortly, Billy. Up and about, back to my job as a policeman.'

'I don't like policemen. They locked me up, yer know.'

'I know that, Billy, but they won't lock you up now I'm on your side.'

'Will I still be Billy Wellington 'cos I know yer supposed ter be called what yer dad's called, only Lucy and

438

Arnold didn't want ter be called what their dad's called so they haven't been. She told me that, so it's true.'

Helen and Daniel stared at him, amazed at such an outburst. 'I really think I'd like you to lose the Wellington name, Billy,' said Helen. 'You'll be called William Earnshawe and I'll be Helen Earnshawe.'

Billy gave this some thought, then said. 'I like Billy Wellington.'

'So do I, Billy,' said Daniel. 'I think it should be up to you what you're called.'

'See,' said Billy, giving his mother a look of triumph. She smiled and was holding up two hands in defeat as Billy said to Daniel, 'Will you always be me dad, 'cos I'm potty, yer know?'

Daniel looked him up and down and he knew that one day his daughters would fly the nest but this young man might well be a responsibility for life. Then he looked at Helen and realised that the reward was well worth it, and from what he'd heard about Billy the lad had an amusing side to him and might be fun to have around.

'Always, Billy,' he said. 'I'll always be your dad, and you'll always be my lad.'

Billy gave this serious thought, then said, 'No, that's not right.'

'Isn't it?'

'No, 'cos you're miles older than me so you'll be dead before me but I'll be old enough to look after meself by then.'

'That's very true,' conceded Daniel, defeated.

Billy gave another smile of triumph and said, 'So, you'll be me dad ... *nearly* always.'